OF YOUNG BRITISH
Jonathan Cape, Secker & Warburg and Vintage

ADAM THIRLWELL
POLITICS
Jonathan Cape (August 2003)

NEW IN PAPERBACK

ALAN WARNER
THE MAN WHO WALKS
(Jonathan Cape and Vintage)

ROBERT McLIAM WILSON
EUREKA STREET
(Secker & Warburg and Vintage)

  Secker & Warburg

www.randomhouse.co.uk

GRANTA

GRANTA 81, SPRING 2003
www.granta.com

EDITOR *Ian Jack*
DEPUTY EDITOR *Sophie Harrison*
ASSOCIATE EDITOR *Liz Jobey*
MANAGING EDITOR *Fatema Ahmed*
EDITORIAL ASSISTANT *Helen Gordon*

CONTRIBUTING EDITORS *Diana Athill, Gail Lynch, Blake Morrison, Andrew O'Hagan, Lucretia Stewart*

ASSOCIATE PUBLISHER *Sally Lewis*
FINANCE *Geoffrey Gordon, Morgan Graver*
SALES *Frances Hollingdale*
PUBLICITY *Louise Campbell*
SUBSCRIPTIONS *John Kirkby, Darryl Wilks*
PUBLISHING ASSISTANT *Mark Williams*
ADVERTISING MANAGER *Kate Rochester*
PRODUCTION ASSOCIATE *Sarah Wasley*

PUBLISHER *Rea S. Hederman*

Granta, 2–3 Hanover Yard, Noel Road, London N1 8BE
Tel 020 7704 9776 Fax 020 7704 0474
e-mail for editorial: editorial@granta.com

Granta US, 1755 Broadway, 5th Floor, New York, NY 10019-3780, USA

TO SUBSCRIBE call 020 7704 0470 or e-mail subs@granta.com
A one-year subscription (four issues) costs £26.95 (UK), £34.95 (rest of Europe) and £41.95 (rest of the world).

Granta is printed and bound in Italy by Legoprint. The paper used in this publication meets the minimum requirements of American National Standard for Information Sciences—Permanence of Paper for Printed Library Materials, ANSI Z39.48-1984.

Acknowledgements are due to the following publishers for permission to quote from:
'The Watershed' from 'Collected Poems' by W. H. Auden, reprinted by permission of Faber and Faber Ltd and Random House. Inc.

Design: Slab Media.
Front cover © Julian Opie 2002
        courtesy of the Lisson Gallery, London

ISBN 0 903141 582

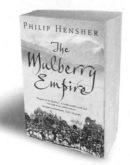 

THE BEST OF CANONGATE'S YOUNG NOVELISTS

NICCOLÒ AMMANITI

I'M NOT SCARED
"Ammaniti's prose is faultless"
Independent on Sunday

LOUISE WELSH

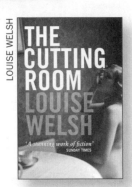

CUTTING ROOM
"Original and compelling"
Daily Telegraph

LAURA HIRD

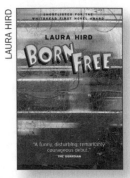

BORN FREE
Short listed for the Whitbread
First Novel Award

MICHEL FABER

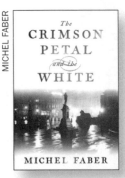

**THE CRIMSON PETAL
AND THE WHITE**
"Irresistibly readable"
Sunday Times

ANNE DONOVAN

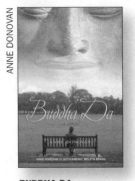

BUDDHA DA
*"A beauty ... very hard to
beat"* Sunday Telegraph

WILL FERGUSSON

HAPPINESS ™
*"A brilliant parody ... bright and very
funny"* Mail on Sunday

YANN MARTEL

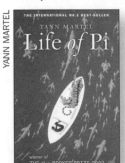

**LIFE
OF PI**
Winner
of
The
Man
Booker
Prize

DAN RHODES

TIMOLEON VIETA COME HOME
"The best new writer in Britain"
Guardian

The debut novel by
Dan Rhodes – one of
Granta's Best of Young
British Novelists
– is out on April 3rd

www.canongate.net

GRANTA 81

Best of Young British Novelists

www.wno.org.uk

Welsh National *Opera*
Cenedlaethol Cymru

SPRING SEASON 2003

The Elixir of Love, Jenůfa, Cavalleria rusticana & Pagliacci

Sponsored by **Coutts & Co**

SUMMER SEASON 2003

Don Giovanni, La bohème, Jephtha

Supported by **WNO** *Partnership*

Venues	Box Office	Spring '03	Summer '03
CARDIFF, New Theatre	029 2087 8889	5 Feb - 8 Mar	17 May - 7 Jun
BIRMINGHAM Hippodrome	0870 730 1234	12 - 15 Mar	
SOUTHAMPTON Mayflower	023 8071 1811	19 - 22 Mar	
MILTON KEYNES Theatre	01908 606090	26 - 29 Mar	
SWANSEA, Grand Theatre	01792 475715	2 - 5 Apr	
LIVERPOOL, Empire	0870 606 3536	16 - 19 Apr	
LLANDUDNO, North Wales Theatre	01492 872 000		10 - 14 Jun
BRISTOL Hippodrome	0870 607 7500		17 - 21 Jun
BIRMINGHAM Symphony Hall	0121 780 3333*		27 & 28 Jun
OXFORD Apollo	0870 606 3500		1 - 5 Jul
PLYMOUTH, Theatre Royal	01752 267 222		8 - 12 Jul

Concert Performances. Repertoire varies at some venues, please check for details.

For further information please phone **0800 328 2357** or find us at **www.wno.org.uk**

INTRODUCTION

This is the third issue of *Granta* devoted to the new work of a group of writers deemed the 'Best of Young British Novelists'. The first appeared in 1983, and the second in 1993. The idea behind each has been to recognize twenty British writers under the age of forty who have showed exceptional promise or achievement, and to introduce the lesser-known among them to a wider audience.

It wasn't originally *Granta*'s idea. In January this year, when our twenty novelists were being assembled by the *Sunday Times* for the by now traditional group photograph, I remembered that I'd witnessed a similar scene in another London studio in the early 1980s. Not the first Best of Young British Novelists, which was still a year or two away, but a promotion called the Best of British Writers, organized by the Book Marketing Council and its chairman, Desmond Clarke. The idea then, quite radical in its day, was to say, 'Look, Britain has all these jolly good writers, and for the getting of your pleasure and wisdom you should be buying more of their books.' All kinds of people, none particularly young and many now dead, climbed up a few flights of stairs to have their picture taken by Lord Snowdon.

As a reporter, I went to write about it for the *Sunday Times*. We had a struggle with John Betjeman in his wheelchair. 'Very kind of you, dear boy, very kind.' V. S. Pritchett was there, and Laurie Lee and Beryl Bainbridge. Disparate kinds of writers: poets, children's writers and essayists as well as novelists. It was odd to see them together; it looked like a piece of cultural nationalism that belonged to the Second World War—Writers Against Hitler. Odd, in fact, to see them at all; we were still in the time when writers were private figures, their public lives mainly confined to what was printed on the page. What they looked like, how they sounded, where they lived, what they believed: these things—always excepting the case of Betjeman—were mysterious to most people outside the narrow world of London publishing houses.

That quiet, and some would argue proper, state of affairs was transformed over the next decade. Literary festivals, bookshop readings, TV shows, marketing campaigns that stressed the writer's persona as much as his or her book—all of these made writers visible and fashionable. The first *Granta* list of Best Young British Novelists—Amis, Rushdie, McEwan (see page 352 for the full list)—was a prominent milepost down that road. How writers performed in public began to be important. Even how they looked. Today you'll hear it said, a popular grudge, that it's easier for a writer to find a publisher if he, and perhaps particularly she, is young and good-looking.

Given the hype that now attaches itself to many young writers and their novels, the first question that arose in my mind when we were planning Best of Young British for a third time was: is it necessary? Times have changed since 1983, and even 1993. Slowly, dimly, I began to see that the hype that now often surrounds authorship made Best of Young British more necessary rather than less. What had been an exercise to publicize the literary novel, at a time when there were few spotlights on this particular branch of culture, might now have a new role as an independent consumer's guide to novelists who deserved to be read in an era where 'a thrilling debut by a young writer of enormous talent' is the standard blurb, and where there are now so many spotlights directed by marketing money and the size of the writer's advance.

We needed, I thought, judges who were wise to the ways of publishing, as well as being good readers, good critics and, where possible, good practitioners. There were five of us, with me in the chair. Robert McCrum, the literary editor of the *Observer* and working on the new authorized biography of P. G. Wodehouse, had a notable track record for finding promising writers, several of whom came good, during his earlier career as editorial director at Faber and Faber. Nicholas Clee, editor of the *Bookseller*, reads new novels constantly for work, and (perhaps surprisingly, given his reading load) for pleasure. Alex Clark reviews fiction for the *Sunday Times* (when the judging began she reviewed for the *Guardian*) and the *London Review of Books*. Finally, Hilary Mantel: not only an accomplished novelist, but also a reviewer of novels for the *New York Review of Books* and the *New York Times*, a great encourager of young writers—and (least, but not unimportant) a woman who lives in Woking, Surrey, where she maintains a sturdy independence from the currents of fashion in London's literary life.

We asked for submissions from publishers and agents and eventually received the work of 139 writers (sixty-two women and seventy-seven men), sometimes still to be published and in typescript. The rules said that entrants had to be citizens of the United Kingdom born after December 31, 1963.

Last summer we began to read.

What were we looking for? Our business was to select the most interesting, original writers of the 'literary novel', though we would also consider shorter fiction, the story and novella, as allowable evidence of a writer's intent in the novel's direction, despite the fact that two writers on previous lists—Helen Simpson and Adam Mars-Jones—had dented this faith by sticking firmly to the short-story form in their careers since. The 'literary novel' isn't an easy thing to define; you know it when you see it. One definition might be 'an artistically ambitious work of fiction, more than 30,000 words long.' Other definitions rely on negatives. It isn't 'commercial' (Archer, Grisham, Harris) and it isn't 'genre' (crime, suspense, sci-fi, fantasy, children). Yes, but on the other hand it might be. Only the brave and foolishly strict would argue that the main pleasure of reading Conan Doyle or Chandler is to find out what happened in the end. Writers can cross boundaries. J. K. Rowling wasn't submitted, though we would have excluded her had she been because in our view, no matter how many adults you see reading her on the tube, she is definitely a children's writer. Other writers were less easy to keep in their boxes. Louise Welsh's *The Cutting Room* is a fine crime novel set in Glasgow. China Miéville is an extraordinary writer of dark fantasy. In the end we rejected both. Personally, I was sorry to see Welsh go.

Emails began to go back and forward between us. Rereading them now I see a punitive streak, as though a restaurant reviewer had got into the wrong kind of restaurant. Of writer A: 'Immense talent, deficient in craft. The punctuation doesn't serve the rhythm, the structure doesn't serve the plot. It has a pungent flavour, but a reader must be careful with a book like this not to confuse the preposterous with the original.' Of writer B: 'An excruciatingly self-conscious writer, but I believe if she could shake herself free of Eng Lit she could be very good.' But sometimes we were in the right restaurant after all. 'I am completely bowled over by Sarah Waters. I read the first 350 pages in one sitting, and only quit when I realized day was breaking.'

We tried to ignore the marketing fanfare which some books had received on publication—not because we were worried that it would persuade us in the book's favour, but because it might encourage our prejudice in the opposite direction. Sometimes a book can live up to its hype.

11

Email from Hilary Mantel, August 9: 'How did this book come to be the "most eagerly-awaited debut of 2002"? Awaited by whom and on what grounds? I am hoping that we discover some person who has been toiling in silence and obscurity, unawaited by anyone except his mum.'

What were we looking for, the Tome of the Unknown Toiler apart? A few critics urged us to find the state-of-England novel. Among books by young novelists Zadie Smith's *White Teeth* is probably the closest England can come to that. We don't, it seems, have young Roths, Updikes, Wolfes and De Lillos—though neither, Jonathan Franzen apart, are the younger Americans much given to the contemporary panoramic sweep. Our novelists like abroad and they like the past; only eight of the twenty we finally chose set their books in modern—i.e. post-Thatcher—Britain, and only five in modern England. Then again, when, since Dickens and Eliot died, have great state-of-England novels been rolling from the press? Instead, we had state-of-sex-and-drugs novels in which self-harming women were a common feature, state-of-marriage novels, state-of-Yorkshire novels.

We met three or four times and decided that one test for writers on the list was a very simple one. Would we have carried on reading their books—for pleasure—if we hadn't been judging them? That seems an obvious criteria, and yet I think there may be one or two writers on the final list whom we admired rather than enjoyed, and one or two left off for the opposite reason. Most of us had been judges in other prizes, and, as Nick Clee remarked, something strange and not easily explained often happens in the judging process. You read a book and enjoy it, and then at the judges' meeting you feel you have been seduced too easily. The reader at home in his armchair is replaced by the literary critic in his hard seat, who finds the book has not somehow been clever, or bold, or original enough. A flaw can be an entertaining thing to discuss, but it can also be a good way of forgetting pleasure.

Our trickiest problem was the weighing of the one-book author against the author with an established career. With a one-book author you are taking a large gamble—what will his second be like, or his third? On the other hand, a three-book author may be getting worse with each book, leaving the brilliance of the original behind. We tried to be reasoned and fair about this, but in the end we chose to back our hunches (and may be proved wrong). After four months of reading, emails and meetings, it was interesting to see how detailed argument about language and narrative strategy boiled down to the straightforward, 'Sorry, but I just couldn't stand it.'

What were we looking for? In the context of Monica Ali's still-to-be-published first novel, *Brick Lane*, about a Muslim housewife in east London, I'd mentioned to Hilary something that V. S. Naipaul wrote or said: that one of the points of a novel was to bring the reader 'news'. Ali's novel was pertinent to now; she'd imagined what such a woman's life might be like. Hilary returned to this in an email:

> This process has made me think what I want from a novel, and I realize that one of the things I want is 'news'—in the sense that you mentioned earlier. It seems to me a reader should expect a novel to take her outside the tight circle of her own knowledge and concerns. News may be from alien places or other eras, properly realized on the page. Or it may be from places and people very familiar, reappraised and reinterpreted, or made strange so that the reader has to think about their meaning. It may be news from the inarticulate, who have not spoken for themselves (or who we can't hear). Or it may be news from the writer's psyche. What it mustn't be, for me, is false news, where tricks of style dress up lack of content, or where inauthenticity creeps through a text—that is what happens when a writer is either insufficiently observant about day-to-day life, or has not imagined their fictional world thoroughly enough. It is not only facts that need rigour; fiction needs it badly.

Many writers lived up to this standard; three of those who did and who nearly made the final list—Nick Barlay, Andrew Crumey and Claire Messud—turned out to have been wrongly submitted by their publishers (they were either too old, or not British). But many more didn't. At our last meeting, one judge mentioned the sense of 'entitlement' that rose from the page, as if knocking off a novel was an easy thing to do. Hilary again:

> Many of the books we have read have left me perplexed. I understand about those books which are shallow 'instant' books, catering to a perceived market. What I don't understand is novels

that aim to last a bit longer, but which are ragged, confused and under-realized... For as long as I've been publishing people have been moaning 'no one does any editing any more'. It's become a commonplace—so much so that you wonder if there ever was a golden age that reviewers are nostalgic for. But if that is so, if there are fewer good editors, or fewer editors with time to spare, writers have an even stronger obligation [on themselves] to give their public something that hangs together... It's as if publishers are leaving their young authors to sink or swim, to get their advice from adverse reviews or a disdainful public. Can that be good business? My private hate are those books with a fulsome acknowledgement to the editor, where it is obvious that the editor has done no more than leave the author's complacency unbruised.

What do our twenty chosen writers tell us about British fiction in this new generation? Perhaps mainly that the novels of young British writers—the good ones—show an energy, a liberty and variety (a spunk which may be the upside of 'entitlement') that many other countries would envy, even the US, where the craft is more professionalized and disciplined. As for the writers themselves, here are some crude demographics: forty per cent are women; twenty per cent have a parent of non-European ancestry; fifteen per cent are Scottish, 7.5 per cent Welsh (the 2.5 per cent is the Welsh half of Peter Ho Davies, a Granta author—I excluded myself from the vote in his case); five per cent Northern Irish.

All very fine and various, and broadly reflecting the country or countries that Britain has become. Less various, however, is the interesting majority (sixty per cent) whose education included the universities of Oxford and Cambridge. The Oxbridge proportion among writers in 1983 was fifty-five per cent, and in 1993, again sixty per cent. There may be a compelling thesis in this. All I can say here is that the most sinister explanation should be resisted: the proportion of Oxbridge-educated Granta judges has shrunk to forty per cent from seventy-five per cent in 1993.

There have been many comparisons with the famous list of 1983, and no doubt there will be more. They do no good at all. That was a special generation. This may be one as well. We have another ten years to find out.   *Ian Jack*

GRANTA

HELEN AND JULIA

Sarah Waters

Sarah Waters was born in Neyland, Wales, in 1966. She studied English at the Universities of Kent, Lancaster and London. She has worked in bookshops and libraries, and in higher education, but began to write fiction in 1995 and now writes full-time. She has published three novels: 'Tipping the Velvet' (1998), which was recently adapted for television by the BBC; 'Affinity', which won her The Sunday Times Young Writer of the Year award in 2000; and 'Fingersmith', which was shortlisted for both the Orange Prize and for the Man Booker Prize in 2002. She lives in London. 'Helen and Julia' is taken from a novel-in-progress to be published by Virago.

'Helen, why don't we put some food together and take it as a picnic to the park?'

'All right,' said Helen.

They packed bread, cheese, apples and lettuce in a check tea towel; Julia fished out an old madras tablecloth they had used as a dust sheet when painting the flat; they put it all in a canvas bag. In one of the streets which ran from their square was a Polish delicatessen: there they bought slices of sausage, more cheese, and two bottles of wheat beer.

'I feel like the leader of a Brownie troop,' said Helen, shouldering the canvas bag.

'You look more glorious than that,' said Julia. 'Like a girl in a Soviet mural.'

Helen imagined herself: square-faced, large-limbed, rather hairy; but she said nothing. They began the walk across Marylebone. The bottles of beer rocked together in the bag. The streets had a bleached, exhausted feel, not unpleasant; they were dusty as a cat's coat is dusty, when it has lain all day in the sun. The cars were so few, one could hear the cries of individual children, the slap and bounce of balls, the sound of wirelesses and gramophones from open windows, the ringing of telephones. Soon, too—swelling and sinking on impalpable gusts of air, like washing on a line—there came music from the Regent's Park band. Julia caught Helen's wrist, grew childish, pretending to tug.

'Come on! Come quick! We will miss the parade!' Her fingers slid down to Helen's, then she drew them away. 'It makes one feel like that, doesn't it?'

'Doesn't it.'

'What tune is it, d'you think?'

They stopped to listen. Helen shook her head. 'I simply can't imagine,' she said—a phrase of Julia's, though she did not notice. 'Something modern and discordant?'

'Surely not.'

The music rose. 'Quick, quick!' said Julia again. They smiled, grown-up; but walked on, faster than before. The park was very close, after all. They went in at the gate at Baker Street, stood on the little bridge that spans the boating lake, deciding where they should sit. The music, here, had lost its raggedness, but also something of its charm. They walked again, and the tune revealed itself at last.

'Oh!' said Helen, and they laughed; for it was only 'Yes! We Have No Bananas'.

The park was filled with people. Old ladies and elderly men had taken the deckchairs that had been set about the bandstand. The women had their skirts drawn tight across their spread-out knees, like skeins of wool about fists; the men had twitched at their trouser legs, exposing socks and ivory shins. They sang to the music, unselfconsciously; they bounced babies, or beat out the rhythm of the tune upon the backs of sleeping children held in their laps. Further away, the park grew livelier. Dogs ran, panting, after sticks and balls, saliva flying from their mouths. Boys charged about with footballs, cricket bats, aeroplanes.

'How well-behaved we all are!' said Julia, as she and Helen spread out their cloth. 'I mean, how well we know what we should do. Like figures in a picture book for children.'

'Or for students of English.'

'Yes! As if everything should have a label. Even the trees and flowers, look. The sycamore, the rose.'

'The cloud,' said Helen. 'The pigeon.'

'The bread. The salad. The knife. May I cut you some cheese?'

'Will you?' Helen's blouse was clinging to her back, where the canvas bag had drawn the perspiration from her. She pulled the cotton free, then kicked off her sandals. She took out the bottles of beer. They were cold, and slid in her hand, deliciously. She set them down.

'Julia, we forgot a bottle opener,' she said.

'Oh, hell. I do so want a beer, as well. Don't you know some terribly clever way of getting the tops off?'

'With my teeth, do you mean?'

'I don't know...'

They turned the bottles in their hands.

'Look, it's hopeless,' said Helen. 'Run and ask those boys over there if they have a knife or something.'

'I can't.'

'Go on. They are sure to.'

'You do it.'

'I carried the bag. Go on, Julia.'

'Oh, hell.' Julia rose, not graciously, took up the bottles, one in each hand; began to walk across the scorched and beaten grass, to a group of three or four lounging youths. She walked stiffly, rather bowed, perhaps only self-conscious, but Helen watched her and thought in surprise, 'She is looking her age. Why, she is almost matronly!' For it was true: Julia, who had always been so slender— who had been, in Helen's mind, almost defined by slenderness, or had herself defined it—had about her now, somehow, something of the angular, wide-hipped, narrow-breasted English figure she would have in earnest in eight or ten years' time... The boys put up their hands to their eyes, against the sun, when they saw her come; they rose lazily from their places, reached into their pockets; one held a bottle against his abdomen as he worked with something at the top. Julia stood with folded arms, more self-conscious than ever, smiling unnaturally; when she came back with the opened bottles, her face and throat were pink. Helen felt filled with tenderness for her. She wished she might take her head between her hands, and kiss her.

'Well done,' she said.

'They only used keys, after all. We might have done that.'

'Never mind.'

They had brought china cups to drink from. The beer was chill, bitter, marvellous. Helen put back her head and closed her eyes. It was five o'clock, but the sun was still fantastically hot upon her face. She said, 'Julia, this is wonderful. Why don't we come here every day?'

'I don't know. We will, from now on.'

'We will, every day, until winter comes. I can meet you, on my way home from work. We can have a picnic every evening, in exactly this spot. We could even have one when it gets cold, if we only dress warmly enough. We can bring our books. You could write here.'

'Yes! It will be lovely.'

'Lovely...'

'That band!' said Julia. The band had finished one tune and started another. 'Tinkling and farting,' she said, idly.

'Tinkling and—!' The phrase was such an improbable one for Julia to have used, it struck them both, suddenly, as hilarious; they lay for quite a minute, convulsed by laughter. Helen thought, 'I'm drunk. I'm drunk, on three gulps of beer!' She looked at Julia and wished again that she might kiss her. 'How I'd like to kiss you, Julia!' she almost said; but she bit back the words, for there seemed something embarrassing about revealing to Julia the fact that she had been made amorous, by beer... Then she thought back to their dreary lovemaking of three nights before and grew ashamed of the fact, herself.

Their fit of laughter left them. Helen wiped her eyes. They turned to the food they had brought, broke the bread, cut the cheese, put back the wax paper wrapper from the slices of sausage; Julia took an apple and rubbed it on her hip, turning it as she rubbed it, dextrously, distractedly. The apple was half pale yellow, half red. 'Snow White's apple,' she said, showing Helen, biting into the red half.

'You always say that.'

Helen lifted a piece of lettuce. There were beads of water still caught in its whorls, from where she had held it beneath the kitchen tap. The green of it was astonishing. It was quite tasteless, however.

'When I was a child we ate lettuce served with sugar,' she said.

Julia laughed. 'You ate everything with sugar. Yorkshire pudding, for instance, with syrup on it. And Christmas pudding you ate with eggs!'

'That was a favourite of my father's... And Yorkshire pudding is jolly tasty with syrup on it. It's only another form of pancake, after all. Isn't it?' She waited. 'Julia?'

'What?'

'Must you look away like that, when we are talking?'

'I didn't know I had.'

'It is like you, to start some idiotic conversation and then to look away.'

'Something caught my eye. I'm sorry, darling. What were you saying?'

'I was saying, that Yorkshire pudding is only another form of pancake.'

Julia blinked. 'Well, I suppose it is, if you look at it like that...'

'How I must bore her!' Helen thought. The thought had sadness in it, but also something that was awfully close to rage; for it *was* like Julia to leave one saying these idiotic things—like leading one into marshy ground, leaping nimbly away before the muddy water rose about her own shoes. Helen had been on country walks with her, on which that had actually happened...

They ate in silence. A little boy dressed only in a pair of shorts came running close to them, closer than an adult would have come. He did a sort of capering dance for a minute or two, then threw himself upon his hands, trying handstands. Every time he fell back, they felt the thud of his feet, and grimaced and winced.

'What self-absorbed little creatures small boys are,' said Julia at last. 'More than girls, don't you think? It's almost enviable, really.'

'Poor Julia. Should you like to throw handstands and cartwheels? Do you feel held back?'

'I might, for all you know.'

'Look at his little chest, how like a bird's it is. I bet it breaks his mother's heart. I bet she pegs out his vests and weeps.' Helen imagined a woman, small as a bird herself, drying her eyes at a clothes line. Absurdly, she felt tears rising in her own throat at the thought. She drank again from her beer.

'That's the way!' called Julia suddenly, clapping. 'Bravo!' The boy had got his feet in the air. He turned his head at Julia's cry, startled to find himself observed; the action threw him off balance, and he fell. He kept dramatically still for a moment, spreadeagled and panting, as he perhaps imagined wounded soldiers lay; then he turned his back to them, pulled madly at daisies, drove his fingers into the ground, making small battle noises. His shoulder blades worked as if furious—as if frustrated by flesh, like the unformed wings of a bird. His hair had been razored at the nape of his neck. Presently his mother called him. She had been sitting quite near, after all. She was not sad and slight as Helen had pictured her. She knocked the blades of grass from his arms and sides as if she might be hitting dust from a carpet, then held out a shirt for him to put on and buttoned it briskly, her chin drawn in. Beside her sat a lumpish girl of about sixteen. She had her foot upon the axle of a pram and was pushing and drawing it back and forth, while a baby wailed thinly from inside it.

Julia rolled on to her back and yawned. 'Thank God I don't have children.'

'I should like it if you did,' said Helen.

'Should you?' Julia raised her head. 'Why?'

Helen blushed. 'I don't know. I don't suppose I would, really.'

Julia watched her for another moment, then lay back down. 'What funny things you say.'

Helen lay back, too, and closed her eyes. The baby cried, caught its breath, cried again. A dog, nearby, barked agitatedly, on and on. From the boating lake there came the creak and splash of oars, the larking about of boys and girls; in another direction, farther off, was the hum of some sort of motor. Concentrating, she heard the scene as, earlier, with Julia, she had observed it: as if the parts had been recorded separately, then put together, perhaps for an educational broadcast upon the wireless...

The band had changed its tune again. She knew the words, and began to sing.

'There's something about a soldier! Something about a soldier! Something about a soldier that is fine!—fine!—fine!'

The canvas bag was close to her side. She reached into it, and brought out a packet of cigarettes, and matches. She never smoked outdoors without a feeling of boldness, of recklessness; now, putting the cigarette to her lip, and lighting it, all without raising herself from her idle position on the grass, she felt more reckless than ever.

'There's something about his bearing! Something to what he's wearing! Something about his buttons all a-shine!—shine!—shine!'

'Give me a cigarette, will you?' said Julia, across the words.

'No,' said Helen, not moving.

'Please, Helen.'

'No. You smoke too much, it makes you cough.'

'What's it to you, how much I cough?'

Helen didn't answer. Julia pushed herself up, and reached, in a rather irritated way, to get a cigarette for herself.

Helen sang on. *'There's something about a soldier! Something about a soldier! Something about a—'*

'Must you?' said Julia.

Helen stopped singing at once. The song went on in her head, however, and as it did there rose up again in her that feeling, that was so like rage, that she had earlier suppressed. 'Why shouldn't I sing?' she thought to herself. '*She* sings all the time. Why shouldn't I? Who am I harming? I'm not like her. She does what she wants, and doesn't care who it hurts...'

The rage grew bleaker. Now she could feel the figure of Ursula Manning, braced, like the demon king in the pantomimes, against the spring that would send her hurtling through the trapdoor on to the stage of Helen's thoughts... 'Don't let me think of any of that, now,' she said to herself, in panic. 'Let me think only about this moment, here. Quickly, quickly. This madras cloth beneath my hand, with the spots of distemper upon it. The prickle of grass against my heels, the cup at my side, the cigarette between my fingers. The sun, how absurdly hot it is. How every small, insignificant thing must burn to ashes, that touches it...'

The sun had sunk, however, was not quite so warm as it had been before. The cup was empty; the beer moved inside her, as if in all her veins: cloudy and sluggish and sour. The dog still barked. The baby still choked and cried. She drew on her cigarette, and rolled to one side, to grind the stub of it into the grass. As she turned from Julia, Julia spoke.

'Helen,' she said. Her tone was rushed and not quite natural. 'Helen, I forgot to tell you. Ursula says she knows a man who might like to write a piece on me—something on the new book—for one of the literary magazines. I've fixed to have lunch with him, on Tuesday.'

'Oh, yes?' said Helen.

'Yes.'

'One of the literary magazines?'

'Yes.'

'Marvellous... Where are you seeing him? Somewhere with Ursula?'

Whoosh! went the trapdoor. 'Yes,' said Julia.

Helen laughed, and turned back. 'Well,' she said, 'won't that be nice for you.'

Julia looked away. 'I thought you might be pleased,' she said quietly, 'that the man wants to write about me.'

'I suppose he's some great friend of hers?'

'Not especially, I think. Does it matter?'

'It just strikes me as odd, that she should go to so much trouble on your behalf.'

'You think someone must go to extraordinary lengths, to get an article written about me?'

Helen did not answer. Her mind, like a diabolical engine, was lurching into life. She did not know what the worst of it was: that this had come; or that it had come while she was unready. She looked at Julia through narrowed eyes, as if vastly knowing.

'So,' she said, 'I suppose you planned to bring me here and make me tipsy, before telling me?'

Julia blushed, in embarrassment or anger. 'Don't be an idiot.'

'Why didn't you tell me sooner, then?'

'I don't know. I forgot. It didn't seem important. It isn't important, is it?'

'Apparently it is, if you have to tell me in this elaborate way— bring me here and make me tipsy. "Show the old girl a bit of a treat, then it won't seem half so bad."'

'What are you talking about?'

Helen sounded absurd, even to herself. But it was too late, now, to be anything else. She lay quite rigid for a moment. Then she sat up, and began to put on her sandals.

'I'm going home,' she said.

'Helen, don't.'

'I don't want to stay. You've spoiled it. It's all quite spoiled.'

'You're being ridiculous.' Julia hesitated, then reached for her own shoes.

'You don't have to come,' said Helen, seeing her move. 'Really, I'd rather you didn't. Stay here, and plan your lunch. In fact, why don't you find some telephone box and call up Ursula Manning, and ask her to join you?'

'For God's sake,' said Julia. She said it sharply. The woman with the little boy looked over, and watched them, puzzled. 'She'll decide we're two bickering spinsters,' Helen thought, as she tugged the strap of her sandal through its buckle. 'Two spiteful, bickering spinsters. "Women shouldn't be so much together," she'll think, complacently. Christ, she's right...'

She put the remains of their picnic in the tea towel, shook the last drops of beer from the bottles and cups, pulled savagely at the madras cloth.

'Move, will you?'

Julia was working at the buckle of her own shoe. 'Let me take the bag,' she said, as she rose.

'I've got it.'

'You carried it here.'

'It doesn't matter, does it?' Helen slung the bag over her shoulder, began to walk briskly away. She heard Julia follow. The woman still watched them; the lumpish girl beside her looked blankly at them, too; even the little boy looked. *This is terrible!* thought Helen. *'Oh*

God, this is agony!' She would have liked to fling herself down, beat her fists upon the ground. She only walked; and when Julia did not catch her up, her misery increased. She thought, 'Now I've made her hate me... Oh, if only she would come and make me stop! If only she would come and tell me not to be such a fool!'

But even as she thought it, she walked more quickly; and Julia did not come: Helen felt her following, at an absurd little distance. They passed about the deckchairs and the bandstand, over the little bridge, into Baker Street; when Helen crossed a road, she ran—she was pleased if there were cars to dodge between, for that meant Julia would be stranded, behind her, at the kerb... They walked like this, all the way to their square. When Helen reached the house, its door was open: she saw with a sinking heart that the man who lived in the flat downstairs from them was sitting on the step, drinking tea from his jam jar, working at something—some small piece of machinery, she thought—in his lap. His daughter was sitting beside him, with one of her rabbits.

'Hullo,' she said, when she saw Helen. The rabbit was white, with eyes of a dreadful pinkness. She lifted it up.

'I say,' said Helen brightly, stepping past. 'Isn't he smart?'

'It's a lady-rabbit, not a boy,' said the girl.

'Soft as shit,' said the man, not raising his eyes. Helen saw then what he had in his lap: a pistol, some soldier's pistol from the war. He was cleaning the barrel, with rags and oil.

The rabbit kicked its legs. 'Can I bring him upstairs?' said the girl.

Helen smiled. 'Not today. We're a little tired, today.'

'Been out on a spree?' said the man, gazing into the workings of his gun.

'Something like that.'

He caught her eye. 'Had your jollies?'

Helen's smile grew rigid. She passed inside, unlocked the door to the flat, left it open behind her. As she began to climb the stairs she heard the girl addressing Julia; and then came Julia herself, exclaiming over the rabbit with the same false brightness with which Helen had: 'My goodness. *What* a beauty...' She sounded like her mother.

They had left the windows closed. The flat smelled faintly sour. Two or three late flies buzzed drearily between the rooms. Helen took the canvas bag to the kitchen, but did not unpack it. She visited the lavatory, and washed her hands. Then she went into the sitting room, installed herself in a chair next to the window, took up a book. The book was one of hers—an anthology of Victorian verse. She enjoyed poetry, but liked it to rhyme. She read at random: some section of Tennyson. The reading calmed her. When Julia appeared and stood in the doorway of the room, Helen felt blank, hard, cool as marble. It was Julia who shook. She said, 'How *could* you make us do that?'

'I didn't make us do anything.'

'I can't stand this, Helen.'

'It's in your power to stop it then, I think.'

'What do you mean?'

'You know what I mean.'

'You can't mean, Ursula. My God! If every time I tell you I'm to have lunch with her—'

'If it's so ordinary a thing,' said Helen quickly, 'why do you have to tell me in such a sneaking sort of way?'

'Why do you think? Because I know you'll behave like this! You twist everything so. You expect me to be guilty. It makes me appear to be guilty, even—Christ! even to myself!'

Helen knew that this was true. But it was beyond her, to admit such a thing, at such a stage. The argument went on. She countered every sensible comment of Julia's with some fresh absurdity of her own; and she spoke coolly, reasonably—now and then laughing, in her hideous knowing way—while Julia grew ever more agitated and upset. At last Julia's voice quite broke. She began to cry. She put her hand upon the door frame and leaned her face upon her knuckles. 'Oh, God!' she said. 'Oh, God, I can't bear it!' The tears spilled from her eyes: Helen saw them fall and strike the leather of her shoe.

She saw them, with horror. It was like the breaking of a spell. For Julia cried often, at moments like this, and Helen—who wept only at nonsense—responded, every time, with the same sort of miserable fright she had felt at the sight of her mother weeping when she was a child. She thought, in a panic: 'Now she will leave me.' She saw herself, alone. 'I will have made her leave me.'

'Julia, I'm sorry,' she said, standing up. Her words were flat, however, though her fear was so great. Julia turned, went into her study, sharply closed the door; Helen heard her sobbing. She put her hands to her stomach: she was sick, at her stomach and her heart.

She thought: 'That's it.' She thought: 'I've lost her.'

But after a minute, Julia's sobs died. Helen heard the click—she thought—of the telephone receiver being lifted from its cradle. And even in the midst of her misery and terror, she began to be afraid—she began to be sure—that Julia must be telephoning Ursula Manning, making some fresh arrangement... She took her hands from her stomach and went stealthily—very stealthily—to the study door; held her breath and listened; but heard nothing...

So the evening wore on. Helen sat with the book of Victorian verse, until the light at the window grew too dim to read by; then she put down the book and sat in darkness. In the flat downstairs the man, the woman and their daughter called out, from room to room; the girl played her recorder—played, endlessly, the same halting nursery tune. At nine o'clock or so, Julia's door opened, and light spilled into the hall: Helen saw her go to the kitchen, heard the sound of her putting water into a pan, making a drink; then she spent some time in the bathroom, then went to bed. She did not speak to Helen, or come to the room at all, and Helen did not call out. The bedroom door was pushed to, but not closed: the light from the reading lamp showed, for a quarter of an hour, and then was extinguished.

After that, the flat seemed darker than before; and the darkness, and the silence, made Helen feel worse, feel choked and defeated and powerless. She had only to reach for the switch of a lamp, the dial of the wireless, to change the mood of the place; but she could not do it, she was quite cut off from ordinary habits and things. She sat a little longer, then got up and began to pace. The pacing was like something an actress might do in a play, to communicate a state of despair or dementedness, and didn't feel real. She got down on the floor, drew up her legs, put her arms before her face: this pose didn't feel real, either, but she held it, for almost twenty minutes. 'Perhaps Julia will come, and see me lying on the floor,' she thought, as she lay there; she thought, that if Julia did that, then she would at least realize the extremity of the feeling by which Helen was gripped... Then she saw at last that she would only look absurd. She got up. She was chilled, and cramped. She went to the mirror. It was unnerving, gazing at one's face in a mirror in a darkened room; there was a little light from a street lamp, however, and she could see by this that her cheek and bare arm were marked red and white, as if in little weals, from where she had lain upon the carpet. The marks were satisfying, at least. She had often longed, in fact, for her jealousy to take some physical form; she had sometimes thought, in moments like this, 'I'll burn myself,' or 'I'll cut myself.' For a burn or a cut might be shown, might be nursed, might scar or heal, would be a miserable kind of emblem; would anyway indubitably be *there*, upon the surface of her body, rather than corroding it from within... Now the thought came to her again, that she might scar herself in some way. It came, like the solution to a problem. 'I won't be doing it,' she said to herself, 'like some hysterical girl. I won't be doing it for Julia, hoping she'll come and catch me at it. It won't be like lying on the sitting room floor. I'll be doing it for myself, as a secret...'

She did not allow herself to think what a very poor secret such a thing would be. She went quietly to the bathroom, closed and locked the door, pulled gently at the string which turned on the bathroom light; and at once felt better. The light was bright, like the lights one saw in hospital operating rooms, in films; the bare white surfaces of the bath and basin and lavatory contributed, too, a certain clinical feeling, a sense of efficiency, even of duty. She was not in the least like some hysterical girl. She saw her face in the mirror again and the scarlet had faded from her cheek, she looked perfectly reasonable and calm.

She proceeded, now, as if she had planned the entire operation in advance. She opened the bathroom cabinet and took out the little silver safety razor she and Julia used for shaving their legs. She unwound the screw, lifted off the little hub of metal, carefully took out the blade and held it. How thin it was, how flexible! It was like holding nothing—a wafer, a counter in a game, a postage stamp... Her only concern was, where she might cut. She looked at her arms; she thought perhaps the inside of the arm, where the flesh was softer and might be supposed to yield more easily. She considered her stomach, for a similar reason. She didn't think of her wrists, ankles or shins, or any hard part like that. Finally she settled on her inner thigh. She put up a foot to the cold rounded lip of the bath; found the pose too cramped; lengthened her stride and braced her foot against the farther wall. She drew back her skirt, thought of tucking it into her drawers, thought of taking it off entirely. For, suppose she should bleed on it? She had no idea how much blood to expect...

Her thigh was pale—creamy-pale, against the white of the bathtub—and seemed huge beneath her hands. She had never contemplated it in just this way before, and she was struck now by how perfectly featureless it was. If she were to see it, in isolation, she would hardly know it as a functioning piece of limb. She didn't think she would even recognize it as hers.

She put a hand upon the leg, to stretch the flesh tight between fingers and thumb; then she brought the edge of the blade to the skin and made a cut. The cut was shallow, but impossibly painful: she felt it, like stepping in icy water, as a hideous shock to the heart. She recoiled for a moment, then tried a second time. The sensation was the same. She literally gasped. 'Do it again, more swiftly,' she said to herself; but the thinness and flexibility of the metal, that had seemed almost attractive before, now struck her, in relation to the springing fatness of her thigh, as repulsive. The slicing was too precise. The cuts she had made were filling with blood; the blood rose slowly, however—as if grudgingly—and seemed to darken and congeal at once. The edges of flesh were closing, already: she put the razor blade down, and pulled them apart. That made the blood come a little faster—at last it spilled from the skin and grew smeary. She watched, for a minute; two or three times more worked the flesh about the cuts, to make the blood flow again; then she rubbed the leg clean with a square of damp lavatory paper.

She was left with two short crimson lines, such as might have been made by a hard but playful swipe from the paw of a cat.

She sat upon the edge of the bath. The shock of cutting, she thought, had produced some sort of chemical change in her: she felt quite unnaturally clear-headed—alive, and chastened. She had lost the certainty that the cutting of her leg was a sane and reasonable thing to do; she would have hated, for example, for Julia, or any of their friends, to have come upon her as she was doing it. She would have died of embarrassment! And yet— She kept looking at the crimson lines, in a half perplexed, half admiring way. 'You perfect fool,' she thought; she thought it, however, almost jauntily... At last she took up the blade again, washed it, screwed it back beneath its little silver hub; put the razor back in the cabinet. She turned off the light, allowed her eyes to grow used to the darkness, then let herself into the hall. She went to the bedroom, pushed at the door, stepped, very softly, to the bed. Julia lay on her side, her face in darkness, her hair very black against her pillow. It was impossible to say whether she were sleeping or awake.

'Julia,' said Helen, quietly.

'What?'

'I'm sorry. I'm sorry. Do you hate me?'

'Yes.'

'You don't hate me as much as I hate myself.'

Julia rolled on to her back. 'Do you say that as some sort of consolation?'

'I don't know.' She went closer, put her fingers to Julia's hair. Julia flinched.

'Your hand's freezing. Don't touch me!' She took Helen's hand. 'For God's sake, why are you so cold? Where have you been?'

'In the bathroom. Nowhere.'

'Get into bed, can't you?'

Helen moved away, to take off her clothes, unpin her hair, draw on her nightdress. She did it all in a creeping, craven sort of way. 'You're so cold!' Julia said again, when she had got into the bed beside her.

'I'm sorry,' said Helen. She had not felt chilled, before; but now she felt the warmth of Julia's body, she began to shake. 'I'm sorry,' she said again. Her teeth chattered in her head. She tried to make herself rigid; the trembling grew worse.

'God!' said Julia; but she put her arm about Helen and drew her close. She smelled of sleep, of unmade beds, of unwashed hair—but pleasantly, deliciously. Helen lay against her and shut her eyes. She felt exhausted, emptied out; she thought of the day that had passed—it was astonishing to her, that a single set of hours could contain so many separate states of violent feeling.

Perhaps Julia thought the same. Her shoulder rose, then sank, as she sighed. 'What a ridiculous day!' she said.

Helen bent her head, as if abjectly, until it rested on Julia's breast. She said, 'I thought you might leave.'

'I ought to,' said Julia. 'It would serve you right.'

'I felt like Othello—like the base Indian, who threw a pearl away, richer than all his tribe.'

'Idiot.'

'I love you.'

'Idiot. Go to sleep.'

'Don't leave me,' thought Helen. She heard the beat of Julia's heart: steady, secret, out of reach. 'Don't leave me.'

Next morning she bathed and dressed after Julia had risen and started work. She did the same thing in the days which followed. The cuts upon her leg were shallow, and fine, and healed quickly: when Julia noticed them at last, they were very faint. Helen said she had scratched herself on the clasp of a suspender, and Julia believed her.

□

GRANTA

DINNER WITH
DR AZAD

Monica Ali

Monica Ali was born in Dhaka in former East Pakistan (now Bangladesh) in 1967 and left with her family during the civil war. She grew up in Bolton and studied politics, philosophy and economics at Wadham College, Oxford. She worked in publishing, design and branding before having children, and started to write whenever her son and daughter 'could be persuaded to synchronize their naps'. Her first novel, 'Brick Lane', is published by Doubleday in the UK in June.

Dinner with Dr Azad

Nazneen waved at the tattoo lady. The tattoo lady was always there when Nazneen looked out across the dead grass and broken paving stones to the block opposite. Most of the flats that closed three sides of a square had net curtains and the life behind was all shapes and shadows. But the tattoo lady had no curtains. Morning and afternoon she sat with her big thighs spilling over the sides of her chair, tipping forward to drop ash in a bowl, tipping back to slug from her can. She drank now, and tossed the can out of the window.

It was the middle of the day. Nazneen had finished the housework. Soon she would start preparing the evening meal, but for a while she would let the time pass. It was hot and the sun fell flat on the metal window frames and glared off the glass. A red and gold sari hung out of a top-floor flat in Rosemead block. A baby's bib and miniature dungarees lower down. The sign screwed to the brickwork was in stiff English capitals and the curlicues beneath were Bengali. NO DUMPING. NO PARKING. NO BALL GAMES. Two old men in white panjabi-pyjama and skullcaps walked along the path, slowly, as if they did not want to go where they were going. A thin brown dog sniffed along to the middle of the grass and defecated. The breeze on Nazneen's face was thick with the smell from the overflowing communal bins.

Six months now since she'd been sent away to London. Every morning before she opened her eyes she thought, *if I were the wishing type, I know what I would wish.* And then she opened her eyes and saw Chanu's puffy face on the pillow next to her, his lips parted indignantly even as he slept. She saw the pink dressing table with the curly-sided mirror, and the monstrous black wardrobe that claimed most of the room. Was it cheating? To think, *I know what I would wish?* Was it not the same as making the wish? If she knew what the wish would be, then somewhere in her heart she had already made it.

The tattoo lady waved back at Nazneen. She scratched her arms, her shoulders, the accessible portions of her buttocks. She yawned and lit a cigarette. At least two thirds of the flesh on show was covered in ink. Nazneen had never been close enough (never closer than this, never further) to decipher the designs. Chanu said the tattoo lady was Hell's Angel, which upset Nazneen. She thought the tattoos might be flowers, or birds. They were ugly and they made the tattoo lady more ugly than was necessary, but the tattoo lady clearly did not care. Every time Nazneen saw her she wore the same look of boredom and detachment. Such a state was sought by the sadhus who walked in rags through the Muslim villages, indifferent to the kindness of strangers, the unkind sun.

Nazneen thought sometimes of going downstairs, crossing the yard and climbing the Rosemead stairwell to the fourth floor. She might have to knock on a few doors before the tattoo lady answered. She would take something, an offering of samosas or bhajis, and the tattoo lady would smile and Nazneen would smile and perhaps they would sit together by the window and let the time pass more easily. She thought of it but she would not go. Strangers would answer if she knocked on the wrong door. The tattoo lady might be angry at an unwanted interruption. It was clear she did not like to leave her chair. And even if she wasn't angry, what would be the point? Nazneen could say two things in English: sorry and thank you. She could spend another day alone. It was only another day.

She should be getting on with the evening meal. The lamb curry was prepared. She had made it last night with tomatoes and new potatoes. There was chicken saved in the freezer from the last time Dr Azad had been invited but had cancelled at the last minute. There was still the dhal to make, and the vegetable dishes, the spices to grind, the rice to wash, and the sauce to prepare for the fish that Chanu would bring this evening. She would rinse the glasses and rub them with newspaper to make them shine. The tablecloth had some spots to be scrubbed out. What if it went wrong? The rice might stick. She might over-salt the dhal. Chanu might forget the fish.

It was only dinner. One dinner. One guest.

She left the window open. Standing on the sofa to reach, she picked up the Holy Qur'an from the high shelf that Chanu, under duress, had specially built. She made her intention as fervently as possible, seeking refuge from Satan with fists clenched and fingernails digging into her palms. Then she selected a page at random and began to read.

To God belongs all that the heavens and the earth contain. We exhort you, as We have exhorted those to whom the Book was given before you, to fear God. If you deny Him, know that to God belongs all that the heavens and earth contain. God is self-sufficient and worthy of praise.

The words calmed her stomach and she was pleased. Even Dr Azad was nothing as to God. To God belongs all that the heavens and the earth contain. She said it over a few times, aloud. She was composed. Nothing could bother her. Only God, if he chose to. Chanu might flap about and squawk because Dr Azad was coming for dinner. Let him flap. To God belongs all that the heavens and the earth contain. How would it sound in Arabic? More lovely even than in Bengali she supposed, for those were the actual Words of God.

She closed the book and looked around the room to check it was tidy enough. Chanu's books and papers were stacked beneath the table. They would have to be moved or Dr Azad would not be able to get his feet in. The rugs which she had held out of the window earlier and beaten with a wooden spoon needed to be put down again. There were three rugs: red and orange, green and purple, brown and blue. The carpet was yellow with a green leaf design. One hundred per cent nylon and, Chanu said, very hard-wearing. The sofa and chairs were the colour of dried cow dung, which was a practical colour. They had little sheaths of plastic on the headrests to protect them from Chanu's hair oil. There was a lot of furniture, more than Nazneen had seen in one room before. Even if you took all the furniture in the compound back home, from every auntie and uncle's ghar, it would not match up to this one room. There was a low table with a glass centre and orange plastic legs, three little wooden tables that stacked together, the big table they used for the evening meal, a bookcase, a corner cupboard, a rack for newspapers, a trolley filled with files and folders, the sofa and armchairs, two footstools, six dining chairs and a showcase. The walls were papered in yellow with brown squares and circles lining neatly up and down. Nobody in Gouripur had anything like it. It made her proud. Her father was the second wealthiest man in the village and he never had anything like it. He had made a good marriage for her. There were plates on the wall attached by hooks and wires, which were not for eating from but only for display. Some were rimmed in gold paint. 'Gold leaf', Chanu called it. His certificates were framed and mixed with the plates. She had everything here. All these beautiful things.

She put the Qur'an back in its place. Next to it lay the most Holy Book wrapped inside a cloth covering: the Qur'an in Arabic. She touched her fingers to the cloth.

Nazneen stared at the glass showcase stuffed with pottery animals, china figures and plastic fruits. Each one had to be dusted. She wondered how the dust got in and where it came from. All of it belonged to God. She wondered what He wanted with clay tigers, trinkets and dust.

And then, because she had let her mind drift and become uncentred again, she began to recite in her head from the Holy Qur'an one of the suras she had learned in school. She did not know what the words meant but the rhythm of them soothed her.

'She is an unspoilt girl. From the village.'

She had got up one night to fetch a glass of water. It was one week since they married. She had gone to bed and he was still up, talking on the telephone as she stood outside the door.

'No,' said Chanu. 'I would not say so. Not beautiful, but not so ugly either. The face is broad, big forehead. Eyes are a bit too close together.'

Nazneen put her hand up to her head. It was true. The forehead was large. But she had never thought of her eyes being too close.

'Not tall. Not short. Around five foot two. Hips are a bit narrow but wide enough, I think, to carry children. All things considered, I am satisfied. Perhaps when she gets older she'll grow a beard on her chin but now she is only eighteen. And a blind uncle is better than no uncle. I waited too long to get a wife.'

Narrow hips! You could wish for such a fault, Nazneen said to herself, thinking of the rolls of fat that hung low from Chanu's stomach. It would be possible to tuck all your hundred pens and pencils under those rolls and keep them safe and tight. You could stuff a book or two up there as well. If your spindle legs could take the weight.

'What's more, she is a good worker. Cleaning and cooking and all that. The only complaint I could make is she can't put my files in order, because she has no English. I don't complain though. As I say, a girl from the village: totally unspoilt.'

Chanu went on talking but Nazneen crept away, back to bed. A blind uncle is better than no uncle. Her husband had a proverb for everything. Any wife is better than no wife. Something is better than nothing. What had she imagined? That he was in love with her? That he was grateful because she, young and graceful, had accepted him? That in sacrificing herself to him, she was owed something? Yes. Yes. She realized in a stinging rush she had imagined all these things. Such a foolish girl. Such high notions. What self-regard.

What she missed most was people. Not any people in particular but just people. If she put her ear to the wall she could hear sounds. The television on. Coughing. Sometimes the lavatory flushing. Someone upstairs scraping a chair. A shouting match below. Everyone in their boxes, counting their possessions. In all her eighteen years, she could scarcely remember a moment that she had spent alone. Until she married. And came to London to sit day after day in this large box with the furniture to dust, and the muffled sound of private lives sealed away above, below and around her.

D r Azad was a small, precise man who, contrary to the Bengali custom, spoke at a level only one quarter of a decibel above a whisper. Anyone who wished to hear what he was saying was obliged to lean in towards him, so that all evening Chanu gave the appearance of hanging on his every word.

'Come,' said Dr Azad, when Nazneen was hovering behind the table ready to serve, 'Come and sit down with us.'

'My wife is very shy.' Chanu smiled and motioned with his head for her to be seated.

'This week I saw two of our young men in a very sorry state,' said the doctor. 'I told them straight, this is your choice: stop drinking alcohol now, or by Eid your liver will be finished. Ten years ago this would be unthinkable. Two in one week! But now our children are copying what they see here, going to the pub, to nightclubs. Or drinking at home in their bedrooms where their parents think they are perfectly safe. The problem is our community is not properly educated about these things.' Dr Azad drank a glass of water down in one long draught and poured himself another. 'I always drink two glasses before starting the meal.' He drank the second glass. 'Good. Now I will not overeat.'

'Eat! Eat!' said Chanu. 'Water is good for cleansing the system, but food is also essential.' He scooped up lamb and rice with his fingers and chewed. He put too much in his mouth at once, and he made sloppy noises as he ate. When he could speak again, he said,

'I agree with you. Our community is not educated about this, and much else besides. But for my part, I don't plan to risk these things happening to my children. We will go back before they get spoiled.'

'This is another disease that afflicts us,' said the doctor. 'I call it Going Home Syndrome. Do you know what that means?' He addressed himself to Nazneen.

She felt a heat on the back of her neck and formed words that did not leave her mouth.

'It is natural,' said Chanu. 'These people are basically peasants and they miss the land. The pull of the land is stronger even than the pull of blood.'

'And when they have saved enough they will get on an aeroplane and go?'

'They don't ever really leave home. Their bodies are here, but their hearts are back there. And anyway, look how they live: just recreating the villages here.'

'But they will never save enough to go back.' Dr Azad helped himself to vegetables. His shirt was spotless white, and his collar and tie so high under his chin that he seemed to be missing a neck. Nazneen saw an oily yellow stain on her husband's shirt where he had dripped food.

Dr Azad continued, 'Every year they think, just one more year. But whatever they save, it's never enough.'

'We would not need very much,' said Nazneen. Both men looked at her. She spoke to her plate. 'I mean, we could live very cheaply.' The back of her neck burned.

Chanu filled the silence with his laugh. 'My wife is just settling in here.' He coughed and shuffled in his chair. 'The thing is, with the promotion coming up, things are beginning to go well for me now. If I just get the promotion confirmed then many things are possible.'

'I used to think all the time of going back,' said Dr Azad. He spoke so quietly that Nazneen was forced to look directly at him, because to catch all the words she had to follow his lips. 'Every year I thought, "Maybe this year." And I'd go for a visit, buy some more land, see relatives and friends and make up my mind to return for good. But something would always happen. A flood, a tornado that just missed the building, a power cut, some mind-numbing piece of petty bureaucracy, bribes to be paid out to get anything done. And

I'd think, "Well, maybe not this year." And now, I don't know. I just don't know.'

Chanu cleared his throat. 'Of course, it's not been announced yet. Other people have applied. But after my years of service... Do you know, in six years I have not been late on one single day! And only three sick days, even with the ulcer. Some of my colleagues are very unhealthy, always going off sick with this or that. It's not something I could bring to Mr Dalloway's attention. Even so, I feel he ought to be aware of it.'

'I wish you luck,' said Dr Azad.

'Then there's the academic perspective. Within months I will be a fully fledged academic, with two degrees. One from a British University. Bachelor of Arts degree. With honours.'

'I'm sure you have a good chance.'

'Did Mr Dalloway tell you that?'

'Who's that?'

'Mr Dalloway.'

The doctor shrugged his neat shoulders.

'My superior. Mr Dalloway. He told you I have a good chance?'

'No.'

'He said I didn't have a good chance?'

'He didn't say anything at all. I don't know the gentleman in question.'

'He's one of your patients. His secretary made an appointment for him to see you about his shoulder sprain. He's a squash player. Very active man. Average build, I'd say. Red hair. Wears contact lenses—perhaps you test his eyes as well.'

'It's possible he's a patient. There are several thousand on the list for my practice.'

'What I should have told you straight away—he has a harelip. Well, it's been put right, reconstructive surgery and all that, but you can always tell. That should put you on to him.'

The guest remained quiet. Nazneen heard Chanu suppress a belch. She wanted to go to him and stroke his forehead. She wanted to get up from the table and walk out of the door and never see him again.

'He might be a patient. I do not know him.' It was nearly a whisper.

'No,' said Chanu. 'I see.'

'But I wish you luck.'

'I am forty years old,' said Chanu. He spoke quietly like the doctor, with none of his assurance. 'I have been in this country for sixteen years. Nearly half my life.' He gave a dry-throated gargle. 'When I came I was a young man. I had ambitions. Big dreams. When I got off the aeroplane, I had my degree certificate in my suitcase and a few pounds in my pocket. I thought there would be a red carpet laid out for me. I was going to join the Civil Service and become Private Secretary to the Prime Minister.' As he told his story, his voice grew. It filled the room. 'That was my plan. And then I found things were a bit different. These people here didn't know the difference between me, who stepped off an aeroplane with a degree certificate, and the peasants who jumped off the boat possessing only the lice on their heads. What can you do?' He rolled a ball of rice and meat in his fingers and teased it around his plate.

'I did this and that. Whatever I could. So much hard work, so little reward. More or less it is true to say, I have been chasing wild buffaloes and eating my own rice. You know that saying? All the begging letters from home I burned. And I made two promises to myself. I will be a success, come what may. That's promise number one. Number two, I will go back home. When I am a success. And I will honour these promises.' Chanu, who had grown taller and taller in his chair, sank back down.

'Very good, very good,' said Dr Azad. He checked his watch.

'The begging letters still come,' said Chanu. 'From old servants, from the children of servants. Even from my own family, although they are not in need. All they can think of is money. They think there is gold lying about in the streets here and I am just hoarding it all in my palace. But I did not come here for money. Was I starving in Dhaka? I was not. Do they enquire about my diplomas?' He gestured to the wall, where his various framed certificates were displayed. 'They do not. What is more…' He cleared his throat, although it was already clear. Dr Azad looked at Nazneen and, without meaning to, she returned his gaze so that she was caught in a complicity of looks, given and returned, which said something about her husband that she ought not to be saying.

Chanu talked on. Dr Azad finished the food on his plate while Chanu's food grew cold. Nazneen picked at the cauliflower curry. The doctor declined with a waggle of the head either a further helping or any dessert. He sat with his hands folded on the table while Chanu, his oration at an end, ate noisily and quickly. Twice more he checked his watch.

At half past nine Dr Azad said, 'Well, Chanu. I thank you and your wife for a most pleasant evening and a delicious meal.'

Chanu protested that it was still early. The doctor was adamant. 'I always retire at ten-thirty and I always read for half an hour in bed before that.'

'We intellectuals must stick together,' said Chanu, and he walked with his guest to the door.

'If you take my advice, one intellectual to another, you will eat more slowly, chew more thoroughly and take only a small portion of meat. Otherwise, I'll see you back at the clinic again with another ulcer.'

'Just think,' said Chanu, 'if I did not have the ulcer in the first place, then we would not have met and we would not have had this dinner together.'

'Just think,' said the doctor. He waved stiffly and disappeared behind the door.

The television was on. Chanu liked to keep it glowing in the evenings, like a fire in the corner of the room. Sometimes he went over and stirred it by pressing the buttons so that the light flared and changed colours. Mostly he ignored it. Nazneen held a pile of the last dirty dishes to take to the kitchen, but the screen held her. A man in a very tight suit (so tight that it made his private parts stand out on display) and a woman in a skirt that did not even cover her bottom gripped each other as an invisible force hurtled them across an oval arena. The people in the audience clapped their hands together and then stopped. By some magic they all stopped at exactly the same time. The couple broke apart. They fled from each other and no sooner had they fled than they sought each other out. Every move they made was urgent, intense, a declaration. The woman raised one leg and rested her boot (Nazneen saw the thin blade for the first time) on the other thigh, making a triangular flag of her legs, and spun around until she would surely fall but didn't. She did not slow down. She stopped dead, and flung her arms above her head with a look so triumphant that you knew she had conquered everything: her body, the laws of nature, and the heart of the tight-suited man who slid over on his knees, vowing to lay down his life for her.

'What is this called?' said Nazneen.

Chanu glanced at the screen. 'Ice skating,' he said, in English.

'Ice e-skating,' said Nazneen.

'Ice skating,' said Chanu.

'Ice e-skating.'

'No, no. No *e*. Ice skating. Try it again.'

Nazneen hesitated.

'Go on!'

'Ice es-kating,' she said, with deliberation.

Chanu smiled. 'Don't worry about it. It's a common problem for Bengalis. Two consonants together causes a difficulty. I have conquered this issue after a long time. But you are unlikely to need these words in any case.'

'I would like to learn some English,' said Nazneen.

Chanu puffed his cheeks and spat the air out in a *fuff*. 'It will come. Don't worry about it. Where's the need anyway?' He looked at his book and Nazneen watched the screen.

'He thinks he will get the promotion because he goes to the *pub* with the boss. He is so stupid he doesn't even realize there is any other way of getting promotion.' Chanu was supposed to be studying. His books were open on the table. Every so often he looked in one, or turned a page. Mostly, he talked. *Pub, pub, pub*. Nazneen turned the word over in her mind. Another drop of English that she knew. There were other English words that Chanu sprinkled into his conversation, other things she could say to the tattoo lady. At this moment she could not think of any.

'This Wilkie—I told you about him—he has one or maybe two O levels. Every lunchtime he goes to the *pub* and he comes back half an hour late. Today I saw him sitting in Mr Dalloway's office using the phone with his feet up on the desk. The jackfruit is still on the tree but already he is oiling his moustache. No way is he going to get promoted.'

Nazneen stared at the television. There was a close-up of the woman. She had sparkly bits around her eyes like tiny sequins glued to her face. Her hair was scraped back and tied on top of her head with plastic flowers. Her chest pumped up and down as if her heart would shoot out and she smiled pure, gold joy. She must be terrified, thought Nazneen, because such things cannot be held, and must be lost.

'No,' said Chanu. 'I don't have anything to fear from Wilkie. I have a degree from Dhaka University in English Literature. Can Wilkie quote from Chaucer or Dickens or Hardy?'

Nazneen, who feared her husband would begin one of his long quotations, stacked a final plate and went to the kitchen. He liked to quote in English and then give her a translation, phrase by phrase. And when it was translated it usually meant no more to her than it did in English, so that she did not know what to reply or even if a reply was required.

She washed the dishes and rinsed them and Chanu came and leaned against the ill-fitting cupboards and talked some more. 'You see,' he said, a frequent opener although often she did not see, 'it is the white underclass, like Wilkie, who are most afraid of people like me. To him, and people like him, we are the only thing standing in the way of them sliding totally to the bottom of the pile. As long as we are below them, then they are above something. If they see us rise then they are resentful because we have left our proper place. That is why you get the phenomenon of the *National Front*. They can play on those fears to create racial tensions, and give these people a superiority complex. The middle classes are more secure, and therefore more relaxed.' He drummed his fingers against the Formica.

Nazneen took a tea towel and dried the plates. She wondered if the ice e-skating woman went home and washed and wiped. It was difficult to imagine. But there were no servants here. She would have to manage by herself.

Chanu ploughed on. 'Wilkie is not exactly underclass. He has a job, so technically I would say no, he is not. But that is the mindset. This is what I am studying in the subsection on *Race, Ethnicity and Identity*. It is part of the sociology module. Of course, when I have my Open University degree then nobody can question my credentials. Although Dhaka University is one of the best in the world, these people here are by and large ignorant and know nothing of the Brontës or Thackeray.'

Nazneen began to put things away. She needed to get in the cupboard that Chanu blocked with his body. He didn't move although she waited in front of him. Eventually she left the pans on the cooker to be put away in the morning.

Monica Ali

After a minute or two in the dark, when her eyes had adjusted and the snoring began, Nazneen turned on her side and looked at her husband. She scrutinized his face, round as a ball, the blunt-cut thinning hair on top, and the dense eyebrows. His mouth was open and she began to regulate her breathing so that she inhaled as he did. When she got it wrong she could smell his breath. She looked at him for a long time. It was not a handsome face. In the month before her marriage, when she looked at his face in the photograph, she thought it ugly. Now she saw that it was not handsome, but it was kind. His mouth, always on duty, always moving, was full-lipped and generous, without a hint of cruelty. His eyes, small and beleaguered beneath those thick brows, were anxious or far away, or both. Now that they were closed she could see the way the skin puckered up across the lids and drooped down to meet the creases at the corners. He shifted in his sleep and moved on to his stomach with his arms down by his side and his face squashed against the pillow.

Nazneen got out of bed and crossed the hall. She caught hold of the bead curtain that partitioned the kitchen from the narrow hallway, to stop it tinkling, and went to the fridge. She got out the Tupperware containers of rice and fish and chicken and took a spoon from the drawer. As she ate, standing beside the sink, she looked out at the moon which hung above the dark flats chequered with lights. It was large and white and untroubled. She tried to imagine what it would be like to fall in love. She looked down into the courtyard. Two boys exchanged mock punches, feinting left and right. Cigarettes burned in their mouths. She opened the window and leaned into the breeze. Across the way the tattoo lady raised a can to her lips. □

GRANTA

GAS, BOYS, GAS
Andrew O'Hagan

Andrew O'Hagan was born in 1968 and grew up in Irvine New Town in Scotland. At secondary school, he became 'a total nightmare to the Sisters of Mercy in their efforts to uphold basic standards of religious education'. After university in Glasgow, he worked on the London Review of Books. In 1995 he wrote 'The Missing', a non-fiction account of missing persons, which was received 'with some enthusiasm' in both Britain and the United States, and in 1999 he published a novel, 'Our Fathers', which was shortlisted for the Booker Prize, the Whitbread, the IMPAC Fiction Prize, the John Llewellyn Rhys Prize, and won the Winifred Holtby Prize for Fiction. He lives in London. 'Gas, Boys, Gas' comes from his new novel, 'Personality', published by Faber.

I came to London after graduation and found a bedsit off Kensington Church Street, a place of antique shops; there was a tree that came up to my window on the top floor and a caged lift down to the street. Early in the mornings I walked across Hyde Park to a swimming pool at Lancaster Gate. There was no one to talk to and London was a mystery, but I loved those first times in the city, reading newspapers and going to lectures near the Albert Hall. I walked across the park as if it were made for the likes of me, people with nothing to do in the morning but contemplate what they might do next.

I saw a job in the *Evening Standard*. It said: 'Assistant Editor Wanted. *St Clare's Review*. Experience required. £8,000 per annum.' My experience was two summers in a television shop back home in Scotland; still, I had an English degree and I cheered myself up on the way to the stationery shop by wondering if I was maybe overqualified for the post of assistant editor. I did some research at the local library. St Clare's had been going since 1915. It looked after the war blinded, giving them houses and holidays and things to fill their time.

The office I first came to smelled of lemon tea and carbon paper. I was interviewed by a Wing Commander Philip Rodney. He had maps of Kent and Sussex on the wall of his private office and slipped me a Mint Imperial during the interview. 'There's not a whole lot to it,' he said, 'though you will have to be good with the old boys. That's a must.'

'I haven't really edited before,' I said.

'Oh, never mind that, it's not *The Times* or anything of that sort. Just a bit of lick and stick.'

'I would give it my best shot.'

'Marvellous,' said the Wing Commander. 'You seem like a good chap. Can you start a week on Monday?'

In this way, I began my working life in the offices of St Clare's. The magazine was a bit of an absurdity. I would often stay late in the office with the lights of Marylebone glowing outside, and I'd hang over the layout desk, sizing photographs, writing captions, forming headlines, for a magazine that nobody was really going to read. It was like one long Monty Python sketch, the magazine for the blind, though it led other and more sensible lives in Braille and on tape, where it was read every month in a plummy voice by an actor Philip had known in the army.

The other departments were staffed mainly by ex-army officers and women in their sixties. There was an officer-corps mentality in the canteen, and some of the women brought knitting to work, and you half expected them to shout you out for air-raid drill at the drop of a stitch. Minnie Hopfield worked in Legacies. She was nearly seventy and she swore like a darts fan and smoked like hell. And yet she was Home Counties posh in the way most of them were: she loved a nice glass of wine, home-made jam, she'd been around the world.

Minnie told me the charity was insanely rich. Ex-servicemen had been leaving money to St Clare's since the 1920s, but the generations who were blinded in war were dying out, and the money, which had been brilliantly managed by a series of chief accountants (the real bosses of the organization), was just growing and growing with nowhere to go. 'It sounds fucking perverse,' said Minnie, 'but the folk upstairs were almost excited when the Falklands happened, I swear. Don't get me wrong, dear: nobody wants a young fellow to lose his eyes, but the charity is dying and it will have to do something. The idea of some new people to benefit did seem, well…it created a bit of excitement. Make no mistake about that.'

I told her she was a terrible person.

'That's as maybe, but as Elsa used to say'—Minnie had been friends in the 1940s with Elsa Lanchester, and she thought that Elsa had been through everything, being married to Charles Laughton and all, and would quote her on any subject, no matter how unlikely a preoccupation for a Hollywood actress—'as Elsa used to say, "One can't feed hens if there's no hens to feed."'

However sublimated, this point had been thoroughly absorbed into the mind of the charity by the time I arrived. I would sometimes run into Sir Edmund Noble, Admiral of the Fleet and Chairman of St Clare's, as I walked down to the strongroom to find some photograph of the wounded at Passchendaele. He was a tall, lean gentleman, high-toned and watery-eyed, and he would stop in front of you as if waiting for a salute. 'Good afternoon, sir,' I remember saying one of those times.

'Are you civilian?'

'Yes, sir,' I said, feeling a bit of a let-down.

'And Scottish?'

'Indeed, sir. Scottish. But I can't help it.'

'No need to help it, my boy,' he said (he didn't care for jokes). 'Some of the best men I've ever met. Good people. You've a lot to live up to.'

'Well, thank you, sir.'

'Not at all. Well, on your way. We won't win the battle standing here.'

Edmund Noble was the man who told Thatcher he could organize a flotilla of ships for the Falklands in forty-eight hours. He had done so, and was known at St Clare's for being closest to those young men, the few we had, who were blinded at Goose Green and on HMS *Sheffield*. He was always asking us to prepare for future casualties. 'Never go to sleep on the job,' he said. 'There's poison gas out there, and barbarians not afraid to use it.'

As for the St Clareites—the men themselves, 'my readers' (as they were not)—I began to spend time with them, walking with them in the countryside, supervising bus runs to here or there, going to reunions, refereeing blind sports, and I became close to some of them. Most had been young men when they were blinded; the last time they had seen the world it was full of smoke and flying dirt, but now they wanted to be guided to peaceful places. St Clare's had taught them Braille, it had given them work, pensions, holiday homes, communities—but it couldn't return them to English normality, the things they craved most and loved.

My job on those days out was to be the eyes, and there is one day I remember better than the others. I was leading a group of veterans of the old stamp, eight of them, half over eighty-five (veterans of Ypres, the Somme and the Dardanelles), three from Dunkirk, and one younger man, Ronnie, blinded by shrapnel during Suez. All of them loved the South Downs. It was something to do with their sense of England: the loveliness of the Downs themselves existed in their memories, but they were also conscious of the sea beyond the cliffs, and of Europe out there. The men seemed pleased to be with one another in the open air and away from their wives for the day, and it felt strange to be thought of as their leader, aged twenty-four, describing the many shades of blue I could see, picking up stones and grass for them to touch and flowers to sniff.

I had named the group the Rodmell Fusiliers, and devised a system for getting them across the Downs: it was to use a clothes pole, with me holding the front of it, Ronnie at the back, and the veterans of the trenches and Dunkirk between us, holding on to the pole as we marched up the South Downs Way. On each trip with this group, I added more stuff I could say, just to make the afternoon work better. I had passages from *The Old Yarns of Sussex* and pamphlets on botany and I would recite poems to liven up the journey over the fields. One of the older men, Archie, had known some of Rupert Brooke's companymen, and walking one foot in front of the other we would go quiet listening to what he remembered.

This one day stands out above the rest. The Rodmell Fusiliers were in good form; they stood beside the van at Lewes in their dark glasses, their knapsacks of lunch on their backs. They never brought white sticks to the Downs. They were old but they were in good shape, apart from the eyes: each man had lived with blindness so long he had mostly forgotten how to think of it as an affliction. They touched things. They listened. They sniffed the air and made the kinds of jokes and said things they knew they could only do in the company of other men.

I drove them first to Charleston. I had been talking about Bloomsbury to some of them—'arty-farty,' they said—and then they decided they wanted to know what it was all about. I parked the van and gathered them at the gate to the house. 'There's a fine pond,' I said, 'and a willow at one side and a stone or flint wall edging the garden part, and a lawn that slopes down there, with formal bushes. Further up there are box hedges and it's all well-ordered.'

'Were they all poofs?' said Simon Gedge.

'More or less,' I said.

'They were COs and poofs,' said Archie. 'The women an' all.'

'Artist folk,' said another.

'Intellectuals,' said Simon. 'Never worked a day their lives. Should shoot the lot of them with the enemy's bullets.'

Inside the house they occasionally stopped complaining while I told them what things looked like. 'Doorknobs in pink and leaf-patterns over the furniture,' I said. 'There's a dresser painted different kinds of green and a fish-carpet. Just under where you're standing.'

'Would give you a sore head,' said Simon.

'Do they have clocks?' said Ronnie from the back.

'No, Ronnie, they weren't that fond of clocks.'

'Were they fond of loos?' asked Archie. 'I'm bursting for a pee.'

Ten minutes later, in the shop, I was trying to describe a Picasso poster. 'I can't imagine it,' said Ronnie.

'Very black eyes,' I said. 'Iberian eyes. Like Picasso's own eyes in fact. So many of his paintings have these very round and very Spanish black eyes.'

'I'll give him black eyes,' said Simon. 'Let's get the fuck out of here, it's boring.'

'You're an ignoramus, Gedge,' I said. I put his hand on my shoulder and got the others to file behind. 'Even if you weren't blind as a bat you'd still be blind as a bat.'

'He's proud of it,' said another.

'There isn't much to see here,' said Simon.

We drove on to Alfriston and I parked the van in the grounds of St Andrew's Church. Archie told us how he knew this village before the Great War. 'I remember the look of it very well,' he said, 'and the Long Bridge over the Cuckmere. My sister and I once scraped our names into one of the stones there with a thrupenny bit.' He put his fingers over the front of his dark glasses. 'You can feel right enough it's a warm day today,' he said. 'I wonder if the Cuckmere gets high like it used to. It used to get very high.'

We ate our packed lunches under the trees. I poured the tea from a flask jammed in the spare wheel at the back of the van, and Simon stuck his finger into his cup. 'Don't be stingy,' he said. 'This cup's half empty. I know you're giving that Ronnie more than me just because he's arty-farty.'

'You can't beat Sussex for weather,' said Jim Nelson. Jim was a Scouser; he'd come with his wife several years ago to live at the St Clare's house at Ovingdean. His skin had seen all weathers and was shiny, ever so white, with little scrubs of red on his cheekbones where the vessels had broken. 'You get a different smell in the air down here.'

'You do that,' said Simon. 'Smell of cow's shite.'

'Very good, smart-arse,' said Jim. 'It's not that. The place smells green.'

'No. I think it's yellow,' one of the others said.

'No, Jimbo. You're right enough. Green.'

'I would say blue,' said Norman Oakley. 'Blue as the day you were born, sunshine.' Norman was the oldest. He was ninety-one. He wasn't married and insisted he be allowed to come on the walks. After I packed away the tin-foil and cups and got the clothes pole from the van we made our way on to the Downs. Norman stood behind me, held the pole tight, and chattered.

'Just say if you want a rest, Norman.'

'Champion, son. Just you lead the way.'

'We've a bit to go today,' I said.

'Step smartly.'

They all liked to talk about being blind. For each of them it was the great subject of their lives. Norman could grow breathless telling you about a mustard gas attack. 'That's the last thing I knew,' he said. 'My eyes were stinging, but not as much as my armpits and my balls. It stings so powerful you wouldn't believe. Then the eyes went out.'

'That's right enough,' said Archie.

'The balls,' said 'Wobble' Gadney. 'I wasn't worried about the eyes. I thought the old knackers would be off.'

Simon and the younger men tended to go quiet when the older veterans spoke like this. They didn't know about gas, but that wasn't why they shut up: it was to let the older men have their say and to respect their seniority. Nobody ever contradicted Norman. He was in charge of his own experience and they left it at that.

I stopped sometimes and laid the pole on the grass. Then I would try to describe the view: the slope of the hills and the sheep scattered about, the occasional butterfly disappearing behind a stone dyke. At one point we found a mound of wild parsley; I picked a bunch and told them to put out their tongues. 'Body of Christ,' I said, and they laughed.

'Born Celtic supporter,' said Simon. 'You're telling us this is parsley. I bet it's shamrock.'

'You'll never know,' I said.

'Definitely parsley,' said Ronnie. 'Our Jeanette could whip up a great sauce for cod out of that.'

'We're not going to have to walk back, are we?' said Simon.

'Just you,' I said.

'Piss off. I'll just hitch a lift back with a sexy woman,' he said.

'I don't doubt it,' I said. 'And she'd need four eyes for your none.'

'You tell him,' said Norman.

'The porter from Ovingdean is collecting us on the other side,' I said. 'Don't worry your poor legs.'

'I could walk from here to the Black Sea,' said Ronnie.

We had a rest beside a rape field and then at Norman's insistence we headed on. The men went on talking about football results and house prices and Ronnie sang a sentimental song about a girl from the Forest of Dean. As we climbed over the Downs the sun seemed to rise alongside us and eventually we could smell the sea. 'Smell that,' said Jim Nelson. 'The Channel.'

I could feel the clothes pole stiffen and the pace was stepped up behind me. 'Steady,' I said. But there was a resolve now to get to the top and I started to tell them how the water looked with the sun making it glimmer for miles.

'Are there boats?' said Archie.

'Nothing,' I said. 'It's clear to the horizon.'

'Very blue?' said Wobble.

'Blue,' I said. 'Changing blues, it's a million wee strokes of paint out there.'

'And you can't see boats?' said Simon.

'Clear,' I said, 'not a single boat to be seen.'

'At one time whole squadrons of RAF would go right over here and that was them off,' said Archie.

We stopped and all listened together as a cricket made its noise beside us in the field. 'Lead on, Mr Aigas,' said Norman.

'Officer Aigas,' said Archie.

'Captain Aigas,' said Jim.

'Herr Kommandant Aigas,' said Simon.

'That's just enough of that,' said Norman.

We were up near Beachy Head. No one else was there at that hour to see the Rodmell Fusiliers marching on the pole, and in an instant the whole scene seemed very dear and quiet.

'Can we sit down for a while?' Archie said. And in that moment I wanted to do better for them.

'We'll go closer,' I said. 'I want you to hear the waves.'

'Yes,' whispered Norman behind me, 'take us closer.'

We went forward and the wind lifted.

'This is a lovely day,' said Norman.

'Sit down here,' I said. 'All of you sit down.' Touching one

Andrew O'Hagan

'Right enough,' said Jim Nelson. 'You can hear the water coming in.' They sat quiet for a moment and they listened for the sound of waves on the beach far below us.

'It's all out there,' said Simon.

'Michael,' said Norman, 'give us some of your words. This is a lovely day. We'll just sit up here for a while. Read something.'

I stood up with my back to the Channel and looked at the old men sitting on the grass.

'In *King Lear*,' I said, 'blind Gloucester is really at the end of his tether...'

'Shakespeare,' said Wobble.

'Yes,' I said, 'and Gloucester's son Edgar, who's in disguise—his father doesn't know who he is—takes him by the hand. His father is blind and he has lost interest in all his hopes and the king has gone mad.'

I paused to think.

'Go on,' said Norman.

'Why is the son in disguise?' said Archie.

'He's in danger,' I said, 'and his mind isn't right.'

'Go on,' said Norman.

'Gloucester wants to end it all,' I said, 'so he persuades Edgar to lead him to a cliff so's he can fall off and die. But Edgar loves his father and only pretends to do it. He keeps him on flat ground but tricks his father into thinking he is indeed on a high cliff and is about to fall. Gloucester can't see the truth.'

The men were quiet. They said nothing for a minute and the sea at my back was calm and almost imaginary, but you could hear the waves coming to wash the chalk cliffs from under us. □

GRANTA

AT THE VILLA COCKROFT

Dan Rhodes

Dan Rhodes was born in 1972, and grew up in Devon and Kent. He went to the University of Glamorgan, where he studied humanities and later took a part-time MA in writing. He has written two collections of short romantic fiction—'Don't Tell Me the Truth about Love' and 'Anthropology and a Hundred Other Stories'. Canongate is soon to publish his novel, 'Timoleon Vieta Come Home', from which this extract is taken. He isn't planning to write more fiction.

They were sitting in front of the house, Cockroft in his deckchair and Timoleon Vieta by his side. It was a warm evening in early spring, and everything was quiet except for the rustling of a packet of nuts and raisins, and Timoleon Vieta's occasional wolfing of rejected Brazils.

Cockroft was trying to remember whether or not he had already told Timoleon Vieta about the time in the mid-sixties when he and Monty 'Misty' Moore had written *Wrens*, a stage musical for all ages about a good-hearted but misguided scientist who was secretly breeding killer wrens the size of emperor penguins in his underground laboratory. Thanks to Monty 'Misty' Moore's treachery it hadn't come close to being staged. Before he started to tell the story, regardless of whether or not the dog had heard it before, he was unexpectedly delighted by the sight of a scruffy, but handsome, young man walking up the track that ran in front of the house.

'That's funny,' he said, stroking his fussily trimmed silver beard. 'Who do you think this could be?' Timoleon Vieta's eyes were fixed on the raisin that had stalled halfway between the bag and his master's mouth.

The cars and jeeps of distant neighbours occasionally went past, but walkers never did. This one appeared to be somewhere around his mid-twenties. He was at least six feet tall, and was wearing old black jeans and a greying black T-shirt that was mottled with sweat. He was carrying a black bag, and his dark hair was looking, rather wonderfully, in pressing need of a cut. At times like these Cockroft kicked himself for knowing next to no Italian. 'Rough stuff,' he confided to Timoleon Vieta.

He smiled and waved at the young man, who didn't smile or wave back, but left the track and walked up the path towards the house. Cockroft had been expecting him to carry on up the track, and was surprised when he stopped just a few feet away from him.

'I have walked from the town,' the young man said quietly, looking not at Cockroft but at the house. 'You should have told me you lived such a long way from everywhere.' He dropped his bag on the ground, and there was a silence as he continued to scrutinize the house through narrowed eyes. 'But I am here now.' From deep inside the dog came the low rumble of a growl.

'Oh, be quiet Timoleon Vieta. Really,' admonished his master.

'What have I told you about behaving in front of visitors?' The dog backed away, but still quietly growled to himself. Cockroft rolled his eyes and shook his head in exaggerated exasperation, stood up and offered his hand.

The young man took it. It felt clammy, and he wondered whether the old man had been playing with himself.

'So,' said Cockroft, trying his best to hide his confusion, 'you have my number.'

'Here.' The young man dug into his pocket, and brought out a card. On it was printed: CARTHUSIANS COCKROFT—CONDUCTOR, COMPOSER, RACONTEUR. Underneath was his address and phone number. On his weekends away Cockroft gave them out like confetti—to handsome waiters, to gondoliers, to strangers he found himself talking to in art-gallery snack bars and in museums, and to almost everyone he introduced himself to on his trips around the bars. The card was always accompanied by an open invitation to visit him at home. A few times over the years people had taken him up on his offer of hospitality in the hills, but they had usually called first to make sure he was going to be in. They didn't just arrive. 'You gave it in Firenze,' he said, his voice monotonous and barely audible. 'When you invited me.'

'Oh,' said Cockroft. 'Yes.' He tried to place the stranger's face, but he couldn't. 'Of course,' he said, smiling as broadly as he could. 'It's so lovely to see you again. I was hoping you could make it.'

'I am thirsty. It was a long walk from the town. Maybe one hour. More. Maybe five or six kilometres. I don't know.'

'Of course. Where are my manners? Do sit down.' He gestured towards his deckchair. As the young man moved towards it Timoleon Vieta exploded with rage, his hackles raised and his barks piercing the still evening air. 'Oh, Timoleon Vieta, please,' said Cockroft, almost firmly. Again Timoleon Vieta moved away and lay down, but he resumed his low growl. Cockroft went into the house.

After a couple of minutes the old man came back out, carrying a tray on which were four glasses, a jug of water, a bottle of sparkling wine and a plateful of chocolate biscuits. By the time Cockroft had assembled the spare deckchair, the young man had drunk all the water straight from the jug and poured himself a glass of wine, having fired the cork over the scruffy lawn and on to the track.

Timoleon Vieta usually chased and returned fired corks, but this time his half-closed eyes didn't leave the newcomer's face. 'You are thirsty,' said Cockroft. The man did not respond.

Cockroft poured himself a glass of wine and sat down. From the corner of his eye he continued his inspection of the unexpected visitor. The young man was almost muscular, and looked weather-beaten and tired. Cockroft wanted to prescribe a rest cure: lots of relaxation, a bit of feeding up, and a lot of very close attention. He went to Florence every once in a while, and tried hard to remember having met the man there. His last couple of trips to the city had been blurs of sex, wine and tiramisu. He was sure he hadn't slept with him though. He would have remembered such a young, firm body. As he looked at the man in the deckchair beside him he was driven half wild with frustration. He wondered whether somebody such as this could ever even have heard of people like him.

What? the young man would cry, slapping his thigh and laughing as Cockroft told him of their existence. *You mean there are men who kiss other men? And enjoy doing it? Oh Cockroft, you come up with the funniest ideas. I've never heard anything so preposterous in all my life, you old comedian.* Or maybe he would just stare at the distant hills, as he was doing now, and mumble without a smile, *Well, nothing surprises me any more.* Either way, Cockroft was sure he was out of luck.

The man grabbed a handful of biscuits from the plate and stuffed them into his mouth whole, not waiting until he had swallowed the first before eating the next. Cockroft took two—one for himself and one for Timoleon Vieta. Cockroft handed the man a cigar, and started imagining they were long-term lovers enjoying a drink and a smoke as the sun went down over the distant hills, and about to enjoy a little, maybe post-coital, chit-chat. He didn't know what to say. He couldn't ask the young man his name, or where exactly it was they had met, without appearing rude. 'So,' he said, after a lot of consideration. 'Where are you from again?' Cockroft wasn't very good at telling where people were from by looking at them, but it was clear that the man was not Italian. He could tell from his accent.

'I told you already in Firenze,' the young man said. He paused for a long time. Then, in a broken whisper, he said, 'I am from Bosnia.'

'Oh, you poor boy. You poor, poor boy.' Most of Cockroft's life was played out against the backdrop of the World Service. It was on the kitchen radio almost every waking hour, and he knew all there was to know about the terrible things that were happening in what had once been Yugoslavia. At least until this conversation he had thought he had known everything.

He certainly knew the names and places. *Slobodan Milosevic. Sarajevo. UN Peacekeeping Force. Mostar. Radovan Karadzic. Mujahedin. Kosovo. Vance-Owen.* He seemed to know everything except, now he came to think about it, who had been fighting whom, who was on which side, what the sides were, which ethnicities were being cleansed, and what the various wars had all been about. He only occasionally read the papers, and tended to daydream through the main news events as they were broadcast on the radio, catching only the barest of outlines. He only ever paid close attention to the short pieces that rounded off the bulletins—like the report about the nine-year-old golf prodigy who had lost an arm in a fairground accident, or the woman who had fallen in love with her rapist and was struggling to have the charges against him dropped, or the man from somewhere outside Osaka who was lobbying *The Guinness Book of Records* to be entered as the loneliest man in the world. He had never really been able to untangle what had been going on just a short way to the east, and events had become so complex that without really thinking about it he had given up even trying to work them out.

He didn't know what to say, but felt as though he had to say something. He tried: 'Which side were you on?' He was sure the answer would mean nothing to him. The Bosnian stared into the distance, seeming to be focusing on a point a long way beyond the horizon that Cockroft assumed was his ravaged homeland. Eventually he spoke, almost inaudibly. 'The side,' he said, 'with the guns.'

'Oh, you poor boy,' Cockroft repeated. He wanted to reach out and pat the young man's hand. His strong hand, with its big, slightly dirty fingers. 'As I was saying to Timoleon Vieta the other day, I can never understand why people can't just get along with each other. It seems so silly, all this fighting.' He held out the bottle. 'More?'

Without taking his eyes from the view, the Bosnian nodded almost imperceptibly, and Cockroft poured two more glasses. It was almost like drinking champagne.

After a bowl of pasta, a few more cigars and glasses of wine and a large glass of brandy, the Bosnian was shown to the guest bedroom, where he fell asleep on dusty sheets. Cockroft packed up the deckchairs, read for a while, kissed Timoleon Vieta goodnight and went to bed pleased that he would have somebody to talk to in the morning.

Because Wednesday had been agreed in Florence as rent day, the Bosnian had made sure he arrived at Cockroft's house on a Thursday. That gave him almost a week to decide whether or not he was going to pay. On the Monday the old man noticed that his guest had been wearing the same clothes the whole time, and that they needed washing.

'Come along,' he said. 'We're getting you some new clothes from the market.' Cockroft filled his wallet, and went out to make sure the pickup was going to start. He had bought the small white four-wheel-drive secondhand when he moved to Italy, convinced that he would need a rugged machine for his new rural lifestyle. It had become as run-down as the house, but it was inexplicably reliable. He also had a little Fiat in his garage, but he had never really liked it, and anyway it hadn't worked for months. He half wondered whether the Bosnian could get it going again. His new friend seemed to Cockroft to be the kind of person who could fix a car. As usual the pick-up started first time, and he left it ticking over. 'I'll just call Timoleon Vieta,' he said. The Bosnian didn't say anything, he just looked away. 'Yes, he loves his trips into town.' He called the dog's name a few times. Eventually he appeared. 'We go everywhere together, don't we Timoleon Vieta?' The dog started scratching at the passenger door. 'Ah. I'd forgotten about that. There's a slight problem. You see, Timoleon Vieta likes to sit in the passenger seat.'

'But there is no problem. He will go into the back.'

'Oh no. He won't be happy in the back.'

'He is dog, right? He is animal?'

'He's fine in the back of the car, but he doesn't like it in the back of the pick-up, you know. He finds it uncomfortable.'

The Bosnian was looking into the distance, seeming to see and hear nothing.

'But I'll see what I can do.' Cockroft lowered the pick-up's back flap and said, in a well-practised falsetto, 'Jump. Jump. Jump up,

Timoleon Vieta.' The dog lay down. 'Jump up.' Timoleon Vieta curled up and closed his eyes. 'No. It's no use. He'll have to come in the front with me.'

'Why not do like this?' The Bosnian went up to Timoleon Vieta, and bent down to pick him up and bundle him into the back. He swept him up, and the moment he did the dog turned from a listless mound into a flailing, yapping whirl of claws and teeth. The Bosnian dropped him. Timoleon Vieta retreated to a safe distance, where he growled and raised his hackles at his master's new friend, who was wiping the dog's saliva on to his jeans, and checking his hand for punctures.

'Let's go,' said the Bosnian. He hadn't wanted to make the trip but had started to be bothered by his own stench, so he had decided to go along with the old man's plan. 'We leave the dog here. He is surviving here no problem.'

'Oh, please let him sit in the front,' implored Cockroft. 'You can go in the back. It'll be fun. It'll be just like your army days all over again.'

The Bosnian, who had decided that he would really rather not have to talk to the old man anyway, climbed up without another word.

Cockroft worried that he had been tactless. He pictured a rainy night, an explosion, and the Bosnian being thrown from the back of a jeep into a quagmire while his comrades lost limbs around him. The old man and his dog got in the front. Cockroft patted Timoleon Vieta's head. Timoleon Vieta looked up at him with his lovely eyes, and wagged his tail. They went into town, Cockroft taking the bends very slowly.

After parking, and leaving Timoleon Vieta in the cab of the pick-up, they went to the hardware store, to the bank and to the market to buy the clothes. At the market the Bosnian performed all the negotiations in what seemed to Cockroft to be fluent Italian. The old man ended up buying him a couple of pairs of jeans, a pair of what looked like army boots, a bundle of underwear, some plain T-shirts and some big work shirts. He steered him towards colours that matched his eyes. The Bosnian asked for, and was given, a hat and a pair of dark glasses, both of which he put on immediately. 'I must be being careful,' he said, without smiling. 'I am not supposed to be being around here.'

They took the bags back to the pick-up, via a cheap barber where Cockroft watched the Bosnian have his head shaved, number one all over. Exhausted, Cockroft suggested they go for a cup of coffee.

The Bosnian needed caffeine. 'I suppose you will be wanting that dog to come with us,' he mumbled.

Cockroft had wanted Timoleon Vieta's company, but he stalled. 'No. He can stay and guard our bags. He'll be fine, so long as we're quick.' Guiltily, he warmed to the idea of having a coffee with just the Bosnian, and he felt a slight buzz as he realized he was being seen out and about with an authentic fugitive. Over his years in Italy he had known plenty of people who shouldn't really have been in the country. They had been Russians, Micronesians, Peruvians and Americans—the chiselled boyfriends of rich expatriates and Italians. Still, he was sure none of them had been a refugee from a war zone. He had never known the illegal people he had met to get caught, so he wasn't too worried about his new friend being snatched away from him by the police. He was sure he would get away with it somehow, just like all the others. Even so, it was quite exciting for the old man.

The cafe was Cockroft's favourite in town, but he wasn't sure why. The staff never showed any signs of recognition when he arrived. They just served him with whatever it was he had asked for, and took his money. He and the Bosnian took a table outside, and ordered a pair of cappuccinos. The Bosnian smoked cheap cigarettes, and the old man smoked cheap cigars. Neither of them spoke.

An argument broke out on the other side of the street. Two men, both with pot bellies and moustaches, were shouting insults at each other, and waving their arms. People walked by as though nothing unusual was happening.

'They are a very expressive race, the Italians,' explained Cockroft. 'You know, they never fight. They use all their energy waving their arms around and shouting at each other, and so they don't feel the need to fight one another.'

One of the men, who was wearing a blue shirt, started poking the chest of the other one, who was wearing a white shirt. 'There might be a bit of poking,' conceded the old man, 'but that's all. It never gets serious.'

The white-shirted man answered these pokes with a punch so hard that it knocked the blue-shirted one to the ground. Blue-shirt got up, clearly dazed, and rubbed his head. The shouting had been succeeded by silence, and they no longer waved their arms so expressively. White-shirt followed up on his success, and landed another punch on blue-shirt's face. Blood ran from blue-shirt's nose, and this seemed to snap him back into life. In a moment, white-shirt had been knocked to the ground, and was being kicked in the belly over and over again. He rolled over, but blue-shirt kept on kicking, his shoes pounding into the other man's back as he struggled to stand up.

'Oh really,' said Cockroft. 'This is no way to behave.'

'I have not seen this for the long while,' muttered the Bosnian. He seemed to be smiling, but the old man wasn't entirely sure. 'It is so beautiful.'

'How can you say that? It's awful. It's mindless violence.'

'But it is not without reasons.' Looking at the fight and not at Cockroft, his voice barely above a whisper, he seemed to be talking to himself. 'We will never know just what it is in these lifes that is driving these people to this. It is more than the simple fighting in the street—it is two lifes, two of the histories on collision. The reasons for this fight is going back for so many, many generations.' He looked, for a moment, at the old man. 'Think about it.'

It was the first time Cockroft had seen the Bosnian seem interested in something. 'Well, whatever their reasons may be, there is never any need for violence.' Cockroft had never been in a fight. Not a real one, with fists. Blue-shirt had white-shirt's hair in his hand, and was knocking his head against a wall.

'But a fight between two men is the most purest form of all conflict. It is simple, and it is beautiful. It is perfect.'

'But they have no dignity, these men.'

'No what?'

'No dignity.'

'What means this word? This *dignity*?' asked the Bosnian.

'Well,' said Cockroft. His mind went blank. 'It's difficult to explain.'

'But you are using this word,' mumbled the Bosnian. 'I think you are knowing what it means if you are using it.'

'Well,' Cockroft thought for a moment. 'It means behaving yourself no matter what.'

'Are you sure?'

They watched as white-shirt wrestled free, and stood a little way away from blue-shirt, catching his breath, his moustache caked with blood.

'Yes. And it means having self-control, and not making an exhibition of yourself.'

'So do you have this dignity?'

'I like to think so. Yes, I do.' Even though the more he thought about it the more he realized he wasn't quite sure what it meant, Cockroft knew that there had been times when he had lost his dignity completely. He wondered whether it was possible for somebody to lose it in private, or whether somebody else had to be watching for it to count.

He wondered whether he had lost his dignity on the summer night he had spent doing the conga alone, wearing nothing but a paper hat from a Christmas cracker, or the time when he had heard on the radio that household dust was in large part flakes of human skin, and had spent hours carefully collecting dust and putting it in a jar so that he might have something by which to remember the object of a recently failed love whom, in his happiness, he had neglected to photograph. He knew for certain that he had lost it in 1976 when, during a particularly difficult time in his life, the police had caught him spraying I SUCK COCKS on a footbridge over a dual carriageway. When the incident wasn't reported in the newspapers he didn't know whether to feel disappointed or relieved.

'And am I having this dignity also?'

'Yes. I think you are.' Cockroft had no idea. White-shirt lunged at blue-shirt.

The Bosnian, having encountered the word many times before, smiled to himself for a moment, with just one side of his mouth. 'But you are saying that these men they are not having this dignity. Well maybe it is better if you are not having it. Fighting is better than not fighting when there is something to fight about. Maybe it is weak not to fight people. This fight it is so beautiful. Like a fucking, I don't know, like a fucking picture or something.'

'It is *not* beautiful.'

'It is beautiful.'

The conversation, in which they had both lost interest, ended. Their attention returned to the fight. After a couple more minutes of grappling, headbutting, kicking and pummelling, blue-shirt walked away, leaving white-shirt lying still on the pavement. Cockroft and the Bosnian made their way back to the pick-up. The Bosnian supposed that the fight had been about a girl—he was sure he had seen the fire of love in the men's eyes. He imagined what she must have been like to have inspired such violence. He pictured her long dark hair cascading over her bare shoulders, her enormous brown eyes and her perfect body. She was far too good for either of them. What she was doing hanging around with those pot-bellied men he would never understand. She was beautiful, and he tried not to think about it.

They drove back to the house, Timoleon Vieta on the passenger seat and the Bosnian lying down in the fresh air. Cockroft rarely felt it was worth making a special effort in the kitchen when there was only him and Timoleon Vieta in the house. Usually he just grazed on bread, fruit and nuts through the day and made a simple pasta dish in the evening, but whenever he had a visitor he rediscovered his culinary enthusiasm. He stopped off at the supermarket for some bits and pieces on the way back from town.

Despite the enormous and meticulously prepared meal, the atmosphere at the table was not what Cockroft had hoped for. The Bosnian, in his new clothes, was quiet, seeming intent on his meal. He answered Cockroft's questions with gestures or the minimum of words. The old man worried that he had spoiled everything by making him sit in the back of the pick-up. The World Service filled the silences.

'You speak very good English,' said Cockroft, hoping to regain lost ground.

'It is so-so,' said the Bosnian, who knew that his English was good.

After the meal the old man poured a pair of very large whiskeys, and showed the Bosnian the music room for the first time. It was Cockroft's favourite room. 'I keep it very tidy,' he said. 'I don't even let Timoleon Vieta sit on the chairs.'

'Then you will not let me sit on the fucking chairs,' the Bosnian said, without raising his voice from its usual, almost whispered, monotone. 'I am below your dog.'

Cockroft was embarrassed. He had not been a good host. He had treated the Bosnian thoughtlessly. He supposed that his world had become so small that he had simply forgotten how to treat guests, that he should have put the Bosnian's needs above everything else.

He knew he should have broken his and Timoleon Vieta's routine without hesitation, and he was ashamed. 'I'm so sorry,' he said. 'Listen. You can sit in the front of the pick-up next time we go somewhere, and I'll put Timoleon Vieta in the back. I'll make him jump up whether he likes it or not. I'll throw a biscuit up there or something.' Cockroft didn't know what else to say, so he said, 'He loves biscuits.'

The Bosnian didn't respond to this gesture. He looked around the room. There was an upright piano with its lid down, and a black leather sofa and matching armchair, and the walls were covered with framed photographs. Cockroft rarely played the piano, a dusty Spelman Timmins that he had shipped over from home shortly after buying the place in the hope that he would hit another creative patch. He never did. His musical about Crufts had never really come together. He had abandoned it halfway through the fifth song, which had been about a basset. His classical piece, *Rape of the Seas*, which he had started to write during a phase of refusing to eat fish, had foundered after he was offered salmon at a dinner party. He had forgotten to tell the host about his diet, and the fish had smelled so good that he had been unable to resist it. He hadn't had the piano tuned since the local blind man had died seven years before, so whatever he played on it sounded somehow diabolical.

The Bosnian walked around and looked at the photographs. In the middle of them all was a big photograph of someone who was recognizably Cockroft in conversation with Paul McCartney. Cockroft, trying hard not to swell too obviously with pride, pointed at it without saying anything.

'McCartney,' said the Bosnian.

'Yes.'

'He is coming from The Wings.'

'Yes.'

'I fucking hate The Wings.' The Bosnian sang, quietly, sarcastically and without tune, '*We are sailing...*'

'Yes, I think that was them.'

'Fucking shit.' He curled his lip slightly. 'I suppose he is your good friend.'

'Yes, he is. He's a lovely man.' Cockroft had met McCartney twice—in passing in Jane Asher's hallway in 1964, when Cockroft had been on his way to meet her brother Peter to talk about the possibility of arranging some music for a flip side, and again when that picture had been taken, in 1973. On their second meeting they had had a thirty second conversation in which Cockroft had reminded McCartney of their earlier encounter, and commented on how Jane Asher's house had smelled of lovely cakes. McCartney had smiled politely, then moved away. 'A really super fellow, Paul. A charming man. A good friend.'

Putting their difference of opinion about Wings down to a culture clash, the old man talked the Bosnian through some of the other photographs. There was a younger Cockroft with a very young David Bowie, with a tired-looking Jimi Hendrix, and standing on the left of a group that included Sammy Davis Junior. A few of the photographs were formal shots, in which Cockroft had a baton in his hand and was surrounded by men in matching blazers clutching electric basses, drumsticks or violins. 'I had my own little orchestra,' he said, pointing at one of the pictures. 'I was a bandleader. I used to be on television all the time. I even made records.' The Bosnian didn't say anything.

They went back to the kitchen table. Cockroft poured even more whiskey into their glasses. 'I'm very famous in my own country, you know,' he said. 'Very famous indeed.'

'Bullshit,' thought the Bosnian, who had never heard of him.

After the Bosnian had gone to bed Cockroft sat with his elbows on the kitchen table, drinking wine and looking at his reflection in the rough old glass of the window. He felt Timoleon Vieta nuzzling him. He slid his chair back, reached down and stroked the dog's head. 'Come here,' he said, drawing the dog into an embrace. After a while the old man kissed him on his muzzle, and withdrew. Then he gently held the dog's head in his hands, and played with his ears. Timoleon Vieta looked up at him, tilted his head to one side and wagged his tail. 'Come here,' Cockroft said again, reaching down to hug his pet.

When he was younger the Bosnian had dreamed of travelling the world and making love to the whores of many nations. Although he always went with the best-looking prostitutes he could afford, many of whom were almost unbelievably beautiful, with big sad eyes and perfect, airbrushed skin, he had encountered some ugly women too.

On drunken nights out, when he had been about seventeen, he and his friends had sometimes competed with each other to see which of them could kiss, for at least two minutes, the ugliest woman. To make it difficult they weren't allowed to pay, so they had to go to bars and discos and other places where these women could be found. A couple of times he had won the contest.

It was with kissing ugly women in mind that the Bosnian went to pay his rent. He imagined it wouldn't be much different.

'We go inside now,' he said to Cockroft, who was sitting outside and patting Timoleon Vieta on the head while half rereading *A Spy By Any Other Name* by Wadham Kenning. 'Now.' Cockroft followed him into the house. 'It is Wednesday. It is seven o'clock. Give me your cock.'

Cockroft knew instinctively that he must not show how amazed he was. It was a line he had used time and time again. *Come and visit me—all you'll have to do is suck my dick at seven o'clock on a Wednesday evening and you can stay as long as you like.* He had thought that everyone had known it was a joke, despite the well-practised poker face he always adopted while making the offer. But not the Bosnian. In Bosnia, it seemed, a deal was a deal and the Bosnian was ready to pay his rent. □

Three voices

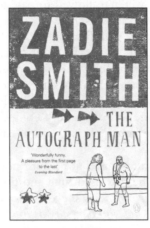

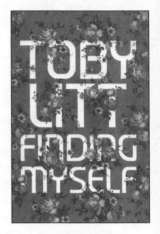

APRIL 2003 **MAY 2003** **JUNE 2003**

One generation

Granta Best of Young British Novelists 2003

Speaks volumes

GRANTA

FIELD STUDY
Rachel Seiffert

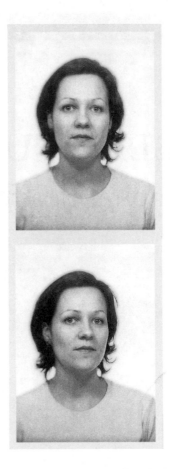

Born in Oxford in 1971, Rachel Seiffert divides her time between teaching and writing. Her first novel, 'The Dark Room' (William Heinemann) was shortlisted for the 2001 Booker Prize, and she has also received a Los Angeles Times Book Prize and an International PEN Award for her work. 'Field Study' was written while she was living in Berlin and will be published as part of a collection of short stories next year.

Summer and the third day of Martin's field study. Morning, and
he is parked at the side of the track, looking out over the rye he
will walk through shortly to reach the river. For two days he has been
alone, gathering his mud and water samples, but not today.

A boy shouts and sings in the field. His young mother carries him
piggyback through the rye. Martin hears their voices, thin through
the open window of his car. He keeps still. Watching, waiting for
them to pass.

The woman's legs are hidden in the tall stalks of the crop and the
boy's legs are skinny. He is too big to be carried comfortably, and
mother and son giggle as she struggles on through the rye. The boy
wears too-large trainers, huge and white, and they hang heavy at his
mother's sides. Brushing the ears of rye as she walks, bumping at
her thighs as she jogs an unsteady step or two. Then swinging out
wide as she spins on the spot: whirling, stumbling around and
around. Twice, three times, four times, laughing, lurching as he
screams delight on her back.

They fall to the ground and Martin can't see them any more. Just
the rye and the tops of the trees beyond: where the field slopes down
and the river starts its wide arc around the town. Three days Martin
has been here. Only another four days to cover the area, pull enough
data together for his semester paper, already overdue. The young
woman and her child have gone. Martin climbs out of the car, gathers
his bags and locks the doors.

This river begins, like so many others, in the high mountains
Martin cannot see but knows lie due south of where he stands. Once
it passes the coal and industry of the foothills, it runs almost due
west into these flat, farming lands, cutting a course through the
shallow valley on which his PhD studies are centred. Past the town
where he is staying and on through the provincial capital, until it
finally mouths in the wide flows which mark the border between
Martin's country and the one he is now in. Not a significant stretch
of water historically, commercially, not even especially pretty. But a
cause for concern nonetheless: here, but even more so in Martin's
country. Linking as it does a chemical plant on the eastern side of
the border with a major population centre to the west.

Martin has a camera, notebooks and vials. Some for river water,
others for river mud. Back in the town, in his room at the guest

house, he has chemicals and a microscope. More vials and dishes. The first two days' samples, still to be analysed, a laptop on which to record his results.

The dark uneven arc of the trees is visible for miles. Marking the path of the river through the yellow-dry countryside. The harvest this year will be early and poor. Drought, and so the water level of the river is low, but the trees along its banks are still full of new growth, thick with leaves, the air beneath them moist.

Martin drinks the first coffee of the day from his flask by the water's edge. The river has steep banks, and roots grow in twisted detours down its rocky sides. He has moved steadily west along the river since the beginning of the week, covering about a kilometre each day, with a two kilometre gap in between. Up until now, the water has been clear, but here it is thick with long fronds of weed. Martin spreads a waterproof liner on the flat rock, lays out vials and spoons in rows. He writes up the labels while he drinks his second coffee, then pulls on his long waterproof gloves. Beyond the branches, the field shimmers yellow-white and the sun is strong; under the trees, Martin is cool. Counting, measuring, writing, photographing. Long sample spoon scratching river grit against the glass of the vials.

Late morning and hot now, even under the trees. The water at this point in the river is almost deep enough to swim. Martin lays out his vials, spoons and labels for the third time that morning. Wonders a moment or two what it would be like to lie down in the lazy current, the soft weed. Touches his gloved fingertips to the surface and counts up all the toxic substances he will test his samples for later. He rolls up his trouser legs as high as they will go before he pulls on the waders, enjoys the cool pressure of the water against the rubber against his skin as he moves carefully out to about midstream. The weed here is at its thickest, and Martin decides to take a sample of that, too. The protective gauntlets make it difficult to get a grip, but Martin manages to pull one plant from the river bed with its root system still reasonably intact. He stands a while, feeling the current tug its way around his legs, watching the fingers of weed slowly folding over the gap he has made. Ahead is a sudden dip, a small waterfall that Martin had noted yesterday evening on the map. The noise of the cascade is loud, held in close by the dense green avenue of trees. Martin wades forward and when he stops again, he hears voices, a laugh-scream.

The bushes grow dense across the top of the drop, but Martin can just see through the leaves: young mother and son, swimming in the pool hollowed out by the waterfall. They are close. He can see the boy take a mouthful of water and spray it at his mother as she swims around the small pool. Can see the mud between her toes when she climbs out and stands on the rock at the water's edge. The long black-green weed stuck to her thigh. She is not naked, but her underwear is pale, pink-white like her skin, and Martin can also see the darker wet of nipples and pubic hair. He turns quickly and wades back to the bank, weed sample held carefully in gauntleted hands.

He stands for a moment by his bags, then pulls off the waders, pulls on his shoes again. He will walk round them, take a detour across the fields and they will have no cause to see him. He has gathered enough here already, after all. The pool and waterfall need not fall within his every one hundred metres remit. No problem.

Martin sleeps an hour when he gets back to the guest house. Open window providing an occasional breeze from the small back court and a smell of bread from the kitchen. When he wakes the sun has passed over the top of the building and his room is pleasantly cool and dim. He works for an hour or two on the first day's mud and water vials, and what he finds confirms his hypothesis. Everything within normal boundaries, except one particular metal, present in far higher concentrations than one should expect.

His fingers start to itch as he parcels up a selection of samples to send back to the university lab for confirmation. He knows this is psychosomatic, that he has always been careful to wear protection: doesn't even think that poisoning with this metal is likely to produce such a reaction. He includes the weed sample in his parcel, with instructions that a section be sent on to botany, and a photocopy of the map, with the collection sites clearly marked. In the post office, his lips and the skin around his nostrils burn, and so despite his reasoning, he allows himself another shower before he goes down to eat an early dinner in the guest-house cafe.

The boy from the stream is sitting on one of the high stools at the bar doing his homework, and the waitress who brings Martin his soup is his mother. She wishes him a good appetite in one of the few phrases he understands in this country, and when Martin thanks her using a couple of words picked up on his last visit, he thinks she looks pleased.

Martin watches her son while he eats. Remembers the fountain of river water the boy aimed at his mother, wonders how much he swallowed, if they swim there regularly, how many years they might have done this for. Martin thinks he looks healthy enough, perhaps a little underweight.

His mother brings Martin a glass of wine with his main course, and when he tries to explain that he didn't order it, she just puts her finger to her lips and winks. She is thin, too, but she looks strong: broad shoulders and palms, long fingers, wide nails. She pulls her hands behind her back, and Martin is aware now that he has been staring. He lowers his eyes to his plate, watches her through his lashes as she moves on to the next table. Notes: *good posture, thick hair*. But Martin reasons while he eats that such poisons can take years to make their presence felt; nothing for a decade or two, then suddenly tumours and shortness of breath in middle age.

The woman is sitting at the bar with her son when Martin finishes his meal. Smoking a cigarette and checking through his maths. The boy watches as Martin walks towards them, kicking his trainers against the high legs of his bar stool.

—*I'm sorry. I don't really speak enough of your language. But I wanted to tell you something.*

The woman looks up from her son's exercise book and blinks as Martin speaks. He stops a moment, waits to see if she understands, if she will say something, but after a small smile and a small frown, she just nods and turns away from him, back to her son. At first Martin thinks they are talking about him, and that they might still respond, but the seconds pass and the boy and his mother keep talking, and then Martin can't remember how long he has been standing there looking at the back of her head, so he looks away. Sees his tall reflection in the mirror behind the bar. One hand, *left*, no *right*, moving up to cover his large forehead, *sunburnt*, and red hair.

—What do you want to say to my mother?

The boy speaks Martin's language. He shrugs when Martin looks at him. Martin lets his hand drop back down to his side.

—*Oh, okay. Okay, good. Can you translate for me then?*

The boy shrugs again, which Martin takes to be assent and so he starts to explain. About the river, how he saw them swimming in the morning and he didn't want to disturb them, but that he has been thinking about it again this evening. And then Martin stops talking because he sees that the boy is frowning.

—*Should I start again?*

—You were watching my mother swimming.

—*No.*

The boy whispers to his mother, who flushes and then puts her hand over her mouth and laughs.

—*No. No, that's not right.*

Martin shakes his head again, holds both hands up, but it is loud, the woman's laughter in the quiet cafe, and the other two customers look up from their meals.

—*I was not watching. Tell her I was not watching. I was taking samples from the river, that's all. I'm a scientist. And I think you should know that it is polluted. The river is dirty and you really shouldn't swim there. That's all. Now please tell your mother.*

The young woman keeps laughing while Martin speaks, and though he avoids looking in the mirror again, he can feel the blush making his sunburn itch, the pulse in his throat. The boy watches him a second or two, lips moving, not speaking. Martin thinks the boy doesn't believe him.

—*You could get sick. The river will make you sick. I just thought you should know. Okay?*

Martin is angry now. With the suspicious boy, his laughing mother. He counts out enough to pay for his meal, including the wine. Leaves it on the table without a tip and goes to his room.

In the morning, a man serves Martin his breakfast, but before he leaves for the river again, the young mother comes into the cafe, pushing her son in front of her. She speaks in a low whisper to the boy, who translates for Martin in a monotone.

—My mother says she is sorry. We are both sorry. That she is Ewa, I am Jacek. She says you should tell me about the river so I can tell her.

Martin is still annoyed when he gets back from the river in the afternoon. Doesn't expect the woman and her boy to stick to their appointment, still hasn't analysed day two and three's samples, half hopes they won't turn up. But when he comes downstairs after his shower, he finds them waiting for him in the cafe as arranged.

The boy helps Martin spread out his maps, asks if he can boot up the laptop. His mother murmurs something, and her son sighs.

—She says I should say please. Please.

—*It's okay.*

Martin shows them the path of the river from the mountains to the border and where the chemical plant lies, almost a hundred kilometres upstream from the town. Among his papers, he finds images of what the metal he has found in the river looks like, its chemical structure and symbol, and he tells them its common name. He says that as far as they know the body cannot break it down, so it stores it, usually in the liver. He speaks a sentence at a time and lets the boy translate. Shows them the graphs he has plotted on his computer. Waits while the boy stumbles over his grammar, watches his mother listening, thinks: *Jacek and Ewa.*

—Where do you come from?

Ewa speaks in Martin's language, points at the map. Martin looks at her, and Jacek clears his throat.

—I am teaching her.

Martin smiles. He shows them where he is studying and then, a little further to the west, the city where he was born. And then Jacek starts to calculate how many kilometres it is from Martin's university to the border and from the border to the town. Martin asks Ewa.

—*How old is he?*

—Nearly eleven.

He nods. Thinks she must have been very young when she got pregnant.

—*He's just about bilingual already.*

An exaggeration, a silly thing to say, and Martin can see in Ewa's eyes that she knows it, but she doesn't contradict him.

—They have it in school now. He is a good student. Not bad as a teacher.

She smiles and Martin is glad now that they came today, Ewa and her son. Pushes last night's laughter to the back of his mind. Sees that Ewa's smile is wide and warm and that her tongue shows pink behind her teeth.

Day five and Martin works his way along the river again. The hot fields are empty, the road quiet. The water here is wider, deeper; flies dance above the surface.

Mid-morning and Jacek crashes through the undergrowth.

—Martin! There you are. I am here.

Martin looks up from the water, startled. He nods then he doesn't know what to say to the boy, so he carries on working. Jacek watches him a while, and then pulls off his trainers, rolls up his trousers, picks up a vial.

—*No! You shouldn't come in.*

—I can help you. You would work faster. I can pass them to you.

—*Shouldn't you be at school?*

Jacek frowns.

—*Does your mother know you are here?*

—She wouldn't mind.

Martin thinks a moment.

—*We don't know enough yet about this metal, you see. It's too much of a risk.*

Jacek avoids eye contact, rubs his bare ankles.

—*You really can't help me without boots and gloves, Jacek. I only have one pair of each. I'm sorry.*

An hour later the boy is back with pink washing-up gloves and a pair of outsize rubber boots, soles caked in mud. He holds up a bag of apples.

—For you. From my mother.

In the evening the cafe is crowded and Ewa is busy, another waitress brings Martin his dinner. His table is near the bar, where Jacek is doing his homework again. New vocabulary, and he asks Martin to correct his spelling. Ewa makes a detour past his table on her way to the kitchen.

—Thank you.

—*No problem.*

He scratches his sunburn, stops. Feels huge at the small table after she has gone.

Jacek brings his mother with him on day six. Ewa stands at the water's edge while her son changes into his boots and washing-up gloves. Midday already, and the sky is clear, the sun high. Martin has sweat patches under his arms, on his back. He watches Ewa hold the front of her T-shirt away from her chest, and then flap it back and forth to get cool air at the hot skin beneath. He sees yellow pollen on her shoes, the hem of her skirt, damp hair at her temples.

They work for a while, and Jacek asks questions which Martin answers. Ewa says very little. She crouches on the bank and looks at the water. Lids down, lips drawn together, arms wrapped around her shins. When Martin says it's time to move downstream, one hundred metres, Jacek says he wants to come with him and Ewa says she will go home.

Jacek watches Martin watching his mother as she wades through the long grass back to the road.

—She used to swim here with my Tata, I think.

—*Your father?*

Martin tries to remember a wedding ring. Sees Ewa's strong palms, her long fingers.

—He is in your country.

—*Oh?*

—He is illegal. Too much problems at the border, so he doesn't come home.

Martin watches Jacek as they unpack the bags again. Fair with freckles. Narrow lips, pale eyes, broad nose. A good-looking boy, but not at all like his mother.

D ay seven and Martin doesn't go to the river. After breakfast he sets up his computer, a new graph template, and plots the data from days two and three. Both agree with day one's graph, with Martin's predictions, and he starts sketching out a structure for his argument, writes a first draft conclusion. The sample results should have come back from the university yesterday, including the mud and weed from day four, which would speed up Martin's analysis. He goes downstairs to the small office mid morning to check for faxes again, but the guest house is quiet, cafe closed, reception deserted. Sunday. So there won't be anybody at the labs, either, but Martin walks out to the phone boxes in the town square anyway.

Jacek hammers on the glass.

—Where were you?

—*Wait.*

Martin holds up one finger, but the phone just keeps ringing out at the other end. Jacek peels his pink gloves off while Martin leaves a message on the lab answerphone. The boy cups his hands around his eyes, presses them up to the glass, watching him. It is stifling inside the phone box and Jacek's hands leave a sweaty streak on the pane outside.

When Martin opens the door, Jacek has his fists on his hips. Rubber boots on the paving stones beside him.

—Why didn't you come?

—*I've finished. I only need to do a couple more tests.*

—Oh.

Jacek picks up his boots and falls into step with Martin. The sun is strong and they walk together on the shady side of the narrow street which leads back up to the guest house.

—*I'm going home tomorrow.*

—Tomorrow?

He looks up at Martin for a second or two, then turns on his heel and runs.

Martin sleeps in the afternoon and is woken by the landlady's husband with a message.

—*Is it from the university?*

—No. From my wife's sister.

Martin stares at the man. Eyes unfocused, face damp with heat and sleep.

—From Ewa. Jacek's mother. She works here. My wife's sister.

—*Oh, yes. Yes, sorry.*

—She says you should come to her house. She will cook you something to eat this evening. To say thank you.

Martin showers and sits down at his computer again but finds he can't work. Looks out at the birds instead, washing in a puddle on the flat roof of the building opposite. The concrete is mossy and Martin wonders where the water came from. He has been here a week and it's been thirty degrees straight through and hasn't rained once. The skin on his back is damp again, and under his arms, and he thinks he hasn't anything clean to wear this evening, so he takes a T-shirt down the hall with him and washes it in the

Rachel Seiffert

bathroom, lays it out on his window sill to dry.

It is still slightly damp when he goes out to find Ewa's. Bottle of
wine bought from the guest-house bar under one arm, map and
address on a scrap of paper from the landlady's husband. There is
a slight breeze and the T-shirt is cool against his skin. He catches
sight of himself in the bakery window as he passes, pushes his hair
down over his forehead a little as he turns the corner. An involuntary
gesture he hopes nobody saw.

Jacek opens the door.
—You're early!
—*Sorry.*

He leads Martin up the stairs, two at a time, cartons of cigarettes
and cake mix piled high along one wall. The narrow entrance hall
of Ewa's flat is similarly crowded: disposable nappies, tuna fish,
toothbrushes in different shades; pink and green and yellow. Jacek
sees Martin looking at the boxes.

—The man we rent from. He keeps things here, we pay him not
so much. Every week is something new coming for him to sell.

A table stands in the middle of the room, a wardrobe in the
corner. Mattress leant up against the wall and draped with a sheet.
The window is open and the radio on. Martin recognizes the song,
a current hit, but can't understand what the announcer says
afterwards. He goes into the kitchen, where Ewa is chopping and
Jacek stirring.

—*Can I help?*
—No!

Ewa pours him a glass of wine and pushes him out into the
bedroom–dining room again.

—Five minutes.

The wind is blowing into town from the river, and Martin can
hear church bells ringing out the evening service.

They eat, Martin and Ewa smiling and nodding, Jacek
concentrating on his food, not worried by the silence.

—*Jacek, can you ask your mother to tell me a little about the
town, please?*

The boy looks up with his mouth full, Martin swallows.

—*I know very little. I would like to know.*

It is not true. He knows what she tells him already, what the boy translates for her about the nine churches, the resistance during the war and occupation, the failed collectivization of the fruit growers during the Communist era.

—There was a jam factory here when she was my age. Everybody was working there, or they were farmers. Apricots, pears, apples and I don't know how you say those small ones. Berries?

Martin asks about the Communist years.

—You want to hear about no food and unhappiness, yes?

Martin rubs his sunburn, and Ewa slaps her son's hands.

—Jacek! Sorry. I don't understand him, but I see he was rude. You translate only, yes? Yes?

Ewa points at her son and then pours them all more wine, offers to make Martin some tea.

—The way we drink it here.

Jacek's translation is sulky, sleepy. Black, in a glass so you can see the leaves floating. Boiling water, hot glass with no handles so your fingerprints get smooth and hard from the holding. Martin looks at the tips of his fingers, Ewa smiles.

—*I didn't know your sister owns the guest house.*

—Yes.

Ewa smiles, Jacek yawns.

—She gives my mother work.

—*And her husband?*

—Tadeusz?

—Uncle Tadeusz does no work.

—Ssh! Not true.

Ewa speaks more herself now, interrupts her son's translations. She tells him her brother-in-law is a plumber. That he put his faith in the church. Her explanations are ungrammatical, sometimes nonsensical, but Martin enjoys listening to her. She says that they built new houses a year or two after the elections, a whole row, right in the centre. New times, new buildings. Flats above, shop spaces below. Brick, solid, good windows. And Tadeusz put in all the pipes, toilets, baths, taps, sinks. He got a loan to pay for all the materials. Copper piping and ceramics, imported from the west. He had the houses blessed when they were finished, but not yet painted. The priest came and threw his holy water around the empty rooms and

Tadeusz was so proud. She remembers the wet, dark spots on the pink-red plasterwork, that it was a hot day, and that the dark spots left white marks behind when they dried.

—He never got paid, Tadeusz, and he cries often now.

Each time he defaults on his loan, and the houses are still empty. A while ago there was new graffiti on the wall of the last one in the row: SEND THE NUNS ABROAD AND THE PRIESTS TO THE MOON.

Ewa looks at Jacek, who isn't listening any more, eyes half closed, head propped in his hands. She whispers to Martin.

—I think Tadeusz wrote that.

Martin feels her breath on his neck as she speaks, can smell wine and soap mixed.

—My sister, she wanted that Jacek and me should live with her. After Piotr left.

—*Your husband?*

Ewa doesn't answer, her eyes are unfocused.

—I couldn't. Not live with Tadeusz. He's not a bad man, but so much bitterness.

Martin is drunk and so is Ewa.

—I don't want my son to be bitter, you see. I want him to like his life, this town, his country.

Martin nods.

—There is not so much here now, but I show him places, take him to the river.

Ewa sighs. They sit with the breeze from the open window on their bright cheeks and Jacek has his head on the tablecloth, asleep.

—I don't make him be at school this week. I think he can't swim in the river now, but it is good that he speaks with you. Has some nice time, learns someone new. More than in a classroom.

Ewa smiles into the middle distance and Martin looks at her. Only half a metre between them, the corner of the table, knees almost touching underneath.

He leans towards her. But Ewa catches him.

—No.

One hand on each of his shoulders, she holds him at arm's length. Martin blinks.

An empty wine glass rolls on the table. Ewa shakes her head.

—Sorry, no.

She smiles and then Martin sits back in his chair again, sunburn itching, sweat prickling in his scalp.

He doesn't look at her and for a minute or so they sit in silence. Jacek's even breathing in the room and the church bells sounding again outside. When Martin looks up, Ewa smiles again.

—I am sorry.

She rights the glass on the table, then covers her mouth with her hand and laughs.

In the morning there is a fax from the department lab. Martin has a hangover, asks for coffee and water to be sent up to his room. His eyes skim the figures, cannot settle. He boots up the laptop, plots the lab's figures on to his graph, though he already sees the disparity between the last set of results and his predictions. Days one to three show serious levels of contamination in mud and water, and correspond with Martin's own data. Day four's samples, however, are almost low enough to be considered clear.

Martin sits on the narrow bed a while, trying to decide if he is relieved or disappointed. The weedy water, the pool under the waterfall: *Clean.* As good as. But the premise of his paper: *Void.* His headache is bad, the day hot already, the shame of yesterday evening still fresh. Martin presses the heels of his palms against his eyes.

He wants to go home, he needs to get dressed. He goes to the bathroom where the window is open, the air much cooler than in his room. He stands under the shower a long time, warm flow on face and shoulders taking the edge off his headache, filling his ears, closing his eyes, replacing Ewa and her laughter with water falling on tile.

The room he returns to is strewn with papers and clothes. Martin works his way round it methodically, folding and sorting into piles. Before he packs, he checks through the lab technician's tidy columns once more, notes the memo at the end of the fax: the weed sample has been sent on to botany.

On the way downstairs, he reasons with himself: if the weed results are interesting, he can propose to further investigate the river fauna in the conclusion to his paper. Over breakfast, he thinks he could propose a joint venture with botany, perhaps. Something to please the department. Zoology might even be interested: the weed may be thriving, but crowding other species out. At the very least,

it is good news for Ewa. She is not working this morning, but Martin
thinks he will leave a note for her, tell her it's okay to take Jacek
swimming again. He finishes his roll. Thinks he made a mess of the
field study, the week in general, but there are still ways to make
amends.

Martin stands in the narrow reception hall with his bags, sees Ewa
happy by the waterfall while her sister calculates his bill. Then he
remembers how sad she looked the day she came with Jacek to the
river, and he is shocked at the satisfaction the memory gives him.

There is paper on the counter in front of him. He has a pencil in
his back pocket, but he doesn't get it out. He pays and picks up his
bags. Tells himself it is too soon to know for certain while he loads
up the car. He has yet to test all his samples, examine all the
possibilities; swimming at the waterfall could still be dangerous.

On the road out of town, he sees Ewa's hand over her mouth,
her eyes pressed shut, Jacek woken by her laughter.

At the border, the road runs parallel with the river for a kilometre
or so, and the traffic moves slowly. To his right, trees grow tall along
the river banks and in his rear-view mirror Martin can see the rest
of the country spread out behind him, dry and flat. His chest is tight
with shame, but the border guard is waving him through now, and
he is driving on again. ☐

GRANTA

THE HARE
Toby Litt

Toby Litt was born in 1968. He grew up in Ampthill, Bedfordshire. He has worked as a teacher, bookseller and subtitler. A graduate of Malcolm Bradbury's creative writing course at the University of East Anglia, he is the author of two books of short stories, 'Adventures in Capitalism' and 'Exhibitionism', and three novels, 'Beatniks', 'Corpsing', and 'deadkidsongs'. He edited the new edition of Henry James's last novel, 'The Outcry', for Penguin Modern Classics. His new novel, 'Finding Myself', will be published in June 2003 by Hamish Hamilton. 'The Hare' is a new piece.

1

For some little while now I have been chasing a hare—buck or doe, I do not know; never yet have I managed to come close enough to check. It is lanky, manky, and quite as rapid as its name. This past month I have pursued the hare through a gallery, my memory, some postcards and a half-dozen books. In recent days, the hare has gone to earth in the British Library; and it is here—seated on this chair, at this desk—that I would like to recommence the chase. (Please excuse the Victorianism of my voice, but I can at present see no way other to make the approach—this task being so obviously illegitimate. I intend, for once, as an improvised Victorian, to ignore the wraiths of contemporary thought; unobjectifiers, soul-suckers.) I will, in this great library—cavernous yet luminous—on this wooden chair, at this wooden desk, attempt to hunt the hare haphazard; to examine the quotidian grasses, to sniff the wind of correspondence, to trace the found tracks of the intentional, to crumble or squidge the meant droppings, and to come—eventually—into the real presence of a real living literary animal-idea, and not kill it.

Wales

Allow me, immediately, to digress; I should like to recall my first encounter with a hare—whether or not it was this same hare I now chase I do not know: I will assume that it was. We were in Wales for our summer holiday: mother, father, myself and my sisters, Georgina and Charlotte. I was at a guess eleven. The antiques trade (my father's) must have been down that year; we usually went to campsites in France, staying in tents that someone else erected—pitched at the start of the season and struck at the end; we never had to touch a belay. This year, it was Wales instead. We were, at the hour I am concerned with, visiting a farm just outside Cardiff, I think; picking up some keys, perhaps. I remember two sheepdogs, an old and a young, both of which we children were warned not to stroke; they worked, were not pets. While whatever transaction it was was taking place, I took myself off for an explore. There was a barn, high-full of hay-bales; and standing in the farmyard, in the thick of its smell, I looked (bored) across to an abruptly rising hillside opposite—where for the first time stood the live hare. It was long and potential-fast, sometimes upright, and here a later quotation intrudes: Auden's 'Near you, taller than grass, / Ears poise before decision, scenting danger.' I realize now, in setting this down, that Auden may not have meant a hare at all; just as likely a rabbit or a man. But, more likely still, Auden was happy—in his early ambiguity—for the reader to infer whatever they wished. And here, the crux left of the watershed, I have from the first wished a hare. In all its liveness, I can't have watched the original Welsh hare for more than a half-minute. Something happened, perhaps it detected— so fine its tremulous senses—my watching, and at a slender lope it was off, up, over the hill, out of sight. It gave the odd baroque to its straight, but was going where it was going and that was for definite. There isn't much else to be remembered from the holiday. We immediately left Cardiff and drove to a farm where the farmer's wife fed us a roast every day: Saturday was beef, Sunday lamb, Monday chicken, and so on through pork, duck and goose (not hare); on the last of the seven days we all of us wondered what variety of animal she had left that she could *possibly* roast (we were sick of roast), and the farmer's wife treated us to an encore of beef. I remember the farmer and his farmhands harvesting with tractors the corn, and this later was the seed of 'Moriarty'—a story from my first book. I remember going up alone into the grain store, and this became the source of a cancelled section of my novel, *deadkidsongs*. A day or two before we left, the farm bull got loose, and was only a four-bar iron gate away from me—its erection pointing toward the plain cows in a nearby field; it had already broken through one dry stone wall in its quest of lust. The following year the antiques trade revived, and we holidayed in Corsica.

3

I am certain the hare is somewhere here in this library, perhaps in many of its places at once—for hares, unlike rabbits and men, are not limited to a single, logical location. There are books through which I know, even before I order and open them, it will have passed. *Brewer's Phrase and Fable*—in which I learn 'It was once thought that hares were sexless, or that they changed their sex every year.' Buck or doe, even the hare does not know. Another book I consult contains the first literary hare I pursued: Kit Williams's *Masquerade*—which began and became a worldwide search for a buried leporine effigy, fashioned (by him) of gold and jewels. Kit himself, unkempt arts and craftsman, lived a couple of villages along the ridge from Ampthill 'where the Princess lay' (Shakespeare, *Henry VIII*, Act 4, scene I, line 28); Ampthill, where I grew up. He buried his golden hare in Ampthill Park, at the foot of Katharine's Cross, set there as memorial to the locally popular Queen, imprisoned in the castle pending divorce by her heir-hungry husband, Henry. Queen, not Princess.

England

My next encounter face-to-face with the hare—though there must have been many now-forgotten glimpses after Wales—was at university. Oxford, in this as in all things, was a perversion; the hare, here, was paraded in its most debased form: jugged. It was also undercooked, by the worst college kitchens in the city, and caused just by itself a small student revolt against the contempt with which our college (Worcester College) treated us. The Food Rep, exploiting the jugged hare incident, and bringing about a brief improvement in the quality of our meals, was the following term elected President of the Junior Common Room. Like all revolutions, ours met disillusion the moment it paused. During the former Food Rep's time and term in office, it was discovered the college had been surcharging all undergraduates on the electricity in their rooms, illegally, since the Second World War. With power of bankruptcy over Worcester College, the President, representative of our revolution, made not even a few polite requests.

5

Joseph Beuys, about whom I first read at university, performed *How to Explain Paintings to a Dead Hare* in 1965 at the Schmela Gallery, Düsseldorf. The gallery in which the hare made its most recent reappearance, late last year, was Tate Modern. In a room dedicated to Beuys, I came across a copy of his *Drawings for Leonardo's 'Madrid Codex'*—a woman-hare, my sketch of which I reproduce below:

A few weeks later, while we were visiting some friends of ours in Sheffield, my girlfriend suffered her second miscarriage. I attempted to distract myself, in a hiatus of respite, by glancing through John Lehmann's *The Craft of Letters in England*—a copy of which, for some reason, was kept on a shelf in the upstairs toilet. Here I found a reference to Jocelyn Brooke, author of 'two impressively morbid short novels'. On coming to the great library a short while afterwards, I ordered up a book by Jocelyn (buck or doe?). It turned out not to be a morbid novel, but a morbid book of verse. The one decent poem was 'The Song of Isobell Gowdie' which contained the lines: 'I shall go into a hare, / With sorrow and sighing and mickle care / And I shall go in the Devil's name / Till I come home again.'

Scotland

The library at this moment resembles nothing so much as a forest— an enchanted forest. And as I notice this, the chairs of the reading room begin to push up in strange columns, and the desks to spread out and settle, as if through long decay. I stand up, step back. I am not as amazed as I feel I should be; transformations were only to be expected. When the trunks of the desks finally touch the whitewashed ceiling, it shows itself to be wrought out as a thick leaf-canopy. I know it is only at night that the library is this empty, and so it occurs to me that an amount of unconscious time has passed. I am awake, definitely, without the excuses of dreaming. The moonbeams are the only infrequent light here—prinking through the canopy, slicing down in crisp diagonals. The air is almost balmy, and as the beams wink out and zip back I can tell that the moon is riding high in a cloud-chased, cloud-ragged sky. The library now resembles nothing so much as the cover of the copy of C. S. Lewis's *Prince Caspian* which I was given to read at Alameda School, Ampthill. The desks have now subsided entirely into the needle-thick forest floor—which, spongy and spicy, beds out a silence that makes steps sound as thuds and thuds as thrums. Although I have no reason to go in any direction, I decide to head towards where the Issue & Return counter once stood. As I walk, I remember and recite the words of the poem, the words taken from Isobell Gowdie's confession, her spell: 'I shall go into a hare / With sorrow and sighing and mickle care / And I shall go in the Devil's name / Till I come home again.' I myself do not turn into a hare, despite reciting them twice more—thrice in total. But I do sight a rapid-moving summat up ahead—a horizontal streak, appearing in front of and disappearing behind the vertical rhythm of the tree trunks; a real rubato, a pulse. It is the hare, I am sure: I decide not to sprint after it, that would for both of us mean humiliation. (The chase is over.) Instead, I call out to it; I call out a name I am far from sure it has or will answer to: 'Isobell!' A hiatus. It is as if there had been a spell and I have uttered the counter spell: the streak stops, in a sighted gap and also in the gaze of a moonbeam, becoming a haunch-supported tower of fur. Its ears are searching for the second sounding of its name, which I then make: 'Isobell!' The hare turns in my direction and hurls its senses towards the source of its loud denomination—all of them falling on me at once; I am savoured, and even also somehow caressed. A third time, in fairy-tale fashion, I call the hare to me ('Isobell!')—and in obedience to the law of three, she comes; not so close that I can touch her, but closer than ever—in a living, inedible form—before. How am I sure she is a she? Sure because confirmation confirms sureness, and because I can't be I if she isn't she. 'I want to speak to you,' I say. 'You can't,' she says, in a soft Scottish voice, 'without you put on the coat.' As she says it I see it: though I can't be completely sure but that it appears at that moment; hanging from a low, hook-like branch—a long coat fashioned from the pelt of surely the largest hare that ever lived. *Sans* hesitation, I step across to it, lift it heavily off the hook and punch my arms into its forelegs. As I do so, I notice that long ears dangle from the hood. No sooner is the coat upon me than it begins to shrink, until coat becomes pelt—and I feel my clothes dissolving beneath it, like meat in the spittle of a fly. I realize that as well as being on the cover of *Prince Caspian*, I have also come to where the Wild Things are. (If I am Max, I am relieved to know that I shall be getting home before my dinner grows cold: *it was all a dream*, while a cliché from outside, is a reassurance when within.) Something else is altering, too: I feel my internal organs lengthen and tumble into place, like grains of tobacco rolling in a cigarette paper. It is from inside out that I realize I am changing, going as Isobell Gowdie at her trial said she did, into a hare. The trunks of the trees give me some marker against which I can judge my height; the hare I am becoming is up high on its haunches, but still its eyes are only four feet off the ground. Sounds stumble towards me, from the deep darkness of the enchanted forest—it feels not as if my hearing is improving but as if the world is rearranging itself so that far is now near. I realize, too, that there are many more noises on the very cusp of audibility—ones I can sense, sense the danger of, but not clearly depict to myself. These almost-sounds are the most useful as they are those made by predators aspiring to silence. I hope at this moment that I will be able to retain such a developed sense when eventually I return to my human form, though cities would be unbearable. But then I realize, and it is the first time I feel horror, that I may have become a permanent hare. The realignment of my muscles feels dreadfully like the relaxation that I have been my whole life yearning towards, as if my new body were a hot bath of fragrant water in which I had just lain down. Isobell, the hare, turns and runs away from me into the enchanted forest. Awkwardly, I follow her— finding my way down the tunnel of her fourfold footfalls; awkward, I am, because I neither know how to move this imposed body nor

do I have any idea of hare etiquette. I am the buck, she the doe—
should I follow or not follow? I do not know. Is there already
romance between us, by mere meeting? And if so, what will it need
to be—a courtship of ludicrous dance followed by long monogamy
proven to science by grief and pining after death? I realize as I come
within sight of her scut, that with each step onwards I feel less
awkward and more afraid of the awkwardness I would feel if
returned to human form. We run for a long time, downhill, through
a hollow that never seems to find a further edge. A librarian
carrying a book strolls along between the wide, wide trunks of the
trees of the enchanted forest. He does not seem in any way lost,
although as he goes he is gazing upwards towards the canopy in
wonderment. Wherever he is he is a long long way away from the
Issue & Return counter. I have time, a little time, to think, and I
realize that it is only now, transformed, that I know the forest as
enchanted; though I should, of course, have known before. The
library also, I sense, as if it were one of the almost-sounds, is or was
an enchanted place. The recognition of enchantment comes, though,
not because I myself have become an enchanted creature (which
should be proof enough), but because I am now alive in a different
version of the world—*more* alive, and the world in turn seems more
of a world; more keenly etched, more exactly sounded, and above
all more powerfully scented. This sense (twitching my new nose) only
fades in slowly, as we descend, like walking into a mist, and I believe
I can understand why: if the intensity of smell-upon-smell-upon-smell
had overtaken me in one instant, it might have killed me, or
rendered me—at the very least—inane with shock. It would have
been like, I can only think to say, being transported, in one's sleep,
into the tympani section of an orchestra halfway through the *Ode
to Joy*. Isobell has now become easily traceable through her scent,
which I find the most delicious of all those attempting to impress
themselves upon me. Symphonic music is the best analogy with
which I can attempt description: a low bass hum of forestness, of
accreted scent (there are many dead things buried here); fleeting
piccolo notes that spatter me for a moment and then evaporate—
like petals brushed across one's eyelids; and all the sounding tones
in between, the pungent dungs, ghostly fungi, motherly mosses,
cinnamonesque barks. We have reached the bottom of the hollow,

the size of which I can no longer estimate—I sense around me extents of forest that may be due to distance or merely to an almost overwhelming intensity of added sensual detail. 'Here we are not at home,' says Isobell. 'We would like it elsewhere more.' And I know where—exactly where she means, to the very hedge and angle and grass-blade; her longing has conveyed itself to me or, more likely, was in me already only waiting to be called forth. I remember that great receptacle and distillation of English nostalgias 'The Old Vicarage, Grantchester': 'Say, do the elm-clumps greatly stand / Still guardians of that holy land? / The chestnuts shade, in reverend dream, / The yet unacademic stream? / Is dawn a secret shy and cold / Anadyomene, silver-gold? / And sunset still a golden sea / From Haslingfield to Madingley? / And after, ere the night is born, / Do hares come out about the corn?' This though is not the summit of Brooke's past-love, that Everestine peak is honey for tea. But just before his death, young Rupert returned for a second and greater thrust at the same image: 'A wind of night, shy as the young hare / That steals even now out of the corn to play, / Stirs the pale river once, and creeps away.' Am I a young hare? I realize that I have no idea. And yet, I feel something more than nostalgia in Brooke's conjured corn: it is an intensified, sensualized homecoming—just as Isobell's spell promised: 'Till I come home again.' And I remember the miscarriage in Sheffield, the sorrow and sighing and mickle care. I grieve again, at great speed that is in no way cursory, for our two lost babies. 'Where is the Devil?' I wonder—if we are going in his name, why doesn't he show himself, or does he show himself only in my altered form? I think, for one awful instant, that I may be losing the instinct of language—for a memory of corn overwhelms me, and it is as if the susurrus of each stem rubbing against each sister stem—all stupendously audible to the long, leporine ears with which I seem to have heard it before—it is almost as if this breeze-borne, breeze-created sound were orgasm. 'We do not belong here,' I say back to Isobell, although I still have no proof or agreement from her that Isobell is who she is. Now that I am as she, her lankiness has become the shape of archetypal desire and the musk of her manky scut, catnip. As one, we move: her thoughts inhabiting my body, my will prompting her muscles; the ground begins to rise, the far side of the hollow finally reached.

7

All along I had been expecting this quest after an image or idea or ideal to end with a confrontation with myself—myself as a hare upon a steep Welsh hillside gazing towards myself as a boy, within a twenty years vacated farmyard. I did not foresee this journeying as a hare towards a hare's longing; neither did I foresee companionship.

Ireland

Fingersmith

SARAH WATERS

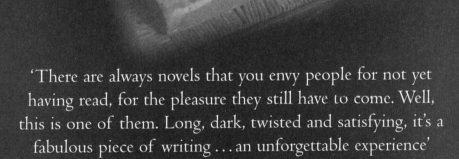

'There are always novels that you envy people for not yet
having read, for the pleasure they still have to come. Well,
this is one of them. Long, dark, twisted and satisfying, it's a
fabulous piece of writing...an unforgettable experience'

Julie Myerson, GUARDIAN

www.virago.co.uk
www.sarahwaters.co

OUT NOW IN PAPERBACK

GRANTA

AFTER CARAVAGGIO'S SACRIFICE OF ISAAC

Rachel Cusk

Rachel Cusk was born in Canada in 1967 to British parents, and lived in the United States until 1974, when the family returned to England. She is the author of four novels: 'Saving Agnes', which won the Whitbread First Novel Award, 'The Temporary', 'The Country Life', which won a Somerset Maugham Award; and 'The Lucky Ones' (Fourth Estate). 'A Life's Work: On Becoming a Mother' (2001) is her personal account of the experience of motherhood. She lives on Exmoor with her family. 'After Caravaggio's Sacrifice of Isaac' was originally written for a BBC series of stories inspired by paintings.

One of the things about having children is the feeling they give you that they know all about you. It's like they've come from inside you and had a good look round while they were there. My son Ian gives me this feeling. I often catch him staring at me when my back is turned, like he's reading something private. Then I think, *he knows*, or *he's found out*, even though when it comes down to it I've got nothing to hide. I say to him, have I got egg on my face then?—something like that, and when he laughs I see that he's still just a boy and that I'm a man, even though a minute before it wasn't clear at all. It sounds a funny thing to say, but it's easy to forget how much children depend on you. It's important for them that you don't lose your authority. My wife said to me, during our bad time, one day he'll thank you Alan, and in those strange moments that seem to come so close to the truth and then don't I believe she might be right. When Ian was a baby we had him circumcized. My wife thought it was more hygienic. I didn't like it, but Sally said to me, he won't remember, they don't remember things. That's the way she is: she won't let it bother her.

I dream about Ian, not the same dream, different dreams, but they're all sort of similar. Like, we're getting on a train, me and him, and I put him on with all our bags and then I get off because I want to buy a newspaper or something and next thing I know the train's pulling away with me still on the platform and Ian looking at me through the window. Or, I'll have a whole dream about something else entirely, and then at the end I'll realize that all the time I was dreaming I was supposed to be looking after Ian and I don't know where he is. My mother left me on a bus once, when I was just a tot. There were so many of us she was always forgetting one. I went all round London on the number 73 crying my eyes out. You'd think I'd *meant* to leave you, she says. Didn't do you any harm, did it? she says. Just like Sally really. I've always tried to be different with Ian, but I sometimes wonder whether it was that trying that made things go wrong in the first place, whether if I'd been like Sally or my mum none of it would ever have happened. What I mean is that loving Ian made me expect more from life. It made me think there were better things out there.

It was right after he was born that I started looking at paintings. After what she'd been through with the birth Sally couldn't bear him near her. His crying made her mad; even if he was at the other end of the house she'd hear him crying and go mad. I didn't know what to think: it was totally unlike her. In the end I had to take unpaid leave off work. I used to take him out and just walk about with him round London, and that's how I first went to an art gallery. I was walking past and I saw a big poster for an exhibition and the picture on it caught my eye. It was a picture of a woman holding a baby. I didn't have a clue what it was then, but just looking at it made me feel things, with Sally at home being the way she was, and so I went in. What amazed me was how many people were in there, at ten o'clock on a Tuesday morning, just looking at paintings when they should have been at work. At least, that's what I *expected* myself to think: you know, lazy sods, arty-farty scroungers. But I didn't think that. I started to, and then I just didn't. It was something to do with Ian. He was asleep in his pram, but his being there was like some kind of passport, some bridge to another place. It felt right being there with him. It was an exhibition of Renaissance art, but as I say I didn't have a clue, I just went round and looked at things and kept getting this feeling of another side of life. You could say it was a call. Looking back to that day I can see now that I might have been a bit confused. I was seeing the writing on the wall with Sally: in my mind I think I was consciously separating myself and Ian from her. When I thought 'we', it was me and Ian I was thinking about. And I worried about that thought, and when I looked at the pictures they told me not to worry, they told me everything was all right. They were sympathetic, if that doesn't sound too silly.

That was the beginning, anyway. I met Gerte a bit later, when I signed up for the evening class she was teaching on the History of Art. Ian was three by then. I was a bit stuck. I'd had all these ideas about art, but they hadn't seemed to come to anything. I was still in my job, even though when I went back after Sally had got better I'd decided to leave. From the first minute back I knew I couldn't stand it any more, I knew I'd changed, and every day I spent there felt like a day wearing shoes that are too small, that cramp and pinch and torture your feet until all you can think about is getting them off. But I stayed all the same. I didn't have the courage to leave. I didn't have the confidence in myself. I just had the dissatisfaction. It took meeting Gerte to give me the confidence to go with it. Once I'd been chosen by her, I thought I could do anything. I looked back at the life I'd lived and thought, how could you have done this and that, how could you have been so ordinary? I was ashamed, ashamed of Sally, ashamed of our house and the things in it, ashamed of our friends and the things we talked about. The only thing I wasn't ashamed of was Ian. Like I say, he was my passport. He was what made me worth something. When Gerte chose me, inside myself I knew that somehow he was the reason; not because she loved him—she didn't—but because I did.

Gerte was from Germany. She taught art history at a university there and she came to England for a year on an exchange programme. She was the opposite of Sally, she was very well educated and delicate and beautiful. Her face belonged in one of those paintings she talked about, a Giotto, a Bellini. Whenever I looked at it I got that feeling, the feeling that everything would be all right. I was obsessed with her from the start. What's funny is that I never felt I was being unfaithful to Sally, even when I actually was. Gerte was better than Sally; it was as simple as that. I was learning about taste and beauty and value, and learning about these things justified what I felt about Gerte. It was a fact; but there are other facts, which don't have anything to do with taste and beauty and value. That's what I didn't see—I never saw it, even when I was standing at the front door with my bags packed.

Gerte spoke to me at the end of the third class. You look at me so much, she said, you'll wear my face away. She said that and then she walked away very lightly, like a ghost, leaving the door swinging on its hinges behind her. The significance of that moment, of her words and her look and the swinging door, seemed to reach right down to the root of my life. I felt that my whole existence was the frame for that moment, in the way that a pond exists for the pebble thrown into it and pulses with its rings long after the pebble has disappeared. I shuddered in just such a way; I felt a force pass through me. I thought it signified something, but now I realize it was a careless, idle gesture, a throwaway remark that I failed somehow to consign to the dustbin. Gerte hadn't yet seen anything in me that she wanted. I hadn't yet roused in her the desire to win, to possess. When I asked to buy her a drink, the next week, she seemed surprised. I was like some mad compass, febrile, sensitive, vibrating to everything she did and said, while she seemed solid and fixed and decided. At the pub she asked me a lot of questions, in the way people do who are bored. I told her things; eventually I told her about Ian. I remember her face, as if something had suddenly caught her eye, something beautiful and rare, something valuable. You love him, she said. Yes, I said. More than your wife? she said. Yes, I said. More than anything. I thought it would be all right, saying that to her, but a feeling of pressure rose in my chest, like I used to get as a child when I'd done something I knew was wrong.

I got so used to that feeling over the next few weeks that I stopped noticing it, it became the atmosphere of my time with Gerte, became indistinguishable from love. Why can't you stay, she would say across the dark, when I rose from her bed to get dressed. You know why, I would say. And she would sigh out my son's name and my heart would pound. Sometimes she spoke about Germany and the life I could lead there with her, and this made me very happy, I made a sort of story of it in my head so that for a while I lived two lives, one actual and one possible. That these possibilities adhered to me filled me with amazement and fear. I felt that without them I would die. How much do you love me, she would say, and because I had the certainty of Ian but not of her I felt that I could encompass him in myself, could speak on his behalf as well as my own. More than anything, I would say.

It's him or me, that's how she put it in the end. If you loved me, you would give him up. Then I would believe that you loved me. She was going back to Germany. Can't I bring him too, I said. If you did I would never know, she said, who you loved more. That's what love is like, when there are no facts. Sally knows about facts. She booked my cab for the airport. When I left Ian cried and ran out of the house after me and held on to my leg. I had to pick him up and carry him back to the house with him screaming. Go to your mum, I said, but he wouldn't, I had to force him off me and shut the door on him. When he looks at me now in that strange way, deep down I always think that it's because he's remembered that night. He couldn't, of course: the way things worked out he wouldn't know any different. I remember Gerte's face at the airport, lit with pleasure at the sight of me, so that I couldn't understand what she said, she had to repeat it over and over. I know now, she said. You can go home to your son. Go on, go home. So I did. Sally was still in the hall. That's when she said that one day Ian would thank me. You're a good man, Alan, she said. □

GRANTA

THE COSTA
POOL BUMS
Alan Warner

Alan Warner was born in the Scottish Highlands in 1964 and published his first novel, 'Morvern Callar', in 1995. 'These Demented Lands' followed in 1997, and 'The Sopranos' in 1998. His fourth novel, 'The Man Who Walks' (Jonathan Cape) appeared last year. He has won the Somerset Maugham, Encore, and Saltire prizes. 'For my generation there was a reaction against a perceived gentility in British fiction, yet I'm sceptical now of the "realist" novel. I've lived in Ireland for six years, which plays havoc nicely with my ideas of belonging to any school or tradition. My writing seems less and less "Scottish", which to me at least is exciting.' A film of 'Morvern Callar' was released last year. 'The Sopranos' will be filmed by Michael Caton-Jones next year; 'under another title I bet!' 'The Costa Pool Bums' is from a novel-in-progress.

The Costa Pool Bums

I'd flown back into Gatwick airport on a usual red-eye charter. A slimy morning sunlight was crawling over the docked night aircraft as I stepped along glass-walled walkways. It was at the Village Inn that I first hooked up with Eisin Park who was to change my life. Like me he was alone, like me, newly tanned. He said his name was Welsh. Like me also, he'd just come back in from Spain, but we didn't see why that meant our holidays were over. This could be the reason why there is such a large and busy twenty-four-hour drinking establishment in Arrivals. Nobody wants to admit their fortnight is over. He bought me a lager. Around us the Village Inn was that confluence of all that makes Britain familiar when you come back.

Eisin's barroom philosophy was immediately above standard. You can learn so much about a person in five pints and I liked him. 'The old man was a plumber and so am I, mate,' he told me first. 'The old man, he called a fitted glass shelf above a sink the "Plumber's Friend". Only a matter of time, the old man used to say, till some heavy object falls off that glass shelf, cracks the basin and they're phoning for a plumber again. My old man used to fit as many of those little glass shelves as he could. Know what the Plumber's Friend is now, mate?'

'No.'

Now Eisin nodded back over his shoulder with a quick jerk towards Boots the Chemist and the Disney Shop. I felt silly but I looked.

'Spanish plumbing, mate.' He set his drink down.

I realized he was nodding to one of the digital flight-information monitors. They don't position monitors in bars in the Departure areas of our great airports. It only encourages the working classes to linger on licensed premises until the last possible moment, destroying the competitiveness of our airlines. But because it was just Arrivals, they had permitted a monitor. It was specifically the departures monitor Eisin was nodding to.

'Not much in Spain except dust and cheap liquor. They don't have any good rock music, same as the French. And most of all they don't know anything about plumbing. Plumbing comes from Ancient Greece. The Romans were great plumbers, I've studied their stuff. Now there's teams of English folk living down in Spain, mate, each one stuck with a plumber who, while we sit here, drinking overpriced beer in England, is already three days late. Lots of opportunities. Do you see what I'm saying to you? I can show you the basics. It starts with a wedding ring at the bottom of a U-bend but if you take plumbing and go to the top of its food chain what do you think you get?'

'Top of the plumbing food chain? I don't know anything about plumbing. Kitchens and bathrooms?' I shrugged.

He smiled, shook his head terribly slowly. 'Top of the chain, mate!'

'Don't have a clue.' I laughed.

'Swimming pools. Top of the plumbing food chain.' He called for two more beers.

Looking back on it Eisin was right. What had we both returned to? Britain and all its mild vices. He was divorced, I'd had my thing. I was definitely not dating two beautiful sisters called Jasmine and Jacaranda. I'd found no lower rungs on any property ladder. Saturdays I sat with no shirt on, staring across my landlord's dirty carpet at morning programmes, filled with genuinely grave concern for my fellow citizens—though I knew I was one of them. I dressed in less than a hundred pounds' worth of clothes, walked to town and stood in second-hand book and record shops believing I represented higher values. Oh, the old dreams were gone, all our guitars sold, we were living imagined lives through younger men in new, glossy music magazines. The guitarists I'd once known had become estate agents. I knew there was more to a healthy society than farmers wearing designer baseball caps. Incredible! Men in thousand-pound suits openly bought porn magazines disguised as lifestyle tracts and Santana had gone and become fashionable, making his vinyl soar in price—even in the smelly, second-hand dumps I hung out in. Like everyone else, the rest of my life I worked. Does it matter at what? I brought in nine hundred a month if I did overtime so I wasn't a yuppie at least.

There was a month's backdated wages in the bank, which Eisin and I hit down on the lower floor at Gatwick with a max daily withdrawal. There were several flights to Spain a couple of hours down the line. We toured around the ticket desks.

I had my passport and a bag of dirty T-shirts and I kept telling myself that I was returning to Spain without having left the airport in the company of a dubious plumber I'd only just met. I was paying for his seat too. When we pooled our cash we had close to one hundred and forty pounds. But I felt more proud of myself than I had in years.

W e'd bought the cheapest tickets, forty-six-quid returns; got two pints' worth in in the Departures Wine Lodge, peed and boarded a completely full aircraft. We must have got the last seats. Eisin warned me, 'No loutish behaviour until after take-off. Just sneeze these days and the dinner ladies of the sky have got you on some air-rage rap. Ban us from your airline if you want, I say, but after you get us to bleeding Spain!'

A bored voice on the public address system announced: *Keep seat belts unfastened. We are refuelling.* A tinkling of seat belt buckle plates sounded as travellers throughout the cabin unbound themselves. An elderly passenger accessing the seat behind us suddenly halted.

'Miss, you must have had an exciting landing, there's ah...something on my seat.'

'I think it was those Scousers,' whispered a stewardess. Her colleague nodded in confirmation. Eisin and I got up on our knees to look over our seat backs.

There was a khaki smear right there in the centre of the garish seat fabric. The old passenger and his two neighbours were forced to stand awkwardly out in the aisle while boarding passengers continued to squeeze by staring, while the stewardess, wearing a rubber glove, bent over and went at the seat with a cloth and basin of hot soapy water.

A group of three females holding excessive hand luggage up high came down the aisle. Their chainmail of blonde hair and dark roots, crunched back severely, matched the tangled gatherings of gold jewellery banded on their fingers, wrists, ears and necks. Mother and daughters shoved onward, the mother wearing the same outfit as her teenagers: white vest tops, struggling mini-skirts, and—showing through the taut cotton polyester—brightly coloured bikinis already in place. The family brushed aft and glanced sourly.

'Hope nobody thinks I did it,' yelped the old passenger.

The women stared but ignored him.

'Turn the gas off at home, love?' the mother yelled suddenly.

'We're disconnected, Mum!' said one of the younger women.

'Ooya. Forgot. And we left Grandad in the hospital for the fortnight, yeah?'

'Ow. It really hurts where I had that tattoo removed,' the younger-seeming daughter growled. She could have been no more than fourteen.

'Shut it. You're better off without him,' her mother clarified.

I whispered snobbily to Eisin, 'Straight to the bottom of the pool with the Argos family jewels.'

Eisin said, 'England's future, mate, dropping h's and popping E's across Europe.'

England's future were now banging and ramming their outsize hand luggage into the roof lockers with such force that the refueller man down under the wing must have been scowling upwards.

In a blast of sickly Everglade's Swedish Pine, the old passenger behind us was finally permitted to lower himself into his damp seat and onto a layer of absorbent paper towel.

Refuelling complete. Fasten seat belts. No smoking.

Behind us the old man groaned, 'And now there *isn't* a seat belt. No wonder they crapped themselves. Miss!'

Both strands of the seat belt had been chopped off and the buckles stolen. Eisin was sniggering like a schoolboy into his hands. The stewardesses returned and tutted, shaking their heads slowly, speculating on the murder weapon. 'Definitely the...Liverpudlian group,' they pronounced.

Meanwhile Eisin was telling me how he used to get away with smoking on flights before he quit. Apparently if one lit the cigarette then held the end down by the sink plughole while depressing the sink-emptying button all the smoke would be suctioned out. The special challenge came in exhaling all your smoke down the open plughole as well. He went on to tell me how he had once dropped his mobile phone down the toilet while carrying out this act and had tried to get the airline to return it. He spoke quite loudly for my tastes and had also reached up and produced a Tesco's sandwich from his bag in the overhead locker. I was puzzled and asked him where he'd got it. It turned out that his flight had landed at five that morning, he'd taken a taxi to the twenty-four-hour Tesco near the airport, then returned to continue drinking in Arrivals.

The Captain's bored voice came over the intercom. *Ladies and...gentlemen. This is the flight deck. Welcome. Hope you'll have a comfortable journey with us this morning. However. We have a problem and are facing a substantial delay.*

A very British groan went up. Eisin looked round and called, 'Anyone with piloting experience?' Playing to the gallery, he chuckled slowly, as if lifting up separate clots from his lungs.

...Learning there is a local dispute between our airline and the baggage handling company we are contracted to...

Eisin and I looked at each other warily.

...At this present time, we are unable to load your baggage onto the aircraft and we're going to miss our take-off slot which could throw us into a several hour delay. I'm asking for young, able-bodied volunteers among you to load the baggage into the aircraft for us all today.

There was a pause, then laughter among the passengers.

'He's joking, surely?' pleaded the old guy.

Eisin seemed impressed by this development.

The volunteers can ring the call buttons in the panel above them. There was a pause, then the captain's voice muttered, as if reading back some crucial air traffic instruction, *Travel insurance will not cover injury.*

The cabin was apprehensive. I undid my seat belt and raised myself to crane back and forth, scanning the grey hair and single mothers ahead and the wrinkled, weary faces behind. The baseball cap of a heavy man wearing glasses up near the emergency exit looked as able-bodied as it got. I slumped back down. The man beside me in the window seat was already asleep, leaning to one side.

'What do you think?'

'Not even at these seat prices am I gonna load up this shower's kit. Look around you—' for once, Eisin lowered his voice, '—golf clubs and suitcases of two-litre lemonade bottles filled with gin! We'll be poking in our hernias on the beach!'

'Be strike-breaking anyway. I'm an old Lefty.'

'Mmm. Me too,' Eisin nodded rapidly. 'When I went broke at least I could start voting socialist again. Up the revolution and down with any exchange rate against the pound.'

Afterwards, complimentary drinks will be served to baggage volunteers, the Captain's voice grumped from the flightdeck.

Our hands raced each other to the call button which pleasingly lit up above us.

We got a polite round of applause as we strode to the forward door. Eisin turned and took a few bows to the long cabin of faces. He was still chewing his sandwich. Up at the front I noticed some Spanish grannies dressed in black. They seemed confused. I believed that it looked as though Eisin and I were being expelled from the plane due to some misdemeanour, while everyone was sharing a delight in this. One of the grannies began to nod aggressively and clap in approval, some kind of seafood resting on unfolded silver foil in her lap.

Down on the tarmac two stewardesses solemnly handed us high-visibility yellow vests. Eisin pretended to look both ways then casually tossed his empty plastic Tesco sandwich packaging into the huge engine mouth hanging beneath the wing, as if it was a convenient litter bin. I laughed. Even though the engine hadn't yet started up, nobody else was amused by this. Eisin rapidly stuck his cropped head into the engine next to the fan blades and retrieved the wrapper.

The stewardesses who had come to supervise our baggage loading looked angry. Both had serious wedding rings on. One grabbed the sandwich packaging off Eisin and clutched it possessively. Walking wonkily in their raised shoes, the stewardesses escorted us in front of the wing, way out to its very tip and then back around behind it. They would not allow us to take a short cut under the wing to get to the baggage hold.

'Why not this way?'

'In case something falls off. On to your head,' snapped the younger-seeming stewardess, who wasn't very young at all.

The unwashed fuselage of the aircraft was painted white but you could see a spreading discoloration both below and above the windows where the reverse thrust of continual, rapid-turnaround landings had thrown up dirt. I'd never been so close up to a jet aircraft. It seemed enormous, especially the undercarriage tyres which sat plump and slightly ominous on the heavily scored macadam.

Two trailers piled high with assorted luggage stood beside a conveyor belt next to the aircraft's baggage hold. It didn't look so very much to me.

'For insurance reasons you're not going to be able to use the conveyor. It's property of the baggage handlers.'

'Another two full trailers are just coming,' the stewardess holding the sandwich packaging smiled.

Eisin took the toughest job. I stood inside the aircraft's belly stacking the luggage across the hold, while Eisin threw each piece up to me from the tarmac. He was strong and had stamina. The cases, holdalls, golf clubs, prams and cardboard boxes bound in parcel tape stopped coming only when Eisin paused to take off his T-shirt; the stewardesses, smirking at him then turning their backs on us to gossip, made him put the plastic reflective vest back on, next to his sweating skin.

I bent back two of my fingernails on the imitation leather suitcases. Drops of sweat fell from my face when I lunged downward to grab the next burden but I felt I was forming a great bond with Eisin. It was he and I alone who were getting this show on the road!

The luggage barely half filled the hold. The ground supervisor, who seemed incapable of helping Eisin chuck up a single suitcase, yelled in at me to stack everything waist-high so there was no chance of anything shifting during the flight. Then I was to buckle the floor straps, section by section.

When we'd finished, I paused at the edge of the hold before lowering my feet the short drop down onto the tarmac. Eisin was getting his breath, leaning forward with his hands splayed on his thighs. The supervisor had been joined by the co-pilot who'd come to oversee the closing of the hold door.

The super laughed. 'The A-Team! Got a future here, boys. When you get back, if you're looking for a spot of overtime?' He was serious. The co-pilot, hands in his black trouser pockets, smiled and shuffled uneasily. He avoided our eyes and instead scrutinized the engine cowling intently. Eisin straightened up and looked around: his eyes followed a taxiing airliner with its fluctuating engine noise. 'Yes, mate. That just about sums England up for me.'

The stewardesses marched us round the wing again and escorted us off British soil.

Back in the cabin, as we dutifully handed back the reflective vests, Eisin and I got a gallant round of applause from the older passengers. With our unexpected and heroic return, the Spanish grannies appeared crestfallen and glanced around.

An engineer was leaning across to the old man's seat behind us, refitting the seat belts. '*Might* hold you in,' the engineer shrugged and rattled off up the aisle with his toolbox. The aircraft doors were pulled shut and locked.

For the next twenty-five minutes the cabin temperature rose horribly.

I looked across the lap of the sleeping man beside me, through the window into the British summer. Outside a ground worker noticed something on the concrete, picked it up, frowned at it, turned his face towards our aircraft with a puzzled look, then threw the part over his shoulder and walked off shrugging. I was convinced this display had been put on for our benefit and that a group of ground workers were now gathered below me, out of sight beneath the aircraft, snickering.

I leaned back, took a breath and said nothing. All around, passengers fanned themselves frantically with safety cards while crying infants smelled. Even without moving I could feel the sweat inside my shirt. Eisin and I had been served a glass of warm water each and had been refused anything stronger until after take-off. With a knowing smile Eisin leaned forward and removed his T-shirt. Immediately a stewardess, who didn't seem to have broken the slightest perspiration, strode from the front of the cabin.

'Sorry, sir. Regulations says you must wear a shirt when travelling.'

'We aren't travelling.'

'Please understand, sir, there are families.'

'We're going to the beach aren't we? They'll see much worse than this on a Spanish beach in three hours'—he slapped his stomach—'or six at this rate,' he added, looking at his watch.

'I'll have to ask you to put your shirt on.'

'I'll have to ask you to put the air conditioning on.'

'Mutiny is in the air!' I snapped.

'And we aren't.'

'Can't have air conditioning until the captain starts the engines up. Sir.'

'Start them up then. Can't he find his keys?'

'An aeroplane doesn't actually have keys and we can't start the engines until we have air traffic clearance,' she smirked, privy to great facts.

I felt I should back Eisin up though I was worried about being thrown off, but even if that happened it would be, like most misfortunes, a story to tell in the pub.

'This only ever happens on charter airlines,' I chipped in. 'Do you really think Concorde is sat over there with millionaires stuck to its leather seats?' I pulled at my sweaty trousers for effect.

'Not unless they're burned on to them,' Eisin sneered.

'Concorde doesn't even fly out of this airport. Put on your shirt, sir, or I'll have to consider you a disruptive passenger.'

'Here we go,' smiled Eisin, head turning round in appeal to his fellow passengers. 'Air rage and they ain't even got us in the bloody air yet.'

'Go on, son,' yelled a mature female voice from behind us. It was the mother of the terrible daughters.

'You've clicked there,' I taunted.

The old guy piped up, 'Miss, this man is not being disruptive, he was just quietly sitting there with his shirt off. If anyone's being disruptive here it's you, miss. This man has just loaded our luggage and it's very, very hot in here.'

There were a few paltry supporting handclaps which petered out as the stewardess moved her orange face from the old man and across the cabin. She turned and walked away up the aisle.

'She fancies me!' Eisin called after her. There was laughter. 'That's why she wants me to put my shirt back on. She can't contain herself!' He smiled serenely, Buddha-like.

Moments later the captain strode down the aisle with the stewardess behind him murmuring repeatedly towards the four stripes of his left epaulette. The captain kneeled down, leaned very close to Eisin and whispered directly into his ear. He had halitosis. 'On a clear day,' the captain took an inspirational breath, 'I can see...everything from up there.'

Eisin shifted uneasily and the captain turned his ear to him. Eisin promised meekly, 'I'll put my shirt back on if you get us down safe.'

The captain nodded. 'You didn't load quickly enough. Missed our take-off slot.' He rose up to his full height, gave the old man behind us a reprimanding glare then announced, 'Sorry about the temperature. Be on our way shortly. When the air comes through you might direct the nozzles backwards and we'll get there quicker!'

The captain ambled up the aisle to the flight deck. On the way he reached out playfully and took a child's ear between the crooked forefingers of his right hand. He pretended to twist each lug accompanying his actions with a crunching sound from his mouth.

Alan Warner

He left a certain tension in his wake. Disturbingly, I clearly heard a young voice say, 'Mum, he's had all his hair cut short but he used to be the singer in that heavy metal band.'

Air still did not circulate through the tropical cabin atmosphere but rumours did. Apparently someone in the long queue for the solitary forward toilet had glimpsed the captain and co-pilot on the flight deck, one man completely shirtless, the other in string vest and underpants.

Then suddenly we were on our way—push back, engine start up, and behold!—lukewarm air stuttered from above our heads through nozzles yellowed with age by the Peruvian domestic routes of the aircraft's middle years. Hands darted up to nozzles as if they were tumbling oxygen masks.

We were a helpless community put in motion together. The aircraft rushed forwards competitively then braked, rushed then braked along and across taxiways towards the threshold of the runway. Stewards and stewardesses struggled to keep their balance while demonstrating safety techniques, the life jacket with its utterly forlorn cherry light and whistle on a string to 'attract attention'. Then the engines began to spool and the cabin crew leapt into impressive harnesses as we swung on to the axis of a glittering runway: two miles, dipping and rising away into green old Sussex; eighteenth-century spires showing above shorn treelines, dark unruly clouds on the perimeter above quarries, beyond the artificially jewelled hinterland of the airport.

I looked out of the window at the wing. As we accelerated it stopped drooping and lifted a few inches, coming alive and tensing in the airflow, as though it had been patiently waiting for speed, its true element. Pushed down in our seats we ascended into sky. The taxiing aircraft I'd glimpsed at the bottom of the runway appeared to halt as we shot upwards, and the middle class bore the working class aloft once more, laughing all the way to the merchant banks.

As the aircraft dipped cutely but kept climbing out, Eisin leaned across me to look down on merrie England's plump pastureland divided up by darker trails of ancient hedgerows as it moved slowly beneath the twisted sneer of the number two engine.

I sighed and tried to relax. The aircraft was holding together. The small clinks and coughs of the other passengers seemed emphasized in the tense, glassy ambience of the creaking cabin. I yawned and my jaw snapped hugely. A scrap of crazily suspended cumulous meandered past the wing tip, which dipped to avoid it, then the seat belt sign plonged off. There was a race for the toilet up front.

As a general rule of thumb in life, Eisin and I knew not to rush at stewardesses for drink but to let them come to you, no matter how slowly. The bashed and dented refreshments trolley looked like it had a few hundred thousand miles of aisle on its clock. After a struggle, two stewardesses managed to engage the footbrake. There was no beer.

'Someone forgot to load it,' the first stewardess smiled. She looked pleased.

'Wouldn't have been cold anyway,' nodded the other by way of compensation.

'What'll you have instead, baggage handlers?'

'I'll have a pint of wine,' Eisin declared.

'We don't have pint glasses.'

'But I do!' Eisin was up in his hand luggage above. He now produced a plastic pint glass. Clearly sickened, but helpless, the stewardess left us with ten small bottles of red wine. We bust the screw tops off and tipped one after another of the bottles into the plastic pint jug.

The captain announced Lourdes as being directly beneath us and therefore invisible to the passengers on both the right and left sides of the plane. 'Nobody flush the toilet!' Eisin cackled up the aisle. The man beside me sighed wearily and closed his eyes. After a few moments, 'Matron', as Eisin called the senior stewardess, switched off the public address and removed a small loudhailer from the Emergency Evacuation Locker.

'Before we go through the cabin with our duty-free and gifts trolley...'

The man beside me jerked awake. One of the stewardesses sashayed up the aisle, her mature torso now tightly bound in a purple-and-aquamarine sarong, stiletto shoes studded with coloured stones. On her head she wore a green-tinted sunvisor secured with an elastic strap. Opaque, horn-rimmed sunglasses were trying to make a comeback over her eyes. A child began to cry. The mother and daughter trio, who'd been ordering a precise battery of Bacardi Breezers, guffawed aloud.

'...We would like to display our range of beachwear and accessories. Jemima and Louise will be our models for you today. For the beach, or just around the pool, Jemima models our handy St Tropez sarong which comes with free, exclusive sun visor.'

Louise appeared from behind the back curtain, wearing a similarly styled sarong in alternative pastels, transparent high-heeled sandals, and a baseball cap bearing the airline's logo. She bore forward enthusiastically, a large, inflatable plastic dolphin beneath her left arm and an inflatable alligator swinging beneath her right. Her catwalk motion encouraged the tails of the inflated creatures to strike out violently at the heads of the passengers in the aisle seats.

'Younger customers today might want a friend for the beach. Ali the alligator perhaps, or maybe a friendly dolphin? We accept all major and minor currencies...and cheques, with or without valid cheque cards.'

'And giros,' Eisin shouted.

The cockpit door opened gingerly just enough for the co-pilot to crane out cautiously, take in the scenario and with a grave nod, retreat. The cockpit door snapped shut.

The two models turned awkwardly at the top of the cabin, the alligator tail severely worrying the Spanish grannies. As the stewardesses made their return pass down the aisle, some passengers on the left began gesticulating and pressing repeatedly at their call buttons. Anxious for a sale, the stewardess abandoned her alligator and dolphin to attend to a customer in a forward row. She bent over displaying where the fake tan ran out up on the back of her thigh. Matron strode forward to assist. Then she turned and shouted through her megaphone, 'Is there a doctor on board?'

'Christ. Every time.' The man beside me opened his eyes and sighed. 'Excuse me.'

Eisin and I jumped up to let our neighbour pass. He tugged up his baggy linen trousers before trudging ahead.

'That's why they call it the Hippocratic oath,' Eisin chuckled.

A passenger in a window seat near the front was having some kind of problem. In a cautious, British way, we all craned over our seats and peered up the aisle. Two of the Spanish grannies, neighbours to the ill person, were moved out to stand jabbering and nodding together in the aisle. The doctor produced ID from his wallet then shuffled in next to the ailing passenger. Things settled down for a moment until we saw the doctor stand, glance at the senior stewardess and, unsubtle though it was, draw his finger across his throat in a decisive cutting motion.

'Christ. Today's first fatality,' Eisin whispered.

Matron lifted her hand to her mouth. The garishly saronged stewardesses began to plead with the doctor who just shrugged helplessly. He selected a series of blue blankets from an overhead locker and, although we had no direct view, it became obvious he was covering the victim with them. Then he squeezed past the curious passengers, back to his seat. The people sitting around us now became solemn in his presence. A noisy child cried louder somewhere as its mother tried to restrain it out of respect. Our neighbour energetically reclaimed his window seat.

'What happened?'

'Elderly gentleman. Cardiac arrest. I'm afraid I had to declare his death.' The doctor began positioning his linen jacket as a pillow against the window.

'Doc! Wasn't the fun and games with the swimwear was it? Too much for him?' Eisin whispered. Strangely, he didn't seem to be teasing. He looked cautiously up the aisle at one of the stewardesses, who was crying now, still wrapped in her sarong. A rogue child was on the loose, taking advantage of the diversion to deflate Ali the alligator and conceal its withered carcass up his football shirt.

'No, no. I couldn't get his eyes closed; that's why there was no point in resuscitation. Never a defibrillator on these charter wrecks anyway. He was barely with us beyond Gatwick.'

'Poor old soul,' Eisin murmured, apparently genuine. 'So you're a doctor? We're going to build swimming pools. I've got the contacts.' He leaned across me, 'Need a swimming pool, Doc?'

'No. Hospital doctor. Can't afford swimming pools and haven't slept for two nights; please guys—keep it down.' He snuggled a cheek into his creased jacket and appeared to fall completely asleep.

Eisin glanced up the aisle. The Spanish grannies, weeping and crossing themselves, were being forcibly ushered back into their seat row, next to the dead man.

'And I thought you were quiet company,' Eisin mumbled to me.

The seat belt sign came on again and the co-pilot's sardonic voice announced, *Ladies and gentlemen, flight deck, beginning our final descent. Be on the ground in about fifteen. Overcast, lovely thirty-one degrees and hardly any breeze...Trust you all...* there was the hesitant, empty acoustic of the flight deck...*Nearly all of you had a pleasant flight.*

He clicked off so everyone could hear the senior stewardess loudly trying to explain to the Spanish grannies that it did not matter that the dead man had his seat belt undone.

The aircraft began to buck and kick its way out of the doldrums and into a very lively ridge of coastal air. There was the sound of a painful impact from within the rear toilet—part of a stewardess's anatomy striking the bulkhead as she tearfully tried to twist out of her sarong and back into her polyester uniform.

A cry now came from one of the Spanish grannies and all of us tried not to imagine the icy hand jumping out from beneath the blue blanket and touching the woman's black skirt.

As we're experiencing a little...uh...a little turbulence could you please ensure your seat belts are securely fastened.

There was a commotion up at the front. The turbulence had dislodged the blanket covering the dead man's heaven-directed gaze. Predicting a repeat of this situation, the old stewardess—thirty-year veteran of the package holiday—leaned across the screaming grannies and placed the horn-rimmed sunglasses over the deceased man's open eyes, before veiling him with the blanket once more.

At the back of the aeroplane the stewardess—Jemima no less—emerged from the rear toilet. Her foot skidded wildly and she grabbed for support. When she yanked back the galley curtain it became clear that Jemima's elegant, non-company-issue shoe had disturbed a large deposit of semi-solid human waste. Some extreme culprit had made highly surreptitious use of the galley's privacy to carry out a dirty protest at the OUT OF ORDER sign that had been taped to the toilet's door, the stewardess's clear ruse to preserve it for their own exclusive use.

A bad odour began to advance through the cabin. This seemed to be the final straw for Jemima who burst into tears again.

'And who is the phantom croucher?' Eisin called out. All eyes flickered to the mother and daughters who seemed unusually subdued. A blanket and more Everglade's Swedish Pine were used to cover the atrocity. 'Soon be out of blankets at this rate,' Eisin drawled unhelpfully.

The turbulent, balmy, health-bestowing airs of the Costa Blanca—which it had anticipated being caressed by—tried to revive the corpse up front with another vigorous shake and test of the airframe, but to little effect.

Through bright vaporous clouds we tipped steeply into a more or less final approach, the fuselage reflected on the silver wing. We leaned forward in the sky as the undercarriage and full flaps were rammed down. Our engines whined smartly and floated us briefly upwards.

The hazy air now revealed the uniform, dull sheen of the deep black Mediterranean visible between the drooped flaps; sun glazed the aluminium wing, its central strip duller and doubtless cheaper to produce than the frictionless boss of the dazzling leading edge. As we travelled forward, descending, we could distinguish a low sea swell burnished by the powerful but still invisible sun. The water was suddenly crossed by a brilliant little fishing vessel trailing a twisting turquoise wake trimmed with white wash. The sea colour lightened and turned toilet-cleaner blue. The sewage-brown wash of the shallows appeared, then a white beach with sun umbrellas and the reassuring formations of high-rise holiday apartments, colourful beach towels drying on every balcony.

The co-pilot seemed to be officiating over the landing necessities. The wing tip dipped and rose as if the bastard was transmitting a Morse code to his hotel ordering what he wanted for dinner. The engines whined then wound down repeatedly as the co-pilot toyed with the runway, considering what it possibly had to offer. Suddenly we all nodded our heads smartly in collective agreement. Speed brakes stood up on the wing showing fragile hydraulics and runway marks streaking beneath; the reverse thrust tested if the engines could take all this one more time; then the sharp scream of the Spanish grannies from the front joined the thrust. The corpse's senseless, sunglassed face leaned slowly forward and its cold forehead touched, with a tender benediction, the stowed and never-used table in the seat back in front of him.

The shaken but triumphant voice crackled above our heads, *No smoking till you reach the terminal.*

Alan Warner

'Terminal being the bloody word,' Eisin droned.

Two ambulances met us. One for our guest and one, with a priest in the back, for the Spanish grannies.

The bus to the terminal broke down twice. When we finally made it to the packed luggage carousel, we discovered that it was another aircraft's luggage Eisin and I had loaded back in Gatwick.   □

124

GRANTA

THE BALANCE
Nicola Barker

Nicola Barker was born in 1966 in Ely, Cambridgeshire, and emigrated aged nine—with her sister and parents—to South Africa. She returned to England in 1981, with her mother. After completing a poor-quality university degree in philosophy and English (which she claims made her 'socially useless') she worked for many years in a bakery in Soho, a bookmaker's off Oxford Street, and then at The Queen Elizabeth Hospital for Sick Children in Hackney, where she spent much of her time sterilizing breast milk. She has published seven books, most recently 'Behindlings' (Flamingo), and her prizes include the International IMPAC prize, worth £70,000. The money made her 'very happy'. 'The Balance' is a new story.

There were five of them remaining and it was all in the balance. But one was only three years old; just a kid. Eli didn't think he really counted. I mean when did an entity, a human being—

A small blob of shite and gristle

—become morally mature? And who decided exactly? The courts? The individual? Did God decide?

Fuck it

The courts of law had always posited sixteen as the 'age of responsibility'—

Before all of the blah blah blah…

Yeah. Please let's not go back there

—but the courts of law—

Frankly

—had only ever really existed as something to define truths against, not as—

A priori

Was that the right Latin?

—not as an actual, a spiritual marker. Let's face it: there was no certainty in law. Never had been.

The kid's name—

To get back to it

—was Bruno. His mother was dead—

Bang-bang / Boo-hoo-hoo / Let's not rehearse it all again / So tired of that stuff

—she'd died with the others, way back at the start. Heaven only knows what the boy had seen and how that would eventually alter things on the main stage—

But bollocks to that, anyway

—And the dad—

To get back to it

—was an un-be-bloody-lievable arsehole—

Monsieur Twatty

—and whenever the kid broke something or screamed or butted like a demonic little ram into your legs, he'd just throw up his hands, helplessly, and say, 'Bruno is German for bear. I guess that's why he pulls this kind of shit.'

First off, Eli couldn't understand why the dad (he generally called him 'The Dad' in his head, but his real name was Danny) always spoke like he came from America. That special emphasis. And the slang. And all the...

Yawn

So far as he knew (and he did know) Danny was born and raised in Basildon. Furthest he ever went—

What? Leave the security of the A127? Are you out of your fucking bush?

—was to London on the coach at New Year's for the sales.

But not any more, mate

He actually thought Hugo Boss was 'The Boss'. 'The Big Man.' He thought Hugo Boss was some kind of deity.

Straight up!

And who in this shithole was to say any different?

Eli smiled to himself. He was in the unenviable position of knowing everything about everything, group-wise. Certainly everything about Danny—

God

And the detail

I am a lone egg frying in a dry pan of detail

Hmmn

Better watch out for my arse-end when the Big Flipper comes

Might get rather...

Uh...

...sticky

—Danny was thirty-four years old—

Ah, Danny.

Cosmopolitan, you say?

That's a drink, mate!

A Yank?!

Hadn't even been to fucking Euro Disney!

Danny supported Chelsea—

No pun intended

And secondly—

To get back to it

—Eli knew for a fact that at least one of the others (her name was Susannah and she was part French but in no way excessively stylish)—

Let historians note this for posterity:

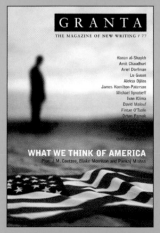

FREE ISSUE OFFER!

Some of the best new fiction, reportage, memoir and documentary photography appears first—often only—in Granta. Each issue is book-sized (at least 256 pages), and illustrated. Many issues are based on a theme like those shown overleaf, which is why each issue has a 'title', like a book. And there the resemblance ends. Granta is a magazine—alive to the present. It is published in book form because writing this good deserves nothing less.

It also deserves to be widely read, which is why, to mark the third in our ten-yearly 'Best of Young British Novelists' issues, we are offering you something special:

➤ A one-year subscription (four quarterly issues worth £9.99 each) for just £24.95, *plus* an extra issue—**ABSOLUTELY FREE.**

➤ That's five issues, worth £49.95, for just £24.95. **YOU SAVE 50% ON THE BOOKSHOP PRICE.**

 **'ESSENTIAL READING.'**

OBSERVER

ORDER FORM

○ **I'D LIKE TO SUBSCRIBE.** I'll get my first issue free, then another four quarterly, book-length issues for just £24.95. In all, that's a discount of 50% on the bookshop price of £9.99 an issue. Please begin my subscription with: ○ this issue ○ the next issue.

MY DETAILS: Mr/Ms/Mrs/Miss _____

_____

_____

03DBG811

TOTAL* £_____ paid by ○ £ cheque enclosed (to 'Granta') ○ Visa/Mastercard/AmEx:

card no: __ __ __ __ __ __ __ __ __ __ __ __ __ __ __ __

expires: __ __ / __ __   signature: _____

* POSTAGE. The £24.95 rate includes UK postage. For the rest of Europe, please add £8. For the rest of the world, please add £15. DATA PROTECTION. Please tick here if you don't wish to receive occasional mailings from other compatible organizations. ○

⫸ **RETURN DETAILS:**

POST ('Freepost' in the UK) to: Granta, 'Freepost', 2/3 Hanover Yard, Noel Road, London N1 8BR. Or, if paying by creditcard: **PHONE/FAX:** In the UK: FreeCall 0500 004 033 (phone & fax); outside the UK: tel 44 (0)20 7704 9776, fax 44 (0)20 7704 0474 **EMAIL:** subs@granta.com

In the beginning there were the five and the French one was not a good dresser

And the one from Basildon couldn't speak German and thought a certain brand of aftershave was holy fucking water

Don't forget the kid. Still shits on a pot. Expects us all to admire it, and fuck me if we don't

—had an improbably long neck and short but rather wide— thick

—almost frizzy hair, which made everything below seem marginally—

Unbalanced

Everything below...

Hey ho...

But enough of all that...

—fragile and undernourished.

Eli was certain that Susannah knew that Bruno didn't actually mean 'bear' in German. Eli knew Susannah knew. But she bit it back every time Danny said it because to correct him, at this stage, would be counterproductive—

So much water / bridge / etc

—she knew she'd have to have sex with him at some point soon and if she put him down over this small semantic issue it might jeopardize his performance. There were no second chances. Things were so finely balanced, after all.

Eli didn't speak German either. But he had pretty good instincts. He glanced over at Susannah as he spoke—

Yes, I am speaking

—She was jiggling the child up and down on her knee. She seemed excessively fond of the child. This depressed Eli. It would make things much harder.

'Little, little Bruno bear,' she sang fondly into his ear, 'we hunted for him everywhere...'

Eli frowned and cleared his throat. He really needed to concentrate. He was in the middle of explaining something to Sushi—

Yup: Sushi. For real

—who was a Japanese—

Hooker

—IT worker for an international bank and—

Hooker

—had just celebrated her twenty-third birthday. He had long since discovered that the only way to make Sushi register anything intellectually was to describe it in terms of action drama.

So that was all five of them;

Count them

Eli, Danny, Susannah, Bruno, Sushi. The five remaining. As far as they knew.

'So imagine that we're in the last scene of the film...' Eli said, dragging his attention away from Susannah and the kid. Sushi was still pretty much focused in on him, which—at this stage—was bloody astonishing. She had no attention span to speak of. Loved kittens. Loved lollies. Loved items of jewellery which looked like kittens and lollies. Loved woolly tartan tights in pastel shades. Shiny shoes with beautiful buckles.

'Awww,' Sushi suddenly said, in her simple, lady-baby jappy-english, 'Don't let it be the end!'

'The end of this film,' Eli conceded, 'But there may well be a sequel. If we're careful.'

'Really?'

Sushi clapped her hands, but up close to her face, and with an almost crazy rapidity.

Eli hated the way she did that. She was twenty—

Sex worker

—three—

Whore

—years old. And she thought she might be gay. Which was very, very inconvenient, all things considered.

Eli (who was thirty-seven and had been a bookbinder, a social worker, had imported high quality incense and was a qualified teacher of the Alexander Technique; which was medically proven as a means of releasing bodily stress and improving posture while relieving certain serious spinal ailments)—

Yeah. Fuck yoga

—continued his story over the tail end of her clapping—

'So the five are left,' he said...

'On top of this big burning building!' Sushi gurgled, wriggling around on the floor where she was squatting.

'Yes. Exactly. Although the fire's something of a red herring...'

She looked confused.

'I mean it's neither here nor there, narratively speaking...'

Still she looked confused.

'Yes! On top of this big, burning building!' Eli caved in.

'And there is nobody left in the whole wide world,' Sushi squealed.

'That's true,' Eli frowned, 'so far as they know...'

'Not a single person to save them!' Sushi reiterated.

Eli scowled, 'Yes. We've already gone into all of that. We're bored with all of that.'

The child suddenly burst into spontaneous song. And loudly. Nobody could identify the tune. There were no tunes, any more.

'Okay,' Sushi parroted brightly, raising her voice, 'We are all bored with all of that.'

'So the leader of the group...' Eli also raised his voice.

'He is like Tom Cruise!'

'Yes. That's it. Tom Cruise circa *Days of Thunder*. Early Cruise...'

'What about...' Sushi mused for a moment, '*Minority Report*?'

She pronounced it clearly and then smiled widely at her own impressive recall.

'No,' Eli wouldn't let her have it. 'Too late. This is before *Jerry Maguire* Cruise. Before divorce Cruise. Before Penelope Cruz.'

Sushi looked confused.

'You're confusing her,' Susannah interrupted boredly. Bruno had climbed off her knee and was now toddling around on the floor. It was getting dark down there.

'It's getting dark,' Susannah murmured softly, but with a slight whiff of dread in her voice.

The child had stopped singing and was now crawling closer to where Eli stood. Eli reached out his foot and kicked him—

On his arse

Hard

Bruno spun across the floor, emitting an unholy howl. It immediately grew lighter.

Eli glanced over at Susannah. 'Sorry,' he mumbled.

'Don't fucking regret it,' Susannah hissed, refusing eye contact. Eli was crestfallen. He peered over at Danny, but Danny was still asleep.

Thank God.

Danny wasn't as cooperative as the rest. He'd been raised a Catholic—

Straight down the fucking line, that one

'*Cocktail*,' Sushi said, as if she hadn't even noticed Bruno's vocal gymnastics.

'Too early,' Eli shot back.

'For Christ's sake!' Susannah was growing impatient, 'just explain it to her.'

Eli took a deep breath.

'Okay. So there are the five of them left, and the one who looks like Tom Cruise...'

'That's you!' Sushi yelled.

'Yes. That's me.'

Sushi laughed, delightedly. Eli noticed how cold he was feeling. Sushi was obviously enjoying the story too much. He really needed to finish it.

'So the one who looks like Tom explains to the others how the principle of karma has been misinterpreted. He explains to the beautiful Japanese one how it has both solidified and kind of...kind of inverted.'

'Now I am getting confused again,' Sushi said, shivering.

'Well do you understand this?' The tone of Eli's voice was suddenly harsher as he moved forward and yanked at the thick chain which tightly entwined her ankles. Sushi gasped, shocked, then smiled again.

She didn't seem to process pain the way the others did—

Weird

If she's a fucking masochist we're truly screwed

—but still he felt it grow warmer. And he could see her feeling it.

'Whatever anybody does, every thought and every action, has its direct consequences,' he continued—

Lost her

Lost her

'And the fewer people there are left, the bigger those consequences are...'

He crouched down in front of her, 'See? There are only five people left. If anybody does anything good, then there will be bad. If anybody does anything bad, then there will be good. It comes in waves.'

Susannah interrupted him, reaching out her hand and gripping on to Sushi's arm as she spoke, 'I am going to have sex with Danny when he awakes, Sushi,' she said, 'and then we will have to kill him. Understand? You will kill him while the boy watches. But we must take a long time over it. A long, long time. Days. Weeks. And you must be strong.'

Sushi nodded. Then she smiled. She understood.

'There will be pain for all of us,' Susannah continued, 'but when we grow wiser, and when we grow greater in number, it should be manageable. It should get easier. Just like before.'

'Do you remember before?' Eli asked kindly, trying to put a lighter slant on it, 'the world before?' Sushi nodded, her eyes wide and glowing—

Ah yes

—She remembers

'And do you remember the story I told you about how the West lived off the Third World, how they ate well so that the others could go hungry?'

Sushi nodded again.

She remembers

The kid was suddenly quiet, and Danny was shifting in his sleep, stirring from his slumber.

Eli grinned and quickly made his hands into a couple of makeshift scales, 'It's all just a question of balance,' he whispered, lifting one arm slowly and then gradually, inexorably, lowering the other. □

What Londoners take when they go out.

Time Out
London
EVERY WEEK

GRANTA

THE JANUARY MAN
David Mitchell

David Mitchell was born in Lancashire in 1969. He grew up around the Malvern Hills in Worcestershire and studied literature at the University of Kent at Canterbury, where he worked at Waterstone's bookshop for a year. He began to write during an eight-year stay in Hiroshima, Japan, between 1994 and 2002. His first novel, 'Ghostwritten', was published by Sceptre in 1999, and won the Betty Trask Award. His second novel, 'number9dream', was shortlisted for the Booker Prize in 2001. His work has been translated into ten languages. He is married and currently lives in Herefordshire. 'The January Man' is a new story.

The January Man

It's so unfair. The worst thing ever just happened, all cause my mum made me take down the Christmas tree. I asked why Julia couldn't do it for once. 'Your sister's got the artistic eye, so she decorates the tree. You undecorate it. I've got to polish the units, and your father's in Oxford, so that leaves you. Won't you just do what you're told without whining for once?' When adults ask you a question you have to answer 'Yes, miss' or 'No, sir' but when you ask them something, they can just order you about and slap another question back.

So anyway, I'd wrapped up the baubles in tissue paper and was coiling up the lights when three things happened, all in one moment. One, Precious Angel jiggled off her spike on the top. Two, she fell to the ground. Three, and I honestly don't know how, but I stumbled in my slippers and trod on her. She made a noise like biting a Crunchie. The living room wobbled a bit like an earthquake, and my ears, eyes and lips prickled hot. 'Bloody bugger!' I hissed over and over like a lawn sprinkler. Precious Angel, made in Venice centuries ago, was—no, is, bloody bugger, is—smashed mirrory eggshells. I prayed to God, hard, to do a miracle, but when I opened my eyes she was still in dozens of sharp bits. I told the Devil he could have my soul if he'd fix her—but I only said it twice, so it didn't count. My mum and dad will murder me. My birthday on January the twelfth'll be cancelled, definitely. All my birthdays, ever.

Precious Angel's broken face was like a little mask on my thumb. She looked so far-away, like my mum hanging out the washing. Could I find an exact same angel in an antique shop or in the Yellow Pages? I get 50p a week pocket money and I've got £28 in the TSB. My parents mightn't notice if it's a slightly different angel. But Julia'd rat on me, for sure. She's in her room now with her stupid friend Kate. They're sposed to be studying for their mock exams but they're playing *Dare!* by Human League. Julia's learnt all the lyrics off by heart but Kate has Simon Le Bon pinned on her ceiling, over her bed, like a pink hairy spider. The Upton Punks'll kick your head in if you say you like New Romantics or even Gary Numan. But he can't be a puff, he's dead futuristic, he's got a friend named 'Five'. Every Thursday after *Top of the Pops* my dad says, 'I wish that little lot would kindly deposit themselves down a very deep mineshaft.' He likes Abba, though he calls them 'The Abba' which makes Julia roll her eyeballs.

So anyway, I scooped up all the bits of Precious Angel in my hanky

137

and put the decorations under the Christmas tree in the bottom of the Narnia wardrobe. Then my mum nagged me to do my thank-you letters. Writing thank-you letters is worse than double maths. I'd rather she just sent all the presents back.

There's adverts for stuff called Superglue that say it fixes anything. Could I glue Precious Angel back together? What a terrible, awful secret. More of a rotten tooth than a secret, one that'll never fall out.

I tried reading *The Stainless Steel Rat Saves the World* to take my mind off what had happened when the phone rang in my dad's office. He's got an answering machine like on *The Rockford Files* but he forgets to leave it switched on. The ringing went on, one minute, two, three. Julia couldn't hear it cause 'Don't You Want Me' was turned up so loud. Mum didn't hear cause she was in the utility room and the washing machine was on its berserk cycle. I crossed the landing. Dad's office is always cool, and smells of cigarettes and filing cabinets. He smokes silver Lambert & Butlers and I like how the boxes smell. His computer hasn't got any games on it, he'd kill me if I touched it anyway cause they cost so much. He writes on a big whiteboard in code, like JAN2ND*RM L.THOMAS/RE:ORDER Q/44*B'HAM/MART (!) SW/CORN&PS/. 'SW/CORN&PS/' is about sweetcorn and peas. My dad's an Area Representative for Iceland, the supermarket, not the country. Iceland give him a Jupiter-red Rover 3200 and change it every two years.

So anyway, I picked the receiver up and said our number. The other person breathed in sharp, like she'd cut herself. 'I can't hear you,' I said, 'and my dad's not here.' Then her baby cried like the end of the world was coming, and she hung up. Must be a wrong number. My dad doesn't know any babies. He's got a pencil-sharpener machine clipped on to his steel desk. You put the pencil in the hole, and turn the handle. I like the smell. My dad only has H pencils. My favourite's 2B. His swively chair's ace, it's like the Millennium Falcon's laser cannon. I aimed over the cornfield towards the cockerel tree and blasted everything between home and the Malvern Hills. Nobody'd notice that Precious Angel was missing if something even worse happened, like a war or volcano or everyone starved.

There was somebody at the front door. I flew downstairs two steps at a time and took the last eight in one amazing bound.

Moron said the pond in the wood was frozen over thick enough to walk on. I didn't tell Mum, cause she'd make me promise not to go on it, then later she'd say, 'Look in my eye and say you kept your promise, Jason.' She says, 'Boys lie all the time, but eyes, never.' That's rubbish. You just stare right back and lie.

So anyway, I said I wanted fresh air cause adults like hearing that. Mum asked what my new black anorak'd done to offend me. The truth is, if you wear black it's like you think you're a biker or hard or something. I told her my duffel was warmer and we left. Moron smells of gravy, wears too-short trousers and lives down Gilbert's End in a cottage that smells of gravy too. Our house smells of alpine air-freshener. Moron's real name is Stuart Moran, it rhymes with 'warren', and when we're alone I just call him 'Stuart', but names aren't simple. Hard kids get called by their first names, like Tom Branch is Tom. Boys one rank lower like Jack Biggs have friendly nicknames quite often, like Bigsy. Next down are kids like me who just get called by their surname. Julia calls me 'Thing' but your own sister doesn't count, cause all older sisters are evil scum, they can't help it. Below us are kids who've got piss-take nicknames like Moron. Nicholas Briar is 'Knickerless Bra'. Being a boy is like being in the army. If you don't use the right name and rank, you end up in a scrap. Girls use Christian names more, and they usually don't fight cept for Dawn Madden who's probably a boy gone wrong in some experiment. Sometimes I wish I was a girl too. If I ever said so, the Upton Punks'd kill me and spray BENDER on my gravestone. It'd be even worse than if anyone knew the poet Eliot Bolivar in the parish magazine is actually me. That was my biggest secret, until I crushed the Angel. If I had one wish, it'd be to wake up tomorrow really old—twenty—with all my problems behind me. Even being Julia's better than being eleven. On her eighteenth birthday last summer she was allowed to go to Tanya's nightclub in Worcester. Tanya's has got the only kryptonite laser in Europe. Grown-ups can buy anything, go to Alton Towers whenever they want and don't worry about ranks or bullying, but they're still always complaining.

So anyway, as we walked to the pond Moron talked about his Scalextric he'd got for Christmas. On Boxing Day its transformer blew up and nearly killed his entire family. He should write to Esther Rantzen on *That's Life* who'll get the shop to swap it for a bigger one, I told him. Moron said it was bought from a Brummie at Tewkesbury Market. I didn't admit I don't know what a Brummie is—it might be like 'Bummer' which is a man who kisses another man. Moron asked what I'd got for Christmas. I'd actually got £12.50 in book tokens, but liking books is a bit gay so I said I'd got the Game of Life. You win by driving a tiny Ford Escort around the board of life the fastest and by getting the most money.

Through the trees we heard kids shouting and screaming, like a zoo with no cages, and we raced the rest of the way. I won cause Moron stepped on a frozen tractor-tyre and his foot got sucked into the mud underneath.

The pond was fantastic, like a massive glacier mint, but dead slippy, and I fell loads before I could skate a whole circuit. I say 'skate' but most of us just slid in our trainers or wellies. Ryan Badger had proper Olympic ice skates but he'd only lend them you if you paid him 5p, though he let Tom Branch and Keith Saunston go for free. Squelch yelled, 'Arse over tit!' at whoever fell over, but Squelch's funny in his head so no one ever thumps him one. He was born too early, Mrs Dendy told my mum. Keith Saunston rode his Chopper on to the ice and kept his balance for a few seconds. He's going to be a stuntman when he grows up. He pulled a wheelie but the bike flew over his head and twisted the handlebars so badly it looked like Uri Geller had attacked it. Then Nigel Baldwin said we should play British Bulldogs actually on the pond. When Tom Branch said 'Okay, I'm on for it,' it was decided. I hate British Bulldogs, in fact Miss Jekyll banned it at school after Sam Lloyd knocked half of Oswald Little's front teeth out, not on purpose. I had to pretend I wanted to play or I'd get called a chicken or a ponce. Our house is on the new estate but most of the village kids live down Winnington Gardens. Winnington Gardens is a big oval of council houses around a green that's muddy even in summer. Its gardens are scrubby, not like on our estate, and its cars are mostly Death Traps. The dogs and houses don't like me. Kids from Winnington Gardens like Ross Wilcox are just waiting for me to come over posh so they can put the boot in.

So anyway, about twenty boys including Dawn Madden stood in a bunch on the frozen pond. Tom Branch and Saunston were team captains, and Baldwin and Bigsy were vice captains. Then they picked us, one by one, like a slave market. I was number thirteen, two after Ross Wilcox. Moron and Squelch were last. Tom Branch and Saunston were joking, saying, 'No, you have 'em both, I want to win!' Moron and Squelch grinned but what else could they do? Baldwin won the toss so our team got to be Bulldogs first, and Tom Branch's team were the Catchers. Coats were put at both ends of the pond for goalposts. The Bulldogs skated to one end, the Catchers to the other. Here we go. My heart was drumming dead loud. You crouch and yell: 'British Bulldogs, one! two! three!', then you charge, screaming like kamikazes.

I slipped, to let the Bulldogs ahead smash into the enemy Catchers. About half our team went down, struggling to slip free before their Catchers pinned both shoulders to the ice for long enough to shout 'British Bulldogs, one! two! three!' Peter Schooling and Sam Lloyd were scrapping and bumped me, but I stayed up. Ross Wilcox homed in, matching my swerves, left and right. He's the fastest sprinter in our year but he's a massive prat. When he grabbed my sleeve, I just grabbed his arm and spun him into hyperspace. Oswald Little did a poxy rugby tackle on me—I spose he wants to keep the teeth he's still got. Baldwin shouted, 'Ye-shaaa, Jacey-boy!' to me when I got through the goal. I felt fantastic. We watched the duels on the ice. About a third of our force had been captured. That's why I hate British Bulldogs—it turns teammates into enemies. It reminds me of that film *Invasion of the Body Snatchers*. So anyway, us survivors charged again. The second pass is much harder than the first, obviously, cause there's lots more Catchers than Bulldogs and they pick off the least hard kids first. I'd already proved I wasn't chicken by getting through the first pass, so when Wilcox and Baz McKay and Dawn Madden downed me, I just lay there. The more you struggle, the more you get hurt. Their faces were red and twisted and it wouldn't have surprised me if they turned into Bull Mastiffs and ripped out my throat. Specially Dawn Madden. She's got cruel eyes like she's Chinese but I think about her sometimes and I can't stop. Something in my pocket went crunch under McKay's knee. It was the Precious Angel bits grinding to powder. Not even Superglue would fix her now. Wilcox punched the air like he'd scored a hat-trick at Old Trafford. I said, 'Yeah, yeah, three against one, well done.' In my heart, I was still a Bulldog. Baldwin and Darren Drinkwater had skated into the thick of the Catchers like punching windmills, but Tom Branch and Bigsy decked them and then Keith Saunston yelled 'Pile-on!' A squirmy pyramid of boys grew higher until we heard a chainsaw roaring through the trees.

It wasn't a chainsaw but Tom Branch's brother Stephen on his Suzuki 450cc scrambler. British Bulldogs was aborted, cause Stephen Branch is in the Royal Navy on a frigate called HMS *Sheffield*, he's got every Led Zep LP ever made and he's shaken hands with Peter Shilton. The older kids gathered around the Suzuki and smoked and stuff. Ross Wilcox started smoking over Christmas. The older kids talked about *The Day After*, a film about the nuclear war. There'll be a winter night that'll last fifty years. When the cans of peas run out, the survivors'll eat each other till only the worst cannibal's left alive.

'When there's a nuclear war,' said Nigel Baldwin, 'I'm going to steal a Pontiac Firebird, drive to Birmingham and watch it from a tower block.'

Ross Wilcox breathed out cigarette smoke and spoke to us middle-rank kids, 'If it hadn't been for Winston Churchill you lot'd all be speaking German now.' Wilcox's always speaking crap, but I didn't say so in case the smokers ganged up with him.

I was dying for a wee so I went to find somewhere in the trees, near the deserted cottage. You mustn't say 'dying for a wee' or you'll get called a puff, you say, 'I'm bustin' for a waz,' and you flob. I'm not very good at flobbing yet, so it hung from my lip and I got gob on my duffel sleeve. I trod through brackeny stuff into the frozen woods. Dead leaves crackled and the mud was crunchy. I like being where there aren't any boys. Pits of gravelly snow lay where the sun couldn't melt it. No good for snowballs. Eat it and you'd cut your gums. Nero killed his guests by making them eat glass grapes, just for a laugh.

So anyway, I stumbled to a holly hedge around the deserted cottage and peed no-handed into that. Holly trees you can't trust, like willows and hawthorns. A green woodpecker came swooping and sat on a spike. The deserted cottage is red brick and has four windows like infant-school kids draw. It's even got a chimney, but there's never any smoke. Houses are heads and windows are usually eyes, but the deserted cottage doesn't give anything away. Magpies sit on its ridge tiles. I was writing my autograph in piss on the frosty ground when the gate swung open. An old woman was there, staring at me.

'I'm really sorry,' I blustered, zipping up my fly before I'd finished. 'I didn't know anyone lived here.' I braced myself for a rollocking. My mum would massacre any kid peeing into her garden.

But she just stared, a mean, sour aunt from black-and-white times. 'Shows what you know.' Her face was shrivelled like a conker soaked too long in vinegar and so was her voice. 'My brother and I were born in this cottage. We've never gone anywhere.' Her throat swung and wobbled like a turkey's. 'You're one of the pond boys, aren't you? You woke my brother up from his nap. He's queer about boys. Some days he loves you dearly, but other times, my, you give him the howling furies.'

'Oh...sorry.'

'You'll be sorrier when the ice cracks. Do you know how many boys are under there now? Eleven, and they're very sorry indeed. Matthew Phipps, the butcher's boy, he was the last. One more for a nice round dozen.'

L unch was fish fingers, chips, sprouts and tomato ketchup. Sprouts make me puke and stink the house out but Mum says I've got to eat five. You hit the bottom of the ketchup bottle until a sudden glollop drowns them and takes their taste away. 'Dad?' I asked.

'Yes?' he answered, mimicking the way I'd said 'Dad?'

'If you fall through ice and you drown, what happens to your body?'

Dad gave my mum that look. 'Why do you ask?'

Put enough details into a fib, it'll become a story. 'In *Arctic Adventure*, this baddie falls through the ice after losing against Hal Hunt, and he gets tombed in by ice. Then in the year 2727 AD he gets found by an alien race who thaw him out again, and—'

My dad held up his hand to say Halt. 'His body would decay and the fish would eat him.'

'Clive,' said my mum, disapprovingly.

'Jason asked a question.'

'Thing's being grotesque,' complained Julia, 'just for the sake of it.'

I ignored her. 'Even cods and trouts? Not just piranha fish and sharks?'

'Uh-huh.' My dad cut his fish fingers into precise fifths. 'Every little fish in the neighbourhood swim'd up. "My turn! My turn! I want my share!" They'd nibble flakes off your poor baddie until nothing was left of him.'

'I thought,' said my mum, 'of doing the guest room in "Zen", after all. "Snowdonia" is a touch bright, I think, for a south-facing room.'

My dad looked at her, sort of nasty, the way he does a lot recently. 'Can't you at least wait until it's warm enough to open the windows before filling the place with paint fumes?'

'May I get down?' asked Julia.

Mum frowned. 'But it's butterscotch Angel Delight for pudding.'

'I'll grab an apple. I've got to get on with my Civil War revision.'

'I wish you'd told me you weren't hungry.'

Just then my dad remembered something. 'Did you go into my office this morning, Jason?'

My sister hovered in the doorway to watch. Grown-ups generally don't bluff kids, except for Mr Prosser our headmaster who hates the whole world. Julia reckons he snarls insults at his bathroom mirror.

'The truth, Jason,' warned my mum.

I must have left the pencil stuck in the pencil sharpener when Moron called. 'Yes,' I said, 'you see the phone was ringing on and on, so—'

'What's the rule about not going into my office?'

'I thought it was an emergency and—'

'What's the rule about not going into my office?' My dad's like iron scissors, sometimes.

'That's funny,' said Julia, unexpectedly.

My dad glared at her. 'What is?'

'When you took Thing to Worcester last week, the phone rang in your office for ever such a long time. I mean, about fifteen minutes. Literally. In the end I had to go in there—the ringing was driving me crazy, and I thought you might have been in an accident or something. I said "Hello" but the other person just put the phone down.'

'That's just like the call I answered!' I said, seeing a way out. 'Did you hear a baby in the background too?'

'Hold your horses, the pair of you!' Dad's voice was an inch from snapping. 'If some joker's making prank calls, I definitely don't want you answering my office phone! If it happens again, just pick up the receiver, cut the line and leave it off the hook. Understand?'

Julia and I nodded.

'I asked you a question!'

'Yes,' we both said.

Julia went, and I wanted to get down too, but I was scared to ask permission. Mum mentioned a special whistle you can blow down the phone at nuisance callers to burst their eardrums, and Dad answered yes, that sounds worth looking into, but in the same way as he says 'we'll see', and 'we'll see' means 'just forget it'. We ate Angel Delight without speaking. Butterscotch flavour isn't as nice as I used to think. Afterwards, I had to do the drying up while my dad did the dishes. He switched on Radio 4 for the weather forecast. Tonight it'll be minus sixteen degrees C in Glasgow, freezing fog'll make for hazardous driving conditions throughout the north, and we can expect temperatures to stay well below zero everywhere except the extreme west. Dad told me off for putting the teaspoons where the dessertspoons go. He stared across the glassy lawn and sighed like he'd entered a competition for the world's unhappiest man. There were icicles hanging on the summer house. I bet they put the cutlery higgledy-piggledy in Stuart Moran's house.

Nobody was on the frozen pond. *Superman II* was on TV, that's why, but I saw it at the pictures on Robin Dukes's birthday ages ago. Superman gives up his special powers just to sit in a silvery bed with Lois Lane. Who'd agree to such a stupid deal, really, in real life? He could fly. He could turn back time.

So anyway, I skated around in figures of eight, slicing lurkers with my light sabre during the nuclear winter. January woods are noisier than you'd think. Rooks go craw...craw...craw...like vague people who can't remember why they came upstairs. Brittle boughs creak like they're polystyrene, twigs snap, farmers' shotguns crack, then echo, like slammed doors, miles away. Do the eleven kids mind me skating on their tomb? Do they want new kids to fall through? Do they miss their parents? Depends what their parents were like, I spose. I made sure no one was spying, laid down and pressed my ear against the ice. I couldn't hear anything, but bubbles were frozen into the ice like an Aero bar. Spose they're speech bubbles? When the ice melts, do the boys' words come out, scrambled up? A pheasant flapped across the pond. The sky was milky with twilight.

David Mitchell

I got up, but my feet flew off, then my ankle bone came whacking down. A crack exploded like an ice cube dropped in warm squash, and splinters of pain shot to my jaw, my middle fingers and the top of my head. You know when you've hurt yourself badly. It's not a one-off pain that dies away. Serious pain stays and stays. I sort of half-crawled, half-snaked off the ice, whimpering. My left foot was just agony and I cried a bit, I couldn't help it. Giant Haystacks would've cried. Headlights from the main road flashed through the flinty trees, but that was half a mile away, and the moon was nearer than that. I tried not to think of the word 'evil', but there's a scarier word than that, it's 'infinity'. Once infinity's got you, you'll never get out.

The knocker on the not-deserted cottage made me think of a sledgehammer smashing ice and bits flying off everywhere. 'Excuse me,' I gasped. Pain made everything underwatery. 'I hurt my ankle.'
'So I see.'
'Can I phone my dad to come in his car and get me?'
'My brother and I don't much care for telephones. Cars can't reach us from the lane. I can see to your ankle, if you want.'
'Yes, please.'
Inside was colder than out, and gloomy as an ocean trench. Bolts on the door behind me slid home. A blurry oblong glowed at the far end of the hallway. 'Down you go,' her voice rippled, 'I'll be along presently.' The floor was stone worn smooth. I hobbled, leaning on the wall, wincing with every half-step. Steep wooden stairs twisted up into blackness. I could see my breath. The hallway seemed to go on and on. I was sinking down it. A dazzling needle of pain went in and out of my ankle with every step.
The living room smelled of mould and musty cardboard, and it was crowded with museumy stuff. An empty parrot cage, a clothes mangle, a towering dresser. The bulb was so weak nothing had a clear shape. No TV, no stereo and no books, nothing new or electric. The wallpaper was Bourbon biscuit brown with Custard Cream wavy stripes and bubbly places where it was peeling off. A gas fire hissed blue, but it was still damp and chilly. Swans made of pear-drop glass swam across the mantelpiece. There were big plants in tiny pots, their pale, blind roots feeling over the rims. So cold! I clenched my muscles and sank into the sofa, trying to find a

position to make my ankle hurt less. She came through a doorway strung with beads holding a china bowl in one hand, a smiley mug in the other. She sat on a stool. 'Take off your sock, then.' The bowl had bread sauce stuff in, which she smeared on to my throbbing ankle. 'This is a poultice. It'll draw out all the pain.'

'It tickles,' I said, hugging myself for warmth.

'It'll be over before it's begun.' Soon my ankle was covered in goo. It crusted over like snot. 'The more you struggle, the more you get hurt.' She handed me the smiley mug. 'Drink this.'

'It smells like coins.'

'It's for drinking, not for sniffing.'

So I swigged back the liquid in one go without tasting it, like you do Milk of Magnesia.

'Is your brother at home?' I asked.

'Where else would he be, Matthew? Shush now, or he'll hear you.'

'My name's not Matthew,' but I couldn't fight the shivery bitterness any more. Odd thing is, as soon as I gave in, I was warmer. I tried to picture my family sitting in their living room, watching *The Paul Daniels Magic Show*, but their faces were wrong, like on the backs of spoons. Down I floated in feathery spirals.

I woke on her saggy sofa. My Timex had stopped, at five past seven, or twenty-five to one, the room was too dim to tell. If it was tomorrow morning already there'd be a manhunt with police dogs. And then when they found out I hadn't been kidnapped, but just been dozing in the deserted cottage, Mr Prosser'd tell the whole assembly, I'd be a laughing stock and even Moron and Squelch'd get picked before me. Bloody bugger, I knew I had better move. My bare foot stuck to the stone floor, and I remembered my ankle. But it was healed. I drew circles with my foot, and put my weight on it—just a twinge. I took out my hanky to wipe the poultice off. Precious Angel powder flew out. The glinty grains hung in the muddied air. I put my sock and trainer back on. Where was she?

'Hello?' I called.

I peered through the beads into a bare kitchen. The beads swayed and clacked. 'Hello?' I called. 'Anyone there?' I tested the back door. Locked, no key, no mat to hide it under even. Back in the living room there was a velvet hood over the parrot cage. I drifted down the hallway to the front door. Locked too, and anyway I couldn't reach the top bolt. 'Hello?' I called up the stairs. 'I have to go home now!' A lakeful of silence. I hauled myself up the creaky steps. My fingertips brushed a doorknob. I knocked and listened—nothing. The doorknob felt like a cold snowball in my palm.

The moon behind the frosted glass was half-dissolved, how the eleven boys must see it. Here she is, under a patchwork quilt. Her dentures were in a pint glass on her bedside table. 'Hello,' my voice trembled, 'I have to go home now.' Nothing. I crossed the wonky floor. The room seemed to have shrunk since I came in. She's so still, still as ladies on tombs. She might be dead. She's got a black hollow instead of a mouth, and shrivelly pits for eyes. If she's dead, I'll need 999. Could I force a window open? Get to the phone box by St Gabriel's or The Swan? But spose they all say it's my fault? Time goes by. Her windpipe bulges as her soul squeezes through. Watch. A blizzard breathes through her mouth, a silent roaring. It hangs in the air, not going anywhere.　　　　　□

GRANTA

THE CLANGERS
Susan Elderkin

Susan Elderkin was born in Crawley, Sussex, in 1968, the daughter of an architect and a pianist. She studied English at Downing College, Cambridge, and creative writing at the University of East Anglia. She won a Wingate scholarship to research her first novel in Arizona, and the result, 'Sunset over Chocolate Mountains', won the Betty Trask award. Her second novel, 'The Voices', is set in the similarly remote landscape of Western Australia and will be published by Fourth Estate this summer. 'The Clangers' is taken from that book. She lives in London.

Crystal slams the fryer on to the gas ring and lets out a joyless sigh. She must make Stan an egg. Stan's world would fall apart if she weren't around to make him a bloody egg. She takes out a wooden-handled spatula from a drawer and drops that on the benchtop as well, making as much of a racket as she can. Then she bangs down the salt and pepper. Stan's hopeless in the kitchen—no surprise there. A few days after they were married she caught him trying to cook a meat pie in a saucepan with the lid on, the gas searing full blast underneath.

Another clanging starts up outside: this one the high-pitched ping-ping-ping of a small hammer against metal. Listen to the pair of us, she thinks. The clangers. *Clang clang clang* all day long, as if this was the only way they communicated these days. Crystal looks out of the window, sees a bright red panel locked in a vice, Stan's long back bending over it. The panel catches a fistful of sunlight and throws out a long-spined star.

Crystal winces. She already has a headache brimming behind her eyes and it isn't even half past seven yet. The bottom of the pan looms blackly before her. All I have to do is crack an egg into it, she thinks. It can't be that bloody hard. Nick it on the edge of the pan. Follow it with another, and another, and another, the whole bloody box of them if I get really in the swing of it, and then I'll whizzy them up into some sort of cross between an omelette and a scrambled-up mess, a few shakes of salt and pepper, maybe a dribble of milk. She goes through the motions, trying not to think too hard. Plops a couple of pieces of sliced white into the toaster. Lays out strips of streaky bacon on the grill. She even makes tea in a pot. When the bacon starts to wriggle and spit she levers open the window and calls out in a billow of smoke.

—Staaaaan!

—Coming!

She closes her eyes and counts to ten. That's how long it generally takes before she hears the sound of him snagging his Blunnies off on the step. By the time she's got to thirteen, his large frame is blocking out the light. She turns around and sees once again how everything seems to droop downwards from his shoulders. You'd think he was carrying the weight of the world in two buckets.

Stan gets to eating without a word, scraping his knife on the plate.

Every so often he looks wistfully out at the car in the yard. When the last bit of yolk's mopped up he coughs a muddied thank you into an oil-smeared fist, dumps his plate on a teetering pile by the sink and goes back out, stooping to clear the door frame.

Crystal leans back in her chair with another sigh and helps herself to a cigarette. Then she gets up and wanders down the hall.

It's not that she worries about him being outside, it's more that she can't quite settle to anything when she doesn't know where Billy is. Behind her half a dozen jobs cry out for her attention: laundry pulled from the basket and left unsorted on the bedroom floor, dishes to wash, shopping that needs to be done. She tugs irritably at her black-and-white polka-dot dress. It never feels right, this dress—the waistline is high of her own waist, and the hem is just high of her knees. And it's got spots on, for God's sake. She doesn't know why she wears it. As for her hair, which is sticking damply to the back of her neck, she's washed it, but the last thing you want to do at this time of year is generate more heat so she's left it to dry naturally and now it's got itself into a right old tangle. Propping the fly screen open at the back door, she steps over to the washing line, helps herself to a couple of plastic clothes pegs and uses them to fix a fistful of loose orange curls to the top of her head.

She's always been a slapdash sort of woman, but it's not through lack of caring. She likes the look it gives her—the frayed, sleepy-eyed look, as if she's only just got out of bed. Men adore her for it. She's been the sexiest white woman in the Kimberley for fifteen years and she'd rather die than lose her claim to the title. She'd certainly rather die than turn into one of those capable, muscular station women who chop up beef joints for the freezer with a butcher's cleaver, bake half a dozen loaves on a Monday and keep a tally of the number of bags of flour left to last them through the wet. Put a bullet in me head, she told Stan, if I ever show a flair for all that crap. Righto, he had said, in full confidence he'd never see the day, and she'd felt his eyes on her arse in her tight jeans, still perched tight and high on her long slim legs: a sure sign of a woman who has her priorities right.

When Billy appears, it is as a little brown speck leaping out from behind a tree. He runs towards the house on invisible paths of his own creation, lifting his face once in a while to check he's on collision course with the house. He's taken his T-shirt off and tied it in complicated knots around his head, sleeves flapping over his ears like a pair of ineffective wings.

Crystal shakes her head in disbelief. This strange creature, her son.

Leaning against the door jamb, her right arm swinging the cigarette to her mouth and away and back to her mouth again, she wonders how she will greet him. Perhaps she'll smile—a big, welcoming smile that invites him to tell her everything, to empty his pockets, show her the stones he has found, because he always comes back with stones. She rehearses the scene in her head, sees them knocking easily against one another as they go down the hall to the kitchen. She'll pour him a glass of milk and he'll eat the toast and Vegemite she's made for him, hungrily, like little boys eat, running out of steam just before he's finished, then getting up from the table and asking to do something else, the skin around his mouth still speckled with crumbs.

Or perhaps she'll tell him off. For stretching his T-shirt out of shape, for not brushing his teeth, for leaving his bed unmade.

Oh, for goodness' sake, Crystal, she thinks. Give the bloody boy a bloody break.

She doesn't need anyone to tell her that this is all wrong: this thin veil of uneasiness that has always hung between her and her only child. They don't touch in the way that a mother and son should touch. Even when he was a toddler and beginning to attract admiring glances from people in the town—the freckles stuck in the shape of a Band-Aid across his nose, one or two stray ones catching on the crag of a narrow, red lip—she was already refusing to believe, in some deep place, that he was anything to do with her. She was still so young herself; she couldn't be expected to step out of the spotlight just yet. By the time he was seven or eight, he seemed to have worked this out for himself, and he'd wrapped himself up in a blanket of wariness that had kept him apart ever since.

It was all there for anyone to see, stored up behind his eyes—penetrating, grey-green eyes, the colour of a stormy sea. Everyone noticed his eyes. Mrs Tucker, his teacher at school, said he'd be a preacher one day, that they burned with an evangelical zeal. Stan said they were a wanderer's eyes—that he'd always be looking for something just over the horizon. Probably never find it, ay. He'd said this cheerfully one Saturday morning as he and Crystal watched their son water the petunias in the front yard—cheerfully and blandly, the way Stan said most things, even when what he was saying was dealing some devastating blow.

Crystal had, of course, dismissed both notions outright.

—They's more like the eyes of the blokes in the Spini on a Friday night, she'd said loudly—too loudly, wanting somehow to ridicule Billy, to make her son more ordinary than her. Pissed as farts and sizing up for a blue. Thassall it is. I'll hev to watch im when he gits older—everyone'll think he's got it in for em. They'll git him into all sorts of trouble, them eyes.

And then she'd laughed, because it was so absurd, so hilarious, this idea that he could ever be a threatening man, her Billy, little skinny Billy, who loved his roos and talked to his stones when he was upset. She'd laughed noisily, nasally, grateful for the release of it, allowing herself to get almost hysterical, and Stan had looked on uncomfortably, large hands hanging.

At moments like this Crystal is grateful to Stan, though she'd never admit it, of course. She knows that Stan is kinder, more honest than she has it in her to be. God knows, Billy deserved more from her than mockery. But given the opportunity, she's got to laugh. There is safety in laughter, a rope to catch on to, and she can't bring herself to let go.

Even before he's cleared the fence, she can hear the words tumbling out of her, an edge sharp as wire to her voice.

—What on god's earth dja find to amuse yerself out there, three hours and not a squeak out of ya, could be lying dead in a gully for all I know, and ya niver take any water with ya, although it doesn't seem to matter, yer like a cow fillin up at a waterhole, drinkin a heap before ya goes out, more than ya think a boy of your size could hold without leakin, and then ya go for eight hours at a stretch—

She shifts her body a little to give him space to pass, then follows him down the hall.

—One of these days you'll jiss not come back. I c'n see it. You'll jiss not come back, and we'll niver know if you ran away or got taken out by a king brown, or jiss crawled under a rock and forgot to wake up—

She's halfway down the hallway before she realizes that the draught at her back must mean she hadn't done up the zip of her dress. She sticks the cigarette between tight lips and reaches awkwardly behind her, trying not to catch loose strands of hair in the teeth of the zip. *Jesus.* Is everyone so slack when they spend all day at home? Then she realizes that she's left her rubber thongs on the step, and she stomps back, gathers them up with an impatient sweep of her arm, slaps the soles together to get rid of any ants, puts them on, slaps back down the hall.

—Billy, are you listenin ter me?

He's at the sink getting a glass of water, his hair a medley of white, blond and gold in the light from the window, luminous against his sun-browned skin. Crystal sits down behind him. She crosses her long legs and accidentally bangs her knee against the table.

—Aw, Jesus.

She rubs the skin where the shadow of a bruise is already threatening to surface. She's got his attention, at least. His eyes are magnified through the distorted, upturned glass. She splays her toes, scrutinizes the orange enamel she painted on them last week.

—Look at them nails. All chipped and jagged. I'll wake up one morning and find I've crossed that line between young n carefree and old n ruined, and there'll be no goin back after that. She gives a little laugh. Whatja reckon, Billy?

She picks a fleck of tobacco from her bottom lip, tucks one arm into her waist, the palm a pivot for the smoking elbow, and tries to get another last drag out of her cigarette, though it's burned right down to the filter. Everything returns to this, her smoking pose, the reassuring to and fro swing giving the moment its purpose.

Gasping for air, Billy fills up again, staring out of the window. Crystal studies him as she smokes. He's hardly ever inside the house, and when he is, he's looking out. Unlike her, he looks as if he expects to see something interesting on the horizon. *There's nothing there,* she feels like telling him, to grip his shoulders and shake him with that fact. *There's nothing bloody there.* Just a big boring desert with nobody in it. Hev ya got something wrong with yer eyes?

He fills up a third time and now he takes his glass and leaves the room. She hears the click of his bedroom door.

—*Billy?*

She grinds the cigarette into the ashtray. Then she looks in the pack to check how many she has left.

This is what she'd tell Billy, if he'd ask her—what she tells herself from time to time, whenever she needs reminding. She was young, naive and pretty. She met Stan in a bar. His hair was thicker then, although already mousy, and he was a bit too lanky in the body to carry off the macho look with conviction; but he had this smile that curled up more on one side than the other. A touch of Elvis, you could say. Hard to spot it now, quite frankly, but it was there, just like it's there on you. And he had these long, long arms that looked like they could wrap all the way around you twice. She even liked the big nose with its extra bulge on the end—like you were getting twenty per cent extra free.

Fact is, she'd been pretty smitten by Stan.

The whole package was all the more alluring, of course, for being seated on a bar stool in the middle of Western Australia. You noticed men there that you wouldn't have missed a blink for back in Sydney. This was fifteen years ago, remember, when most men in the outback referred to you as sheila, and when you came across one that didn't you reckoned you'd got yourself a pretty good lurk.

Now, sitting at the kitchen table, she almost manages a smile. Perhaps it's a good job Billy isn't here, after all. She shouldn't take the piss out of the outback fellas when he's one of them himself, after all. She catches a glimpse of her smiling face reflected in the kettle, and closes her mouth abruptly. She gets self-conscious about her crooked incisors, way too prominent for her small mouth. Beginning to stain at the edges too.

She and her friend Elise had been travelling around Australia for two months by then—four weeks as jilleroos on a station in New South Wales, fencing, tagging, drenching—then over to Fremantle to stay with Uncle Jack and Auntie Pam, and now they were on their way to Darwin, not intending to stop in the godforsaken stretch after Broome, but all anyone could talk about on the bus was the rodeo at Fitzroy Crossing—the highlight of the Kimberley year, they said.

Some year they have out in the Woop Woop, she muttered to Elise, but they decided to give it a go, got tizzed up in their moleskin shirts and hitched a lift on the back of some station hand's ute.

The place was swathed in dust. It coated your tongue and settled in the corners of your eyes. Here and there a blade of sunlight sliced through, showing up a swirl of motes, golden splinters of hay. Cattle with hot, runny noses brayed and butted each other's hindquarters, eyeing the commotion from their pens with shifty eyes. There was a smell of beer soaking into the earth. Bandy-legged men in chaps and Akubras knocked a finger against the worn rims of their hats as they swayed past. Crystal prickled with excitement. She narrowed her eyes against the sun, ripped the pull-ring off her can of Emu and tossed it on the ground. She was a match for these men. She knew it. She hitched a foot on the rung of the fence, mimicking their stance. Beside her stood a row of horses, steaming, placid, their eyes covered with back cloths. Crystal laid her cheek against a flank, sucked in the warm smell of horse hair and horse manure, until someone wrested her back roughly by the shoulder.

—Mind yer face, mate.

A brown leather boot presented itself an inch from her eye. A gun went off. The cloth on the horse's eyes was whipped away and immediately the creature reared up, transformed into a maddened brumby. Its nostrils flared and eye whites rolled as it leapt into the circle and within seconds had flung the rider over its shoulders, kicking its back legs higher than its head. Crystal was thrilled at the dangerousness of it all. Only as the thrown rider scrambled quickly to her feet and leapt out of the ring did Crystal realize she was a girl of about her own age, two long plaits uncoiling when she flung her hard hat off. The men yooped and wolf-whistled and clapped and Crystal swigged her beer and fought for their eyes. Yes, she had met her match.

At the end of the day she and Elise jumped on the back of another ute and sang their way into a hotel bar, arms looped over the sweat-sodden shoulders of men and women they didn't know. Everyone was very drunk by then. Dirt-smeared faces reeled on undecided legs. There were flailing imitations of a dance. Every few minutes came the crash of a glass on the floor. Plenty of men turned to look at her, but he was the only one who lifted his Akubra, the action implying she'd come here expressly for him. She smiled and took the bar stool next to him. Only then did Crystal realize that his eyes, the same faded blue as his jeans, were barely able to focus, and he'd probably mistaken her for someone else.

Still, she was here for the ride, and she wasn't going to cop out now. Besides, she had something to prove. She raised her voice, shouted orders at the barman, flung her hair around. She cast off her old reserve so easily she wondered why on earth she'd been hauling it around for so long. Conversation with her new blue-eyed friend was fairly monosyllabic. He was clearly a man more used to having the elements for company than other human beings. He had a desiccated face, everything dried and dusted, scabbed over and peeling off. His sun-blasted lips were more brown than red. Freckles cropped up in unusual places—on the lobe of an ear, in the crease of an eyelid. His eyes were patient and soft with something hopeful about them. He reminded Crystal of a dog tied up outside a shop. He offered her an Extra Strong mint and when she said no he shrugged and helped himself, then looked around, sucking noisily to make her laugh. The mint made him sneeze and his hat fell off. He ran a hand through his hair and found a stray cigarette lodged inside a curl. He turned it over in his fingers.

—That's a worry. I don't smoke. Do you?

Crystal said yes. He put it in her mouth and lit it. Then he gave her his hitched-up smile.

She had presumed he was a stockman taking part in the rodeo, and it wasn't till later he told her he was a panel beater—see, look at the oil on me hands, it never comes off—holding up ten black-rimmed nails for her inspection. But by this time it was half a dozen beers later and she didn't give a toss what he did. When he offered to escort them both to their room, Crystal, high on this unexpected chivalry, whispered to Elise to take a run around the block. Stan propped Crystal against an outside wall, slipped his hand inside her jeans and cradled her wet crotch with his fingers.

—So he had this lopsided Elvis smile, you see—a flicker of borrowed sexiness stuck on him like a badge, she says out loud. But he had no idea that he had it. At the time I thought that was endearing, but now I'd prefer him to *know* what he has. The awareness would be more attractive. He isn't very clued up, your dad.

Probably niver heard of Graceland in his life, as a matter of fact.

She sits up straight, embarrassed to catch herself speaking to an empty room, and looks out the window again. The shiny red bonnet gapes open like a jaw. She can't see him from here but he'll no doubt have his head stuck inside it, the radio in there with him, his big, cavernous nostrils investigating all those dirty pipes. Stan Saint, the man that she'd married.

She flicks her ash in the sink.

And so they'd fucked against the wall—or at least they'd tried to fuck, neither of them managing to get the angle quite right. He was much taller than her, and he had to either bend his knees or stick his bum out. At one point a bit of him got caught in her zip, and he'd yowled and yowled in pain. She'd put her hand over his mouth.

—You've got beautiful hair, he'd said afterwards as he tucked himself in, leaving her to disentangle herself from jeans that shackled her knees. —Pretty. The colour of five o'clock wheat.

That was what did it. So simple, so childlike, a snatch of poetry from the heart of this sun-roughened man with big, bungling hands. There was more to him than the others. He seemed to know how lucky he was to have done what he'd just done.

I'd niver met a man who treated me with respect before, she'd tell Billy, if she could. You should've met me dad. Then you'd see how it all makes sense.

She wished he'd hang around long enough to listen. Surely he was old enough to hear these things by now.   □

GRANTA

POSTCARDS FROM BRITAIN
Stephen Gill

Stephen Gill was born in Bristol in 1971 and began
to take photographs in the mid-1980s. These
pictures come from a series taken in different parts
of Britain over the past three years. A book of his
photographs will be published by Chris Boot in 2004.

The Plague Village,
Eyam, Derbyshire

Junction of
Kingsland Road
and Old Street,
East London

Between Wakefield
and Huddersfield,
South Yorkshire

Young mother's unit,
North Shields,
Tyne and Wear

The Lawns day
centre, Weymouth

The Mall, Cribbs
Causeway, Bristol

Sainsbury's superstore,
East Filton, Bristol

Pedley Street,
East London

Telephone kiosk
and pillar box
restoration yard,
Merstham, Surrey

Annual Portuguese
wine tasting, Royal
Horticultural Halls,
Central London

Costa Coffee bar,
The Mall, Cribbs
Causeway, Bristol

Harwich, Essex

City farm, Bratley
Street, East London

The old graveyard,
Cairndow, Argyll

Between Grantham
and Skegness,
Lincolnshire

B&W Bowers & Wilkins

> CLEANSED

One damn good song

I'm moving on

Listen and you'll see

www.listenandyoullsee.com

To hear B&W loudspeakers and find your nearest retailer, please call 01903 221 500 or visit our website.

GRANTA

LEADING MEN
Peter Ho Davies

Peter Ho Davies was born in Coventry in 1966 to Welsh and Chinese parents. He studied physics at Manchester University, and English at Cambridge, and after three years working in publishing in Britain and Asia, moved to the US in 1992 to take an MA in creative writing. He is the author of two short-story collections: 'The Ugliest House in the World' (winner of the John Llewelyn Rhys and PEN/Macmillan Prizes in the UK) and 'Equal Love' (a finalist for the Los Angeles Times Book Prize). 'Leading Men' is taken from his first novel, 'The Bad Shepherd' which will be published by Granta Books next year. Davies currently directs the graduate programme in creative writing at the University of Michigan.

Outside, a technicolour sunset is giving way to the silvery sweep of searchlights, as a hand tugs the blackout curtain across the sky. There is a scraping of chairs and then the snap of a switch as the projector starts up. The room fills with the sharp chemical smell of acetate, the ionized stink of scorched dust.

'Lights,' Rotheram calls, and the lamps are extinguished. The makeshift screen—a bedsheet tacked to the wall, ironed creases still visible—blooms white. An image comes into view, blurred, then twisted into focus. Clouds. Gauzy, cotton-wool clouds glide across the screen, and then the camera dips beneath them, and there's the city, spread out like a map. The screen fills with gothic script, *Triumph des Willens*, and beneath it, in shaky subtitles, TRIUMPH OF THE WILL.

The watching men flicker in the reflected light from the screen. They're seated in a rough semicircle; a handful of dining chairs flanking a cracked leather armchair. Only the armchair faces the screen squarely. The men in the dining chairs are half turned away from the film, looking back towards the projector, narrowing their eyes against its glare, studying the figure at their centre.

On the screen behind them, Adolf Hitler rides through the streets of Nuremberg in an open car. Crowds throng the side of the road, their arms thrusting into the air, the Heil Hitler salute rising and falling like a great wave. In the car Hitler, himself, holds his arm up, not at the same sharp angle as the salute, but tipped back at the wrist, fingers slightly arched, as if balancing a silver tea-tray overhead. The screen dissolves to a shot of Hitler on a podium as a battalion of men, gleaming spades on their shoulders, march past in powdery sunlight. Beside and a little behind him on the stage is a severely handsome man, slimmer and taller than the Führer, and in the next scene, this same man is at a lectern, a glinting microphone before him, passionately exhorting the crowd. His hand saws the air, a shining lock of hair falls across his brow. He ends his speech by crying *Seig Heil*, over and over and over until the crowd rings with it.

The reel runs out, and as the film is being changed a hand reaches out of the gloom and offers the figure in the armchair a cigarette. He fumbles it out of the pack and bows his head to take a light. There is the flash then flutter of flame and in it his face is momentarily visible. Older, gaunter and more dishevelled, it is still recognizably the man in the film: Rudolph Hess, former Deputy Führer of the Third Reich.

Peter Ho Davies

The film had been Rotheram's idea. He'd seen it first in 1936 in Berlin, taking a tram across town to a cinema in a district where he didn't think anyone would know him, not telling his mother where he was going.

She had been pressing for them to leave Germany for months by then, ever since his grandparents had fled to France the previous year. 'But they're Jewish,' he'd told her, as if she might have overlooked this fact. 'We aren't.' His father, long dead, had been, but his mother was the daughter of German settlers in Canada who'd sent her back to the motherland to study in Göttingen, where she'd met his father in 1912. In the eyes of Jews, the eyes of his father's family, say, who had spurned his father's marriage and only supported him and his widowed mother from a distance, he wasn't one of them. Yet in the eyes of the Nazis he was.

He'd been set against leaving, even after seeing a man beaten in the street, the previous week. It had happened so fast—the slap of running feet, a man rounding the corner, hand on his hat, chased by three others. Rotheram had no idea what was going on even as the boots went in—the kicking action so reminiscent of football he expected a ball to fly out between their feet as if from a tackle—and then it was over, the thugs charging off, their victim curled on the cobbles. It was a crowded street, and no one moved, just watched the man roll on to one knee, pause for a moment, taking stock of his injuries, then pull himself to his feet and limp hurriedly away, not looking at any of them. *As if he were ashamed,* Rotheram thought, *or afraid of us.* It was all over so fast. He'd barely understood what was happening—later he couldn't even be absolutely sure the man was Jewish—and yet still he felt as if he'd failed, not a test of courage, not that, he told himself, but a test of comprehension. He felt stupid for having not understood, stupid for standing there gawking like all the rest. Too slow on the uptake to even have time to fear for himself. But when he told his mother she clutched his hand and made him promise not to get involved in such things. To her it was yet another reason to emigrate, but he refused to run. He shook her off in disgust, explained that he hadn't been afraid, but she told him sharply, 'You should have been.'

So he had gone to see the film, gone to test himself, to prove something. He arrived early and slipped into a seat to one side and

196

towards the rear, hoping it would be a small crowd, but by the time the film began the theatre was nearly full. He sat through the first half-hour with his shoulders hunched, his arms crossed tightly to avoid any contact with the fellows sitting on either side of him. They were with their girlfriends—it had been a mistake to sit towards the back—and when after about ten minutes the boy to his left started to kiss his girl, Rotheram hadn't known what was making him more uncomfortable, the film or the couple. He was actually grateful when someone behind them harrumphed loudly and hissed, 'Show some respect,' although it made him very conscious of being watched himself as he watched the film. When twenty minutes later the boy on Rotheram's right tried something, he distinctly heard the girl slap his hand away. By then, though, he was caught up in the film. The fervent, joyous crowds on the screen seemed to merge with the crowd around him in the theatre. How he wanted to be one of them. It might have been the two couples flanking him, but by the time the film was over he felt violently lonely. He wanted to have even a bit part in this great drama, and for just a moment in the darkened cinema, invisible in his seat, he felt as if he did. But then the lights came up and he hurried out, panicked by the sudden piercing thought that, if he could, he would want nothing more than to join the Nazis. In his haste he trod on the toes of one of the girls, fleeing before he could apologize, fleeing from her little hiss of anger, her pointing finger. Outside he must have run a mile feeling as if the crowd were at his back, ready to kill him for stepping on some girl's toes.

That was the day he realized he and his mother would have to leave.

It was her old Canadian connections that made it possible for them to come to England. Rotheram wondered what his father, killed at Verdun, would have made of that. Conceived in 1915 during his father's last leave, Rotheram had never met the man, although he still kept his frayed campaign ribbons pressed in his wallet, as proud of them as he was ashamed of having run from Germany.

He'd shown them, with a kind of shy defiance, to Colonel Hawkins one night in 1941 shortly after he'd been seconded to the Political Intelligence Division as a document translator. 'Ypres?' The old man had whistled in admiration, pointing to one decoration. 'Lord, we might have traded potshots. Staunch soldiers, those fellows. Took everything we threw at them.' Rotheram's mother had been killed in the bombing a few months earlier and it was the first time he'd talked about his father to anyone since.

'Neither fish nor fowl, eh?' Hawkins said when he told him his background, and Rotheram nodded. He still wasn't sure what he could call himself—not German, not Jewish—but serving under the CO these last three years he'd felt for the first time as if he weren't running from something, but being led somewhere. In 1941 the war seemed as good as lost, the papers filled with defeats, yet Hawkins was winning small victories every few days across the interrogation table. The first story Rotheram heard about him was how he once questioned a suspected spy for thirteen hours, only cracking him in the end when he told the man he was free to go, told him in German that is, and saw the fellow's shoulders sag in relief. Hawkins made winning the war seem a matter of wit and will, and Rotheram had been thrilled when the CO selected him, personally, from the translation pool to sit in on interrogations. Hawkins spoke excellent German himself, of course, but he didn't always want to let on to the prisoners. 'It helps sometimes to let them think they know more than me.' Springing his German on them when they weren't expecting it was just one of his simpler tricks.

Hawkins enjoyed having a third party in the room. 'It complicates things in interesting ways. Means it's not just one against one—which is what they're expecting, what they're braced for—there's you to figure out as well. The middle man, the go-between. You're helping me, of course, but in a sense you're their translator, too.' Hawkins liked to begin by staring at the prisoner directly, craning forward over the table, never glancing at Rotheram as he translated. Some of the men would flinch, would start to look to Rotheram, offering their answers to him. These would never last long. Others, though, kept their eyes defiantly on Hawkins, and these he'd lull, gradually twisting in his seat, and directing his questions to Rotheram, until the prisoners too began to switch their attention to him. 'They lower their guard a smidgen when they talk to you,' Hawkins explained to Rotheram. 'Lets me watch them more closely.' Over the months they came up with other stunts. A couple of times, Hawkins had Rotheram translate so sloppily that the infuriated prisoners lost patience and broke into English themselves. Later, he began leaving Rotheram alone with a prisoner, stepping out to the toilet, while Rotheram offered the man a cigarette, warned him what Hawkins was capable of, advised him to talk: 'It's nothing to be ashamed of; anyone would.' He posed as a British student of German literature, professed an affinity for things German. 'You've a talent for sympathy,' Hawkins told him, but in truth he despised the prisoners, loved to see Hawkins break them. Once they'd reversed the roles—boredom, as much as anything, dictating their tactics—and Hawkins had played the sympathetic one, hamming it up so much Rotheram thought he was being mocked. He listened from behind the door as Hawkins offered the prisoner a smoke and warned him that Rotheram was a German Jew, implacable in his desire for revenge. The man had talked before Rotheram had even come back into the room. He'd felt a stark thrill, but afterwards in Hawkins' office he'd told him, again, that he wasn't a Jew, and Hawkins had eyed him carefully and said, 'I know, I know, old boy. It was just a ruse. No offence intended.'

'None taken,' Rotheram had told him, but then he'd asked, 'Why do you think he believed it though?' And Hawkins had said quietly, 'The reason most men here believe anything. Because he was terrified it was true.'

'If it bothers you,' he added after a moment, 'we won't try it again.'

'No. It's just the inaccuracy I can't stand. I never wanted to be what the Nazis said I was.'

Hawkins had smiled. 'But dear boy, there's always a silver lining. If they hadn't said you were a Jew we wouldn't be on the same side.'

And Rotheram had laughed. He couldn't say if loyalty to one man could grow into patriotism, but the harder he worked for Hawkins, the more prisoners he questioned, the more British he felt.

But by February 1945 there were fewer and fewer prisoners at the London Cage and Rotheram was missing the interrogations. He'd been agitating for a transfer since Christmas. Quayle and his gang had been flown to France in December and most of the interrogation was being done in Paris now, or by roving teams near the front. According to Hawkins it was a miserable detail, Paris or not. So many men surrendering, thousands a day—it was nothing but paperwork. 'And they know they're beaten,' the CO said disdainfully, tapping a pile of recent reports in his in-box. 'This lot'll tell you anything you want to know. No sport in it.'

'Yes, sir,' Rotheram said. 'But what about the "needles"?' He meant the brass, the higher-ups, the order-givers hiding among the surrendered. The Nazis in the haystack.

'Those fellows aren't going anywhere, believe me.'

'And the snatch squads?' There was talk of small advance units, a dozen or so men foraging ahead of the front trying to catch certain individuals before they fled, or killed themselves, or vanished in Soviet hands. 'They need interrogators to go on those missions,' he said, and the other nodded.

'But I need you here, dear boy, to help put the jigsaw together.'

They were trying to identify defendants and witnesses for the prospective war-crimes trials planned for Nuremberg. The pieces of the puzzle.

'You don't believe me,' Hawkins said, when Rotherman remained silent. 'Come on. We spend too much time ferreting out other people's secrets to keep them from each other.' He leaned across the desk, offering a cigarette, and after a second Rotheram took one. He fished a match out of his pocket, stood to offer the other a light.

'I was wondering if this has anything to do with my father being German,' he asked, sitting back.

The CO shook his head, slowly. 'No,' he said. 'Although if I were you I'd be grateful not to have to see what's happening over there.' He paused and studied the tidy desk before him, and when he spoke again it was with bluff embarrassment. 'It's just that there's a sense that Jews ought not to be a big part of the process. To keep everything above board, so to speak. To avoid it looking like revenge. Can't stick a thumb on the scales of justice, and all that.'

Rotheram inhaled deeply, the tip of his cigarette flaring. He shook his head.

'Even if I were Jewish,' he said, tightly. 'I'm not sure why it should make me any less impartial than a Frenchman or a Russian.'

Hawkins gave him a sharp look, and then shrugged. 'I know you don't like it, and I'm sorry. I will speak to the higher-ups. But this is the way ahead for you now.'

Rotheram had nodded and gone back to the dry work, processing the boxloads of interrogation reports coming in from France, filing them, cross-referencing them. Despite his training as a lawyer, or perhaps because of it, he much preferred the face-to-face work of questioning suspects to building cases on paper. Nine times out of ten he knew he could have conducted a better interrogation. He spent half his time jotting down questions that had been left unasked; questions that—at best—someone else would ask without knowing what answers to look for.

There wasn't even much doing at Kempton Park by then. The autumn before he had been used to heading down there two or three times a week, to the old racetrack where the POWs were processed, for a 'chat', as they called it, with the more interesting and recalcitrant cases. In March he begged permission to make another visit and persuaded the local MPs to give him a captured uniform and put him in with the unprocessed men to eavesdrop. He'd bagged a captain and two lieutenants posing as non-coms when he was rumbled. He had a rib broken before the guards could get to him.

Hawkins was furious when he heard about it. 'First you bombard me with transfer requests, now you take a stupid risk like this. Why would you do that?' Rotheram was silent. Hawkins studied him, then lowered his voice. 'Seriously, my boy, do you ever ask yourself the question? What do you think you were playing at?'

Rotheram shrugged. 'I was going round the bend, sir,' he said. 'Sometimes it feels like I'm the bloody prisoner here.'

Hawkins smiled thinly at that.

'Then you should be able to fake it better. How did they spot you, by the way?'

'Lice,' Rotheram said, making a face. 'I didn't have any. They saw I wasn't scratching.'

The other shook his head.

'And how's the rib?'

'Sore, but I can work.'

'All right. You want some excitement, then?'

'Sir?'

He began writing out a chit on his blotter.

'I'm giving you a staff car, sending you on a little trip. You're off to Wales, my boy.'

'Wales?' It sounded like a joke. Rotheram wanted to go east, not further west, further from the action.

'Think of it as a little holiday,' the CO said drolly. 'You're going to see Hess.'

Rotheram was silent for a moment, watching Hawkins's pen move across the page.

'Rudolph Hess?'

'No, Rudolph ruddy Reindeer. Who do you think?'

Rotheram had seen Hess once before, in Germany in 1935. He was the only party leader he'd ever glimpsed in person. It was at a football match. *Hertha Berlin v. Bayern Leverkusen.* Hess had arrived with his entourage a little after kick-off. There'd been a popping of flashbulbs, a stirring in the crowd, and then the referee had blown the whistle and stopped the game for the players to give the Heil Hitler salute. Players on the Hertha team Rotheram had supported all his life. Hess had returned the salute smartly, and gone back to signing autographs. He'd been Deputy Führer then, a post he'd held until 1941 when he'd flown to Britain. It had been a sensation at the time—was he a traitor, was he on a secret mission?—but now Hess was almost an afterthought.

'Even if he has any secrets left they'd be old hat by now,' Rotheram observed.

'He still has at least one, apparently,' the CO said, placing the travel orders on top of a thick file. 'We don't know if he's sane or not. He's made two attempts to kill himself and he's been claiming selective amnesia for years. Says he has no recollection of anything important. Not of his mission, not of the war.'

'He's acting?'

'If so he's doing a splendid job. He's been maintaining the same story pretty much since the crash-landing in Scotland.'

Rotheram looked at the file on the desk between them, the dog-eared pages bound together with ribbon.

'What makes you think I'll be able to crack him?'

'Not sure you will, my boy. Plenty of others have had a go. Medics, intel fellows. The Americans.'

'But you don't trust them.'

The CO sighed.

'Hess is the biggest name we have so far, and if there's to be a trial, he's likely to be a star in it. Only not if he's gaga. Not if he's unbalanced, you follow? It'll make a mockery. The problem is, if we don't put him up it'll smell fishy to the Soviets. They're convinced he came here to conclude a peace between us and the Germans to leave them free to concentrate in the East.' Hawkins shook his head. 'The one thing for sure is if he does end up in the dock, we'll be the buggers building the case. I just want someone I know to have a look-see.'

'This isn't exactly what I had in mind when I asked for a transfer.'

'In which we serve, dear boy,' the CO told him with a shrug. 'You're going up the wall, so I'm giving you something.' He smiled but then leaned forward again, suddenly impatient. 'You want a role in the trial. You want to play a part in that? Well, this is the beginning. Do this right and you might do yourself some good.'

Rotheram pulled the file into his lap, where it rested heavily. He plucked at the ribbon.

The POW Department had authorized newsreels and films for prisoners two months earlier, as it turned out, so it wasn't hard for Rotheram to get his idea approved. It hadn't been difficult to find a copy of the film either. The censor's office had impounded more than a dozen at the start of the war, and the CO had smiled slyly as he signed the requisition order.

'Very nice,' he whistled, admiringly. 'The play's the thing, eh? Makes me wish I could be there to watch you spring your mousetrap, Hamlet.'

But as Rotheram drove west in his dilapidated staff car—all the depot sergeant could be persuaded to spare for a mere captain—it occurred to him that Hess, and not himself, was a more likely Hamlet. He was the one with the antic disposition, after all. The broken-down suspension of the Humber jarred Rotheram's bandaged ribs and made the silver canisters of film on the passenger seat beside him jingle like a giant's loose change.

It had been warm in London, a bright spring morning that lasted as far as Shrewsbury. But crossing the Brecon Beacons into Wales felt like crossing into winter. By the time he arrived, the metal of the film cases was so cold it stung his fingers as he carried them in from the car. He walked up the gravel drive to the manor house, remembering something Hawkins had once told him, that the gentry had put in gravel to announce their visitors. He had a moment to take in the ivy-bearded brick, the leaded windows cross-hatched a second time with safety tape, and then he heard the bolt draw back on the heavy oak door.

'Ah,' the pinch-faced lieutenant who met him declared, 'I see you've brought our feature presentation.'

The lieutenant, a doctor in the RAMC who introduced himself only as Mills, showed him into the parlour, where a projector had already been set up. 'You've eaten already?' he asked brusquely, but Rotheram shook his head. There'd been only a meagre ploughman's at a sullen pub outside Oswestry. The doctor looked disconcerted. 'Well, look, not to be inhospitable, but could you possibly wait, old chap? Unless you're ravenous, I mean. Only he's an early riser, so if you want to show it this evening, best start soon.' He smiled apologetically. 'Not to rush you, but I can't promise he won't nod off, otherwise.'

'It's fine.' Rotheram began loading the film. His fingers were so cold they trembled and it took him long minutes to thread the first reel through the sprockets.

'Nervous?' Mills asked. 'He doesn't bite.'

'Cold,' Rotheram said, rubbing his fingers. 'Those will have to be turned,' he added, indicating the neat row of chairs and making a circling gesture. 'So that we can watch him.'

'Right you are,' the other replied agreeably enough, although he didn't offer to light the fire in the grate.

Finally the film was ready, and Rotheram ran it forward for a few seconds, watching the test numbers flicker and count down, and then the opening shots from a plane descending over the city, the image pale in the still-bright room.

'Action,' Mills called jauntily, leaning over one of the scroll back chairs.

Rotheram snapped the machine into reverse and the camera lifted back through the wispy clouds, the mediaeval rooftops dwindling, the sound track discordant and garbled. He'd run the whole thing for himself the night before in his office at the Cage, partly to make sure the film was whole, partly to refamiliarize himself with it, waiting until everyone had left for the evening, ashamed of being caught, as if he were watching pornography.

'All right,' he said, and Mills opened the door and announced gaily, 'Tonight's performance is about to begin.' Someone must have been waiting for the signal, for less than a minute later there were footsteps in the passage outside.

Rotheram expected a guard to come first, but it was Hess himself stepping into the drawing room as if it was his home. He was greying and more drawn than Rotheram recalled from his pictures, his nose as sharp as a beak and his cheek bones swept up like wings under his skin, as if his face was about to take flight. Out of uniform, in a navy blue cardigan darned at one elbow, he seemed stooped, retired, more a shy uncle than the fiery Deputy Führer. His shirt was pressed and buttoned to the throat, but he wore no tie, and Rotheram recalled he'd made two suicide attempts, according to the file: once opening his veins with a butter knife he had stolen and sharpened on an iron bedstead for a week; a second time hurdling a third-storey banister. He was limping from that fall still, as he approached and held out his hand. Rotheram looked at it, and slowly held out his own, but to one side, gesturing to the armchair. Hess ignored the insult, taking his place with only a wry, 'Vielen Dank,' to which Rotheram found himself automatically mumbling, 'Bitte.'

Two burly MP corporals followed Hess into the room; one taking a seat flanking him, the other carrying a salver with decanter and glasses which he set on the sideboard. Last through the door was a delicate featured officer who Mills ushered over and introduced as Major Redgrave.

'I gather we have you to thank for the evening's entertainment, Captain.'

'I hope it'll be more than that, sir.'

'You've seen it already?'

Rotheram nodded, although he didn't say where.

The corporal appeared at his elbow, proffering glasses on a silver tray.

'Scotch, sirs?'

'And how do you propose to manage this?' Redgrave asked softly, when they all had drinks.

'I'll run the film, observe his reactions, debrief him afterwards.'

'You think you'll perceive if he's lying?'

Rotheram watched the corporal bend down beside Hess and offer him the last glass on the salver.

'I hope so,' he said, slowly. 'There are signs to look for.'

Redgrave exchanged a glance with Mills. 'You know we've tried pretty much everything. Over the years.' He said it gently and without impatience and it occurred to Rotheram that it was meant to comfort him, that they expected him to fail.

'Yes, sir.'

'Very well, then,' the major told him. 'Can't hurt to try. Whenever you're ready.'

Redgrave took a seat halfway between the screen and Hess, lowering himself stiffly, tugging up his trouser legs by the creases. Hess smiled at him questioningly, but the major just shrugged. Rotheram motioned Mills to draw the blackout curtain against the sunset, then threw the switch and took a seat across from the lieutenant and the major, studying the man in the armchair.

Back in London the CO had offered Rotheram this job as if it was a plum, but until this moment he had felt like little more than a glorified delivery boy. Now here was Hess, one of the leading men of the Party, right in front of him. And it occurred to Rotheram, stealing a glance at the screen, that the last time Hess had been in prison was after the Putsch. He'd been Hitler's cell mate. He'd taken dictation of *Mein Kampf*.

Initially, Hess seemed entertained, watching the stately procession of staff cars, the pageantry. It was a captivating film, Rotheram knew, queasily fascinating in the way it made the ugly beautiful. He could see the two corporals were rapt—one of them moving his mouth to read the subtitles—and Mills and Hawkins kept swivelling their heads back and forth between the screen and Hess as if at a tennis match. But it was no effort for Rotheram to keep his eyes on the prisoner. The whole scene, since Hess had entered the room, seemed unreal. He couldn't quite believe he was in the man's presence, like the night he thought he glimpsed Marlene Dietrich getting into a taxi in Leicester Square, but afterwards could never quite be sure. If he took his eyes off Hess, he thought he'd disappear.

Hess himself watched with interest, but without comment, sipping his whisky, his foot occasionally keeping time with the music. Only once did Rotherham notice the other man's gaze drifting towards him, then flicking away almost coyly. At the first reel change, he seemed inclined to talk, started to lean forward, but Rotheram, wanting to keep the film moving, busied himself with the projector. Hess accepted a cigarette from Mills, and the major asked him if he knew what he was watching and he said, yes, yes of course. He recognized Herr Hitler, he understood that this was Germany before the war. He said he admired the marching. But when Redgrave asked if he remembered being there, he looked puzzled and shook his head.

'Your English is good,' Rotheram called from where he was bent over the projector, threading the next reel by the light of a small desk lamp. He didn't like the others asking too many questions.

'Thank you,' Hess told him. *'Und seiner Deutsch.'*

Rotheram looked up sharply and a loop of film slipped off the reel he was removing, swinging loose.

'I only meant you do not seem to need the subtitles, Captain.'

Rotheram recoiled the reel hurriedly.

'Of course, perhaps I should be complimenting you on your English, instead.'

Mills barked out a little laugh and then looked puzzled. 'I'm not sure I get it?'

'It's not a joke,' Hess said pleasantly. 'I'm asking if Captain Roth-eram'—he drew the name out—'is German? A Jew perhaps?'

Rotheram felt the others turning to look at him, the major sitting up straighter. He kept his eyes on Hess, but felt himself colouring in the darkness.

'Well,' Mills said. 'I'd never have guessed.'

'You have to know what to look for,' Hess said nonchalantly, as if it were a parlour trick.

'But Jews can't be German, Deputy Reichsführer,' Rotheram told him flatly. 'Or did you forget that also?'

Hess's lips twitched, a small moue.

'Besides, you're wrong.'

'My mistake.'

'I'm not Jewish.'

'Yes,' Hess said. 'Thank you for clarifying that.' He smiled around the room. 'I gather it's one thing we have in common.'

'Unlike thousands, tens of thousands of people—' Rotheram began angrily, but the major cut him off.

'Captain,' he called, with a weary shake of the head. 'Let's press on, shall we?'

The second reel moved to the evening events of the Reichstag, a grainy sea of flags waving in a torch-lit parade, and finally to the footage of Hess himself, starkly pale under the floodlights, rallying the crowd, leading the ovation until his voice cracked with the effort. In the drawing room, Rotheram watched Hess closely, saw him flinch slightly, his nostrils flaring, as his younger face stared down at him. His eyes widened as he watched, and he seemed to clutch himself, his crossed arms drawing tighter, his leg hitched higher on his thigh. The tip of his cigarette glowed in the dark, and his smoke twisted up through the projector's beam like a spirit. At the next break, he called for some light and said he needed to stretch his legs. He rose and walked twice around the room quickly, his limp jagged, his head bent.

Mills tried to join him. 'Are you cold?' But Hess waved him away, and the doctor approached Rotheram instead.

'How much longer?'

'One more reel.'

'Good. I don't want him too agitated.'

Rotheram looked up.

'Isn't that the point?'

'It's your point, my friend. My job's to keep him healthy. I don't want him stressed or over tired.'

'I understood—.'

'You understood wrong,' Mills hissed. 'And don't be thinking you can go around my back to the old man. He and I have an understanding.'

Rotheram looked up and saw the major watching them.

'Do you mind?' he asked Mills steadily. 'I'd like to start this.'

Mills turned abruptly and barked at one of the corporals to light a fire. There was a clatter of coal from the scuttle and for a few seconds they all watched as the flame caught.

The final reel showed Hitler addressing the crowd, and Hess sank against the seat cushions, as if he were trying to smother himself in the chair. Rotheram, glancing round, noticed Redgrave and Mills thoroughly engrossed in the film, watching the younger Hess, the one formed from shadow and light. The scene had moved to Berchtesgaden, Hitler's Bavarian retreat, and Hess appeared, lounging on a sunlit terrace, smoking. Rotheram felt a sharp craving for a cigarette himself, but suppressed it. Turning back, he found Hess watching him. Their eyes met for a moment—Hess's dark, but shining in the light from the screen—before Rotheram had to look away, back to the film. Almost shuddering with excitement, he tried to decide if the man was crying. But when he brought himself to look again Hess was steadily stubbing out his cigarette.

Afterwards, pacing the room once more, Hess repeated that yes, of course, he recognized himself on the screen, so he must accept that he had been there. Yet he had no memory of the events depicted.

'No memory?' Rotheram asked. 'None at all?'

'Perhaps one,' Hess said.

'Yes?'

Hess gave a small smile. 'The opening reminded me of my flight here, to Britain, the clouds over Scotland.'

'And yet you seemed agitated during the film,' Rotheram observed. 'Disturbed.' The room seemed very still now without the tick and whir of the projector.

'I wouldn't say so. Troubled, perhaps.'

'Troubled, very well. Why?'

'Troubled that I can't remember, of course. How would you feel if you were shown and told things you had done that you had no memory of? It is as if my life has been taken from me. That man was me, but also like an actor playing me.' He touched the side of his head gently with his fingertips as if it were tender. 'I do not have these memories'—he gestured to the empty screen—'his memories.'

Hess sniffed abruptly. The chimney was drawing poorly. Mills raked through the coals with the poker, making them spit.

'But you would like to have them?' Rotheram asked.

'Perhaps. I'm told the war is almost over, Germany near defeat. I should like such memories of happier times.'

'The film made you happy? You enjoyed it?' Rotheram pressed.

'Not happy!' Hess cried. He raised his hands in frustration, let them drop with a sigh.

There was a moment's silence and then Mills said quietly, 'You're tired.'

'Yes,' Redgrave added. 'Perhaps it would be best if we conclude this evening, turn in.'

'Major,' Rotheram began, but when he looked at Redgrave's hangdog face he stopped. He had been about to say that this was his interrogation, but it occurred to him suddenly that Mills was right. As far as he and the Major were concerned it was no

interrogation at all. It wasn't that they thought Rotheram couldn't
determine if Hess were mad or otherwise. They thought it was
irrelevant. That unless Hess was raving, or foaming at the mouth,
he'd be put on trial. They believed the decision had already been
taken. That was why they couldn't see any point in this. It was a
sham in their eyes and worse, to continue it a cruelty.

They expect me to find him fit, Rotheram thought slowly, *because
they believe I'm a Jew.*

He became aware that Redgrave and Mills were staring at him,
waiting.

'I suppose I am finished,' he muttered.

Only Hess was not. He was standing at the pier glass scrutinizing
his own reflection. Turning his head from side to side to study his
face in the narrow mirror.

'Not happy,' he repeated softly. He ran a hand through his lank
hair, held it off his brow. 'It's hard to admit one is an old man.' He
smiled bleakly at himself.

Rotheram spent a sleepless night.
It was all so unreasonable. He knew next to nothing about
Judaism, beyond the fact that he wasn't one. He'd always resented
his grandparents, in truth, refusing to write the thank-you letters his
mother asked him to send in reply to their begrudging gifts, and
secretly pleased when they fled to Paris in 1935, as if this proved
something. Even when his father's pension had suddenly stopped two
months after they'd left, Rotheram had been convinced it was just a
mistake. The Nazi bureaucrats were fools, too dense to understand
a subtle distinction like matrilineal descent, something his mother had
explained to him in childhood. He was in his second year of law at
the university, and he'd gone to Herr Professor Bremer, who'd given
him top marks in the last exam, to explain the situation and ask his
advice, but when he tried to register for classes the following term he
was told he wasn't eligible to matriculate and realized he was the fool.
It made him think of a moment, years before, when as a boy of
thirteen or fourteen he'd asked his mother yet again why he wasn't
Jewish if his father was. Because the Jewish line runs through the
mother, she'd told him. Yes, but why? he'd pressed her, and she'd
explained, a little exasperated, that she supposed it was because you

could only be absolutely sure who your mother was, not your father, and he'd gone away and thought about that deeply and narrowly, as a teenager will, and finally come back to her and asked if she was sure his father was his father. She'd stared at him for a long moment, then finally slapped him hard across the mouth. 'That sure,' she said.

Just before her death she'd told him how she'd been spat on in the streets of Berlin in 1918. 'After Versailles,' she said. 'Because I was a Canadian. That's what your grandparents could never forgive. That I was a reminder of the enemy, the men who'd killed their son. I wasn't German enough, for them.'

In her possessions, after her death, he'd found a photo of his father he'd never seen before. It must have been taken on that last leave, because he looked gaunt, his uniform loose, his features sharpened almost to caricature, no longer the smiling, slightly plump figure in a close-fitting uniform that Rotheram had seen in earlier poses. This was his father, he thought, and the figure had seemed to rebuke him.

And yet the following week he'd gone ahead and anglicized his name.

He called the CO first thing in the morning. It was Sunday and he got him out of bed to tell him he'd decided to return to London.

'You've made up your mind about Hess?'

Rotheram paused.

'Not really. No, sir. But I'm not sure under the circumstances that I'll be able to.' He was unconvinced of Hess's madness, he explained, and yet reluctant to find him sane.

'So spend some more time. Take another run at him.'

'I don't think that'll do any good,' Rotheram offered.

'But why, for heaven's sake?'

And finally Rotheram was forced to admit that, in part, he was reluctant to find Hess sane because the thought of confirming Redgrave and Mills' assumptions rankled.

'Let me get this straight,' the CO said slowly. 'You believe you can judge Hess, fairly, rationally, but you're concerned that others won't see that judgement as impartial, because they suspect you're Jewish. Those are the horns of your dilemma?'

'Yes, sir.'

'Well, but do you ever think you might not be so impartial, after all.'

'I'm sorry, sir?'

He heard Hawkins take a sip of tea, and then another. Finally, he asked, 'Tell me, my boy, honestly now, don't you ever think about your family? Your father's people, where they are, what's happened to them?'

Rotheram was momentarily taken aback. He began to say 'No' and stopped. Hawkins had told him to recognize the pause before answering as a lie. But if he said, 'Yes' now, it would seem no more the truth. So he was silent, which as Hawkins had taught him might mean a man was holding something back, or simply that he didn't know.

'I'm sorry, sir,' he repeated. 'You'll have my report Monday morning.'

There was a long pause at the other end of the line, and Rotheram felt acutely that he'd disappointed Hawkins. But when the other spoke again he sounded brusquely hearty.

'No need to hurry back, my boy. There've been some new orders, as a matter of fact. The POW department want someone to visit their camps up in North Wales. Something to do with screening, and the re-education program. Thought you'd be just the fellow to liaise with London. Anyhow, the orders should catch up with you there later today, or tomorrow at the latest.'

Rotheram, gripping the receiver, told him stiffly that he understood, and he did, although dully, as if his head were still ringing from a blow. The CO had been flattering him with this mission, he realized; more than that, it was a consolation prize. The decision had already been made, but not by Rotheram. Hess would be going to the trial, but Rotheram wouldn't. The closest he'd come to Nuremberg was the image of the city on the screen.

'You will be missed,' Hawkins said softly. 'But really, that stunt at Kempton.' He laughed ruefully. 'That's what you get for playing silly buggers.'

Rotheram was silent and the CO filled the pause by asking, 'By the way, how is Rudi, the old bastard?'

'Probably as sane as you or I,' Rotheram said, and the old man laughed again.

'Well that's not saying much, dear boy. That's not saying very much at all.'

Rotheram put the receiver down, and went in search of some breakfast.

He found Mills and one of the corporals lounging at a long wooden table in the kitchen, washing down charred toast with cups of tea from the largest china teapot he'd ever seen. The lieutenant, his mouth full, pointed to it, and Rotheram nodded.

'There you are,' Mills said swallowing and setting a cup before him. 'So what's your plan for today?'

'I'm leaving,' Rotheram said simply. 'Appears I was wasting my time. Perhaps everyone's. New orders should come through this afternoon.'

Mills nodded for what seemed a long time, and finally pushed over the toast rack.

'Go on,' he said, when Rotheram hesitated. 'The butter's local, and we've also got this.' He slid across a crystal jar. 'Honey. Special rations on account of our guest.'

Rotheram lifted the lid, dipped his knife and studied the honey before he spread it thickly on his toast and took a bite. The rich sweetness was incredible. He wondered that he could have forgotten the taste. How long had it been since he'd had honey? 'Good, eh?' Mills said, and Rotheram nodded as he chewed.

'No hard feelings about last night.'

Rotheram took a mouthful of tea, shook his head. 'Only I'm not Jewish,' he said.

'Of course not, old chap.'

Rotheram detected a hint of the bedside manner in the way he said it, but the thought of explaining his history to Mills was suddenly exhausting.

Mills was silent for a moment, then brightened suddenly. 'If you're waiting for orders this afternoon, your morning's free, yes?'

Rotheram looked up slowly.

'Why not come along with us, then?' He gestured to the corporal. 'We're taking Hess for a Sunday drive. He likes a little fresh air every so often.'

'I don't need another crack at him, you understand.'

'I know,' Mills said, grimacing slightly. 'It's not just for you. The thing is, he asked if you'd come.' He laughed awkwardly. 'Seems he's a little bored with our company.'

And so thirty minutes later Rotheram found himself in the front seat of an open-top staff car, the corporal, whose name was Baker, at the wheel, and Mills with Hess beside him in the back seat. The car reminded Rotheram uncomfortably of Hitler's tourer in the film.

The drive seemed to restore Hess. He had been subdued when he had climbed into the car, pausing on the running board to tuck his red woollen scarf into the collar of his sweater and wrap his greatcoat around his knees before sitting down. But now, Rotheram half turned in his seat, saw the colour return to the older man's cheeks. Hess noticed his scrutiny.

'How do you like my gift from Mr Churchill?' he asked jovially, indicating the car. 'It's just the thing for the beautiful Welsh countryside wouldn't you say?'

'Why do you think you're in Wales?' Rotheram asked coolly, but Mills broke in with a shrug.

'No need to be coy. We ran into some locals at a crossroads on one of these jaunts last month and he recognized the lingo. Bit of a cock-up, really, but at least they didn't recognize him.'

It was still chilly, but the sun had come out and Hess slipped on a pair of dark glasses.

'He recognized Welsh?' Rotheram asked, sceptically. He was addressing Mills, but Hess answered impatiently.

'Where else in the British Isles do they speak another language? My father lived here for several years, in fact. I should have known the country from his descriptions.'

Rotheram nodded, although this was not in any of the file material he had read, and he realized he had no idea whether it was true or a fantasy.

'His first wife, Elizabeth, was a Welsh woman. He was steward to a bishop, and she was the housekeeper, I believe. She died, though, after only a year of marriage—a chill she caught walking—and he returned to Germany to open a hotel in Hamburg, where he met my mother. She's buried in a cemetery, somewhere near Cardiff, I understand. Who knows, if she'd lived, she might have been my mother, and I a Welshman.'

'You'd prefer that? To be Welsh rather than German?' Rotheram asked, humouring him. He didn't believe a word of it, and judging by the way Mills rolled his eyes at him neither did the doctor.

'I don't know. Perhaps. How do you prefer being British, Captain?'

Mills gave a little wincing smile, but Rotheram wouldn't rise to the bait.

'Besides,' Hess went on thoughtfully, 'perhaps I am Welsh now, a little.'

'That's hardly the party line,' Mills sneered. 'To think a few months' stay in a country is a claim to nationality?'

'Call it sympathy. Isn't Wales where the ancient Britons retreated to? When the Romans came, I mean. Wasn't this their last resort? Even Churchill, I understand, had plans to pull back here if we had successfully invaded. What did he say about your home guard? They'd make Britain an indigestible hedgehog for any invader! Well, this would have been the lair of the hedgehog, eh?'

'Wales, the land of retreat? Or defeat?'

'Of last stands, perhaps,' Hess offered.

'Which makes you Welsh?' Or else mad, Rotheram thought.

'So.'

They rode for some time in silence after this, driving uphill along a narrow lane between high stone walls. Finally the track opened at the brow of a ridge into a small dirt yard. The view, tumbling hills, speckled purple and yellow with heather and gorse, spread before them.

They climbed down to admire it, while the corporal steered the huge car through a five-point turn—so laboriously that Mills felt the urge to direct him.

'You never said what you made of our film, Captain?' Hess asked, companionably.

'I thought it was vile lies. Rabble-rousing propaganda.'

'You think so?' Hess mused. 'That it incited the mob?'

'You don't?'

'Yes, yes, I suppose so. But the mob was only a tiny number really. A few thousand out of millions who saw the film. Not very efficient if its goal was to rouse. You saw it in Germany?' he asked suddenly and Rotheram, caught off guard, nodded slightly.

'A film like that,' Hess went on slowly, 'does something much more important than stir the few, I think. It makes the rest an audience. It makes them viewers. Passive, you see? You watch a film, you sit in a cinema, you see things, you feel things, but you do nothing.' He leaned closer. 'That film made our actions a drama to be watched, and talked about, as if it were only happening on a screen, on a set. Forget incitement. That's the power of film, to draw a line, between those who act and those who watch.'

Rotheram shook his head. He looked for Mills, but now he was helping Baker wrestle the canvas roof of the car into place.

'You disagree, Captain? It had some other effect on you, perhaps?'

'Tell me something,' Rotheram said, turning to him. 'Let's grant, for the sake of argument, that you have no recollection of why you came to Britain. Why do you *think* you came? You must have wondered.'

'I was on a secret diplomatic mission, as far as I can determine.'

'Yet you can't recall the details, and no one else from Germany has tried to fulfill the mission since?'

'I imagine you have other theories, Captain,' Hess said drily.

'Some say you were—forgive me—crazy before you crashed. That you were already unstable when you decided to fly here.' Hess was impassive. 'Others that you'd fallen out of favour somehow with Hitler, that you felt your position, your life, threatened. They say you ran.'

'Would you like me to be an exile, is that it, Captain? Another sad refugee? Should we sympathize with each other, now, is that the form this takes? Why yes. It's all coming back to me now. I'm remembering, remembering. *Mein Gott*, I'm really a Jew. How could I have forgotten.'

He started to laugh, then saw the blunt fury in Rotheram's face and checked himself, put his hands together as if in prayer.

'Why won't you believe me when I tell you I'm not a Jew?'

'Why won't you believe *me*?' Hess smiled. 'But for the sake of— how did you put it?—for the sake of argument, let's grant that you are not a Jew. But if not, tell me, why do you hate me so?'

'Why!' Rotheram asked in a strangled voice. 'Because you and your kind, drove me from my home, accused me of being a Jew—' He caught himself, suddenly conscious of Mills's approach.

'But, Captain,' Hess asked leaning close, 'what does that say about the way you feel about Jews?' He pivoted smoothly to Mills. 'Ah, Doctor, I was just suggesting a stroll to the captain.'

Mills nodded. 'If you're up to it.'

Hess shrugged. 'It's downhill. If the corporal would be so kind to meet us at the crossroads?'

Mills gave a wave to Baker, and the car rumbled back down the lane, while Hess lead them through a kissing gate on to the hillside.

'You're sure this is all right?' Rotheram asked, pulling Mills to one side as Hess went ahead slowly.

'Quite. We've done this walk before. It's the bugger's favorite. The locals are all at chapel this time of a Sunday morning, and believe me he isn't likely to escape.' He gestured at Hess who was gingerly lowering himself down the path. His limp was more apparent now than in the house. When they drew level with him he was already breathing hard.

'We can go back,' Mills said, putting a hand on his shoulder. 'If you're unwell. Don't want *you* getting a chill, after all.' He grinned at Rotheram behind the other man's back.

'The Herr Doctor is concerned about my health,' Hess told Rotheram, shaking Mills off. 'He watches me so well, so that I won't catch cold, or stub my toe...or fall downstairs.'

Mills coloured at this reference to the latest suicide attempt.

'I just want what's best for you.'

'Yes, yes.' He paused before a steep stretch of the path that had been washed out by rainwater.

'Perhaps?' He raised his hands, and for a second Rotheram thought it was a gesture of surrender. Then he saw Mills duck under one arm, and he bent to let Hess lay the other across his shoulders. In this way they eased down the slope, silent apart from Hess's panting, now that they were so close. The old man was surprisingly heavy, Rotheram thought. He felt his arm weighing down on the back of his neck. The faint scent of aftershave wafted from Hess's collar.

When the slope was more gentle, he lifted his arms and Rotheram was glad to step away, pressing a hand to his bruised ribs.

'Thank you, gentlemen. Now, where were we?' Hess said. 'Oh, yes, the doctor. He does take fine care of me, but Doctor, don't you find that difficult?'

'Well, you're not always the most cooperative patient.'

'No. Forgive me. Don't you find it a...' He searched for the word. 'A conflict.'

Mills shook his head gravely. 'My oath as a doctor—'

Hess held up his hand. 'Forgive me again. I didn't mean this conflict. Your *hypocratishe* oath, I know. We have this in Germany. Every doctor has this. No. I mean is it not a conflict that you are keeping me alive in order for your government to kill me?'

'What makes you say that?' Rotheram asked quickly.

Hess looked at him.

'*You* know, Captain Roth. It's why you're here. To decide if you can try me. Let's see. Can we, can we?' Hess furrowed his brow, held his palms out before him like an unsteady pair of scales. 'But, yes, of course, why not?' He laughed. 'But, I ask you, why bother—you want to kill me, just kill me.'

Mills, put out, had walked ahead a little.

'Doctor! I've shocked you with my talk. And on such a beautiful morning. My apologies. Please. All this talk of death, of killing. Of course, I don't mean you should kill me. Besides, I'd do it for you, if you'd let me.'

'You want to die?' Rotheram said.

'You want to kill me?' Hess asked, mimicking his tone. 'Yes, yes. I want to die. Does that seem mad to you? In which case does that mean you shouldn't try me and kill me? Or does it seem sane, under the circumstances, which would mean that you should?'

Rotheram had pulled up beside Mills, a little below Hess on the slope, and now he found himself looking up at him, as if he were on a stage.

'Do you feel you deserve to die?'

A shadow crept over them and Hess glanced up at the clouds. When he looked down again his smile had faded.

'Perhaps,' he said softly. 'If I fled as you say. That would be shameful, wouldn't it? But deserve, don't deserve, I just want to. I have no one left, you understand. I don't remember my wife, my children. I don't remember my country. I told you, my life has already been taken. I'm already half-dead.'

Mills sighed and shook his head, but Rotheram was rapt.

'You're still trying to decide about me,' Hess said.

'Was that true before?' Rotheram asked. 'About Wales, your father?'

'Can't you tell?'

'I just wondered if you remembered it, or if someone told you.'

'Or did I make it up? But you can't tell, can you? And you can't tell about me and my faulty memory.' He shook his head. 'You know why? Because it doesn't matter. All those signs you look for. Dilating of the eyes, for instance?' Hess took his dark glasses off and folded them away. He goggled at Rotheram. 'Those only matter if the subject cares about being believed. I don't care, because whether you believe me or not...' He shrugged. 'Kaput!'

'Oh now,' Mills began, but Hess didn't take his eyes off Rotheram.

'You want the truth about me? First you tell me, am I right, or not?'

It occurred to Rotheram that he had been the last to know this truth. Even Hess was there before him. He found himself nodding slowly.

'So,' Hess sighed. 'I thank you for this honesty.'

'Your turn,' Rotheram said.

Hess studied him for a moment. 'Indulge me. One last question. Then I promise to tell you what you want to know.'

'What question?' Rotheram asked tiredly.

Hess peered into his face. 'You know already.'

As if from a long way off, Rotheram heard the scrape of a match beside him as Mills lit a cigarette. He took a long breath, and shook his head.

'Some think I'm a Jew, but I'm not. Not to myself at least. Still, perhaps that doesn't matter, the way I see myself, not compared to the way others see me. Not when the way you see me is a matter of life and death.' He shrugged. 'Is that an answer?'

'An answer? No.' Hess gave a crooked smile. 'But maybe the truth.'

Rotheram looked up. 'Well then, I believe we had a bargain.'

'Quite. So am I unbalanced?' Hess held his arms out from his sides, and took a few steps like a tightrope walker, narrowing the distance between them. 'Am I faking my amnesia?' He leaned close and Rotheram could feel his breath against his cheek. 'The truth is I—don't remember any more.' He stepped back, smiling apologetically. 'Do I remember the Nuremberg rally, or do I remember that film? Maybe yesterday I remembered the rally, but today all I remember is the beautiful footage. Six months from now, a year from now—if I live that long—maybe I won't even remember how I remember.' He gave a short laugh. 'We really do have something in common, you and I. The same dilemma. Are we who we think we are, or who others judge us to be? It's a question of will, perhaps.' He glanced away for a moment, over Rotheram's shoulder, and then back, meeting his eyes. 'How can you hope to judge me, Captain, if you can't decide about yourself?'

He held up his hand before Rotheram could answer.

'If you go now,' Hess said softly, 'you may outrun him.'

Behind him, Rotheram heard Mills whisper slowly, 'Oh, bloody hell.'

He turned to where they were looking. A bull had appeared on the hillside below them. For a second Rotheram was stunned. Where had it come from? Had it been hidden in the shadows by the wall, or lying in a shallow dell? It trotted steadily across the field, not more than twenty feet below them, and as Rotheram watched its dark velvety head swung round—he saw the pale curve of its horns turn—to study them.

'Hell,' Mills said again. The cigarette which was dangling from his lower lip, fell to the ground. 'Bloody bloody bleeding hell.'

It occurred to Rotheram that Hess, slightly higher and looking past them, would have seen the beast before any of them. He wondered if all his talk had been simply a way of distracting them while the bull approached.

'Come on,' Mills was saying. Rotheram felt his hand on his arm.

'I believe he's seen us,' Hess noted calmly. 'Gentlemen, I'm fifty-two, and with a limp, I might add. I can hardly outrun him, but you might. If you go now.'

Rotheram felt himself fill with disgust. What foolishness! To lose the prisoner to a bull.

'Are you coming?' Mills hissed.

'The corporal can shoot it,' Rotheram said, searching beyond the bull, but although he could make out the car over the stile at the near corner of the field, there was no sign of Baker, perhaps gone for a smoke or a piss. Rotheram and the doctor were themselves unarmed, standard procedure with a prisoner, but even if Rotheram had had his service revolver he doubted he could stop a charging bull with it.

'Even if the good corporal were to see us,' Hess said, 'he would need to move very smartly to get a clear shot. And,' he added wryly, 'I'm not so confident of his marksmanship. Not on a Sunday morning.'

'Come on!' Mills had already started to edge towards the stile in the far corner of the field, but even as he took a step in that direction the bull moved almost leisurely to cut him off. Its bulk seemed ponderous, but it was flanking them, Rotheram noticed, shocked by the animal intelligence, angling up the slope, avoiding charging uphill at them. In a few moments, he saw, it would be above them. It was already close enough for him to see that its dark coat wasn't smooth, but kinked with tight woolly tufts, the black curls licking around the base of its horns. He could smell it too, a rich smoky scent on the breeze.

'Go now, please,' Hess told Rotheram.

Before he could make up his mind, Mills took to his heels. He'd seen what Rotheram had seen, and spotted also that the route to the near corner was now open. Rotheram felt Hess's hand on his back. 'Really, there is no need to die for me, Captain. It would be foolish, no? To die for a dead man? If you thought I was innocent, or mad, maybe...'

He pushed again, but weakly, and Rotheram stood fast. He was trying to decide if he could carry Hess (he doubted it given the condition of his ribs) or perhaps draw the bull off.

'Captain.' Hess was raising his voice now. 'I really must insist.' Rotheram, glancing away from the bull, saw the determination in his face. He tried to steel his own will, to keep his eyes on the old man's but he could hear the hoof beats now, and just as at the film show he found himself turning, looking over his shoulder. 'Wouldn't this be easiest for all of us?' Hess whispered urgently. He was fumbling with the buttons of his greatcoat, drawing out the bright red scarf that had been tucked into his collar. With a final feeble shove, not much more than a pat on the back, he set Rotheram in motion towards the stile, and himself hobbling towards the bull, the scarf flourished behind him on the breeze like a signature.

Rotheram found himself running—it came so easily, his legs adjusting to the steep slope of the ground—chasing the doctor, making headlong for the stile. It crossed his mind that he couldn't remember the last time he had run. He made a point of walking out of the building during raids in London. He must have run since that time he fled the film show in Berlin, he thought, but he couldn't recall. It troubled him because, even as his rib seemed to grind in his side, even as he heard the thunder of hooves behind him, he found he rather liked running, the wind in his face, the blood beating in his head. It made him feel so suddenly alive, he couldn't imagine why he had ever stopped.

Sensing the beast closing, he veered sharply for a low stretch of the wall, his arms bracing him as he swung his legs over the top and tumbled into the soft unmown verge of the lane. Looking up, he saw the bull's galloping momentum carry it past, saw Mills clattering over the stile into the arms of the corporal, as the beast broke off its chase, tossing its great glaring head.

He climbed to his feet, favouring an ankle he must have skinned on the wall, and looked uphill. There was no sign of Hess.

For a sickening moment Rotheram stopped searching for the man, and started looking for a prone body, but then he saw him, upright on the hillside, waving. Rotheram felt a rush of relief and then almost immediately an overwhelming flood of disappointment that left him light-headed and sagging against the wall.

He watched numbly as Hess hobbled downhill and Mills scurried to join him.

'Are you all right?' the doctor called.

'An old man wasn't worth his trouble, apparently,' Hess cried. 'The black beast didn't want anything to do with me.'

'But are you all right?' Mills insisted. He sounded panicked, almost hysterical, but to Rotheram Hess looked better than he'd ever seen him. He seemed braced. His eyes gleaming, his cheeks as rosy as his damned scarf.

'Really, Doctor,' he was saying cheerfully. 'I'm perfectly fine. Your concern is appreciated. Although,' he smiled ruefully, 'I doubt very much you can actually save me from anything, in the long run, you know.' He smiled at them both. 'Is that the car?'

They watched him limp down the lane towards the corporal. They looked at each other for a moment and then quickly away, before they followed, Mills staggering just a little. 'Awful thing,' he muttered under his breath. 'Running before the enemy like that.' And Rotheram nodded and told him softly, 'It's all right.' And yet for one moment, he couldn't conceive how the war was being won. □

GRANTA

ROOM 536

A. L. Kennedy

A. L. Kennedy was born in the north-east of Scotland. She has written four collections of short fiction and three novels (all published by Jonathan Cape), along with two books of non-fiction and a variety of journalism, including a column for The Guardian. She has won several prizes. She also writes for the stage, radio, film and TV. She has sold brushes door-to-door and now lectures part-time in the creative writing programme at St Andrew's University School of English. In 1993 she was listed among Granta's Best of Young British Novelists. She is now ten years older. 'Room 536' is taken from a novel-in-progress.

How it happens is a long story, always.

And I apparently begin with being here: a boxy room that's too wide to be cosy, its dirty ceiling hung just low enough to press down a broad, unmistakable haze of claustrophobia. To my right is an over-large clock of the kind favoured by playschools and homes for the elderly, the kind with bold, black numbers and cartoon-thick hands that shout what time it is whether you're curious or not. It shows 8.42 and counting. Above, there is a generalized sting of yellow light.

8.42

But I don't know which one—night or morning. Either way, from what I can already see, I would rather not be involved in all this too far beyond 8.43.

In one fist, I notice, I'm holding a key. Its fob is made of viciously green plastic, translucent and moulded to a shape which illustrates what would happen if a long-dead ear were inflated until morbidly obese. I only know that it's actually meant to be a leaf, because it is marked with an effort towards the stem, the ribs and veins that a leaf might have. I presume I'm supposed to like this key and give it the benefit of the doubt because people are fond of trees and, by extension, leaves. But I don't like leaves, not even real ones.

I'll tell you what I do like, though: what I adore—I'm looking right at it, right now and it is gorgeous, quite the prettiest thing I've seen since 8.41. It concerns my other hand—the one that is leaf-free.

It is a liquid.

I do love liquids.

Rising from the beaker to the jug in that continually-renewing, barley-sugared twist: falling from the jug into the beaker like a muscle perpetually flexed and re-flexed, the honey-coloured heart of some irreversibly specialized animal. It's glimmering and, of course, *pouring*—a drink *pouring*, hurrying in to ease a thirst, just as it should. I put down the jug and I lift up the glass, just as *I* should.

I presume it's filled with some kind of apple juice and, on closer acquaintance, I find this to be so—not very pleasant, but certainly wet and necessary. The air, and therefore my mouth, currently tastes of cheap cleaning products, unhappy people, a hundred years of stubborn cigarette smoke and the urine of young children, left to lie. Which means I need my drink. Besides, I really do have, now I think about it, a terrible thirst.

225

'Terrible weather?'

I'm swallowing ersatz fruit, not even from concentrate, so I can't have said a word—it wasn't me who spoke.

Terrible thirst: terrible weather—but the echo is accidental, I would have to be feeling quite paranoid to think it was anything else. Nevertheless, the remark feels intrusive—as if it had access to my skull—and so I turn without even preparing a smile and discover the party responsible tucked behind me: a straggly, gingery man, loitering. He has longish, yellowish, curly hair, which was, perhaps, cute at some time in his youth, but has thinned now into a wispy embarrassment. I can almost picture him, each evening, praying to be struck bald overnight. God has not, so far, been merciful.

Mr Wispy's expression attempts to remain enquiring although he says nothing more and I do not meet his eyes or in any way encourage him. He is the type to have hobbies: sad ones that he'll want to talk about.

Checking swiftly, I can see there are no windows, which may explain his lack of meteorological certainty. There's no way that either of us can know what the weather is doing outside. Then again, Straggly has the look of a person habitually unsure of things: it may be he's stolen a peek beyond the room and already *has* prior knowledge of whatever conditions prevail—monsoon, dust storm, sleet—he may simply hope I'll confirm his observations.

Of course, I have no prior knowledge, not a trace.

There is a fake cart rigged up, beyond us both—it's clearly made of stainless steel, but is burdened with a feminine canopy and fat, little flounces of chintz. Inside, I can make out a seethe of heat lamps and trays of orange, brown, or grey things which ought to be food, I suppose. The whole assembly smells of nothing beyond boredom and possibly old grease.

'Really dreadful... Yes?' He tries again: maybe harping on about the weather, maybe just depressive, I can't say I care.

'Appalling.' I nod and angle myself away.

But Straggly has to chip in again. 'Tchsss...' He seems to be taking the whole thing very personally, whatever it is. And I notice there's something slightly expectant in the scampery little glances he keeps launching across at me. It could be that he will give me a headache soon.

'Ffffmmm...' He nods, as if his repertoire of noises has any meaning beyond his own head.

But I can't deny that he is also speaking English, just about—which is a clue. I can probably assume that I'm in a hotel somewhere English-speaking. Either that, or I've been ambushed by Mr Wispy who is himself English-speaking and has guessed that I am, too, and I could, in fact, be anywhere at all.

Meanwhile, he's continuing to linger inconclusively and I do hope this won't blossom into some weird expression of long-term, national solidarity. To help him move on, I try to sound forbidding, although I will never discover what I'm trying to forbid: 'Ghastly. Almost *frightening.*'

That seemed to go well, though. He edges back a step, and another, then bolts into a crestfallen retreat. I feel I am safe to believe our exchange is exhausted.

Around me, various groups and solitaries are hunched over bowls of cereal, plates of glistening stuff, collapsing rolls. The carpet is liberally scattered with a sort of bread-related dandruff: each table has its dusting, too, along with a thread or so of unconvincing foliage in a throttled vase. At uneasy intervals the walls display reproductions of old European advertisements: a British hotel, then. This particular level of grisliness could only be fully achieved in the British Isles. And this surely must be breakfast—8.44, no 8.45, in the morning then, and breakfast in a cheap, British hotel.

I'm home. Perhaps.

Their backs to a wall, a shouting wife and inaudible husband are picking at mushrooms and sausages, 'We have to get a gas grill. That was the loveliest meal I had when we were there, the loveliest. That was the loveliest meal.' Her partner chews and chews while I try not to imagine the finer and finer paste he is producing. 'And that continental...continental...continental...'

Continental **What?** *Quilt? Breakfast? Lover? Self-improving language course?*

She is never going to finish and I'm never going to know and he is never going to swallow—I can tell. I do not wish to think of them travelling freely across the globe, dementing people, everywhere they go—driving them into gas grills for relief. I refill my glass and concentrate.

Then I remember, with aching clarity, an air steward blocking the ragged perspective of an aisle and dancing his arms through the usual safety drill: the oxygen mask for yourself before your gasping children, the floor level guides to coax you through darkness and smoke. He was enjoying himself, sweating only a little with all of those swooping indications in time to the comforting script. Then he tried to put on his For Demonstration Only life jacket and failed comprehensively.

I watched, couldn't stop myself watching, while his previously smooth hands stuttered and the rubberized yellow crumpled and began to look unhelpful—like a grubby bib. By the time he was meant to be tying a firm double bow at his waist (and then moving on to display his inflation tubes, his convenient whistle and nice light) his drawstrings were only tangling perversely and the more he jerked them and smiled to reassure, the more everything twisted and snagged. His head dropped then and he fought at the jacket outright, a neck blush rising to his hair. Full blown knots had developed now, his fingers scrabbling round them, wetly impotent. He blinked up for a breath and I grinned at him—what other expression was possible, but a pleasant, encouraging grin?—and something about the moment made it plain that we both knew he was now demonstrating a true emergency. This was precisely the way that we really would panic and fluster and take too long as the plane went down. This was how we'd be trapped in the dark, inanely struggling. This was how we would stare, while horrors struck against our wills. This was how we'd be plunged into water and feel every trace of protection ripped easily adrift. He was showing us how we would die.

The demonstration ended, but he stayed where he was, puzzled by himself, almost tearful, the jacket still round him, lopsided, improperly tied.

This is a recent memory, it tastes close at hand.

So I am, once again, grinning pleasantly and thinking that I must have been somewhere and must now be coming back, which is new and important information and a cause for joy.

But I am still thirsty.

Now I already have a substantial glass, filled and in my possession—probably 300 millilitres, or even a drop in excess. I've left a decent interval between the meniscus and the brim—anything else is antisocial and draws attention—but even if the juice were slopping right up to the top, it wouldn't be enough. A litre might begin to be enough, might start to feel refreshing, a litre and nothing less. So I need to down this while I stand, refill, down, refill again and then sit somewhere secluded, rehydrate. You have to be undisturbed to rehydrate. I presume I am safe in believing that this is the usual snatch-all-you-can rolling buffet sort of situation and no one will intervene when confronted with naked appetite.

As it turns out, I'm not wrong.

Clutching glass number four, I wander through the wreckage and mumbling, keeping an eye out for somewhere bearable to sit. The place seems clotted suddenly, nothing unoccupied.

I may have a little toast later, if there is toast. I can only assume I have money to buy some, it's unlikely I'd have come here otherwise.

'Ah...?' *Again.* Mr. Wispy is flapping one hand annoyingly above an empty seat. The only visible empty seat. 'A-ah...?' He keeps repeating that one sorry, wheedling vowel.

I could just stand.

On either side of him lurk what can only be his children: a surly-looking blonde girl of maybe eight and a smaller, darker boy. Happily, neither of them has inherited his hair. They are both intent on squeezing the contents from several tiny plastic containers of jam and then spreading the resultant mess across random objects.

I could dodge back to the fruit juice counter.

I could run.

'You won't disturb us. Really. It's all right.'

'I will.'

'No you won't.'

'I think I will.'

'No-o.'

The children lose interest in smearing the milk jug and the girl sucks at her palm, eyes me appraisingly.

'Perhaps for a moment.' I edge past the worst of it. 'Like pustules, aren't they?'

Father Straggle swallows less than happily.

'The jam packets—when you squeeze them out, they're just like...well, they're a little like...' I give up, sit and sip my apple juice in the silence. Five or six swallows and breakfast will be done. Except I still feel below my volume, somehow, a glass or three owing, nagging me.

'Whee-HA. Whee-HA.' Of course he has an abnormal laugh, why would he have a normal one ? How often would he get the chance to use it with his life? '*Pustules*. Whee-HA.'

In any case, it's ugly and should be stopped, 'So... You're leaving?'

He is sombre again, flushed, and softly offers, 'Coming back.'

'Uh hu.'

The little boy nudges me under the table, his hand unmistakably adhering as it leaves my leg. I'm wearing jeans—they look new—new jeans and a T-shirt. My forearms have a vague tan. The boy tries again. I engage him with my best patient-and-open-fun-loving expression. Sooner or later, this always works. I am a person other people warm to—without exception, they all warm. My lack of memory, if I were in a film, would mean that I am a killing machine, patiently trained by some dreadful governmental agency and soon my amnesia will evaporate in a bloodbath of conscienceless combat and burning cars. But I know I'm not any variety of machine. I am a human being, a proper one. And I am likeable—almost unnaturally easy to like. The boy turns shy under my attention, but is not truly uncomfortable. The girl glowers with some vehemence. She would take me more time.

'Amelia. That's not how we behave.'

'She's fine. Don't fret. Tired perhaps. Not used to strangers.' I gulp down the last of the juice, preparatory to moving off—somewhere I may have a room with other resources and no jam. Father Straggle's ears are almost scarlet—he is obviously a man who prefers that his children should be polite, which is admirable, but such hopes can be taken too far. He is patently furious now, insisting on being annoyed, so I become placating. 'Amelia. That's a lovely name.'

At this, the girl gives me a slightly wounded flick of her eyes and stares at the tablecloth. She expected me to know her name, then. She expected me to remember. So we've met before.

On a flight? Inside an airport? Hotel foyer? At 8.35?

I do recall an airport and scuffling about in the usual way as I waited to be off to somewhere else—wasting time in the record shop, thumbing through the DVD's.

'Tell me, *Lesbian Tarts Having Sex*—what's that about?'

The counter man sleepy, or drugged-up, or clinically bored, 'Hm?'

'*Lesbian Tarts Having Sex*—seems a bit vague. I mean, I wouldn't want to end up buying something I wasn't sure of. Does it have harpsichords? Or skating? Folding chairs? Do any characters feign amnesia as a ruse?' I was in that running-off-at-the-mouth mood, chirpy, in need of a chum to banter with.

The counter man was not my chum. 'Do you want to buy it.'

Even as I opened my mouth again, I realized he might be misinterpreting my chatter as a come-on of some kind, which it wasn't, not in any way.

'Of course I don't want to buy it—where's the mystery in it, the imaginative flair?'

Actually, he wasn't responding as if he was being seduced—he was barely responding as if he was still alive. 'You don't want to buy it.' He was, in all respects, monotone.

'No. I have no desire to make a purchase.' And I removed myself before I could say something else.

Or:

I really said, 'I wouldn't buy that DVD if it was the last one on earth.'

And then he said, 'You know what you can do.'

And then I said, 'Fuck myself and make a video of it called *Fucking Myself*.'

I can remember both endings, which is tricky. But I think I'm more convinced by the first. I think I told him I had no desire to make a purchase and then left. However it played out, there were no children anywhere near me at that stage—I would never have used offensive language and referred to sexual acts had there been any young folk present. I have standards.

'Amelia?' I try not to look like someone who is thinking of bad words and begin to make amends with the daughter, which is good of me because I will have done her no genuine wrong. She had thought of me as a friend, perhaps, and I've seemed to be slightly non-friendly, forgetful, nothing more. That's the sort of behaviour my brother detested when he was her age. Me, too. It's nothing serious, but even so, 'Amelia, I hope you have a pleasant journey home. Are you looking forward to it?'

'Mummy likes it better at home.'

'Oh.' Thank God, they have a mother: they're not wholly
dependent on Wispy Dad.

'Well, that's good then.'

But Wispy Dad can't resist getting involved, of course. 'Their
mother is still in our room. Tired.'

*Well, that's understandable, I'd be eternally bloody exhausted if
I was married to you.* 'Travelling is a strain.'

At the food cart, a woman is shovelling out what could be eggs.
Even from here, I can see them shudder and slide. They unnerve me
in a way they should not—because eggs ought to have no particular
power over me—and I realize that I'm about to have a feeling,
something unpleasant, an episode. What I can only imagine as a
huge, grey lid is threatening to close on top of me. This means that,
far too soon, I may cry, or become unsteady, or find myself vomiting.
Without doubt my head is, once again, about to let me down. There
will be pain involved: there always is: and it will be bad unpredictable
pain: it always is. After so many years, I can recognize the signs.

I softly stand and the boy glances at me, definitely glum to see
me up and off. 'Good bye, you.' No idea what his name is. 'Good
bye, Amelia.' Amelia kicks at nothing and ignores me. 'Good bye…'
I move forward and brush against a restraining hand—who else but
Dad, standing, wriggling from foot to foot. He ought to know he
shouldn't do this, not now. I am becoming urgent and so is my head.
Wispy adjusts his gesture into one half of a handshake, faintly
pleading, and, courteous to the last, I clasp his soggy fingers and
soggier palm. 'Good bye.'

'Good bye, Hannah.'

'Yes.' *We exchanged names across the board, then, how extremely
chummy and civilized.* 'That's me away then, bye.'

'Great to have met you. Sorry about the ah… children.' He licks
his lips with an odd, little grating sound, as if he is made of
something peculiar.

'Yes.'

'The way they are, ha?' He seems not to grasp the essential
intention of saying goodbye. 'Well. Hmm. Goodness… Blow me.'

Not in a million years. 'Yes.'

'Safe home.'

'Yes,' I nod—which sparks up a layering sensation, the impression of being loosely, poorly stacked—the head is growing delicate and I don't move it again, but pause—wring out a grin—and finally he does first loosen his grip, and then abandon it.

'Good—uh...bye.'

Although I fear he may snatch in again.

I withdraw as smoothly as I can. 'Good bye...all of you. Really.' Trying to balance myself at the top of my neck, not picturing my personality starting to slop out over my sides, running down to my chin.

Which carries me past a last view of Wispy's vaguely stricken offspring and off on a wavery march for the doorway, then out, a passageway (passageways lead to staircases and lifts, they are my friends) through a fire door and into a foyer complicated with several queues—not helpful—but, yes, here is a lift.

When I stop, the momentum of my thoughts sends them rushing forward, pressing and wetting the backs of my eyes. I raise my key to aid steadier inspection—it is attached by a chain to leaf number 536: fifth floor, then.

And, thankfully, no one else is with me when the doors whump shut and seal me in the queasily rising box. The surrounding walls are mirrored from waist height up which suggests an illusion of space and must be a comfort to claustrophobics, but which also does— due to the laws of physics—have one truly horrible consequence: I can see myself. Not only one self, of course: from a few especially disastrous angles my right selves and my left selves reflect each other unrelentingly. On both sides, I can watch my head diminish along an undulating corridor of shrinking repetitions until I finally coalesce into one last, pinkish drop of light. This aches.

It isn't fair. All I wanted to do was find 536 and take care of my head, but instead I'm trapped inside this 3D *memento mori*—staring at eternity while it howls graphically away, before and after (as if I were an extra in some truly sadistic, educational short) and all that I'm fond of as me is cupped up in this single, staring instant—which isn't enough. Look at me—this is the only point where I'm recognizable, where I make sense—beyond it, I'm nothing but distortion and then I completely disappear. What is this?—*a Jesuit lift*? I am not at an appropriate moment to be metaphysical. For Christ's sake, I was only trying to cut out the stairs. I didn't ask to be forcibly reminded that I don't want to die, not ever, no thank you very much. I am not well and terrified and I don't have the room to be either properly.

So I am not in quite perfect condition when the lift shunts open and gives a gloating little *ding*. Meanwhile, my sweat gets a chance to chill in the passageway where small metal plaques with arrows are waiting for me, all set to suggest hypothetical directions.

589–543, this way: 502–527, that way: 518 over there.

I'm taking little runs to blind ends, finding corridors that loop round on themselves, cupboards, fire escapes, while the floor starts to pitch down quietly beneath my feet, as if I were aboard some ghastly submarine.

The world cannot be as this is, I refuse to accept it.

*589–543 this way. But they were **that** way before.*

I deny the existence of this hotel in its current form. I deny the existence of this hotel in its current form.

528, 529, 530... which is encouraging, fairly, I should be okay, it can't be far—

500.

Bastards.

I deny the existence—

I'm not going to be sick.

I deny the existence of this hotel—

533, 534—

in it's current form.

I deny—

535...536.

536.

Well, well.

Slowly. Approach it slowly, it may move. Don't let the key chain rattle, make no sudden cries, but, as soon as I'm ready...hold the bloody handle, grab it, key in the lock, key in the lock, right in, in, okay. And. Turn. Turn everything.

The room agrees to be opened and it is, indeed, my room—here is my bag on its floor, lolling open, and this is my own, my personal alarm clock, ticking primly by the raddled bed: the soft, the horizontal, the wanted bed. There is nothing better than being bewildered and unhappy and very tired and then discovering you have a bed.

'Could I, uh...I'm in Room five three six, I wonder could you tell me if I'm checking out today...five...thirty...six... That's right, three six. *Five three six.*'

I will admit that I had expected someone who worked in a hotel might be able to keep a grip of perhaps one room number, now and then, but I won't be snappy, that would be unconstructive and would not reflect my mood. I have slept for two blank hours—nearly two and a half—slept through, I can only assume, the whole of my head-related distress and every threatened intimation of death and doom. I am quite fine now and, had I been calmer, I would have known— the whole source of my earlier trouble was tiredness.

As I let myself be comforted, there comes a dull clunking on the line—perhaps the receptionist playing with loose teeth. She mutters a name.

'I'm sorry, *who?*... Oh. And I'd have to check out at twelve?... *Eleven?*'

Why do they do that?—Twelve is bad enough, but now everybody wants you outside in the snow by eleven. Try checking in before five and see what it gets you: a bloody lecture: your bags in a cupboard somewhere until it's dark: that's what. 'In that case, could you be very kind and give me the room for another day?... Well, no, not *give*. Just...the usual arrangement. You have my credit card?... You *do?*'

Good. That's a good sign. Cash is a bad sign—credit is good. 'Then that's all very fine then, isn't it? That's all extremely fine.'

Above the window comes a laboured thunder, like a broad stone being rolled in overhead. I get up gently, examine my view.

Dove blue clouds, a gold edge to them and spindles of light behind. Nearer there is a fat concrete tower, topped with the scoop of a radar dish, revolving, and a runway and the slanting rise of a plane, charcoal-coloured. Another stone grinds by.

Which is disturbing. I could swear that I'm on my way home, so why am I still at the airport? Reproachful on the felty, dun carpet, my bag is waiting—it can usually explain.

Dishevelled contents, the clothes have been worn. Still, they seem to be nobody's clothes but my own and—

I need to be sick, immediately.

Thank God the room is tiny—it means the en suite facilities are close. □

PRISONERS OF CONSCIENCE APPEAL FUND

Providing relief for non–violent victims of religious, ethnic and political oppression

The Prisoners of Conscience Appeal Fund joins Granta and its readers in congratulating the 20 Best of Young British Novelists.

We would also like to pay tribute to the writers we have helped over the years. One such man is Sami, a Sudanese writer and publisher. He was arrested on seven different occasions for writing articles criticising the Sudanese government and its policies.

During each arrest he was blindfolded, forced to do hard labour (he was 65 years old at the time of his last arrest) deprived of food, water and medicine. Sami is a diabetic and without essential treatment, his health deteriorated badly. He was only released when the authorities feared that he might die in custody due to his worsening condition. Despite the huge difficulties Sami faced in attempting to leave the country, he finally arrived in the UK to undergo a vital lung operation, which saved his life. The Fund contributed to the costs of his treatment.

Without the generosity of individual donors it would be impossible to help as many people as we do. In the words of John Simpson CBE (our Patron and former editor of Granta):

> "I never cease to admire the strength of the human spirit
> in adversity, but it helps when someone cares"

We rely entirely on charitable donations. Please help.

Prisoners of Conscience Appeal Fund
Granta Appeal, FREEPOST NW5 944
London SW9 9BR
Tel: 020 7738 7511   Fax: 020 7733 7592
info@prisonersofconscience.org   www.prisonersofconscience.org

Registered Charity No. 213766

GRANTA

LOOK AT ME, I'M BEAUTIFUL!
Ben Rice

Ben Rice was born in Tiverton, Devon in 1972 and raised
there. The son of a schoolmaster and a pharmacist, he
attended Blundell's school where he wrote 'quite a good
poem about a frog' and then went to Newcastle University
to read English literature. Later, at Oxford, he was
encouraged to write by the poet/don/editor, Craig Raine. He
travelled to Australia on a writing scholarship and visited
Lightning Ridge, the opal mining community where his
girlfriend had grown up. The experience resulted in his
novella 'Pobby and Dingan' (Jonathan Cape) which he
wrote back in London while working in an off-licence. It
has been published in many languages and won a Somerset
Maugham Prize in 2001. He lives in London with his
partner and their six-month-old son. He is adapting two of
his stories for feature films. 'Look at Me, I'm Beautiful!'
is a new story.

Well, when I got back it was late and your father was sitting alone in the living room by the fire looking very calm and clean, and quite pleased with himself too, and the first thing I noticed was that he had taken off his waders and replaced them with desert boots. There was something rather annoying about him sitting there so calmly at a time of crisis, and I was just about to tell him that I hadn't come back to stay, and that I was only stopping by to pick up some things to take back to Gwen's, and that I was going to ruddy well spend the night there, if not the whole week, when he stood up and held out his arms and started to apologize for being so awful and going to that blessed koi show on our anniversary when he really should have been taking me somewhere special.

I was past listening to his grovelling, of course. I mean, the number of times he'd made lame attempts to appease me so that he could spend more time with the koi! Anyway, I was just about to tell him it wasn't going to rub, when suddenly and quite out of the blue he declared that he had decided to give up keeping fish once and for all.

'Shove your fish, Pete Joplin!' I said.

And I laughed in his face and told him that I wasn't in the mood for jokes. In fact I almost started to cry again. Then your father said if that was how I was going to be then he would have to jolly well prove it, and so he said: 'Follow me then, if you don't believe me, Annie. Come on, I want to show you something,' and he skipped outside. Well, I reluctantly followed him, and when I had joined him by the carp pond—or crap pond, as I rechristened it—he asked me if I noticed anything out of the ordinary.

I looked it over and saw no difference at first. Nothing at all. I mean it was the same hideous thing as far I was concerned and looked less like a pond, really, than something for drowning horses in.

'I'll give you a clue,' your father said.

And then I noticed.

There were no fish in it. No fish at all. It made no sense and I stared at the pond, agog.

'What? You haven't sold them?'

'No, no,' your father said, and he folded his arms and looked rather smug. 'I gave them away!'

'Gave them away? For nothing?'

'No. Not for nothing, Annie. For us,' he said and he put a hand on my shoulder, which I shook off, of course.

'To Mike Westerly?' I said. 'Are you insane, Pete? They're worth ten thousand pounds.'

'Not to Mike, Annie,' he said.

'Who then?'

'Aha!' he said, tapping his nose with his finger, the way he does.

'I don't get it,' I said. 'Why would you give them away?'

'Because I love you,' your father said. 'And because you and I are worth more than ten grand, my love,' he said.

'What else?'

'This thing just happened,' he went on. 'This really bizarre thing. It was really something.'

And then your father told me what had happened on the way back from the koi show but before he did he made me promise that I mustn't tell anyone else about it and I suppose I really ought not to tell you now.

'Cross your heart and hope to die?' said your father.

'Oh, just get on with it, will you, man?' I said.

So, your father said that he had set off for the koi show that morning in a foul mood after our row, but that when he got there the 'electric atmosphere' soon took his mind off it, and he cheered up a great deal now that he was in his element. And when both he and Mike Westerly won prizes for their fish he cheered up even more. Yes, he had won a highly commended in one of the categories apparently, and Mike won runner-up for supreme champion or something which is supposed to be a tremendously big deal.

On the way home your father drove slowly, out of respect for his Piscean passengers, and of course he and Mike were very jolly, and the two of them droned on a lot about fish and talked about their ponds and their filtration units and whatnot, and just outside town they stopped for a few drinks and got a bit tipsy and sang a few koi songs. Don't even ask.

Your father said it was late by the time he stopped to drop off Mike, and that as they were shaking hands, Mike asked him if he fancied coming in for a quick nightcap. Your father, being your father, said he thought about me for a minute and the blazing row of that morning and wondered for a second if he really ought to, but then told Mike that he didn't see why he shouldn't have just a quick one and besides he wanted to see the underwater sound system that Mike had installed in his pond so that he could play Beethoven to his fish. Yes, underwater Beethoven. That was what it had come to. Me escaping to poor Gwen's and crying for hours on her shoulder, and your father going to Mike Westerly's for a nightcap and to play Beethoven to his fish!

So anyway your father helped Mike Westerly carry his fish up the path and into the house. As soon as Mike had stepped inside, however, he sensed there was something wrong. 'What is it, Mike?' said your father. Mike Westerly didn't answer. He drew a driver from his golf bag, and holding it over his shoulder like a meat-club, he eased open the living room door.

'Holy Christ!' he said.

Mike's living room was a bombsite, apparently. His fish trophies were scattered round the room. Someone had raided the drinks cabinet and spilt half a bottle of burgundy on the carpet and there were drawers open and furniture upturned and paper everywhere. Yes, the place had been completely ransacked.

Mike Westerly's first thought, of course, was that someone had broken in. A few months ago, you see, he had caught some yobbos from the estate trying to steal his fish. One of them had got away with a Kohaku named Prince that was worth three thousand pounds. The little vandals had also trashed his garden and decapitated the little white Buddha who sat on a marble plinth overlooking the pond. Well, at the time I remember thinking: 'Good on the yobbos!'

Anyway, Mike's second thought was that there was no sign of his wife.

'Emma? Emma? Emma?' he called out. But there was no answer. So poor Mike Westerley bounded upstairs two at a time, without using the banister. He was worried, I suppose, that she'd been attacked or tied up or something by the intruders. Your father rushed to the phone and dialled nine-nine-nine, but while he was on the line to the police Mike suddenly came bounding back down the stairs carrying a strange bundle in his arms, and he was effing and blinding and screaming at your father to open the French windows. 'Open the doors, Pete. Open the effing doors. Quick!'

Your father slammed down the phone and darted over and opened the doors and I think it was at that moment that he realized that what Mike was carrying was a koi carp wrapped in a blanket. Yes, a fish. He didn't have a lot of time to take it in, though, because in seconds Mike Westerly had dashed into the garden with it and over to the pond. Your poor father just chased after him crying: 'Mike? Mike? What's going on? What the hell was that fish doing upstairs? Is she still breathing?' and all that kind of thing. But then both of them suddenly stopped in their tracks. And Mike said, 'Oh no. Oh dear God!'

You see, it was his wife, Emma. She was lying in the steaming pond on her front with her face in the water and her arms dangling down at her sides and she was entirely naked. She was pale too—almost blue, your father said—and they were sure she was dead because some of Mike's carp were nibbling at her toes and that suggested she had been in the water for some time. Can you imagine?

Mike was so shocked he fell to his knees and covered his face with his hands, the poor man, and your father was just about to kick off his shoes and jump in after her, when the woman suddenly raised her head. Yes, she did, she stood up and spat out a jet of water and said: 'Surprise, my darling! Surprise, Mike! I'm in the pond. I'm in it. And I'm absolutely bloody starkers!'

She was far from dead. On the contrary, she was alive and very drunk, completely blotto in fact, and your father told me it was not until then that he suddenly twigged what the mess in the living room and all the bottles was all about and why Mike had come downstairs with the fish. Emma, he realized, had taken the fish out of the pond, and put it in their bed. And she had put herself in the pond in its place. The poor woman was absolutely out of her tree.

'Emma? What are you doing? Get out of there!' poor Mike Westerly shouted, but all his wife did was swear at him and say: 'Mike, look at me! Look at me!' Yes, apparently she just kept yelling: 'Look at me, Mike! Look at me! I'm beautiful. Look at me, you eff-ing this and that, you twit! You haven't looked at me in so long, you whatnot,' and she kept yelling at Mike that he never even looked at her any more because he was too busy looking at his fish and so now why didn't he just look at her long and hard. 'I'm beautiful, you silly old this and that!' she shouted. 'Look at my boobs, look at my lovely you-know-what. You stupid this and that, I'm beautiful and you never even ruddy notice!'

Mike Westerly took his hands down from his face and he kept trying to hush her and tell her to be quiet because she would wake up all the neighbours and apparently there were indeed lights going on next door and someone started shouting at them to keep it down. Well, your father said Emma Westerly didn't take a blind bit of notice. She didn't even seem to have realized that he was there. She just kept standing in the water flashing her bits and shouting out that she was prettier than the fish by a mile, and then she started to swim out into the middle of the pond, crying: 'Look at me, I'm swimming! Look at me, I'm beautiful!' and then Mike told her very firmly to get out because your father was there and besides she was affecting the pH levels, and even a tiny change in temperature might upset the fish and cause irreparable harm.

That was enough for Emma Westerly. Frankly it would have been enough for me too. She screamed at him and told him to go and, you know, shove himself, and good on her. Then she announced that she was going to defecate in the water and he could see what that did to his pH levels.

By now Mike Westerly was so worried that her behaviour might be stressing his fish that he jumped into the pond and tried to pull her out, which made absolutely no sense at all to me, but your father said that it was one of those moments when nothing was really making sense. Yes, he threw himself into the water and your poor father was still so numbed by what he was seeing that all he could do was watch helplessly as Mike grappled with his slippery wife and tried to drag her out. He was having a little trouble, apparently. I mean he isn't exactly the most robust of men, and I think his waders had started to fill up with water, and he had to call out to your father to help.

And so now it was your father and Mike Westerly trying to get poor plastered Emma, who is normally such a restrained quiet woman, you know, and who isn't exactly in her physical prime, although your dear father says she isn't entirely out of it either, trying to get poor Emma out of the pond, before she damaged the fish or worse—though I don't think this thought ever occurred to her husband—drowned herself.

A couple of policemen arrived at this point, an older officer and a young chap with acne who it turned out was a trainee and used to go to school with you—Harry something, I think it was. No, Barry. Anyway, they'd heard the shouting coming from the back garden and had broken down the gate. I suppose they got a little more than they bargained for. Instead of a couple of adolescent oiks from the estate they were faced with two middle-aged men and a naked woman having some bizarre kind of aquatic wrestling match, while around them at least seven huge fish were going into trauma, flashing their tails and leaping about like God knows what.

When your father and Mike eventually got Emma out of the pond, and your poor father, soaked to the skin, had finished explaining to the police that this was purely a domestic matter and that he had mistakenly thought someone had broken in, but it was just that his friend's wife was a little drunk that's all—as soon as he had said all this, they all mucked in to help cart the poor woman up the stairs. All the way up she was screeching obscenities, apparently, and trying to grab hold of the banister and whatnot.

It was some time before they managed to bundle her into the bedroom and lay her on the bed and throw some towels over her, and even when they had finally succeeded Emma Westerly carried on shouting. And so the senior policeman very gallantly sat down beside her on the bed and did a good job of trying to soothe her, and then pretty soon she was snoring and dead to the world.

Mike and your father thanked the police and apologized again for the false alarm. And then everything was quiet and back—well, not to normal—but back to something resembling normality. The fish was in the pond, Emma was in bed. Mike Westerly came into the living room and caught his breath. Your father poured him a drink from the decanter, and Mike took it, and then he suddenly began trembling like a washing machine and burst into tears. Your father tried his best to comfort him and told him 'these things happen' and then realized how daft that sounded because of course these things don't happen, hardly ever—well not like that anyway. But then Mike said something else.

'I can't believe Emma did that to me, Pete,' he said. 'I can't believe she took my fish out of the pond. She could have killed it, the stupid effing woman could have killed my fish.'

And I think it was at that moment that your father had what he calls his Road to Damascus experience. He said the more he looked at Mike sitting there complaining about his wife, the more he felt his stomach churn and he didn't know it if it was the drink or what but he thought he was going to vomit. Yes, at that very moment all he wanted to do was get out of there. So your father excused himself politely and said he ought to leave Mike to it and get on home. And Mike Westerly made your father promise that he wouldn't tell a soul about it all, not a soul, not even me! And they embraced and slapped backs and your father eased Mike off him and quickly left the house.

He was in the car and heading for home, when he did something quite extraordinary. He was still soaking wet and shivery of course, and needed a good hot shower, but instead of taking the turn for our house, he drove up to the canal basin car park. Then he unloaded his fish one by one from the back of the car and carried them carefully over to the towpath and set them down next to each other. He mumbled a few parting words, and then, wasting no more time, released them all into the canal. Can you believe it? Just like that. He said that once he had decided it was the right thing to do, he didn't stop to think about it. He didn't even think about the money he was throwing away. He said he never wanted to see a carp dealer again, or have anything to do with his friends from the koi society. All he knew was that he wanted the fish to swim right out of his life.

Well, the fish didn't swim away at first but sort of lingered by the bank rubbing shoulders. They were still a little dopey and under the influence of that elbowgin stuff your father used to sedate them whenever they had to travel anywhere. Anyway he had to bend down and stick his hand in the canal and splash it around quite a bit, and eventually they flicked their tails, turned their noses north, and swam sleepily off into the night. They moved together, the whole shoal of them: oranges, whites, reds, Kohakus, Goromos and whadyamacallit, Sankes; they swam through the reflections of trees, beneath a group of coots. And then they made for the cow bridge. Well, your father rushed up on to the bridge and leaned over the side like a boy playing Poohsticks. He watched the fish approach the bridge and then he rushed across and saw them come out the other side and he kept staring after them as they headed on up the dark canal in a sort of procession. When they had disappeared around the corner he stood there, shivering, thinking he could still see some of them. And when he was finally sure that he couldn't, he turned around and walked back to the car.

So that was your father's story, and what could I do after hearing it all but gape at him as if he were an exotic fish himself? I mean when I came back from Gwen's I had expected to find him in the throes of his midlife koisis—you know—trimming an anal fin in the bath, or nursing a slime coat at the very least—but to find the pond empty, and then to hear how and why!

Your father and I hugged and made up and went back into the living room eventually, both of us in a bit of a daze. And before we went to bed we had a drink and toasted Emma Westerly. But I kept watching your father closely, I think I was half expecting him to dash out of the house with his holding net at any moment and go running up to the canal in pursuit of the fish. He didn't, though. No, instead he sat calmly and kept saying how relieved he felt now that the fish were gone and how the next day he was going to drain the pond and build a tennis court over it.

I can tell his calmness is fading though. Since that night all he's done is rattle on about this tennis court plan. I keep telling him not to be so rash, that a former pond is hardly the best place to lay down the foundations, but your father is adamant. He says the rashness is all part of it. He says it's all about making a bold symbolic gesture, a straight swap. We will be 'doing an Emma Westerly', he says.

That poor woman! I can't help thinking how brave she was. I'd fled to Gwen's like some hysterical schoolgirl, but she'd tackled the problem head first.

I saw her on the High Street yesterday, and she pretended she hadn't seen me. 'Emma!' I called out. 'Emma, it's okay, I just wanted to tell you how much I admired—!' but by the time I crossed the street she had disappeared. □

GRANTA

HERE WE GO

David Peace

David Peace was born in Ossett, West Yorkshire, in 1967. He graduated from the former Manchester Polytechnic in 1991. He taught English in Istanbul and Tokyo from 1993 until 2001. His first novel, 'Nineteen Seventy-Four', was published in 1999 by Serpent's Tail. He followed this with 'Nineteen Seventy-Seven', 'Nineteen Eighty' and 'Nineteen Eighty-Three', completing his Red Riding Quartet (all published by Serpent's Tail) — four novels set in the West Riding around the time of the serial killer known as the Yorkshire Ripper. 'Here We Go' is taken from his next novel, 'GB 84', set during the 1984–85 miners' strike, which Faber will publish in 2004.

Monday March 5–Sunday March 11, 1984

Terry Winters sat at the kitchen table of his three-bedroom house in the suburbs of Sheffield, South Yorkshire. His three children were squabbling over their scrambled eggs. His wife was worrying about the washing and the weather. Terry ignored them. He took an index card from the right-hand pocket of his jacket. He read it. He closed his eyes. He repeated out loud what he had just read. He opened his eyes. He read the card again. He checked what he had said. He had been correct. He put the card into the left-hand pocket of his jacket. He took a second card from the right pocket. He read it. He closed his eyes. He repeated out loud what he had read. He opened his eyes. His children were taunting each other over their toast. His wife still worrying about the washing and the weather. They ignored him. He read the card again. He had been correct again. He put the card into the left pocket. He took another card from his right pocket. He read it. Terry closed his eyes. Terry Winters was learning his lines.

They had their breakfasts across the road from the County Hotel on Upper Woburn Place, Bloomsbury, London. Four tables of them. Full English. No one speaking. Everyone hung-over—

Everyone but the President. He was on the early train down from Sheffield.

They mopped their plates with the last of the bread. They put out their cigarettes. Drained their teas. Terry Winters paid the bill. They got four cabs down to Hobart House. Terry paid the drivers. They pushed through the press and the sleet. They went inside.

The President was waiting with the news from South Yorkshire—

Solid.

They had their last cigarettes. Looked at their watches. They went upstairs—

The Mausoleum—

Room sixteen, Hobart House, Victoria.

Bright lights, smoke and mirrors—

The anti-terrorist curtains always drawn, the matching carpet and the wall-length mirrors, the tables round the edge of the room. In the middle—

No-man's-land.

The Board at the top end with their deputies.

The National Union of Mineworkers at the foot of the table.

Fifty people here for the Coal Industry National Consultative Committee—

But there was no consultation today. Just provocation—

More provocation. Real provocation—

Fifty people watching the Chairman of the Board let his deputy get to his feet.

Terry Winters didn't sleep. None of them did—

It was never dark. It was always light—

The bright lights on the train back north. The TV crews outside the NUM headquarters, St James's House. The fluorescent lighting in the foyer. In the lift. In the corridors. In the office—

Always light, never dark.

Terry phoned Theresa. *Click-click.* Told her he didn't know when he'd be home. Then he got out the files. Got out his address book. His calculator—

He did his sums—

All night, again and again, over and over.

First thing next morning Terry Winters was across in the Royal Victoria Hotel with the finance officers from each of the union's twenty separate areas and groupings. Terry made them all stand up before the meeting could begin. He made them search the room for hidden microphones and bugs. He made them frisk each other.

Then Terry Winters drew the curtains and locked the doors. Terry made them write down their questions in pencil and seal them in envelopes. He made them pass the envelopes forward.

Terry Winters sat at the head of the table and opened the envelopes one by one. Terry read their questions. He wrote the answers in pencil on the other side of their papers. He put the answers back in the envelopes. He resealed them with sellotape. He passed them back down the table to the individual authors of each question—

The finance officers read the answers in silence, then returned them to be burned.

Terry Winters stood up. Terry told them how it was—

The Government would come after their money; hunt them through the courts.

He told them what had to be done to cover their tracks—

Nothing on paper; no phone calls; personal visits only, day or night—

He handed out sheets of codes and dates for them to memorize and destroy.

The finance officers thanked him, then returned to their areas.

Terry Winters went straight back to St James's House. Straight back to work.

He worked all day. They all did—

Each of them in their offices.

People coming and going. Meetings here, meetings there. Deals made, deals done.

Breaking for the *Nine o'Clock News, News at Ten, Newsnight*—

Notebooks out, videos and cassettes recording:

'I want to make it clear that we are not dealing with niceties here. We shall not be constitutionalized out of our jobs. Area by area we will decide and in my opinion it will have a domino effect.'

Cheers again. Applause—

Domino effects. Essential battles. Savage butchery.

Then it was back to work. All of them. All night—

Files, phones and calculators. Tea, coffee and aspirins—

The Communist Party and the Socialist Workers arguing in the corridors—

The Tweeds and the Denims at each other's throats. Their eyes. Their ears—

Shostakovich's Seventh Symphony on loud upstairs in the office of the President—

All night, through the night, until the brakes of dawn—

Terry put his forehead against the window, the city illuminated beneath him—

Never dark—

You couldn't sleep. You had to work—

Always light.

Head against the window, the sun coming up.

The troops were gathering on the street below him. The Red Guard in good voice: 'SCAB, SCAB, SCAB—'

The dawn chorus of the Socialist Republic of South Yorkshire.

Another cup of coffee. Another aspirin—

Terry Winters picked up his files. His calculator.

Terry went up to the tenth floor. To the Conference Room—

The National Executive Committee of the National Union of Mineworkers.

Terry took his seat at the right hand of the President. Terry listened—

Listened to Lancashire: *'There is a monster. It's now or never.'*

Listened to Nottinghamshire: *'If we're scabs before we start, we'll become scabs.'*

Listened to Yorkshire: *'We are on our way.'*

For six hours Terry listened and so did the President.

Then the President stopped listening. The President stood up with two letters—

It was their turn to listen to him now.

The President talked about the secret December meetings between the Chairman and the Prime Minister. He talked about their secret plans to privatize the coal industry. Their secret nuclear, electric dreams. Their secret hit lists—

Their open and savage schemes to butcher an industry. *Their* industry—

For then the President spoke of history and tradition. The history of the Miner. The tradition of the Miner. The legacies of their fathers and their fathers' fathers—

The birthrights of their children and their children's children—

The essential battles to come. The war that must be won.

The motion from South Wales was before them—

'It is now the crunch time,' said the President. 'We are agreed we have to fight. We have an overtime ban. It is only the tactics which are in question.'

They listened and then they voted—

They voted twenty-one to three to endorse the striking areas under Rule 41.

It was the only vote. The only vote that mattered—

The vote for war.

The President put a hand on Terry's shoulder. The President whispered in his ear—

Terry Winters nodded. Terry picked up his files. His calculator.

He went back down to his office. He closed the door.

Terry walked over to the window. He put his forehead against the glass. He listened to the cheers from the street below. Terry closed his eyes.

Terry Winters opened his front door. His family were asleep upstairs. The lights off downstairs. Terry quietly closed the door. He stood his briefcase in the hall. He caught his face in the dark mirror: Terry Winters, the Executive Officer of the National Union of Mineworkers; Terry Winters, the highest non-elected official in the National Union. Terry applauded himself in the shadows of South Yorkshire, in the suburbs of Sheffield—

In his house with the lights off but everybody home.

The Yorkshire Area Executive had defied the High Court injunction on picketing; the pickets continued to fly. The Yorkshire Area had been found in contempt of court; the bailiffs had been dispatched—

The Yorkshire Industrial Action Fund already exhausted.

The President sent Terry and Mike Sullivan back to Area Headquarters in Huddersfield Road. This time they weren't alone—

Two thousand from the Yorkshire coalfield had answered the President's call; 2,000 miners here to defend the battlements of King Arthur's (former) Castle, ringing the black, stained bricks of the Yorkshire HQ—

Four thousand eyes watching and waiting for the bailiffs.

In an upstairs room Terry and Mike shredded papers.

There were scuffles outside. The men attacked photographers and camera crews. The police stepped in. Punches were thrown. Arrests made.

Clive Cook brought in more boxes. Terry and Mike shredded more papers.

There was a sudden, huge cheer from the men outside—

Terry and Mike went to the window.

Clive came back with the last box. He said, 'The Board's abandoned the action.'

Monday March 26–Sunday April 1, 1984

Terry stood on the platform. He stamped his feet. He rubbed his hands together. He had a first-class seat on the first train down.

The train was ten minutes late.

David Peace

Terry found his seat. He ordered coffee. Breakfast. He checked his files:

National Coal Board vs National Union of Mineworkers: NCB High Court action against the NUM's pension fund investment policy.

Terry checked his notes:

Union constitutionally opposes investment of funds overseas and in industries that compete with coal.

He checked his sums:

£84.4 million annual contributions from members; £151.5 million from the NCB; £22.4 million in pensions and £45.2 million lump sum payments to be paid annually; £200 million for investment.

The President would be representing the Union. Himself. The President would be conducting their defence. Personally. The President would be waiting for Terry. Himself. The President would be counting on Terry—

Personally.

Terry put away the file. He picked up the complimentary copy of *The Times*:

MORE MINERS JOIN STRIKE AS PICKETS INCREASE; BRITISH STEEL CUTBACK 50% AT SCUNTHORPE; MINER FOUND HANGED—

Terry felt sick. Terry looked at his watch. Terry changed carriages—

Terry sat at a table in second class as the train pulled into King's Cross.

Terry Winters knew they would be waiting for him. Watching him.

The President had not come to ask for help. He did not want help. He did not need help. The President had not come to beg. He did not want charity. He did not need charity. The President had come only to hold them to their word. To have them keep their promises. Honour their pledges. The President had come only to collect. To collect what was his—

From the steelmen. The lorry drivers. The railwaymen. The seamen. The promise and the pledge to cease all movement of coal—

By road. By rail. By sea—

To cut off the power stations. To shut down the steel works—

The whole country.

This was what he had come to collect and the President meant to collect it.

254

The Union took over the TGWU. They ordered tea. They ordered sandwiches. They listened to the report. The daily update:

Thirty-five out of 176 pits still working; tailbacks on the MI and A1 as pickets took revenge on the roadblocks; fresh trouble at Coal House; arrests at 300 plus.

The President was in his court suit again. The President was impatient—

'This case is going to go on forever,' he said.

'But we knew this,' said Paul.

'Forever!' he shouted. 'While the Right are up there plotting and scheming.'

'You're taking on too much,' said Dick.

'Ballot. Ballot. Ballot,' said the President. 'That's all I ever hear.'

'We shouldn't be down here,' said Paul. 'We should be up where the fight is.'

'We've been set up,' whispered the President. 'Set up.'

'Let me take care of the pension fund,' said Terry.

The President looked up at Terry Winters. The President smiled at Terry. He said, 'Thank you, Comrade.'

There was a knock at the door. One of the President's ladies came in. Alice said, 'They're waiting for us.'

'No,' laughed the President as he rose to his feet. 'We're waiting for them—

'Waiting for their unconditional support; for the movement of all coal in the British Isles to be blocked—

'Then we cannot lose,' said the President.

Everybody nodded—

Kiss me.

'Not one single piece of coal will move in the whole country without our say-so. We will picket out every pit. We will close down every power station and steelworks.'

Everybody nodded—

Kiss me in the shadows.

'We will bring the Government to their knees. We will make her beg.'

Everybody nodded—

Kiss me, Diane.

'We cannot lose,' said the President again. 'We will not lose! We shall not lose!'

Everybody stood up. Everybody applauded—
Kiss me in the shadows—
Everybody followed the President. Down the corridor. Down to business—
Kiss me in the shadows of my heart—
To Victory.

It was April Fool's Day and it was snowing outside. Terry Winters lay in the double bed. He could smell Sunday lunch. He could hear the kids fighting. The little tempers rising. The little fists flying. The President had been fuming too. The President had been raging. The Iron and Steel Trades Confederation had very predictably denied him. Betrayed him! The President demanded revenge. The President would be on *Weekend World* again today. The President would let the whole world know what he thought of those who would deny him. Those who would betray him, his members and their families. Judases. Terry turned over in the double bed. He looked at his briefcase with the broken strap. The one he never used now. The papers piled up on the dressing table. Terry got out of the bed. It was cold. He put on his slippers. His dressing gown. He went across to the bathroom. His cock was sore when he pissed. He flushed the toilet. He washed his hands.

They'd taken Terry Winters' office apart. Everything in it. Everything—
The carpet off the floor. The cabinets. The bookcase. The desk. The telephones. The chairs. The blinds. The lights. The portrait off the wall—
It had been Terry's idea.
These were paranoid times at the headquarters of the National Union of Mineworkers. Even more than usual. The press and television coverage was almost all hostile and negative. Even more than usual. Every question returned to the issue of a national ballot and democracy—
Democracy. Democracy. Democracy—
Even more than usual.
Terry took three aspirin. Terry picked up his files. His calculator.
He walked down the corridor. He didn't take the lift. He took the stairs up.
Len frisked him at the door. Len told him to leave his jacket outside.

Terry took off his jacket. Terry went inside—

This room the same as his room. The portraits gone from the walls. The carpets—

Just the plastic chairs and the plastic tables remained. Melting—

The heating on full. The lights all on.

Terry drew the curtains.

The President looked up. He whispered, 'Thank you, Comrade.'

Terry nodded. He took his seat at the right hand of the President. He listened—

No ballot. No ballot. No ballot—

Listened to the schemes and the plots. The counter schemes and the counter plots:

'Without Durham,' said Gareth, 'the moderates haven't got the numbers.'

'You rule it out of order,' said Paul. 'We'd get 12–9 our way. Possibly 13–8.'

'The simple majority proposal is going to derail them anyway,' laughed Dick. 'They'll agree to hold a Special Delegate Conference just to buy themselves more time.'

'Then come the SDC,' said Paul. 'Then we'll have them.'

'I'll talk to Durham,' said Sam. 'I'll make sure they deliver for us.'

Everybody looked up the table. Everybody looked at the President—

'Then it's decided,' said the President.

Everybody smiled. Everybody clapped. Everybody patted each other on the back.

'There's just one more thing,' said the President—

Everybody stopped clapping. Everybody stopped smiling.

The President stood up. The President stared around the room. The President said, 'They are opening our post. They are tapping our phones. They are watching our homes.'

Everybody nodded.

'This we knew. This we had come to expect from a democratic government.'

Everybody nodded again. Everybody waited.

'What we didn't know and we didn't expect is that we also have a mole.'

Everybody waited. Everybody shook their heads.

The President looked round the table. The President said, 'A mole, Comrades.'

Everybody shook their heads again. Everybody looked down at the table.

The President nodded to Bill Reed. Bill Reed stood up. Bill edited *The Miner*—

Bill Reed stared at Terry Winters as he said, 'Contact of mine, very well-placed. Told me they're boasting they've got someone on the inside. Here and in Barnsley.'

Everybody else stared at the table. Their hands. Their fingernails. The dirt there—

Terry Winters stared back at Bill Reed—

Bill Reed said again, 'They've got someone, Comrades.'

Bill Reed sat down.

The President said, 'I need strategies. I need ideas.'

Terry coughed. He said, 'It could be disinformation. Create mistrust. Paranoia.'

The Tweed next to Dick said, 'And so could that remark, Comrade.'

Mike Sullivan put his hand up. He said, 'Do we have any actual proof?'

The President stared at Mike. The President said, 'We have proof, Comrade.'

Everybody looked up. Everybody waited.

'The proof is on the face of every policeman on every picket line,' he shouted. 'The smile that says, *We knew you were coming—*

We knew you were coming before you even did!'

Everybody waited. Everybody waited for Terry—

Terry stood up. Terry said, 'Thank you, President. I have drawn up a code that will allow the areas and branches to contact us here at the Strike HQ using our existing telephone lines and numbers. I intend to reveal the code to you here and now, though I would ask you to write nothing down but rather to commit the details and instructions of what I am about to say to memory. On returning to your areas you are to brief the panels verbally and in turn instruct the panels to brief their local branches in the same manner. I repeat, nothing is to be written down. I shall now reveal to you the code—

'Pickets will henceforth be referred to as apples. I repeat, apples—

'Police are to be referred to as potatoes. Repeat, potatoes—

'Henceforth, branches will be requested to supply X number of apples based upon Y number of potatoes at a given site. Likewise branches can request extra apples from HQ in response to superior numbers of potatoes. Our brothers and sisters in the railways are henceforth to be known as mechanics—

'I repeat, mechanics—

'Members of the National Union of Seamen are henceforth plumbers. Repeat...'

The one day they won. The next day they lost—

The Judge said the President had not been acting in the best interests of the 350,000 beneficiaries of the Pension Fund. The Judge ruled the President was in breach of his legal duty. The Judge ordered the President to lift the embargo on overseas investments. The Judge threatened to dismiss the President from the management committee of the fund, if he did not comply with his orders.

Terry Winters hailed a cab outside the High Court. Five of them squeezed inside. The President on the back seat in the middle. Flaming. Furious. Terry looked at his watch. They weren't going to make the four o'clock train. The President wiped his face with his handkerchief. He hated London. The South. Terry turned to look over the driver's shoulder up the road. Nothing was moving. The President gently touched his hair. He said, 'That's British justice.'

Everybody nodded.

Terry Winters put his briefcase on his knee. He opened it and searched through it. The President was watching him. Terry looked at his watch. He searched through his briefcase again. The President leaned forward. He said, 'What is it, Comrade?'

Everybody nodded.

Terry Winters looked at his watch again. Terry checked his case again. Terry said, 'I think I must have left one of the files at the court. You'll have to let me out.'

Everybody nodded.

Terry stopped the taxi. He got out. He gave Joan the fare and the tickets. He said, 'Don't worry about me. Don't wait for me.'

Everybody nodded—

Everybody except Paul. Paul shook his head. Paul watched him go—

Disappear again.

David Peace

Monday April 16–Sunday April 22, 1984

Terry couldn't keep up. He was exhausted. Diane was too much for him. She was insatiable. He fell over on to his back. He was out of breath. He hurt. She rolled on top of him. She mounted him. She rode him. He groaned. He moaned. She smiled. She laughed. He cried out. She screamed. He came. She lay beside him. He had his eyes closed. She took his cock in her hand. He opened his eyes. She stroked his cock. He closed his eyes again. She whispered, 'You got a code word for him, Mr Executive Officer?'

Terry knew the President blamed him. The situation was extremely dangerous and nobody dared predict what would happen next. The families would not be starved back. Troops could be used to move coal stocks—

The greatest good for the greatest number.

The situation was extremely dangerous and the President blamed Terry. Blamed him for everything. Terry had told the President he'd take care of it—

Take care of everything. Terry had told the President they would win—

They had lost.

Terry put his forehead against the window of his office. Terry closed his eyes. Terry knew the President blamed him. Blamed him. Blamed him—

Back to the Big House for Terry.

The phone on the desk rang again. It never fucking stopped.

Terry picked up the phone. *Click-click.* He said, 'Executive Officer speaking.'

'Terry? Thank Christ for that. It's Jimmy. I'm trying to get hold of the President. No one will tell me where he is. What's going on?'

'Not allowed to give out information over the phone. New directive.'

'Look, just listen. I'm down in London. We've just come out of a joint policy meeting. The Board have just told us they're willing to sit down with you all. Talk. Face to face. No messing about. I'm trying to set something up for next Tuesday—'

'What's to bloody talk about? He was on *Weekend World* saying they should use troops to move stocks. Told Jimmy Young he'd got more constructive things to do with his time than talk to us. There's Tebbit all over the papers talking about denationalization. You'd be wasting the President's time, Jimmy—'

'Terry, listen. No compulsory redundancies and they'll drop their initial timetable. That's a fucking climbdown in anybody's book. It's a victory for us.'

'Us?'

'For the whole movement. For the NUM. For the President.'

'What do they want?'

'I've got a letter from them saying what I just told you. But they want a response. And they want it as soon as possible. Then we'll talk about setting the time and the place. But I do need to speak to the President.'

Terry drummed his fingers on the desk. He said, 'Get their letter to me by courier. I'll make sure the President sees it—'

'He'll thank you, Terry.'

'I'll ensure you have our response by the end of the day,' said Terry. 'Personally.'

Terry put down the phone. Terry stood up. Terry smiled to himself—

Terry knew the President blamed him. Blamed him for everything—

But not for long.

Terry couldn't keep up. He was exhausted. Christopher and Timothy were too fast for him. They were incorrigible. Louise fell over on the flagstones. She started to cry. She looked around for her daddy. Terry stopped chasing after the boys and the football. He walked back across the lawn. Louise pointed at the graze on her knee. Terry bent down. He kissed it better. He picked her up. He held her. Theresa came out of the house. She was carrying a tray of barley water. Ice clinked in the glasses. She looked at Terry—

She didn't speak. She never did. Theresa Winters just smiled—

He didn't speak either. He never dared. Terry Winters just smiled back—

He winked at his wife. He was going to amaze them all.

'The fuck is this, Winters?'

Terry looked up from his figures. Paul Hargreaves was standing
before his desk. Len Glover in the doorway. Paul holding out a piece
of paper—

A letter. *The* letter.

Terry put down his pen. He took off his glasses.

Len stepped inside. He closed the door.

'Is there a problem, Comrades?' asked Terry.

Paul banged the letter down on to Terry's desk—

'Yes there's a problem, *Comrade*,' he said. 'The fucking problem
is you.'

'Have I done something wrong?' asked Terry.

Paul stared at him. He tapped the letter. He said, 'You changed this.'

'Did I?' asked Terry. 'Did I really?'

Paul reached across the desk to take hold of Terry. Len pulled him
back—

'What do you mean, *did I?*' shouted Paul. 'You know fucking well
you did. You're such an arrogant bloody prick, Winters. Arrogant
and—'

'Then I apologize,' said Terry. 'I apologize to both of you,
Comrades.'

Paul made another lurch towards the desk. Len held him back—

'It was a fucking opportunity and you fucking killed it,' screamed
Paul. 'Dead. There's nothing now. No meeting. Nothing. I hope
you're fucking pleased with yourself, *Comrade*. Dead in the water.
Nothing. Fucking satisfied now, *Comrade?*'

'I made a mistake then,' said Terry. 'I thought the President said
pit closures and job losses were not negotiable. I thought I was
simply restating our position. I'm sorry.'

Len let go of Paul. Paul stared at Terry Winters—

Terry smiled at Paul Hargreaves. Terry smiled at Len Glover—

Len shook his head. Len opened the door. Paul pointed at Terry—

Paul said, 'I'm on to you, Winters.'

The President stood up behind his desk. Stood up in front of the huge
portrait of himself. He walked round to where Terry was sitting.
Handed Terry a tissue, hand on his shoulder. The President said,
'People make mistakes, Comrade. It's what makes them human.'

Terry blew his nose. Terry dried his eyes.

'I believe you had the best intentions of the movement in your heart, Comrade.'

Terry sniffed. Terry nodded.

'This time you are forgiven, Comrade.'

Terry stood up. Terry said, 'Thank you. President. Thank you. Thank you—'

The President walked back behind his desk. Back in front of the portrait.

Len held open the door for Terry—

'Thank you,' said Terry again. Terry went downstairs for his coat—

Terry Winters knew he was on a short leash.

Terry got his coat. Terry took the lift down to the foyer—

They were waiting for him.

Terry sat in the back of the car between the President and Paul—

No one said a word.

They drove to Mansfield. They parked near the Area HQ. They parted the crowd—

They went inside. They walked through the room. They sat at the top table—

Ray spoke. Ray said, 'Get off your knees—'

Henry spoke. Henry said, 'You are mice not men—'

Paul spoke. Paul said, 'You are on strike officially—'

The President spoke to them. The President scolded them. The President shouted, 'YOU DO NOT CROSS PICKET LINES!'

They got up from the table. They walked through the room—

There was no standing ovation—

No applause. No songs. No autographs. □

SUBSCRIBE NOW!

One year's subscription to *indobrit* for only £12
(cover price £14)

name _____

address _____

town _____

county _____

postcode _____

email for confirmation _____

Start issue: January-April 2003 *indobrit* 1

GIFT SUBSCRIPTION

message: (max 100 letters) _____
_____

name _____

address _____

town _____

county _____

postcode _____

email for confirmation _____

**Please send a cheque made payable to Indobrit
Magazine for £12 per subscription with this form
to:** Indobrit Magazine, Subscriptions, 5 Argyll
Mansions, 303 Kings Road, London SW3 5ER

next issue

**THE WATER ISSUE
ISSUE 2 OUT APRIL 28, 2003**

**INC.
HYDROTHERAPY
THE BEST BATHROOMS
WATERSIDE LIVING
WATERSPORTS
JUSTINE HARDY ON YOGA
STEPHEN ARMSTRONG ON BUYING
A SECOND HOME
AND THE BEST BEACHWEAR!**

Get wet with...

indobrit

GRANTA

LILA.EXE
Hari Kunzru

Hari Kunzru was born in 1969 and grew up in Essex, near junction 26 of the M25. Later he took degrees in literature and philosophy, and did 'the usual rubbish jobs' while trying to get a book published. His journalism has appeared in The Guardian, Wired, iD, The Economist and the London Review of Books. He is music editor at Wallpaper magazine and a contributing editor at Mute magazine. In 1999 he was named Observer Young Travel Writer of the Year. His novel 'The Impressionist' was published in 2002 by Hamish Hamilton and has been translated into sixteen languages. He lives in London. 'Lila.exe' is from a novel-in-progress.

It was a simple message.
Hi. I saw this and thought of you.
Maybe you got a copy in your inbox, sent from an address you did not recognize; an innocuous two-line email with an attachment, lila.exe. Maybe you obeyed the instruction to
check it out!
and there she was; Lila Zohar, dancing in jerky quicktime in a pop-up window on your screen. Even at that size you could see she was beautiful, this little pixelated dancer, smiling as the subject line promised, a radiant twenty-one-year old smile
just for you.
That smile. The start of all your problems.

It was not as if you asked for Lila to come and break your heart. There you were, doing whatever you normally do online; filling in form fields, downloading porn, *interacting*, when suddenly up she flounced and everything went to pieces. For a moment, even in the middle of your panic, you probably felt special. Which was Lila's talent. Making you believe it was all just for you.

But there were others. How many did she infect? Thousands? Tens, hundreds of thousands? Impossible to count. Experts have estimated her damage to global business at almost a billion US dollars, mostly in human and machine down time, but brute financial calculus does not capture the chaos of those days. During Lila's brief period of misrule normality was overturned. Lines of idle brokers chewed their nails in front of frozen screens. Network nodes winked out of existence like so many extinguished stars. For a few weeks she danced her way around the world, and disaster, like an overweight suburbanite in front of a workout video, followed every step.

Of course the whole thing made her famous, beyond even her mother's wildest imaginings. Lila was already a rising star, India's new dream girl, shinning up the greasy lingam of the Mumbai film world like the child in the conjuror's rope trick. But while Lila's mother had thought through most eventualities, she had not factored the march of technology into her daughter's career plan. Mrs Zohar was decidedly not a technical person.

And so Lila found herself bewitched, the girl with the red shoes, cursed to dance on until her feet bled or the screen froze in messy blooms of ASCII text. Yet despite what her proud mother may have thought, she was a surface effect; mere window dressing. The real action was taking place in the guts of the code, a cascade of additions and subtractions, iterations and deletions, an invisible contagion of ones and zeroes. Lila played *holi* and her clinging sari diverted everyone's attention from the machinery at work under her skin.

A chain of cause and effect? Nothing so simple organized the pattern of her summer. It was a time of topological curiosities, loops and knots, never-ending strips of action and inside-out bottles of reaction so thoroughly confused that identifying a single point of origin is almost impossible. Where did it all go wrong?

Arjun Mitra first saw a computer when he was ten years old. It was a 286 PC and it belonged to cousin Hitesh, whose father, concerned for his son's education, had brought it back from a business trip to America. Hitesh improved himself by playing solitaire and trying to beat his high score on a side-scrolling game which involved bombing villages from a helicopter. Mostly the machine sat grey and untended in Hitesh's bedroom, humming portentously. Arjun's family was staying in Bombay for a week, and while Hitesh was in the next room watching action movies he could spend hours undisturbed, exploring the extraordinary object. It was like stumbling through an alien landscape. Path not found. Sector not found. He was asked questions which made no sense. Abort, retry, fail?

He felt like a hero on a quest. When he pressed a key and the cryptic pulse of the DOS prompt exploded into graphics, the suspicion was planted in his mind that something inside the machine must be alive. It was a suspicion that had never quite left him.

Before you can legitimately point to something and cry 'It's alive!', the thing in question needs to satisfy up to a hundred criteria, the exact number depending on which scientist is standing next to you as you point. Is that blob capable of motion? Or reproduction? Does it consume and grow? Does it wriggle if you poke it with a stick? By the age of thirteen Arjun knew there was nothing actually alive inside computers. The machines failed the life test on several grounds, notably reproduction. But they persisted in hinting at something mystical, the presence of a vital spark. A computer booting up is creating itself *ex nihilo*, each stage of activity generating the grounds for the next. A tiny trickle of electricity to a dormant chip allows it to take a roll-call of components, which then participate in a simple exchange of instructions, a setting out of terms and conditions that generates a more complex exchange, and then another, tier after tier of language coming into being until the display of a holiday photograph or the sweep of a pointer across a spreadsheet become intelligible gestures, their meaning reaching all the way back down into binary simplicity, into changes of electrical state on a silicon wafer.

Arjun was intrigued by this yes–no logic, by the way that ones and zeroes could give birth to the unexpected. Hungry for more computer time, he would beg or steal it where he could; libraries, college labs, the houses of richer or luckier schoolfriends. He particularly loved to run simulations. Anything would do. Commercial god-games; cities and armies; a simple world of different-coloured daisies; clusters of digital cells switching each other from red to blue. Watching populations of computer creatures grow and die, he found himself meditating on scale, wondering in a teenage way if his own world was nothing but a stupendous piece of programming, a goldfish bowl system running for the amusement of other cosmically bored teens.

True or false?

Whichever, he found himself in retreat from it, buffeted by puberty, stricken by the awkwardness of interacting with other people. People were a chasm, an abyss. Their violence, their vagueness, their unknowable motivations and their inexplicable changes of mood had by some nightmarish process been woven into a social world into which he had been summarily thrown. Why would nobody understand? They were making no sense. At last, having laid hands on his own machine and desperate to regain a sense of control, he became a computing hermit, fleeing into a place where communication was governed by clearly laid-out rules. Logic gates. Truth tables. The world of people could go and rot. He closed his bedroom door on it.

His life could have progressed in any number of different directions had he not, one evening, left a floppy disk in his computer. When he started up the following morning his screen suddenly went blank. He pressed keys. No response. He rebooted. The machine ran slow. He rebooted again. And again. Finally, after an interminable crunch and stutter from inside the case, a message appeared in front of him.

u r a pr1z0n7r ov th3 l0rd$ ov m1zr00L

He shut down and restarted, but the problem only got worse. His computer had been reduced to a pile of scrap metal. To get it running again he had to reformat his hard drive, which meant that he lost all his data. Everything. Months of work erased by this catastrophic visitation.

If you don't understand all you have to do is ask. Arjun started to research what had happened and found that he had been hit by a thing with a name: the carnival virus, a string of code that had hidden itself in an innocuous floppy disk and had used his computer to make copies of itself. Every restart had given birth to another generation. Life.

Like their biological analogues, computer viruses stand on the ill-defined boundary between living and non-living. There is not much to a biological virus, just a strand of nucleic acid surrounded by a coat of protein. It drifts around until it can attach itself to the outer wall of a cell, then finds a way to smuggle a sample of itself inside. Once through the door it diverts the cell's biosynthetic machinery from doing what it is supposed to be doing—building copies of the cell—and fools it into making copies of the virus. Is it alive? Not exactly. But almost.

Arjun soon found that information on computer viruses was hard to come by. Even a sketchy idea of where they originated was impossible to discover without his own Internet connection, and in India that was then an impossibility. By writing off for disks and magazines and making occasional cripplingly expensive calls to foreign bulletin boards he managed to get hold of a few code samples, which he studied like religious texts. In the privacy of his bedroom he created several simple viruses, careful to keep back-ups of his data in case (as happened once or twice) he accidentally infected his own machine. He taught himself assembly language, and by his late teens had begun to excel in all sorts of more conventional programming tasks. His parents, who were worried by his reclusiveness, his bad posture, his unwillingness to play sports or bring friends round for tea, began to see an upside to his obsession. Computers were the coming thing, Mr Mitra would remind his colleagues at the firm. *My son will be an engineer.*

It was only when Arjun went to college, and at last had proper access to the data riches of the Net, that he was properly able to satisfy his curiosity. He started to burrow into the underground, logging on to chat rooms and IRC channels, navigating with a thrill past the braggarts and hypers, the ranters and flamers and paranoiacs who infested this grey area of the computing culture. All the time picking up, filtering. Searching for information which would allow him to control something new, reveal the location of a hidden tool, point him towards the construction of another toy.

Screw you lamer, don't come running to me when it wipes your hd, i just distributed the thing. Well anyway enjoy d00ds, cya at my next release...

That was the style. If you had knowledge you wore it with arrogance. You put down the pretenders and the fools like a dashing musketeer, a programming dandy. Arjun was shy. Even online, hidden behind the anonymity of a screen name, he was no player. He did not feel confident about what he knew. For a long time he just lurked, watching and listening, gleaning information about security flaws, vulnerabilities, techniques, exploits. But in the true underground, the untraceable underground of temporary private channels and download sites with shifting addresses, exchange was everything. If you didn't give, you didn't get.

So, feeling trepid and illicit, *badmAsh* started to appear on virus exchange boards, offering to trade code for code. To his pleasure and surprise he found that people wanted what he had got, and he soon became popular, respected. One night it dawned on him that behind the bluster most of the other traders were not that talented. Most of them were handymen, tinkering with already-existing routines. They were not the originators, the architects. *badmAsh* became something of a star.

Further blurring the borderline between life and not-life, the Internet had brought computer viruses into their own. While floppy disks had remained the primary transmission vector, rates of infection were low. Now that files could be sent over phone lines, the number of incidents soared. From his college terminal Arjun watched in fascination as malicious code flared up like a rash on the computing body of the world, causing itching and discomfort to a public educated by science-fiction and the cold war to regard the convergence of machines and biology with uneasy reverence. Computer virus. Sublime terror.

Arjun himself had little time for science fiction. For him it was all Romance. *Pyaar*. But being the hero of the Vx boards was a sterile thing in some ways, because the point of being a hero is to get the girl, and on the Vx boards there were none. Not one. Not even anyone pretending to be one.

Pyaar. Pyaar. Pyaar. Throughout South Asia it's impossible to get away from it. Perhaps the rise of Love has something to do with cinema, or independence from the British, or globalization, or decadence, or a furtive observation of backpacking hippy couples by a generation of young people who suddenly saw that it was possible to grope one another without the sky falling on their heads. There are those who say Love is just immorality. There are those who believe it is encouraged by amplified disco music. There are even those who claim that the decline in arranged marriage and the cultural encouragement of its replacement by free-choice pair bonding has to do with the obsolescence of the extended family in late capitalism, but since this is tantamount to saying that Love can be reduced to Money, no one listens. In India (the most disco nation on earth) Love is a madness, an obsession, and is broadcast like the words of a dictator from every paan stall and rickshaw stand, every transistor radio and billboard and TV tower. While Arjun tried to concentrate on public key cryptography or the Hungarian naming convention, it kept knocking on his bedroom door like an irritating kid sister. Will you come out and play with me? He would have paid no attention to it (after all, what could be vaguer and less logical?)

but sickeningly all its absurd rituals and intricacies seemed to lead back to something he wanted, something he had grown to crave with a longing bordering on panic.

Touch.

Love was the price of touch. Love was the maze through which you had to find your way. In the May heat, when the heavy air was already like a hand on his body as he lay awake at night, he could feel the need for another person as a hard ache inside, an alien presence which had formed in his chest like a tumour.

As somebody who interacted with people almost exclusively through his computer, he knew that he had limited his options, touchwise. In the absence of practical lab work, he concentrated on the theory. When he was not studying he was at the cinema and on the journeys from one to the other he ran simulations in the form of daydreams, preparing for the moment when he would take his place among the lovers, when he would dare to open the door that separated him from tactile life. Unconsciously he assembled a kind of composite, an ideal girl collaged together from bits of film stars and long-range glimpses of students at the nearby girls' college. Hair and eyes. Floating chiffon. Laughter.

Lila Zohar.

As far as it is possible to piece together, the sequence of events runs like this.

At 21.15 PST *badmAsh* appears on *#vxconvention*, which at the time is running on a server belonging to a private Internet service provider in Indonesia. By 21.28 PST he has completed a negotiation with a regular user known as *Elrick21* to swap a copy of a packetsniffing utility for a compressed file containing a list of around a million email addresses, the kind of list that spammers use to send people messages about penis enlargement, great investment opportunities, requests for urgent business assistance and hardcore pornography. In return for the home phone number of pro golfer Tiger Woods (which *badmAsh* acquired as part of a batch in a previous trade, and which *Elrick21* thinks 'would be cool just to have'), he also acquires a list of a dozen or so IP addresses belonging (claims

Elrick21) to computers on to which, unknown to their owners, he has installed a piece of software known as a remote access trojan.

Between 21.32 and 21.37 PST *badmAsh* attempts to communicate with these machines. Only one responds, a PC physically located in the *banlieux* of Paris which its owner, a junior doctor called Patrice, has hooked up to a broadband connection so he can play Second World War flight sim games. Patrice sometimes thinks he would rather be a fighter ace than a medic with a crummy apartment in a bad part of town. Patrice tends to leave his computer on all the time. Right now (it is early on Thursday morning in Paris) he is still at the hospital, and so is not present to watch *badmAsh* establish communication with the trojan, send a set of commands to his machine and take control of his email software.

Between 06.50 and 09.23 CEST, the time when Patrice returns, spots through a haze of tiredness that something weird is happening and pulls the power plug out of the wall, his computer sends email in a constant stream, contacting hundreds of thousands of people around the world to say

Hi. I saw this and thought of you.

At 14.05 KST fifteen-year-old Kim Young Sam, who is playing truant from his English class at Seoul Science High School, comes back to his bedroom with a bowl of microwaved instant noodles and wonders why he has mail from France. He opens it and clicks on the attachment. Nothing happens. Ten minutes later, when his computer sends copies of the email to everyone in his address book, he does not notice because he has fallen asleep.

Kelly Degrassi, insomniac, mother, receptionist at the offices of the Holy Mount Zion church in Fort Scott, Kansas, opens and clicks.

Darren Pinkney (dairy farmer, Ballarat, Australia) clicks.

Altaaf Malik (student, Lila Zohar fan, Hyderabad, India) clicks and is disappointed. No pictures.

Ten minutes after the first mail went out from Patrice's computer, forty more people have unknowingly distributed it to their friends and contacts. Half an hour later 800 have done so. By the time Patrice phones technical support at his Internet service provider to say that he thinks something might be wrong with his connection, *Lila01* has made her way around the world. □

GRANTA

IN TIME
OF WAR
Philip Hensher

Philip Hensher was born in south London, where he still lives. He was educated at Oxford and Cambridge, where his doctorate was on eighteenth-century English painting, and worked for six years as a clerk in the House of Commons. His novels are 'Other Lulus' (1994), 'Kitchen Venom' (1996) which won a Somerset Maugham Award, 'Pleasured' (1998) and 'The Mulberry Empire' (2002) which was shortlisted for the W. H. Smith Literary Award. His short stories are collected as 'The Bedroom of the Mister's Wife' (1999). In addition he wrote the libretto for Thomas Adès's opera 'Powder Her Face'. He 'is the youngest writer in the "Oxford Companion to English Literature", "Who's Who", and A. S. Byatt's "Oxford Book of the English Short Story"'.

The Germans had only stayed one night. Fred was glad of it. They had arrived in a mood of resentful ruddiness, and had kept it up until their departure the next morning. Here, at the southern end of India, they had seemed discordant and unwelcome. Fred's eye had grown used to a different human scale, of seven-stone Dravidians in crowds, and even his morning reflection in the wardrobe mirror had started to strike him as indecent. The manager of the lakeside hotel, perpetually tapping away in his office, trying to get onto the Internet, had apparently taken the same view. Far from being pleased at this addition to his only guest, he had looked the two Germans up and down and done his best to get rid of them immediately; he refused to offer them any discount although the hotel was empty, and when they grudgingly gave way—there were no other hotels for miles— he showed them to the worst room. Fred had glimpsed it when the door had been left open earlier that day, and knew it was horrid, dark and dirty, with a view over the kitchen dustbins. It was quite unlike his top floor room, empty and light with a balcony giving over the bay. Perhaps it was kept for such a purpose as this, and a minor colony of cockroaches tenderly nurtured with titbits.

The war, a few hundred miles to the north of here, had emptied the hotels of India. All that long hot night Fred sat by the side of the lake, thinking nothing very much, enjoying each new eruption of complaint from the Germans over the food, the towels, the beds, the light-switches. It was as interesting as observing the battles of small-scale wildlife. They ignored him entirely. There was the noise, calm as milk, of the lake lapping at the shore beyond the villa's veranda, and, he knew, absolute starry darkness. Moonless unfeeling felt. And in the morning, when the Germans paid their bill with voluble outrage and departed in a taxi, a white Ambassador which with its squashed rounded front and faint edge of engine complaint reminded him as always of an old boxer trundling into a boastful retirement, Fred and the manager enjoyed a moment of sly, unspoken satisfaction. The manager sat on one of the benches, and raised a smiling eyebrow at his only guest. For a moment they sat companionably listening to the car groan up the track, the ghosts of two quite different smiles on their faces. And, when the car's noise had quite faded away, the manager turned to the lake and visibly gave himself up to the luxuriant, old-fashioned poetry of the day. It was as if he were quite alone; Fred found that obscurely flattering. Yes, on the whole he thought he would stay a while longer here.

When people told Fred that he was a dizzy tart, he could not plausibly contradict them. But if they referred, as they so often did with mild distaste, to his 'gang', his 'crowd', his 'cronies', he was in the habit of giving a short smile and say 'It's more of a posse, really.' He was always rather pleased to know that the arrival or assembly of the posse in one of their five regular London bars attracted not just attention, but often alarm. They had gravitated towards Fred, one by one, until he was at the centre of a little court; noisy, handsome, and scathing, they were the object of envy from strangers who, finding them impermeable by duller or plainer applicants, generally described them as a clique. Fred was rather thrilled by that, and even egged on acquaintances when they voiced their resentment; he had always preferred the company of foreigners to that of his own nationality, and the posse, made up as it was of half a dozen nationalities, might have been assembled from the far corners of the earth for the sole purpose of making him shine in public. His most cherished evenings were those which began at eight in a Soho bar, and ended twelve hours later, as the posse lay about on the sofas of some bewildered boy they had somehow acquired on their yellow-brick route, and shouted, indefatigably, with laughter.

As the years had gone by, however, the posse began to shrink, as one after the other, the foreigners took a graceful bow, and returned to their birthplaces, summoned by promotion, love or duty. Christian, who for years had been intermittently pursuing some tiny academic point in the British Library, finally found the munificence of the German government exhausted, and had to take a job as an administrator in the Pinakothek at Dresden. Max went to Chicago for three months to take the lead in a new play, was 'discovered', and never came back. Each departure was marked by a Soho bender in the grand style, and from time to time a new member of the posse was acknowledged to fill a gap. Still, Fred's posse was not what it had been, and sometimes, at thirty-five, he was uncomfortably aware that those who had remained were the least adventurous and dashing of the original group. If they had done very well in a crowd, as Fred's intimates they were apt to disappoint. From always being the one who would pursue the evening to its last possible moment, Fred became the one who, quite often, would go home before closing time. When two of the staunchest members of the posse fell in love with each other, and starting living a life of quiet domesticity in which hellraising had no place, Fred had said to himself that enough, really, was enough. He decided to take radical action before he found that his social life had diminished to a quiet pint up the road on his own in a cardigan, farty old Alsatian at his feet.

Fred had always longed to have a career of a random and implausible nature, the despair of his parents, but in the event had worked steadily for the same clothing chain for fifteen years. He had slowly risen to a position of some importance, managing all the chain's London shops. Just as he had decided that the state of his social life justified some radical alteration, an event took place which would, he quickly realized, make this possible. The firm he worked for, which for many years had existed almost outside fashion, the dowdy butt of urban jokes and the safe choice of country matrons, was acquired by a conglomerate. The conglomerate was newly under the control of a viciously successful young American designer. Fred knew what that meant.

It would not be true to say that Fred, in those fifteen years, had not changed. In some respects, he had altered a great deal. His name, which at school had seemed a name which might have been borrowed—and actually was—from a great-uncle, somehow changed its nature at some point in the early Eighties. As Freddie, Fred rode the snobbish aspirations of the time; it was now perfectly incredible to him that he had once gone to nightclubs with a cricket sweater draped around his neck. Later, as the fashion changed, he reverted to Fred, which in the interim had become a name of fascinating urban style. With his name, he scrupulously altered his dress, his behaviour, even his accent.

Two months after the takeover, he was summoned by the new director of the subsidiary—a mild, nervous man whose milky blue eyes, disconcertingly suggesting, of all things, grief, would not connect with Fred's. Fred learnt, after hearing a great deal about the future of the company, that he was being sacked. The future of the company, naturally, now could not interest him and afterwards he wondered why the man had told him about it.

The news did not surprise him. He was one of the last of the long-serving staff of the company to be dismissed in this way. Nor did it worry or frighten him; he saw in this sacking an opportunity to carry out the change in his life he had come to see as necessary. The settlement was extremely generous, amounting to fifteen months' pay; the new owners were impatient to begin work, and had little stomach for legal arguments.

With this neat exchange of years for months, and months for money, Fred saw a way to do something he had always wanted to do, and prepared for departure. He let his flat, bought a plane ticket, and packed his bags. He had it in mind, for the first time in his life, to take a holiday for some other purpose than acquiring a suntan.

'It was either there or Morocco,' he said to the posse. 'There was just this great deal going on with flights to India for some reason.'

'That'll be because they're in the middle of a war,' someone said. 'You dizzy tart. At least you've got the combats, I suppose.'

'Of course,' he said, 'I'm not about to discover myself, or anything.'

They grinned at the idea that there was anything much of Fred to be discovered. Like the globe, by the beginning of the twenty-first century that terrain had been thoroughly gone over by all sorts of amateur explorers.

Fred had arrived at the hotel in the dark. It had seemed like a good idea, back in England, to have a butch unplanned sort of holiday, rather than one with coaches and an itinerary. His vague general idea of working around the coast of the southern half of India had deposited him at Kollam towards the end of the afternoon. He didn't quite know why he'd left the train here; perhaps it was for no better reason than that every time he heard someone mention the town, they gave it a different pronunciation. Quilon, Kwee Lung, Co-Lamb, Column. The ragged guide book had not been enthusiastic, saying only that it was a convenient point from which to explore the surrounding countryside, and Fred almost immediately saw his mistake. It was a dirty, squat, scrubby little town, like any other. He hailed an auto-rickshaw, and told the driver to take him to a good hotel; tomorrow he would set off to somewhere better. 'Where are you coming from?' the driver asked after a mile or so. 'Trichy,' Fred said absently; the driver fell into a puzzled silence, but it was five minutes or so before Fred saw his mistake, and said 'I mean, I come from England.' The driver left the answer where it lay, wary of a man who was unsure of his origins, and they drove on in silence.

There were, it seemed, no hotels of any sort here, and they drove out of the town into dark, wooded country. The driver seemed confident, and Fred did not query their direction. 'Not very Thomas Cook,' he said to himself, but it was hard to be ironic on your own. After half an hour or so, they turned off the main road onto a rough track. By now it was dark, and the only light came from a few bungalows set back from the road. The few people they passed peered curiously into the back of the rickshaw; a European, now, in this time of war, counted as an event for them. Drowsily, Fred entertained the possibility that there was no hotel here; that he was about to be robbed and murdered.

But the rickshaw climbed the slope, whinnied a little at the crest of the hill, and, taking a steep descent into almost complete darkness, came all at once upon the villa. The rickshaw stopped, and the driver unloaded the bags. Fred offered him a hundred rupees, which he took without comment and drove off without waiting as the manager came out. Previous hotels had treated him like instant royalty on his arrival, with a train of anxious-eyed bearers carrying ornamental drinks and floral garlands, promises of reduced rates and volumes of handwritten commendations. This man seemed quite indifferent; he did not even call Fred 'my friend'. No one offered to carry Fred's bag for him; indeed, no one else emerged as they went into the hotel. Still, it proved cheap, and the top-floor room plainly furnished and clean. The silence all around was absolute; for one night it would do. He went early to bed, and slept without dreaming until eight in the morning.

Fred made his way downstairs to breakfast. He wandered about the ground floor of the hotel, looking for something which might be a breakfast room before noticing that on the lawn in front of the hotel at the edge of the lake a single table had been laid with white linen, clean and much-darned, and plastic-handled cutlery. There was no one around. He sat down, looking at the lake, the low sun, the forested hill at the far shore. In a moment, someone appeared. It was not the man from the night before, but a younger man. His hair was slicked down, and he appeared to be wearing a purple velvet suit and a green cravat. He was carrying a pot of coffee and a jug of milk, which he set down in front of Fred. Without inquiring further, he went back into the hotel, and in stages, brought out a breakfast; a plate of that pink-orange Indian fruit with its cotton texture and faint feety smell of Parmesan, a salty glass of brine-coloured lime juice, and a hot dish, a soft pancake filled with a sort of potato curry. Fred ate it all steadily, his eyes on the eventless lake. It was almost like being in hospital, your life and your meals going on without your making any kind of decision or request. But more beautiful. A boat drifted into view, a small canoe with a couple of fishermen in it. They raised their hands, and Fred waved back. There was nothing to do, and nothing to think. When he had finished, and the dishes cleared away by the velvet dandy, he lit a cigarette peacefully.

The day passed without narration or commentary, and for most of it, Fred sat by the lake, watching the sun move through the sky. He fetched his book, but after a few minutes, his attention lapsed; there was nothing in the landscape to watch, but all the same he watched it. Some time after ten, he remembered his camera, and got that from the room. Over the next hour, he took fifteen or so photographs, hardly moving from his chair; it was just when the view struck him as suddenly beautiful that he raised the camera, and photographed what he saw. Sometimes, he was photographing something new: a cormorant landing on a floating branch, or a fishing boat. But mostly he was photographing the same thing, the lake. He could see how corny the photographs were going to look. It was more like a tribute to beauty than a record of it. Lunch came in the same way breakfast had, without consultation, and it was all delicious. Afterwards he fell asleep for a time in the sun. He considered going for a walk, and actually got up and strolled round the grounds; but then decided that it was too near sunset, and sat down to read a page or two more. The sunset held his attention like pornography. It was odd to see a whole day like this, and when it was over, he gave a sigh, and went inside to shower and rest before dinner. He had more or less forgotten that he was supposed to go on today, to the next place. Beyond the lake— beyond the hill—out there—the world was burning, the earth was beginning to roar. For the first time, perhaps, in his life, Fred felt something of this; felt something of all that, out there.

The next day the Germans came, and quickly went. Apart from that, the days passed in much the same way, with no kind of disturbance. It was only on the fourth, or perhaps fifth, day in the hotel that he came down in the evening and there were two tables set for dinner, and Fred felt a small tang of surprise and disappointment. He had grown used to the hotel being at his disposal alone. Five minutes later, a girl emerged. She was white, densely tanned, and tiny in her backpackers' vest and khaki cargo pants; she looked at him, her nose wrinkling, and grinned. He started mildly—he supposed he must have been staring—as if some unobserved animal had slinked itself about his calves.

'You had a quiet afternoon,' she said. 'Snoring, you were, when I got here. I thought, there's a man without a care in the world.'

'You should have woken me up,' Fred said, absurdly.

The girl raised an eyebrow. 'I don't suppose you've ever met someone who the first thing they said was about your snoring.'

'No,' Fred said, reflecting that this was not so; that quite often, the first proper conversation he had with someone had begun with a breakfast complaint about his snoring, after the brisk Soho pickup, the taxi snog, the efficient one-off shag. No, it was quite often the first thing someone said to him. 'Second impressions are best. Shall I sit here?'

'Don't mind,' she said. Fred picked up his knives and forks, and transferred them to her table. For some reason, everything seemed to strike this girl as faintly amusing. 'Where have you come from?'

'England,' Fred said.

'Just now, I meant,' she said.

'Oh, right,' he said. Where have you come from, he thought; where are you coming from; where do you come from. Odd, that. A silence fell, and then he suddenly noticed that it was his silence.

'Sorry,' she said. 'Boring question, I know. People always say that when they meet you here, where have you come from, where are you going. Sorry.'

'That's okay,' Fred said. 'Madurai, it was. No, Trichy.'

She made a gesture with her hand, as if winding up an invisible crank, encouraging him to go on. 'It was nice,' Fred said helplessly, and smiled, shrugging.

'How long's it been?' the girl said.

'Long?' Fred said.

'You're funny,' the girl said. 'Don't look so scared, I'm not going to eat you. I mean since you've been in India, since you've opened your mouth and had a conversation, you know, with words. Me, it's just a couple of weeks, I'm still normal, I can still talk, you know, but I've seen it before. After a bit, you get so you can't talk or you can't stop talking, one or the other. I've seen it before, don't worry, I don't mind. Oh boy, that man, where was it, Madras, I just said hello, and it was like you'd pulled a plug out, he couldn't shut up, and then, half an hour later, following me down the road, couldn't shut up. You're the other way, I can tell. Hello!' she said abruptly in a Minnie Mouse voice, grinning and waving with both hands from three feet away. 'My name's Carrie, what's yours?'

'Fred,' Fred said. He was appalled.

'Ooooh,' the girl said. 'Here comes dinner.' But then the waiter, who had been coming out of the villa with a tray of food, appeared to think twice and turned back. 'Ah well,' she said, and a silence fell. 'Why don't you say something, then?'

'You know,' Fred said. 'People are always saying to me, why don't you say something. Well, not always, but I can remember a few times when someone's said it to me and I couldn't think of anything to say back. I did German at school, years ago now, and I don't know why—well, yes, I do, it was that or geography or technical drawing and I thought you'll never know when you'll need a bit of a foreign language, do you. Four years I did it, but the only thing I can remember is the one afternoon Mrs Thornton, she was the German teacher, was saying *Fur um durch gegen entlang bis ohne* and what's the last one, Frederick? And I just sat there and then she said Why don't you say something and I said What would you like me to say. Funny really because there have been quite a lot of occasions in my life when someone has said to me Why don't you say something and I always say back What would you like me to say. And you know what. They never tell you. There was once a boy, and I'd been seeing him for a while, a year or two even, suddenly said to me that he'd met someone else, and then we had the why-don't-you and what-would-you-like conversation, Richard his name was. But what would you say? Good luck, I hate you, oh, fancy that. And then a month or two back, when I got the sack, I knew it was coming, I did, so I didn't have anything much to say, and my boss said just that. Why don't you say something. Funny really. It doesn't matter who it is, but they tell you something; you know it's coming, whatever it is, or you don't know it's coming, but there's nothing to say. And they want you to say something. They always do. And you don't know what to say, and they don't know what to say, but still they say it. Why don't you say something. Why don't you say something. And sometimes you want to shut your eyes and close your mouth and say nothing, because there's nothing to say. That's what I think.'

Fred stopped talking for a moment; he was almost out of breath. It was eight in the morning, the next day, and he was alone in his room before breakfast. A sound had attracted his attention, outside, and he cocked his head and slowly lowered the fist with which he had been making his point to the empty room. The bed was rumpled with his sleep, the blue canvas bedspread tossed to the floor; on the bedside table was the green plastic flask of boiled water, his watch, and his untouched book. The noise came again, a call. Before he went through the open balcony door, he looked quickly around the room. He didn't know how loud he had been—it would have been nice if there had been a telephone there to blame if his monologue had been overheard. Stealthily, like someone stalking a cockroach in the dark, he went step by step through the doors, onto the balcony, into the day. Down there was the girl from last night, her face upturned like a flower, her hands behind her back. He waved uncertainly down at her.

'Hello, Mr Fred,' she called up. 'Look!' She spun round and pointed, there, there, there, lake, trees, villa, before turning back to him with a great smile. The morning woke again for him with the clean magic it had displayed the day before, and she had woken it for him with her sorceress pointing. 'Look!'

'I know,' Fred called, smiling despite himself. 'Yes, I know.'

'Oh, you're dressed,' Carrie said. 'Come down. I was just thinking—'

'Hang on,' Fred said. It was true, it was beautiful; the long lax passage of the days had veiled the lake's beauty without him noticing, and the girl had shown it to him again. He hurried, gratefully. As he came out onto the lawn where she stood, she was already talking.

'—wouldn't be a bore, I mean, I was going to head off today, but I might as well stay, and I've got no plans otherwise. You're not going on today are you? You didn't say. I mean why not. It could be fun, the guide says it's fun.'

'I'd love to,' Fred said, divining that at some point she had suggested something. 'But I wasn't listening.'

'You're funny,' Carrie said. 'You're not going on anywhere today, that's all I was saying.'

'No,' Fred said. He didn't know how long she'd been standing there, but now that there were two of them the velvet fop came out to lay the first stages of their breakfast.

'So I was wondering,' Carrie said, 'if you'd like to go somewhere together today. It could be fun. Did you get a newspaper today? I didn't get one.'

'No,' Fred said. 'I don't think they give you one here.' He stopped talking, and just looked. 'It's lovely here.'

'Laavly,' Carrie said, making a joke of it.

After breakfast, they had agreed to drive to Kollam together, and somehow Fred didn't mind the idea now. He had never been a solitary person, and already his lone travelling started to appear like a curious and uncharacteristic interlude, like—what it was—a holiday. He waited on the steps of the villa. Carrie might prove the beginning of some new posse, as if in a week or two he and she and five others, friends yet to be made, would be hilariously trolling the bars of some South Indian city.

It was true, what she had said, that this hotel did not supply you with a morning newspaper. Every hotel he had stayed in until now had done so; the luxurious and rather extravagant mock-Moghul palace in Madras, the overstaffed but dusty towers in Trichy, Madurai, Tanjore. They had been local papers, but still they were the same stories, the same slow terror that was on the front pages of every newspaper in the world in these black months. He had never been a habitual reader of newspapers; he preferred the sort of magazines which depicted the lives and taste and marriages of rich people. Even *Hello!*, however, seemed to find itself discussing threats and violence and bloodshed among distant people; even breakfast television's chipper sequence of innuendo and natter was intruded into, once an hour, by a minute or two of sinister declarations, of brisk body-counts. It could not be avoided, the outside world, and Fred had not missed the free newspaper.

But all the same in his mind there was something which had not been there before, an expanse stretching behind the immediate and particular events of his life and his journey. It was like the lake, stretching away like a backcloth. Sometimes, in the last few days, he had found himself envisaging the crump and soar of munitions flying over borders only a few hundred miles to the north of the quiet Keralan lake. At first the images of war were as clean and swift as Hollywood fireworks, but he could not prevent the camera in his mind zooming in; the imagined kapow of the rockets always seguing into the noises people made. The thoughts ran their course, and perhaps for the first time in his life Fred found the vivid imagery giving way to intense fruitless speculation about the wrongs and grievances which had led to this. He had not been paying attention, and could not answer his own questions, never having thought that they might one day become urgent to him. The questions would not go away. It surprised him; he surprised himself.

Waiting for Carrie outside the empty hotel, the train of thought ran its course, but then it was exactly the unenvisaged emptiness of India which encouraged such speculations. Involuntary and inept, they were provoked by absences; the painful absence of cadres of European tourists. The floral tributes were disconcerting enough, but it was a single, recurrent gesture which most unnerved Fred. As he walked down a road in a temple town, perhaps, a row of faces would turn slowly and watch his progress, and on his return, would monitor that, too. It happened again and again; it was like a slow-motion film of the crowd at Wimbledon swivelling their necks. The acclamations and curiosity his presence inspired puzzled him at first—it felt more like a burden than a pleasure, this sudden celebrity—but then he had noticed that there were no other Europeans around, or very few. It was then that he started to think about the war.

Fred was not a stupid man, but the furniture of his mind was randomly and unhelpfully arranged, as if it had been supplied by others; a flat-pack of furniture parts without the tools necessary for assembly, and instructions only in Japanese. And perhaps the sense that his mental furniture had been supplied by others was not so false. He felt that what he knew had been generously donated by the posse and people like them, and he had acquired very little by his own efforts. His knowledge was spasmodic and surprising. For instance, Fred knew, or felt he knew, a good deal about eighteenth-century Venetian painting, or at least many of the names of the painters; not something one would have predicted from his appearance, but the knowledge that, say, there were three separate painters called Tiepolo had been imparted by long hours listening to Christian talking about his studies. It was all rather like that. None of it, apparently, had arrived by the more conventional routes of reading a book or a newspaper, and now Fred wondered how it was that he had ever come to know the name of the prime minister without, as far as he remembered, anyone ever mentioning it over a vodka-and-red-bull in a gay bar.

Most painfully, he realized that he knew nothing about politics and nothing about this war which now seemed so urgent to him. The acquisition of such knowledge had certainly been circumscribed by the fact that the posse, in general, tended to regard the subject, if it ever arose, as evidence of social unacceptability, of the speaker being, as they said, *sad*. The long years of neglect had not struck Fred until he was alone in India, without even the doubtful aid of the posse to keep him up to date with information about the state of the world. In the first stages of his holiday he had taken to reading the newspapers left outside his door in previous hotels. He made an effort, but it was too late. The stories, with their long and lordly allusions to the BJP and the STU and the FRD ('Fred!' he thought, like the dizzy tart he was) were opaque and, over a series of brow-wrinkling breakfasts, did not become less so; it was like switching on a soap opera twenty-six years into its run, or listening to an inconsiderately detailed conversation between friends about people you didn't know and would never meet. On the third such attempt Fred's attention had wandered towards an impenetrable but well-drawn cartoon of two politicians grappling with an octopus—he didn't have a clue who the politicians were, but he could recognize an octopus when he saw one—when he became aware that a waiter and the waiter's underling were hovering by him.

'Komflix?' the waiter said.

'Yes,' Fred said faintly. 'Yes, lots of conflicts in the newspaper.'

'Komflix,' the waiter said more decisively, and went away. Five minutes later he returned with a bowl of some yellow sugary mush.

Fred accepted it and gave it a forensic poke or two. Cornflakes. Bugger.

The driver came promptly at ten, and the driver's inquiries began while Fred and Carrie were still settling themselves.

'You have left your children behind sir madam?' the driver said.

'No, no children,' Fred said.

'Honeymoon?' the driver asked.

'No,' Carrie said. 'No, we're not married to each other, we're just friends. We just met.'

The driver digested this. 'You are married, though, sir?'

'I was married,' Fred said. 'My wife died, though, five years ago. She was killed in a car crash.'

A reflective silence fell in the car. Poor Fred! Poor wife of Fred! And then Carrie, all at once, without any encouragement, told Fred the story of her life.

Fred had only taken this journey once, in the opposite direction, and although he remembered it being a long trip, it seemed longer today. Twice, he interrupted Carrie's story to lean forward and make sure that the driver really was taking them to Kollam. Perhaps there were, after all, no variations in pronunciation; perhaps Kollam and Quilon and the rest were in fact different towns. But the driver twice gave that side-to-side wobble of the head, whatever it meant. Not yes, not no; probably no more than 'I am proposing to rook you of an embarrassingly small sum of money'.

It might not even be that. It was so strange, time; it passed more slowly when everything was interesting; it passed more slowly when everything was boring. Outside the car, everything he saw was interesting—cripples, crops, crowds, temples. Inside the car, Carrie was talking about a boy who loved her more than she loved him which was a bit sad when you came to think of it.

'And that's how I got here,' Carrie said eventually. Fred looked up. They had come to a halt. She shrugged, smiling a brave practised sort of smile.

'I wait for you,' the driver said.

'No,' Fred said. 'We don't know how long we'll be.'

'Best to wait,' the driver said. 'No problem.'

'It's best if we pay now,' Fred said.

'Pay later,' the driver said. 'I can wait, no problem. One hour, two hours, I wait.'

Later, Carrie suddenly said 'That's so sad.' Fred was watching a bullock in the middle of the road, and the devout graceful choreography of the flocks of orange rickshaws around it. First, he thought Carrie was summing up her life story; then he realized she must be talking about the driver waiting.

'Not really,' he said.

'It is, though,' she said earnestly. 'I'm sorry, I didn't know about your wife. You don't have to talk about it if you don't want to.'

'My wife?' Fred said. 'Oh, my wife, the car crash. No, I always say that—I should have warned you—it's not true. I just say that.'

'It's not true?'

'No, not at all. I only say it because it shuts them up. They always ask if you're married, and then just keep on asking and asking, but if you tell them your wife's dead, they stop out of respect.'

Carrie just turned and stared. 'It's not true?'

'Afraid not.'

She stopped, and gaped, and then, all at once, began laughing uncontrollably. Around her, Indians stared at the laughing woman.

'We seem complicated to them,' Fred went on. 'A boy said that to me, a few days ago, in Madurai. "Complicated, Europeans," he said. I didn't know what he meant. "Wife, girlfriend, boyfriend, divorced—" he said. You could see what he meant. They get married and then they have children and then that's it. We seem to have complicated sorts of arrangements. They understand a dead wife, though.' Fred shrugged. The boy in Madurai, he reflected, had not in fact said 'boyfriend'.

'I think that's terrible,' Carrie said. 'You're terrible, Mr Fred. You really are. What's your dead wife's name?'

'Fifi,' Fred said. 'They don't often get so far as to ask that, though. It really does shut them up.'

'Fifi, Christ,' Carrie said. 'And no wife? None at all?'

'No, none,' Fred said. 'Sorry, I should have warned you. They always ask. You should try it. It really works.'

'We can't both say it,' Carrie said. 'It would look like the widow's outing. And they wouldn't believe me. I just don't look the type. I don't look like I've known pain and suffering.'

'Do I?'

Carrie turned and looked him up and down, as if he were a horse she was proposing to buy. 'Oh, I would say so,' she said. 'Deep pools of suffering, lots of silent pain in your soul, yes, I would definitely say so. You're deep, Mr Fred, deep and secret and sorrowful. No one ever told you you're a man of mystery?'

'You see that clock?' Fred said, overpoweringly embarrassed. 'It says here it was put up in 1911 when George V visited.'

'Swot.'

Deep pools of suffering and silent pain in the soul; and the clock, a fifteen-foot replica of Big Ben, reminded you that some things were only good when they were very big. Dicks, for instance, he attempted—but no, you couldn't be smutty on your own either. Fred turned his attention to a roadside fruit stall. It was a sad little stall with just three sorts of fruit on it, each arranged in a series of neat pyramids on sheets of newspaper. By the stall, a boy squatted. All around the town, the forests grew, laden with fruit; the oranges and durian and mangoes glowed in the leafy dark like festival lanterns. But on the streets of India there was only warty, dried, shrunken fruit to be had, piled up in hopeful pyramids. He supposed the best went straight to Sainsbury's, and the children of India reached five foot two and stopped growing.

He was about to suggest buying some oranges to Carrie, but she had been taken by something else. On the other side of the road, two figures were making their way through the crowd; Europeans, a boy and a girl like them, but weighed down with rucksacks—the girl, who led the way, was actually carrying two, the second over her front. The boy was wearing the thin Indian skirt, the lunghi, and both had beaded and braided hair. Under their loads, they were bent down towards the earth, and did not see Fred or Carrie, or seem to notice how anyone was looking at them. Carrie, her mouth open, watched them go towards the railway station.

'Someone you met?' Fred said, when they had disappeared.

'Oh, no,' Carrie said. 'I was just looking. They wouldn't want to speak to us, anyway, I know the type. You know, they've come to see the real India, they're not going to speak to someone just because they've got the same white face. And they're not tourists, they're travellers.'

'I'm a tourist,' Fred said. It seemed odd to him that nothing Indian seemed to interest Carrie; only him and other tourists. 'I go to beauty spots and send postcards home and I buy souvenirs. I'm too old to be a traveller. I thought you were a traveller though.'

'Oh, no,' Carrie said. 'I'm too rich to be a traveller. You'd know I was a tourist if you'd seen my luggage.'

'I was asleep. Do you like India?'

'Ooh, yes,' Carrie said. 'I can't believe how cheap it is.'

'Yes,' Fred agreed, though whenever India had started to mean anything to him, it was the glimpse of a monkey cavorting through a wild orchard of roadside pepper-trees, not cheap but unbuyable, free. 'Yes, I like a bargain.'

They set off, walking in a slow way without map or plan. There was nothing much to be seen in this town. They had different guide books, but when they paused for a moment to compare possibilities, they laughed to find out that both books said only that Kollam was a useful place from which to explore a network of canals. Not much of a recommendation for a town, Fred said, that you could easily get out of it. So they wandered aimlessly, and soon found themselves in a street full of ironmongers.

'I started this game,' Carrie said, as Fred was examining a tiffin-pail with a degree of scrupulous curiosity he had never, quite, been capable of faced with even the lewdest of temple statuary. 'It was in Madras. Every day, I'd sit and watch the backpackers go up and down, and after a while, I started a competition, you know, for Backpacker of the Day. I gave them points and the one who came out on top won the competition for the day.'

'What do you think that's for?' Fred asked.

'I don't know,' Carrie said. It was a round tin box. 'You could keep things in it. You're not listening.'

'I'm listening,' Fred said.

'They got a point if they were carrying a copy of *Lonely Planet* while they were walking, and for stupid hair, and for wearing Indian clothes and looking stupid in them, and for the size of their rucksacks. There was one boy who had a rucksack which was so big he couldn't get through the door of the backpacker cafe in Madras. And for having a conversation about where they'd just come from and where they were going to and telling you where you should go to and where you should have come from, that was another point.'

'I've never met anyone like you before,' Fred said. He surprised himself, saying that; and it was not true. It would have been more true about any other person in this town; but those people, watching them as they walked, those he had not met.

Carrie stopped. It was just another ironmonger's, and what she picked up was just another tiffin pail. The shopkeeper, at the back of the dingy little space, wearily raised himself from his accounts book to deal with them. When she set it down, and turned to Fred, he thought he saw what might be the beginnings of tears in her eyes. 'Don't say that, Mr Fred,' she said. 'I'm not going to fall in love with you. I always know whether I'm going to or not, straight after I meet someone.'

'I didn't mean that,' Fred said. He was astonished, and now he felt that perhaps he been right after all. No, he had never met anyone like this before, and he was glad of it.

'You don't know what you meant,' Carrie said. Anyone else might have sounded angry. 'Let's talk about something else.'

'Okay,' Fred said. 'Those backpackers, those ones, there. How many points would you give them?'

'Oh, we've done that,' Carrie said. 'Well, all right, four. Maybe five if they were Swedish. I know. Do you know what language they speak here? No, nor me.'

Fred attracted the attention of the shopkeeper. 'Malayalam, apparently,' he said.

'Ma, lay, a, lam,' Carrie said slowly. 'Hello! How do you say hello in Malayalam?'

The shopkeeper told them; they repeated. 'And goodbye? And thank you? And how do you ask, How much is that?'

At this last, the shopkeeper produced a bubbling stream of syllables. He gazed at them with a schoolmaster strictness, waiting for their repetition.

'All right,' Carrie said aggressively, turning her head as they left the shop. 'We were only asking. Hey, Mr Fred. Will you buy me some oranges?'

Fred was tickled. 'They're not that nice,' he said soberly. 'I bought some a few days ago, but they were old and dry and full of pips. You don't want them really. The thing is, I only bought them because I liked how they'd set them out. But they weren't very nice.'

'I'm trying to guess what you do for a living,' Carrie said.

'I'd tell you if you asked,' Fred said, reflecting that she hadn't asked.

'Whatever it is, it's something where you get to say, I liked how they'd set them out, all day long.'

'That could be anything, though,' he said.

'No, not anything,' Carrie said. 'For instance—' she thought, '— for instance I don't think vets say it that often.'

'I like how you've set them out,' Fred said. 'Animal medicines, maybe. Or a line of anaesthetized hamsters.'

That was the way in which the afternoon passed. They looked at everything, and it all looked back at them. They had a glass each of iodine-flavoured Limca in the empty dining room of a blowsy hotel with posters of Switzerland on the walls; Carrie said the smell of the drink reminded her of swimming lessons at school. She had not had it before, and couldn't promise that she'd have it again. 'It's nice, India,' she said disconsolately. 'It's not as nice as Australia. It's nicer than China though.'

'Have you been?' Fred said, glimpsing the United Nations or something, all in a row, arranged in order of niceness.

'China smells,' Carrie said.

On the way back to the car, she started a game, of sorts.

'Would you rather be blind or deaf?'

'I've played this one before. Blind. People are sorry for you. They get annoyed with deaf people.'

'Would you rather be a hammer or a nail?'

'A hammer.'

'That's horrible.'

'But only because I'm really a nail.'

'That's okay then. Would you rather be rich or famous?'

'Rich.'

'You're horrible. Would you rather have a cat or a dog?'

'A cat. You don't have to bother so much about them.'

'A cat,' she said, and from the way she just repeated what he'd said, he could see that she was taking in the possibility that horrible was what he might actually be. A cat; because you don't have to put yourself out on its behalf. It was true, but also horrible.

'Is that it?' Fred said.

'No,' Carrie said. 'Would you rather be gay or black?'

'Gay or black?'

'Okay, would you rather have a dead wife called Fifi or no wife at all?'

'The question doesn't arise,' Fred said, his heart hardening. In any case there was the driver waiting for them. How nice was India, or Fred, or Carrie? Nicer than China?

'You're not going to have to choose between being a hammer and a nail either,' Carrie said. 'The question never arises. That's not the point. Why doesn't it arise?'

'Well, I'm a homosexual,' Fred said, sidling into the car as their driver held the door open. For a moment it seemed as though Carrie was about to get in through the same door, and he started to shift along to make room for her. It was strange to get into a taxi with no shopping. But then she was walking around to the far side of the car after all, with regal, almost ballerina-like steps; the driver, caught by surprise, ran round to open the other door. There was nothing wrong with saying that you were homosexual, but he felt as if he could only have said it to Carrie when his heart felt cold and hard towards her. It made no sense; he knew of no kindness or care in himself which would have prevented him from saying it. She should have said something encouraging and sympathetic as she got into the car, that was the conventional thing, however little he needed encouragement, but in fact what she said was merely 'It wasn't really worth it, was it, that town?' She said it in quite a different voice, and he had to agree; it was, unmistakably, her mother's decisive voice, wherever or whoever her mother might be. He hadn't heard it before.

All the way back, she carried on playing the game, but with a party brightness in her tone which kept him at a distance, obediently choosing at her whim, and it was only when she had been reduced to making him decide whether he would rather be an orchid or a lawn (a lawn, natch) that she finally observed that he might have mentioned it earlier. There was nothing accusing about the way she said it; she simply shrank back a little from her social manner as if deflating. It was an absurd complaint; the fact was banal and presumably conspicuous. All the same, her comment made him see that in her life, his existence would count as in itself interesting and perhaps even pitiable. In London, among the shrinking posse, the fact had been ordinary, and in India the least exotic of his qualities had been his habitual practise of sodomy. It had been years since he had had a conversation like this one. She was doing her best.

'Have you got a boyfriend?' she said, as the car turned off the main road and onto the succession of dirt tracks which led to the hotel.

'No,' Fred said. 'Not my sort of thing, love.'

'I've got a boyfriend,' Carrie said accusingly.

'That's nice for you,' Fred said.

'It is,' Carrie said. 'It's very nice for me.'

'I'm happy on my own,' Fred said.

'And that's nice for you too,' Carrie said.

Then silence fell, and afterwards Fred could never understand how that was. It was as if he had a clear idea of someone, a different Fred, who would change the subject and, at this pitch of hostility, would ask Carrie if she'd seen a newspaper recently. He imagined himself, suddenly well-informed, explaining the international situation to her. There was a Fred in his mind, in the silent car, who could talk about the violence and destruction to the North. If everything, every other thing in his life had been different, he could now at this moment have smoothed things over between them by exposition, setting out the wrongs on each side, the history of grievances lit up as he talked. This was a girl who knew nothing, and that other Fred could have enlarged her life by showing her what she had never listened to; the reason the world was as it was. He had never talked in such a way, and, much as he wished to do so, he could not start now. They travelled in silence, since once her games had come to an end, neither could supply anything in their place. All at once they were together in front of a door—her door, not his—and her key was in her hand.

'I'd never have thought—' she said. 'I mean—' she said, admonishingly '—Valentine's Day.' She shrugged, opened her door, stepped through it, and closed it. To be alone was astonishing. She had been presenting him with choices all the way back, as if there were choices a person could make, but the choice she hadn't offered him was the important one. Would you rather be the person who loves? Or the person who gets to be loved? Would you rather be a man who can talk; or a man who can listen? He asked himself the questions. He didn't know the answers.

How far from home was he? He had no idea. The only unit of measurement he had was the memory of one of the posse—Christian, was it?—moaning that with the prospect of a shag, he'd gone all the way to Brighton, a good hundred kilometres. It had been a funny story; Fred heard Christian's voice, saying 'a good hundred kilometres'. He tried to see London and Brighton on a map, tried to multiply that hundred kilometres over an imagined globe to work out how far India was from London. He couldn't do it. A hell of a distance, though, to travel in order to discover that he was bored with that lulling womanly subject of love, whether one person loved a second more than the second loved the first. Though he had devoted hours of his conversation to the subject, he now felt unutterably bored with its future applications, and felt in any case that nothing much in his life had prepared him to discuss love with authority. Deprived of that, however, he had nothing else to turn to. He could hear the vague rumbling music of inquisitive, knowledgeable speech, but a man who, like him, could not turn those swells and crescendi into words, into an explanation of war and politics and the world, would always be vulnerable to the easy exchange in which someone boringly says 'Do you love me?' and the other boringly replies 'No', before the silence of incapacity falls. Millions of books and films, billions of individual dreams had found love and nothing else interesting enough, and, until now, the prospect of it and its attendant physical acts had been enough to keep him talking, all his life. Carrie shut the door, and he saw the terrible poverty of it. Their lives; there was nothing in them but a CV, and a lot of going on about love.

She wasn't at dinner. He didn't blame her. It didn't seem important; after all, he would see her the next day. The night had descended, and the lake, which had so delighted him, put away for him to play with tomorrow. The dinner, too, which he ate self-consciously and with faintly embarrassed attentiveness, turned out to be exactly the same sequence of dishes as the night before and the night before that. It hadn't disappointed him until now, this unambitious regularity. Carrie had just fallen asleep, he assured himself. But when he came down the next morning, she had gone, and he was, again, the only guest in the hotel. There was a note waiting for him, on the single table set for breakfast on the lawn, in an actressy hand. 'I've gone,' it said. 'I just felt like it. It was so nice yesterday. You never know, maybe—here's an orange for you. C.'

That seemed like an incomprehensible joke, here's an orange for

Philip Hensher

you, and it was true that she was a girl to whom incomprehensible jokes came easily. But after all it seemed that she meant exactly what she said. Perhaps people mostly did. Because here, across the lawn, came the waiter in his green velvet jacket and his silk cravat solicitously bearing before him a single orange, glowing like a jewel, one courtly hand behind his back. Where, when, had she bought it? The waiter placed it on the table and smiled. Fred peeled it and ate it pensively, self-consciously. It was dry and old and full of pips, as he had told her it would be.

'Very good,' he said finally, trying out a smile.

'Another?' the waiter said, and brought his other hand from behind his back, bearing another orange, and as if choreographed, the manager of the hotel, the two cooks, the kitchen boy and two other men, old and bent, who he didn't recognize at all came in solemn procession from the door of the hotel, each of them bearing in each hand an orange with stately precious care. There was no mockery on their faces, no sign that it was anything but rational to request fourteen oranges, but as they approached and piled up the fruit in a perfect pyramid before him, he felt some hostility in the gesture which was not Carrie's, but India's; a gift like the hotels' garlands to show that it was time for their solitary guest to go. He had been inspected, somehow, and shown that he had brought nothing; he felt it was going to take him weeks and months to discover what they so lucidly saw, what it was that he had been given, what he had to take back with him. ☐

298

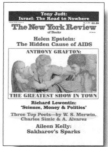

GRANTA

THE DREAMED
Robert McLiam Wilson

Robert McLiam Wilson was born in 1964. He has written three novels: 'Ripley Bogle' (1989), 'Manfred's Pain' (1992) and 'Eureka Street' (1996). He has also written a non-fiction book about poverty in the UK, 'The Dispossessed' (1992). He has made several television documentaries for the BBC, though he is 'a very bad filmmaker'. It also seems to him that his work is much more popular in translation—his books have been translated into fifteen languages. He is married, lives in Belfast and owns a black-and-white cat. 'The Dreamed' comes from his forthcoming novel, 'The Extremists', which will be published by Secker & Warburg in 2004.

The old man woke abruptly, like a man surprised, like a man chased or cheated out of sleep. He breathed rapidly and stared unhappily at the slits of cold sunshine that sliced his bedroom walls. He lay still on his left side for some moments, peering at the room.

Taking a deep, reluctant breath, he turned slowly on to his back and looked at the young man in the bed beside him. The youth slept on his back. He slept deeply and strongly almost as though he might never wake. The covers were drawn high up to his chin and his face was turned sharply in the opposite direction. The old man could only make out a jumble of thick dark cropped hair and a smooth pale jawline.

With infinite patience and care, the old man stepped out of bed. Silently he stood at the bedside and tried to lean over the sleeping form that he might see more of the face. The young man stirred slightly and more of his features became visible. The old man stared curiously.

Young of course. As he grew older, he struggled to judge the age of young men but at least this one didn't seem to be quite a teenager. Perhaps twenty or so. A fine face, not unhandsome, wiped smooth by the characterless tonality of all young men's sleep. The old man was relieved that he was not quite a child. The boy's pale skin looked English but if the old man struggled to judge their age, he almost never guessed their nationality. The pale skin meant only that he was unlikely to be Mediterranean.

The old man shrugged neutrally to himself. Silent as a spy, he gathered his clothes and went downstairs.

As he dressed and cooked breakfast, he congratulated himself on waking up first. It would have been much more embarrassing, even dangerous if the youth had woken first. It was much better that he had not woken to find himself in bed with an elderly stranger. At that thought, the old man's mood darkened. He put more bacon in the pan to dispel the sudden qualm. Young men were always hungry. Young men were eternally hungry.

He had nearly finished getting the breakfast ready when he heard movement from upstairs. His pulse quickened as he heard the bed creak. He laid the table nervously. Some minutes passed and then there were footsteps on the staircase. He reminded himself that he had locked the doors of any rooms that contained a television, video or computer. The young man had an unlocked path between bedroom, bathroom and kitchen. There was no electrical equipment to be found anywhere there. Nothing that could lead to unfortunate incidents.

The old man poured coffee into cups and heard the footsteps pause on the staircase. The youth had evidently stopped halfway down the stairs. Perhaps he thought he had heard something. The old man picked up the frying pan and clattered it loudly on the hob. A moment's silence and the footsteps slowly resumed.

He tried to calm himself and regulate his breathing. It was more important to appear calm than actually to be calm. It wouldn't matter that he was terrified if the boy could only believe him master of this situation. The footsteps had come close to the kitchen door and stopped again. The old man listened, imagining that he could hear the youth breathing on the other side of the door. He waited, feeling only an infinite reluctance. Nothing.

He loudly scraped breakfast on to two plates and sat down, shifting his wooden chair demonstratively. He almost smiled.

'*Qui va la?*'

French. Good. The voice was trying to be firm but failed to disguise its quaver. The old man spoke firmly, calmly.

'*Ami. Restez calme. Venez. J'ai prepare un repas si vous avez faim.*'

There was a moment of silence and then the door pushed open slowly. The old man pressed a welcoming smile on to his face. The young soldier stared at him in confusion and fear.

'Come and eat something,' the old man said.

'Who are you?'

'Sit down. We'll talk over breakfast.' He saw that the young man's nostrils twitch at the aroma of the bacon. He gestured at the empty chair before which a piled plate lay.

The soldier sat down warily. His grubby boots scraped on the floor. He flinched nervously and glanced quickly at the other man. He looked embarrassed to make such noise. He murmured something inaudible. The old man gestured to his plate. 'Go on. It grows cold.'

The young man ate with rapid relish.

'More?'

'Thank you. Yes.'

The old man gave him some more bacon.

'Excuse me sir but who are you and what is this place? Are you French? Was I wounded?'

The old man smiled confidently.

'Something strange has happened. Something wonderful.'

The old man told him where he was. The young soldier was bewildered to find that he was in England. The old man ignored this and questioned him. He gave him cigarettes and coffee.

His name was Christian. He was a twenty year old medical student from Lyons who had only been in the army for six months. His regiment had been bypassed and surrounded. It had been a slaughter. Few had surrendered. He had watched many Frenchmen die. He asked the old man if he knew how the battle had ended.

'Yes, I know.' The old man replied.

'Who won?' asked Christian.

'What year is it?'

'What do you mean?'

'What year is it?'

'What kind of question is that? Are you crazy?'

'Just tell me what year it is.'

'You know what year it is.'

The old man closed his eyes unhappily. 'Is it 1940?' he asked.

'Yes, of course it is.'

The old man opened his eyes and looked at the young Frenchman. He tried to smile.

It took hours. It took almost the whole day. Initially, the young soldier demonstrated a rapid series of entirely predictable responses; laughter, concern about the old man's sanity, bewilderment, the idea that it was an elaborate regimental joke, irritation that the joke had gone too far, anger, fear, disbelief, mockery and general perturbation.

As the hours passed and the day grew dark, the old man evinced his number of proofs. Slowly, one by one, he unlocked doors to the other rooms. He showed the man books published sixty years on, histories of the Second World War. The soldier thought they were fakes and that the old man was part of some kind of elaborate German interrogation.

He showed him a television set. The boy reeled in horror, but he had heard of such things and the Germans were famous for the technological advances. The old man showed mobile phones, computers, laptops, CD players, microwaves.

He made the boy promise to stay with him and then drove him around the city. The boy stared in open-mouthed silence. The old man explained like a tour guide, momentarily feeling happier than he had in days.

It was nearly nine when he started making some dinner. He had told Christian to watch television until dinner was ready but after twenty minutes or so the young man drifted back into the kitchen and hovered unhappily.

'I don't understand.'

'Nor do I.' The old man replied gently.

'It's...' Christian stopped searching for something with the required emphasis. 'It's impossible to believe.'

'Do you believe it now?'

'Yes.'

The old man stopped and put out his hand. Uncertainly Christian grasped it. They shook hands. The Frenchman did not release the old man's hand. The pressure increased. He looked into the stranger's old eyes.

'Does this mean...? Does this mean I died?'

The old man tried to make his voice warm. He returned some pressure to the young man's grasp.

'Yes, I think so.'

'Christ.'

He felt the boy's grasp weaken. He held his hand tighter, insistently, pressing, recalling him. Christian's face was white, his lips trembling, unable to form a proper expression.

'You are here now. You're alive. Does it matter? Welcome back.'

The boy's knees sagged slightly. The old man put his free hand on Christian's shoulder, steadying him. He heard a clutch in the boy's throat.

'Don't be afraid. You're here. Accept it. Be glad.'

His voice sounded like a sports coach exhorting greater effort from some recalcitrant athlete. He felt the numbness of the young man's shoulders, the remoteness, the self-absorption of his fear. He squeezed the young man's neck until it could only have hurt. The young man pulled back a little, hand still clasped. He looked pallidly into the old man's face.

'What I don't understand...'

The old man smiled and squeezed his hand encouragingly.

'Yes?'

Christian did not return the pressure of the old man's hand and there was something like accusation in the crease of his forehead.

'What I don't understand is that you don't even seem surprised?'

The old man dropped his hand abruptly. He turned back to the dinner he was preparing. He shuffled a pot listlessly. His face turned away from the young man. When he spoke, his voice was flat and he did not turn round.

'It's not my first time.'

His first time was on the morning of October 24, 1945. He had more than avoided the war. He had almost entirely missed the war. He left Oxford in May '39. After three months in Bologna, he returned to start the research he had had always desired and dreaded in equal measure. A day later war was declared. A month later he joined the faculty group of scientists and researchers pressing for a War Department research group. Two months later his mother died. Six months later he joined the War Office Research Unit and moved back into his childhood home.

He did no real science. He was a bureaucrat. He allocated resources, mineral, mercantile and human to the various technological projects that gained or lost favour in the fluvial fortunes of the British war. Sometimes he tried to communicate his impressions or opinions on the value or utility of these bellicose projects. No one listened. The prime minister had his own fetish for technology. He was a regulator of supply. He was a gauge.

Somewhat to his shame, he even began to enjoy this work. When all projects clamoured for the same basic goods, it was a matter of some delicacy to direct the flow. He learnt an algebraic instinct for how the bare estimates of necessity he received differed from the amounts of materials that would actually keep those projects alive.

Obviously he saw no fighting. Even German bombing stayed out of his way (in later years he almost came to think that this was not accidental, that they had bombed paths around him). He saw wrecked buildings and rubbled streets but he saw no explosions, no casualties, no dead. When he was at work, the area was not bombed. When he was at home, the neighbourhood was not bombed.

He was perturbed to find the world around him more beautiful than it had ever been. The war made the sun brighter, the clouds more luminous, the trees more generous.

On VE day, he was invited to stay at the department for the foreseeable future. He agreed without thought and worked late that day.

He had grown used to casualty figures and projections of all kinds. He had even seen economic breakdowns of casualty figures. How much British casualties cost the economy, how much it cost on average to kill Germans. He was perturbed in only a minor way.

He had a great gift for not thinking. He distrusted empathy, he distrusted the way his eyes could fill with reasonless tears. Why weep over suffering that didn't belong to him? What was the possible use of such a habit?

When the Americans dropped two of their spectacular new ideas on Japan he felt the blast a little more. It made his head itch in a peculiar way, a sensation only increased by colleagues openly wondering how soon they would have to drop these things on Moscow.

But he soon stopped thinking about it. He had discovered his talent for not thinking years before and used it now as a conscious and utile skill. Now he applied technique.

When he started to read government documents about the Jews, he found it harder to avoid reflection. When accounts appeared in newspapers, his head itched again. When he saw photographs, his mouth dried for what felt like forever.

Although he could not avoid thinking about it, he tried to lock the door in his brain behind which such thoughts lodged. But he rode home one day on the underground train and saw some schoolboys sniggering over a newspaper, yelping in excited surprise and delight. Their concentration was intense and unwavering. He watched them for ten minutes and then glanced down at the newspaper as he disembarked.

He never forgot standing on the platform as the train rattled out of the station, reeling, nauseous, unable to breathe.

The boys had been looking at a line of blurred naked Jewesses, their hands pressed to breasts and pudenda as they walked in single file past desultory groups of German soldiers.

That night he dreamt for the last time.

When he woke the next morning to find Sylvain in the bed beside him, his fright had been noisy and spectacular. The Frenchman's bellowing response had been no less impressive. In many ways it had been a stroke of luck that the first one had been French. His French was adequate and their countries had been allies after all. A German might have been troublesome that first morning.

Sylvain was a *maquis*. A Resistance fighter from Grenoble. Resourceful, decisive and intelligent. He had been trapped in a firefight while trying to plant land mines on a railway line. He remembered nothing after the first few moments when he and his comrades had returned fire, crouching in the poor cover of a trackside ditch.

Sylvain was convinced that he had been wounded and arrested. He inspected his body minutely. He was full of predictable doubts and suspicions of what the Englishman told him. He was evidently being tortured by the Gestapo with some new disorientating method. Or he had been wounded in the railway line gun battle and flown to London and the Englishmen was trying to discover whether he was some kind of double agent for the Germans. Or that the Englishman was merely mad.

When he saw a city undeniably English, undeniably four years after the last date he could remember, he was impressively calm. He must have been wounded and merely lost his memory or been in some kind of coma. When he came to believe the Englishman when he said that he knew nothing other than Sylvain had suddenly appeared, he decided that the last act of his amnesiac self must have been to break into this man's house and climb into bed beside him.

The Englishman seemed a little cracked and Sylvain suspected that he thought there was something magical to the occurrence. He concurred with Sylvain's theory but the Frenchman saw something furtive and frightened in his eyes when they spoke of it.

He stayed there for ten days. He contacted the British authorities and a mild fuss ensued. Stories even appeared in newspapers. There was some difficulty in making people believe his extraordinary story though that improved when the French Embassy checked and found that much of it was verifiable right up to that gun battle at the railway line. Sylvain had been declared dead in 1941. He had a brother still living. He stayed ten days when he might easily have left sooner.

He said goodbye to the peculiar Englishman, still troubled by his manner, embarrassed that he had stayed so long, that he had been so oddly reluctant to leave. He arrived in Paris that night, his unease steadily growing. His brother met him, weeping hysterically, unable to believe that he had been returned so.

Within a week, Sylvain had met with some of his surviving comrades. Their awkwardness shamed him. He guessed that they were either perturbed by the whole event and that some even suspected he was hiding some kind of secret collusion with the Germans. He wondered if the British had suspected the same thing. He knew that the man closest to him of his old colleagues was avoiding him.

He went to the man's home.

It was a meeting that Sylvain refused to remember in the years that followed. He had had to fight his way into the house and then his old comrade had simply pointed a pistol at him. Sylvain asked him if he thought he had collaborated with the Germans. Was that what the gun was for?

'That's not it.'

'What is it, then?'

The man's face was immobile with horror.

'I buried you. I buried you with my own hands.'

Before he left Sylvain suggested that they dig up the spot where his friend had buried him. His friend told him he had already done that just a few days before. Sylvain was too frightened to ask but the man told him anyway. There was nothing there, he said. Nothing at all.

He returned to England three days later. He spent a day sitting on a train station bench watching the English hurry by. Before the evening had grown quite dark, he stood on the doorstep of the house of the man in whose bed he had woken. As he raised his hand to knock on the door, he knew that he had come to a junction. If he found the man alone, life could continue in some way that was welcome to him. If the man was not alone (as his instinct had told him since the day after he left), his life would change in ways he could not yet number.

The old man often thanked the chance, if chance it was, that Sylvain had been the first.

He never forgot the joy he felt to see him standing on his doorstep that night, the gratitude when the Frenchman's first words were, 'Have more come?' He actually wept.

Three more had come in the twelve days since Sylvain had left. The first had been a terrified Englishman whose name he had never even learnt. The boy had sneaked away the night after he arrived which meant that his perplexed host had woken up beside a new Frenchman, Paul a sailor from Marseilles. Paul had stayed for six days. His host had not told him everything, he had frankly lied by omission and before he left had asked him to tell no one what had happened.

The morning after Paul's departure, the man had woken to find a boy in a filthy Wehrmacht uniform curled in foetal sleep beside him. The thing he had already begun to dread.

It had been difficult but manageable, the German spoke some few words of French and frankly, the boy's terror helped. The man bought a German–English dictionary and they tried to communicate. He was the current guest when Sylvain came back. The man had a moment's concern about what the Resistance fighter might make of this but Sylvain merely said that it was good that he had come back since he spoke some German.

Sylvain moved in for a year. Everything improved. Nothing would have been possible without him. Within a fortnight he had set up a system that changed very little in the next half century and more.

Gunther left ten days after Sylvain's arrival. It took a while but with Sylvain's *maquis* experience, false documents were found and Gunther returned to Germany with a carefully invented story filling in the disappeared years since his death near Kiev in 1943.

The evening after Gunter left was one of the happiest. He and Sylvain dined uproariously.

He woke up the next morning beside a twenty-four-year-old sailor from Newcastle whose ship had sunk in 1941.

It became a habit. Certain immutable laws quickly became apparent. A new arrival could only appear once the previous returnee had left. The old man could never stay awake to witness the actual appearance or materialization (he tried in a guilty way a couple of times and failed—such experiments could cost a life). There were never any women. Or children. Though some of the soldiers were so young as to be near children.

There were never any weapons. Rifles and pistols were gone. Even knives they had concealed in boots or clothing did not return with them. The men were never wounded or bleeding. They always woke whole (or as whole as they had been before the last thing they could remember). Few were sick. Few missed limbs.

There were no non-combatants. No civilians. They were all soldiers, sailors or pilots.

Perhaps the strangest thing in that first year was the readiness of their acceptance. Of course there was fear, amazement, denial and disbelief but on the whole not as much as might have been expected. Even the quality of their joy at their safety was muted, uncoloured. As though something had drained the expression of their stronger more egoistic emotions.

Though not all spoke of it, they all seemed to be quickly aware that they had died. Some spoke of unsurvivable bombardments or air attacks. Some remembered thoughts of finality. Of the end.

There were varying degrees of mysticism. Largely, the men tried to avoid too much excitement and he felt that they often kept various thoughts to themselves. The calmness that he and Sylvain began to show was a great help. The men responded to that most of all. They were mostly quiet men, disliking noise and strong feeling.

Some cut up rough. Some were nearly violent, their fear was so strong. Sylvain's strength and courage always prevailed and as they grew more experienced, they found that they could calm even the violent without force.

Their trust of these men was remarkable and as more men came, the trust came quicker and stronger. He felt that this was only partially attributable to his growing experience. He felt there was something else. Each boy who woke in his bed was in effect a little less surprised than the one before.

After a few months he arranged to work only three days every week. He claimed a research project that he intended to publish. Sylvain got a job with the Department of Works.

After a year more than sixty men had returned. A dozen had been given new identities—the Russians in particular—but most had returned to their previous lives with varying explanations for the biographical gaps long and short: imprisonment, illness, debilitating injury, general amnesia. Sylvain began contemplating a rule for men returning to their previous selves. Two years was the upper limit, he felt. Anything longer was too hard to explain away. In the months that followed several disobeyed those rules. Sylvain knew that as the war grew more distant, the problem would grow.

That brought the conversation both men had overtly avoided. How long would this continue? When would it stop? The both knew and did not want to acknowledge their certainty to one another.

Those who had already come and gone started to come back, to re-establish contact. Sylvain forced the man to get a telephone. More and more men came back, telling them that they had tried to stay away but had felt somehow drawn. Sylvain was surprised by the depth of the Englishman's reluctance to see these men. He dealt with it. The men started to meet in hotels and cafes, in each other's homes (it became clear how many of them no matter what their nationality had settled in the same city or even close by). Sylvain stopped telling the Englishman when he had met the others.

And still the men kept coming, the French, the English, the Germans, Americans, Italians and Russians, the pilots, the artillery men, the infantry and the parachutists. As the Englishman and the Frenchman became more proficient, the men stayed for a shorter time—were moved out more quickly, often with the assistance of those who had already been through their hands. By default, a kind of network was set up.

They realized that the returners weren't confined to the dead of the recent war when a British soldier murdered in Palestine arrived in the Englishman's bed the morning after he read an account of his death in a newspaper. He started to dread the arrival of the dead of other wars. The Great War. The Franco Prussian. The Napoleonic.

The very next arrival was a *poilu* who had died in 1916.

After that the man tried to regulate his thoughts. To gain some form of control. He felt innumerable guilts about this—that he was trying to restrict the gift to the dead of only one war. It was simply much easier for a man to re-enter the world a year or two after the last date he could remember than thirty years or a hundred. Even Sylvain spoke unasked of the necessity of this. The Englishman realized how clearly his friend had been thinking about his habit.

After two years more than one hundred and thirty men had come and gone.

One night Sylvain, who had been writing and preparing documents for weeks past and obviously having meetings with the other returnees, told the Englishman he was leaving. He also said he had come to some decisions, that he had some suggestions. He told him that they had to increase the frequency, bring more men back. The man would have to give up his job. Sylvain and several of the other men had arranged to set aside money which would replace his salary and fund the men who returned. The man watched him palely.

'Jesus, you can't give me orders. This is not the Resistance.'

Sylvain slapped his hand loudly on the table.

'That's exactly what this is.'

He never dreamed again. His sleep was a dreamless blank. He knew that people who said they didn't dream merely couldn't remember their dreams. He knew that everyone dreamt. But he felt or hoped perhaps that his sleep was a true void, a different thing. Such a claim of uniqueness was hardly excessive under the circumstances.

It sometimes amused him how quickly the thing had become mired in bureaucracy. It always amused him to think of how intricate it grew, how humourless, how pompous. It was a very modern miracle in that way. It brought an awful lot of admin.

There were two sets of bureaucracy, or rather more correctly there was a bureaucracy of procedure and an organizational bureaucracy. The old man only involved himself in procedure. Over the years, the technique of processing the young men had improved to something close to mechanical ease. Created by Sylvain in the first couple of years, the procedure was simple. The night before, newspapers, books and radios that might disturb a returnee (and later devices that were incomprehensibly modern) were placed in locked rooms. The old man tried his best to wake first. They were quickly fed. The men always suffered hunger of an unusual intensity and food calmed them (particularly as the old man began secreting measures of sedatives therein sometime in 1948). Written accounts of the phenomena were translated into every language they could think of and handed to those who spoke a language the old man could not (he and Sylvain were still often flummoxed—Hausa, Catalan, Djboutin).

When the newest man arrived, Sylvain would be informed of his name, nationality, unit, time of death. At first, Sylvain would come and take the boy away himself, but after a few years he usually delegated. He would send someone of the boy's own nationality, close in age and type. This grew easier as the pool of returnees grew. It would be explained to the boy that he had to leave so that others might come. Usually he left that same day.

The old man embarked on the study of several languages; French, German, Russian, Italian. He was soon proficient and had picked up rudiments of others. Since he had never left England he often surprised the few outside people he met by his fluency in the languages of countries he had never even visited. The unease of his replies to their remarks made many suspect some mystery. But never the right one.

He became expert in the armies and regimental dispositions of many wars. He often recognized shoulder or collar flashes in the uniforms of the young men asleep beside him and could roughly guess when and where they had died. Particularly true of the Russian divisions slaughtered wholesale in 1941 and '42. Soon he knew more than any of the men who woke beside him.

There was an emergency set-up for boys who were unmanageably terrified or possible violent. Sylvain had made sure that several men lived in houses close by. On the morning of an anticipated arrival, two or three of them were always ready for a hurried call (unknown to the old man, they would actually be waiting in a van forty yards from the front door). If the boy proved dangerous, they would rush in and subdue him. If the problem was intractable as happened once a year or so, the youth would be sedated and taken away after dark.

The old man never knew precisely what was done with these men but guessed that they were held until they could be released without harming themselves or others.

There was a network of handlers and their back ups of every nationality. Some men showed a real gift for the work and helped accelerate the process. Sylvain picked them with skill. The rate of throughput increased further. Soon it was at least two men a week.

Of course, as the numbers increased and the pool of men who had left became larger, the other bureaucracy increased in scope. The old man liked to call the men who had left 'the dearly departed'. He thought that this was a good joke. Perhaps, under the circumstances, the best possible of all jokes. Sylvain's meetings with the other men were soon formalised, soon structured. Boards were set up, committees. The old man sometimes wondered how much of this was because of Sylvain's *maquis* experience, those fierce administrators, those robust organisers. Sylvain gave the old man fewer and fewer details. He was increasingly aware of the man's discomfort in talking about or talking to the men who had left. With typical unsentimentality, Sylvain made no enquiries.

As the years passed the bureaucracy of the departed had become magnified, monstrous. Much of it was in the form of open, charitable trust. Fundraising mostly took place within the group of departed but several investment companies were set up and increased the proceeds judiciously. Businesses run by the departed burgeoned. No man leaving the old man's house needed to look for work.

By 1952, almost all the returnees were paying a semi-formal tariff on their income to one of Sylvain's organizations. By 2001, the old man made a guess that the simple income of the returnees must amount to a minimum of 192 million pounds. Five or ten per cent of that would be considerable. That did not count the investment accounts and various businesses.

It became a secret society, a ghostly mafia, a discreet empire. It endorsed schools and clinics, university scholarships and addiction centres. The old man liked to mock the organization as it grew. He lampooned its power and success, its great sincerity and commitment. It relieved the sensation of peculiar remoteness he felt towards the departed men. It sharply underlined the detachment he craved.

The organization disguised a truth that he found troubling. It was the mere exemplification of the togetherness of the departed, of their unusual brotherhood. One of the strangest things about those who had left was how easily they found each other. Some of it was obviously because he would send a new boy to one of those already returned so a form of society naturally arose. Some of it was naturally because of the growing bureaucracy but there were other incidents—chance meetings, men marrying sisters without knowing the other's secret. Two of the men had even become homosexual lovers before they realized.

Often two returnees who had never met could walk past each other on a crowded city street and stop to speak to one another for a reason neither knew.

They seemed to sense some mark in each other, some trace.

And how successful the men were by and large. How intelligent, decent and well-paid. What stable families they built. What legions of children they had. Conspicuously, the Russians were often more troubled, struggled more with alcohol and suicide. This did not surprise the old man. He liked the Russians. Sometimes he told himself that the Russians were his favourites.

But he preferred not to think of their lives after they had left him. Their successes and their failures, their wives and their children. Their wealth and their poverty. He could recall hundreds of them as they had been in their few days in his house and liked to recall the pleasant, intelligent ones. But he tried not to think of them as departed. His motives were mostly a mystery to him. He preferred this.

One thing he particularly abhorred was Sylvain's habit of documentation. Sylvain had kept scrupulous archives. He believed the old Frenchman still oversaw this task personally. There were now five co-ordinators; French, English, German, Russian and Miscellaneous (that *miscellaneous* always made the old man laugh, not kindly). Each one kept his own records and figures but all data was still passed to Sylvain who kept a voluminous overall digest. Sylvain had picked up the statistical habit. He knew all the numbers, all the factions. He knew the exact total of returned men. He knew the monthly rate of returnees, their nationality predominances and sequences, costs per man.

He knew the average income of the departed. The marriage status. The children and now grandchildren. He knew which were the most common professions among them. He knew how many had gone mad or died. He knew how many were untraceable. He knew the total worth of all the income, capital and investments of all arms of the organization. He knew how many crimes they'd committed and how many bastards they'd fathered.

The old man thought often of these files, of this archive. As far as he knew he was never openly named. Even the introductory videos and literature he passed out to the new boys avoided mentioning him by ludicrous circumlocutions. He had never asked. Sylvain had guessed early that this was best.

He still wondered how these documents read. What kind of literature did they represent? What kind of testament? He knew that the vastness of the bureaucracy was Sylvain's attempt to dilute the occult strangeness of the whole phenomenon. He knew the Frenchman had always hoped that double-entry book keeping would render everything more thinkable.

The only fact or statistic that the old man could quote verbatim from this strange archive was that nearly two hundred of the men had ended up long or short term in psychiatric institutions for trying to tell the truth.

The new boy, Christian, was surprisingly buoyant. The day after he appeared, he suggested that they eat lunch in the garden. It wasn't really warm enough but it was sunny, and the old man could not summon the energy to object. The boy's appetite had ebbed a little and the volumes of food were less astounding than the day before. He chatted happily.

Occasionally, he made insufficiently awed remarks upon what he had learnt that morning. Is that true, he would ask about some confirmation-requiring detail. But, as often was the case, it wasn't the atomic bombs or the slaughter of the Jews. It was flight times between New York and London. It was computers and mobile phones. It was cured tuberculosis and the reattachment of severed limbs. It was breast augmentation and pornographic films.

He was delighted by the moon-landings as they all had been for the last thirty years or more. It seemed to appeal to them in some way he barely understood. Maybe it helped them feel less peculiar, contextualized their own surprising journey.

The old man asked him how he felt about how his war had ended. The French boy seemed a little embarrassed, as though the old man had made a gaffe. He smiled uneasily. Somehow it didn't seem surprising, he said. In some way, it was hard to care. He already felt that it was such a long time ago. It was hard to get too excited.

The old man watched him as he basked in the cool shine between the trees. Christian would be one of the successes. He was suited to what had happened. He was already formulating his new self, liberated from bonds older than death. He was reinventing. He hadn't simply been brought back to life, he was being rewritten. He was getting a second draft. The men who understood this could achieve anything.

'The air is beautiful.'

He inhaled with ostentatious pleasure. He breathed like he ate, with wilful reckless hunger. 'I feel like it's the first air I've ever breathed.' He laughed again, needing to share his delight.

They were in some ways like the newly born. The mad bite of their relish was evident and enviable and they were as needy and attention-absorbent as babies. He was almost never alone. They required vigilance and would become querulous if they did not know where he was. They panicked when they were left alone for too long. When baby alarms had first become popular, he had amused himself by thinking how useful he would find such a device.

The energy necessary for their care meant that he often craved solitude but found it insupportable. The nights after one of them left were usually dreadful. He thought of this as he listened to Christian babbling in the autumn sunlight.

'Are you too cold?' the boy asked.

The old man peered at him over the tightly pulled collar of his heavy overcoat.

'I'm fine.'

'You seem cold.'

'Don't worry about me. Finish your lunch.'

The young man continued eating with jocose obedience. He was so ready to obey to give pleasure and be liked. The old man was finding it harder to resist the boy's promiscuous goodwill.

'A man will come to meet you later. His name's Alain.'

'Was he...? Is he one of us?'

'Yes.'

'Very organized.'

'Yes.'

The young man smiled and set his knife and fork down on his plate with an absurd conclusive clatter.

'It's a little like being at school.' He smiled delightedly when the old man laughed.

'Yes, a little.'

'I suppose there is much to learn after all.'

'Yes.'

'He is a good teacher, this Alain?'

'They are all good teachers.'

'And you do none of this teaching?'

The old man started to stack the plates in a pile. Christian faltered again, his instinct told him how little the old man liked to be questioned.

'Of course, it is more important that you do your other work.'

He stared keenly at the old man who stood up and picked up all the dishes he could carry.

'The work that only you can do.'

The old man took the dishes into the kitchen and put them in the sink. Wearily, he filled the basin with water. He heard Christian bringing in cups and glasses behind him.

'I'm sorry.' The young man said. 'You must admit I have not asked many questions under the circumstances.'

Yes, the old man certainly had to concede that.

But the question that Christian congratulated himself on eschewing was that question that almost none of them asked. How? *How?*

His habit. He had felt better after he had named it, found some way of referring to it with Sylvain that did not involve stunned peroration or awed euphemism. Naming it made it more bearable, infinitely more quotidian. And *habit* was such a good word for it. When he saw how little Sylvain liked it, he knew he had found the right phrase. Habit suggested monotonous accumulation and private vice all at the same time. It was a bad habit he had. He had an eight-a-month habit. It was a habit he could not give up. It was like cracking his knuckles. It was only smoking or drinking.

The other words were such bad ones, he felt. Miracle. Magic. Marvel. Phenomenon. Anomaly. Aberration. Oddity. His life was resolutely non-miraculous, he felt sure. The most confirmed sceptic or atheist, the world's most rigorous rationalists or literalists lived lives that contained more of the glitter of the bizarre or unworldly than his own dull days. His life was aggressively prosaic. The problems caused by this miracle, the work brought by it was mostly administrative, mostly practical.

His life lacked magic. His life needed more magic. Or more God. This sentiment, this resentment grew as he aged. He could have done with a little rejuvenation himself, a little being brought back to life.

He knew that most of the men formulated superstitious or religious explanations. The Russians were the most prepared to see the work of God, the Japanese simply the least surprised (or perhaps some of the Irish). Men mostly attributed the magic or miracle to him. One Russian boy had frankly asked, 'Excuse me, sir, are you God?' They treated him with awe. No matter how calmly he behaved, no matter how mundane his words and actions, they persisted in thinking him magical or holy. The cabbalistic admiration was suprisingly one of the easiest things to bear in their attitude to him.

There were sceptics too, scientists, thinkers. They were almost worse. They believed him to have some gift or capacity and refused to believe that he could not control it. They thought him even more special, more unique than the superstitious peasant-boys found him.

Their theories were multiple and absurd. Concentrations or gaps in life force, a time warp centred through the old man. An alternative reality or universe, the door to which he could open. As the nineteen-fifties passed into the nineteen-sixties and the culture of the developed world was saturated by the endless banality of science fiction, his life grew rather harder in this respect. UFOs, collective consciousness endlessly made flesh, alien portals for returned abductees. In the end, he decided that he preferred the believers.

Some wondered openly if it was a matter of him or his house. His bedroom, even perhaps just his bed. They tried to guess where the magic or oddity might reside. The old man firmly believed that it was him and that no matter where he slept he would wake with these boys. Nonetheless, he remained in that same house, that same bedroom just in case. He had the bed repaired and extended its natural life through a series of mutinous carpenters. He had slept in the same bed for more than fifty years.

He himself didn't like to investigate too much, to think too deeply about it. He was still good at not thinking and he knew that thinking was what had got him into this trouble. He feared that understanding would bring some onerous new addition to the duty, to the eternal obligation.

For that is what it was. An obligation—an endless burden. It was such a *job*. Such a task. This unpleasant feeling was not entirely unfitting. The more professional he was—the more men he could help. But he never lost his resentment of this duty. He daydreamed sometimes of irresponsibility, of leaving it behind. He had done enough. He had reawoken all these men. He had done his bit. It was someone else's turn. He had fantasized idly but never seriously thought about it (he was always now conscious of the terrible danger of seriously thinking about things).

In any case, that number was never high enough, the number of men who had come back. He had kept an instinctive mental record and no matter how brisk and professional he became, no matter how rapid and successful the throughput, the processing, the terrible smallness of that number shamed him almost to panic. There was no retirement target possible. He could never fix on a number that would be enough.   □

GRANTA

MARTHA, MARTHA
Zadie Smith

Zadie Smith was born in north-west London in 1975. She attended Hampstead Comprehensive School and then King's College, Cambridge. She is the author of two novels, 'White Teeth' and 'The Autograph Man' (both published by Hamish Hamilton), and is the recipient of a Guardian First Book award, a Whitbread First Novel award and the James Tait Black Memorial prize. She is presently a Radcliffe Fellow at Harvard University. 'Martha, Martha,' is a new short story.

Though the telephone is a perfectly useless indicator of most human qualities, it's pretty precise about age. From her tiny office on the third floor, Pam Roberts looked through a window and correctly identified the Martha Penk she was waiting for, a shrimpish girl pushing twenty-two, lost down there. She had on a red overcoat and cream snow boots, putting her weight on their edges like an ice skater; she seemed to waver between two doorways. Pam opened her mouth to call out 'Miss Penk!' but never got to make the curious sound—abruptly the girl turned the corner and headed back down Apple towards the river. Pam went to her own door, opened it, worried her chapped lips with a finger, closed it again. The cold was just too extreme; today the first snows were due, opening performance of a show that would last a dreary, relentless four months. Besides, she had her slippers on. Miss Martha Penk, who appeared to believe that two bedrooms and a garden could be had for a thousand dollars a month, would figure out her second mistake soon enough, come back, discover the bell. The confusion was common; it arose from the higgledy-piggledy arrangement of the ground floor—a busy bookshop and a swing-doored optician obscured the sign that told you of the dentist, the insurers, the accountant and Pam's own dinky realty business at the top of the building; also the antique elevator that would take you to them. Pam tapped her door with a knuckle, warning it she would return, and crossed the room to the filing cabinet. On tiptoes she slid open the top drawer and began flicking through files, her Mozart swelling behind her. She sang along with that section of the *Requiem* that sounds so very like 'OH I SEE YOU WILL GO *DOWN!* AND I SEE YOU WILL GO ALSO!', although it could not be this for the words are Latin. As she sang she ground one of her Chinese slippers rhythmically into the carpet and pressed herself into the metal drawer to reach for something at the very back: 'OH I SEE YOU WILL GO DOWN, OH! I SEE YOU WILL GO DOWN! ALSO! ALSO!'

Pam found what she wanted, closed the cabinet suddenly with an elbow and sat down in a fat armchair opposite a lithograph of Venice. She put a foot in her hand and said 'Phee-yoo! Now, *there* you go,' pressing relief into a sore instep. She started picking out every third sheet or so from the listings and laying them on the floor before her in a small pile. At the opening of the 'Lacrimosa' she removed her slipper entirely, but then hearing someone gallop up the stairs, replaced it and quickly rose to greet a large, dark, bearded man in a sheepskin overcoat, who stood bent at the knees like a shortstop, trying to recover his breath in the hallway. He took a step towards her, looked up and frowned. He paused where he was, supporting himself with a hand on the door frame. Pam knew exactly why he had come and the two spoke at the same time.

'This temping agency?' he asked, a heavy accent, quickly identified by Pam as Middle-Easterny. A Middle-Easterny scarf, too, and a hat.

'No dear, *no*,' said Pam, and let her glasses fall to her chest from their chain, 'It's above the *other* Milliner's Books, right? There's two Milliner's Books—you need the one on the corner of Apple and Wallace—this is the wrong Milliner's, this is above the *children's* Milliner's—I don't know why they just don't say that to people—'

The man groaned pleasantly and hit his temple with the hub of his palm.

'I make mistake. Sorry, please.'

'No, they just didn't say, they never *do*. It's not *you*, dear, it's them—people always come here by mistake, it's not *you*. It's two minutes from here. Now, you go back down, turn left, then immediately right, you can see it from there. I've got somebody who just did the *exact* same, but *exactly*—only vice versa—she's gone to...'

A further thundering on the stairs and three more men, younger, also bearded. They stood bent like their friend, panting, one man crying the involuntary tears of a Massachusetts winter. They stared at Pam who stared frankly back at them, with her hands on her makeshift hips, up there where her black linen trousers began, high under the breasts. A black T-shirt and cardigan finished the thing off. Pam was a recognized doodlenut when it came to clothes, buying the same things over and over, black and loose, like a fat Zen monk. She didn't mind. Her moustache was moist and visible—oh, so let 'em *stare* was how Pam felt about it. Young men did not register with Pam any more.

'My friends,' explained the man, and with his friends began the descent, emptying out a demotic mystery language into the stairwell. Miss Penk must have passed them on the bend. A moment later she was in the room apologizing for her lateness.

'Sorry I'm late, I'm sorry,' she said, but did not look sorry. Her face, very black, could not blush, and her accent, to Pam's ears very

English, could not apologize. She stood in the centre of the room, clumsily divesting herself of the loud red coat. She was short, but more muscular, more solid than she had appeared from three floors up. A cheap-looking grey trouser suit and some fake pearls were conspiring to make her older than she was. The buttons on the jacket looked like rusty spare change.

'No, I saw *you*, you see,' began Pam warmly, coming forward to catch what was falling, a scarf, a woolly hat, 'There's *two* Milliner's—did you see those men? On the stairs? They did the exact same thing—and I saw you down—'

'The lift's broken, it don't work,' said Martha, and now lifted her head and reached out a hand. Pam felt faintly interrupted, but took the hand and gave it a double-handed shake.

'Pam Roberts, we spoke on the phone. It's so good to *meet* you!'

'I'm Martha,' she replied and quickly freed herself. She passed a smoothing hand over her own short ironed hair, cut in a flapper's style, a helmet brilliant with some kind of polish. A concrete kiss curl had been plastered on to her left cheek. Pam had never seen anything quite like it in her office before.

'Well. Now, did you come from far? Are you nearby?' Pam asked, a question that had a little business in it.

'Near, yeah,' said the girl, firmly. She stood oddly, hands by her sides, feet together, 'A hotel, it's called The Charles? It's just like by the river—it's just if you go down by—'

'Oh, I know where it is—it's *very* nice.'

'It costs too much, man,' said Martha, tutting loudly, removing a pair of childish mittens, 'But I came right from London and I didn't have any place arranged—I just arksed the taxi to take me to the nearest hotel—I been there a week, but I can't afford it for much longer, you know?'

Usually Pam would use these minutes in the office to ascertain something about likely wealth, class, all very gently—what kind of house, what kind of taste, what kind of price—but she had been wrong about English accents before, not knowing which were high class, which not. Or whether high class meant money at *all*—if you watched PBS as Pam did you soon found out that in England it could, often did, mean the exact opposite.

'It *is* such a nice place, The Charles. They really do things properly there, don't they? They really make the best of that location, I think. I stayed there once for a realty conference, and I really appreciated the standard of the breakfasts. People talk about pool this, steam-room that, but in actual fact it's the little things, like a *breakfast*. A good hot *breakfast*. But my *God* the price isn't any fun—Martha, we'll have you out of there in no time, I promise, especially if we find something empty—'

'Yes,' said Martha, but rather too quick, too desperate, 'How long would it be before I could move in somewhere?'

Pam felt herself immediately on surer ground and slipped down a gear into patter, 'Well, as I'm saying, dear, it depends on whether the place has people in it at the *moment*—but even then, we can turn it around very *very* quickly. It just needs to happen so that everybody wants to make it work, that's all. Don't worry, we'll find something that works. And if it doesn't work, we'll cut it loose and go on to the next,' she said loudly, clapping her hands and glancing at a clock on the wall, 'Now, I've got about two hours free—it's really very dry at the moment so there's *plenty* to show.' She bent down to scoop the remembered listings from the floor, 'I think I understand what you're looking for, Martha, I received your letter, I have it right here—Wait—' Pam reached over to her stereo like a woman with one foot each in two drifting boats; she punched at a couple of buttons to no avail, 'Sometimes it gets a little loud. Funny little machine. It's completely wireless! It's like a single unit stereo for single people, very liberating. You can't really adjust it without the remote, though, which is a little frustrating. And I find it gets louder sometimes, do you know? Sort of when you don't expect it?'

'Classical,' said Martha, and looked at Pam and the surrounding office with determined reverence, 'I want to listen to more classical music. I want to know more about it. It's on my list.'

And this she said in such a way that Pam had no doubt that there was such a list, and that renting an apartment *today* was somewhere on it. The girl had a manner that was all itinerary, charmless and determined, and Pam, a Midwesterner by birth, had the shameful idea that she might go far, this Martha Penk, here on the East Coast.

'Oh! Well, I don't know what there is to *know*, really. I mean, I don't know anything at *all*. It's the violins that do it for me, I guess, the way they sound like somebody's crying? The "Lacrimosa" means crying, I'm pretty sure. Lachrymose—that's from the eye, isn't it? But are you at the university?'

'No!' said Martha but her face at last released a flood of undisguised pleasure, as when a girl is told she could be a model or an actress or do whatever she does amateurishly, professionally, 'I wish! Maybe one day. I'm looking for that next level—qualifications, getting forward, raising myself, my consciousness. But that's like a dream, yeah, for me at this stage?'

She looked serious again, began enlisting her hands in her speech, drawing out these 'levels' in the air, 'It's about stepping a bit further, I mean, for me, I really want to improve myself while I'm here, go up a bit, like listening to different music, like that.'

'*Well*,' said Pam brightly, and sounded her desk with her hand, 'We'll just have to find you the right place where you can do that. Hmm?' But Miss Penk had returned her attention to the CD case, and Pam found herself nodding into the silence, and talking to fill it, 'Oh, I just like all kinds of music, really. I am just the *biggest* fan of music. Cuban, classical, hillbilly—or whatever you call that sort of close harmony singing? A lot of jazz...don't know a thing about it, though! Oh *my*. Maybe I can't be improved. Too old to be any better than I am,' said Pam in a saccharine sing-song, as if it were a proverb.

'Yeah,' said Martha, the sort of absent yes that a silly proverb probably deserves. She took the sleeve notes out of the case and opened them up.

'Now,' said Pam, struggling a little, 'From your letter I understood you were thinking around the thousand mark—but that's really a little *low*—I mean, I'll *show* you those places, Martha, but I can't guarantee you're going to *like* them. I mean, they're not there to be *liked*,' Pam said patiently, and gathered up her car keys from her desk, 'But we'll find something that works—we just need to get a handle on it. I'd like to show you a big place that's going for two thousand, maybe—maybe lower—it's negotiable with the present owner. In more vibrant times, it's worth at least three. It'll give us some idea anyway. I'm here to make it work for you, so, I'm going to be led by you...'

Outside a plane roared low like some prehistoric bird, Pam shuddered; Martha did not move. Pam tried jostling her keys expectantly in her hand; Martha put down the CD case leaving the notes unfolded and walked over to the window. From behind she was an even more neatly made girl than from the front, everything tight and defined, fighting slightly against the banal restraint of polyester.

'We'll take my car, if that's all right,' tried Pam, anxious that Martha should not open a window but unwilling to ask her not to. It *was* hot in the room, but it was that time of year: you either fried or you froze. But Martha had already tugged on the sash, in a second her head was out there in the open air. Pam winced. She hated to see people lean all the way out of a window like that.

'Do you get a lot of university people? Students?'

'Oh, *yes*. At the beginning of a semester, certainly. Students around here have some money to spare, if you know what I mean.'

Martha took her plastic pearls in her hand and twisted them.

'They must be amazing. Focused people.'

'Oh! Well, yes, I suppose. Certainly, they're *bright*. There's just no denying that. But I'm afraid,' said Pam in her own, overused, comic whisper, 'They can be pretty *obnoxious* as well.'

'There aren't any black students,' Martha said in a tone somewhere between statement and question. Pam, who was in the middle of forcing her arm though a recalcitrant coat sleeve, stopped in her position like a scarecrow, 'Well, of *course* there are students of colour, dear! I see them all the time—I mean, even before the affirmative action and all of that—I mean, there's *always* been the basketball scholarships and the rest—though it's much, much better now of course. They're *completely* here on their own steam *now*. Lots of Chinese young people too, and Indian, many. Many! Oh, there's plenty, *plenty* of people of colour here, you'll see,' said Pam and switched off her desk lamp. 'But have you been to America before?'

'Only Florida when I was twelve. I didn't like it—it's quite vulgar?' said Martha, and the word was most definitely borrowed in her mouth. Pam, who also occasionally borrowed words, recognized the habit and tried to look kindly upon it.

'Florida and Nigeria are the only places I've been, really, out of England,' continued Martha, leaning yet further out, gazing across the square, 'And now here.'

'Oh, are you Nigerian?' Pam asked, kicked off her slippers and began to replace them with treasured walking boots. When people remarked that Pam had become 'so *hard*' recently or suggested that she'd turned into a doodlenut since her divorce, they often meant these boots and nothing more than these boots.

'My parents.'

'Penk, it's very unusual, isn't it?' said Pam to Martha's back, 'Is that a Nigerian name?'

'No.'

Nothing further came. Discovering her remote control behind a coffee cup, Pam stopped the CD and then approached, reaching briskly around Martha to close the window. Clearly, the girl blew hot and cold; in the end Pam just needed her name on a contract, nothing more. Even that was not essential—plenty of people take up your whole afternoon and never call again; Pam called them her one-day stands.

'Look at that sky. It's gonna snow any minute. You know, we should try to get going before it really starts to come down...'

With a simple, businesslike nod Pam indicated the coat that Martha had left draped over the photocopier.

About a half-hour later the two of them were completing their tour of Professor Herrin's house, climbing back down the stairs into his open-plan ground-floor lounge. The place was big, but in some disrepair. The carpets felt springy, damp. Mould was the overarching theme. Martha was stepping over an empty cat-food can, and Pam's voice was taking on the fluidity of a woman who feels she is moving down the home straight of her anecdote, 'He's just a very, very impressive man. Not only is he a Professor of Chinese, he holds a law degree—can you imagine—he's on all *kinds* of boards, I'm sure he plays that piano—When the *President of the United States* wants advice on China, the *President*, mind you, he calls up Professor Herrin. It's such a pleasure talking with that man about *Taoism* or, I don't know, *science* or health matters... So many men, they just don't achieve anything at *all*—they don't *expect* to—beyond *business* or a little bit of *golf*, maybe. But there's no attention to the spiritual side, not at all. I mean, his wife, well, actually his wife's a little peculiar—but the mind just boggles to think about living with a man like Professor Herrin, I mean, the attempt to satisfy him, *mentally*...and it's *such* a beautiful house, a little fusty; but—have you seen this? He carved it, he really did. He's a Zen Buddhist, death for him is just an *idea*. He *made* the bookshelf—and of course that would all stay here—he would just want to know from you how many of his books he'll have to store, I mean how much shelving you would need, and so on. He's already in New York, and he's intending to be there until at *least* next February. He's a sort of an *expert* on relations between the races,' whispered Pam, 'so he feels it's important to be in New York right now. In its hour of *need*, you know.'

'I don't have any books,' said Martha, opening the screen door and stepping into a small walled garden, 'I'm going to get books, though, prob'ly, I'll—Oh, it's snowing—it must've started when we were in there. It's on the ground, look.'

Pam turned to look and already the ebony sheen of Martha's hair was speckled white, like dusting on a chocolate cake.

'This house feels sad, man,' said Martha, and lifted one foot off the ground. She reached behind herself and grabbed the ankle, pressing the foot into her buttocks. First one leg, then the other.

'Does it?' asked Pam, as if the idea had never occurred to her, but her passion for gossip was stronger then her instinct for business, 'Well, actually his wife is very peculiar, a terrible thing happened to her. Terrible. It's partly why they're moving again—she can't stand to be in one place, she *broods*. Now, aren't you *cold* out there?'

Martha shrugged, crouched, and tried sweeping a half-inch of snow into her hands, began packing it. Pam sat on the piano stool and stretched her legs out in front of her.

'His wife, Professor Herrin's wife—it's such an awful story—she was in *China*, about twenty-five years ago, and this young man stole her bag. Well, *naturally* she reported it—and what do you think? Two months later when she got back to America, she heard he'd been executed, can you imagine? What that would *do* to a person, it's just terrible. It's a terrible weight to bear.'

'She shouldn't have said nothing,' said Martha, and appeared to think no more about it.

'Well,' considered Pam, pushing her glasses up her nose, 'I think it's quite a difficult marriage—I think he's quite eager to leave this place, so I imagine he'd be flexible vis-à-vis the rent, Martha. Martha?'

'Yeah? Sorry, what?'

'Now, Martha, let's talk now. What are you thinking—are you at all...?'

Martha took her half-packed snowball and threw it limply at the wall.

'I can't afford it. It's too much. Loads too much. Why does it smell weird out here?'

'*Okay*...well, now I wanted to ask about money,' said Pam slowly, coming to the opening and hugging herself against the chill, 'I mean, are we talking about savings? You're very young. Or will you be working? Just so I have some *idea* of how much space we have to manoeuvre.'

Martha stayed where she was in the garden but put both hands out in front of her, awaiting whatever came. The flakes were massive, consistent and quick, as if the snow was not merely falling but being delivered, like manna, because people needed it.

'I've been left some,' said Martha quietly, 'In a will. My uncle passed. Basically, it's enough for a year. A thousand a month, two bedrooms and a garden, yeah? Maybe a bit more, maybe. I need space for people. To come.' She paused. 'If they want.' Suddenly she seemed agitated, even panicked; she attacked her bottom lip with her teeth and looked up and over into the next garden, 'People who might visit, you get me? But this is too too big, I can't afford it. I can't. Don't you have anything I can *afford*?'

It looked for a moment that the girl was about to cry—out of instinct Pam hurried towards her—but by the time she stepped outside Martha had already recovered herself, turning to peer now over the back wall towards the piercing towers and stark white crosses of the university. She seemed calmly framed by them and remote, a figure in a plastic snowstorm.

'Something a bit further out, maybe,' offered Pam a minute later as they climbed back into the car.

'If I had all that education,' said Martha, fastening her seat belt, 'Believe me, I wouldn't live somewhere like *that*.'

'Oh no?'

'I'd live somewhere *new*.'

'I see,' said Pam tersely, starting the car and welcoming the automatic resuscitation of the stereo, Mozart and his death song as background filler. 'Well, each to their own, I suppose, Martha, that's what this business is about, of course. Actually, I used to live on this street, at the top end, at this end, in the more modern architecture,

333

and I must say I found it very pleasant for a long time. Though I also enjoy—I have a sort of apartment now, downtown, and that's also very nice, in a different way.'

'You used to live in one of these big houses?' Martha asked, with unseemly incredulity, and as she spoke they drove past the very house. For the first time in months Pam resisted the urge to inspect the curtains, the lawn, the little things he'd changed for somebody else.

'Why'd you go?'

'Circumstances. My circumstances changed. I guess you could say that.'

'How?'

'My *gosh*, you *are* a nosy parker. I'll guess I'll have to tell you my dress size next. '

'I'm just arksing, you don't have to answer.'

'You should be a lawyer or something, it's like being cross-*examined*.'

'So why'd you go?'

Pam sighed, but in fact she had, some time ago, designed a speech to answer the question, whoever it came from, 'Well, I suppose at my age, Martha, and especially in the light of the events of last September, I just think you have to make things work for you, work for you *personally*, because life is really too short, and if they don't work, you just have to go ahead and cut them loose, and that's basically—'

'I'd love to be a lawyer,' interrupted Martha, 'My friend is a lawyer. She has a house like that. Big-up house. We used to get the bus together to school. Now she's a big lawyer. That's like the best thing you can be.'

'You know what?' said Pam, drumming the steering wheel and preparing to lie, 'I like what I do. I don't think I'd change it to be a lawyer for all the tea in China. I really don't. I guess that's just me.'

Martha pulled down the passenger mirror, licked her finger and began to reshape her kiss curl.

'She's my role model, Kara—she definitely took it to the next level—as a young black woman, you know? She didn't get caught up in a lot of the things you can get caught up in—kids and that. She took it forward. That's where I'm aiming for—if you don't aim high, there's no point, really.'

Martha wound down the window that Pam had just closed and Pam felt she might just scream if the girl kept letting the outside in everywhere they went.

'Now, *good* for her! And good for you, too. God knows, when I was your age, all I did was have children, oh *my*. I've *three* girls. But it's such a different world. I wouldn't even want to bring up children in this world now. My *gosh*, it's really snowing. That's a couple of inches since we left the office.'

They drove twenty minutes and then parked a street from the one they wanted so Martha would have an opportunity to see a bit of this new neighbourhood by foot. It was cold beyond cold. Everything laid out like a promise, delayed for summer; bleached porches, dead gardens, naked trees, a sky-blue clapboard house, its rose-pink neighbour. Part of the East Coast realtor's skill is to explain what places will look like when the sun finally comes.

'And this just goes the most *incredible* orange when the fall comes. It's like the whole city is on fire. Just life, life, life *everywhere*. Now: the couple we're about to see,' said Pam, walking briskly ahead, 'They are just darling. Yousef and Amelia. He's Moroccan and *so* handsome and she's American, just American, and they have such a beautiful daughter, Lily.'

'Where they going to go, then, if I move in?'

'They're moving to Morocco. It's just what we were saying, they don't really want to bring up children in this country, I'm afraid. And frankly, I can understand that. They're *artists* too, so, they're a little bit flaky. But *very* sophisticated. So witty, and they make you feel comfortable right away, you know? Now, Martha, I've shown so many people this house, but it's a little too small for a family and a little too big for a single person, so it's awkward—but it's *perfect* for you—now, what *is* that—'

There had been a babbling noise the past minute or so, excited foreign voices, and as they turned the corner Martha saw some snow come flying and guessed at children, but the next second revealed the depth of the voices—these were bearded men, with dark, ashen skins—and the argument was over design, a snowman. It was incompetently begun, a tall upturned cone upon which a future head would never sit. And now work had stopped entirely; at the sight of the two women, the men froze and looked at their gloved hands and seemed to find themselves ridiculous.

'But those are the men!' cried Pam when they were not five yards out of hearing range, 'From my office. They just came just before you. But isn't that *weird*? They're making a snowman!'

'Is that what they were doing?' asked Martha, and dug into her pocket for a mint she had quietly lifted from the bowl of same in Pam's office.

'Well, what *else* were they doing. You know, Martha, they've probably never seen snow. Isn't that amazing—what a thing to see!'

'Grown men playing in the snow,' said Martha, but Pam could not be dissuaded from the romance of it, and it was the first anecdote she told as they walked through the door of 28 Linnaean, a canary-yellow first-floor apartment with two porches, front and back, nestled behind a nineteenth-century police station. Yousef was handsome as promised, curly-haired and with eyes many shades lighter brown than his skin; he was frying something with a great deal of chilli in it and offered his elbow for Martha to shake. Amelia was very skinny and freckled, with an angular hip and a toddler perched on it. She had the kindly, detached air of a young mother, the world outside the screen door having grown distant and surreal, brought to her only in tiresome reports from other people. But she good-humouredly let Pam hustle her to a window at the front of the house and followed the direction of her finger.

'Over there, can you see? They're making a *snow*man! Egyptian or Iranian or *something*. They were so *sheepish* about it. They were so embarrassed. I don't think they've ever seen snow before! And I saw these men, an *hour* ago in my *office*. It's the same men. But the *exact* same. Martha doesn't think anything of it, but I think it's darling.'

'That *is* sweet,' conceded Amelia, and hitched Lily up over her shoulder.

'Amelia—' said Pam, suddenly, taking a step back from her and appraising a small bulge around her middle, 'Now, are you pregnant again?'

'NO,' called Yousef from the other room, laughing, 'She's just a fat girl now! I feed her too much!'

'Four months,' said Amelia, shaking her head, 'And I'm going to have it in Morocco, God help me. Hey there, Martha. Do you think you'll take this place off our hands? *Please* won't you, please? We're totally desperate!'

'I don't know yet, do I?' said Martha very fiercely and made the odd, contemptuous noise with her teeth again. Lily reached out a doughy pink hand for Martha's face; she flinched from it.

'Oh,' said Amelia, reddening, and battling Lily's tiny kicking legs, 'I didn't mean to—'

Pam almost blew up right there—she just *could not* understand what kind of a girl this was, where she came from, what kind of conversation was normal for her. She drummed her fingers on the patch of wall behind her—as close an expression of suppressed fury as Pam ever managed.

'Martha, I'm sure Amelia only meant—'

'I was really joking, I didn't—' said Amelia, putting an incautious hand on Martha's shoulder, feeling a taut, inflexible muscle. She soon retracted it, but Martha continued to look and speak to the spot where the hand had been, 'I didn't mean that, I mean I meant I think I want to be nearer the university, nearer all of that, yeah? It's very alone up here, if you're alone, isn't it?'

'Well, you know, there's a very convenient bus—' said Amelia, looking over Martha to Pam who was performing a minimal mime with her thumbs to the effect that she did not know the girl well nor could she explain her.

'I'll look around,' said Martha, and walked away from them both, down the hall.

'Look everywhere,' said Amelia feelingly. She let Lily loose from her struggle, laying her on the floor. 'Please, feel absolutely at liberty.'

'Oh, she will,' said Pam rather tartly, but Amelia did not smile and Pam was mortified to see that she had thought the comment cruel. Without any skill, Pam turned the conversation to the problem of noisy plumbing.

At the other end of the apartment, Martha's walk changed; she was alone. She moved through the two big bedrooms, loose and alert, examining the strange foreign things in them: Arabic writing, meaningless paintings, and all those touches that rich people seem to use to look poor: wood floors, threadbare rugs, no duvets, all blankets, nothing matching. Old leather instead of new, fireplaces instead of central heating, everything wrong. Only the bathroom was impressive; very clean, white tiled. It had a mirror with a movie star's bald light bulbs circling it. Martha locked herself in here, ran both of the taps full blast, and sat on the closed toilet seat. She took a worn-looking, folded photograph from her coat pocket and wept. She was crying even before she had unfolded it, but flattening it out now against her knee made it almost impossible for her to breathe. In the picture a grinning, long-lashed boy, about eighteen months old, with a head like a polished ackee nut, sat on the lap of a handsome black man. Neither the picture nor their mutual beauty was in any way marred by the fact that both of them had sellotaped their noses to their foreheads to give the impression of pigs' snouts. Martha turned over the photograph and read what was written there.

> Martha, Martha, I love U
> And I'm trying 2 tell U true
> For this New Year 2002
> I am going to be there for U
> I know that U have many dreams
> And life is not always how it seems
> But I want U 2 put me 2 the test
> And I will do all the rest
> Together we will get so much higher
> Through my love and our desire
> Don't give up on what we've got
> Cos Ben and Jamal love U a lot!

It took another five minutes to recover herself. She rinsed her face in the sink and flushed the toilet. She came close up to the mirror and gave thanks to God for her secretive skin that told nobody anything; no flush, no puffiness. She could hear a great deal of laughter the other side of the door and wondered what they were saying about her; especially *him*, who was probably the worst, because he'd married like that and those ones that marry white always feel even more superior. She hadn't expected this. She didn't know what she'd expected.

'Martha!' cried Pam as she appeared again in the kitchen-lounge, 'I thought you'd been eaten by something. Eaten by a bear.'

'Just looking around. It's nice.'

Pam sat on a high kitchen stool beaming at Yousef, but he was busy pulling a giggling Lily out from under the sofa by her ankles.

'So you've had a good look around—she's had a good look around, Yousef, so that's something. Now,' said Pam, reaching down to the floor to get her bag, 'I don't want to hurry anybody. It always helps to get to know each other a little bit, I think. How can we make this work, for everybody?'

'But I don't know if I—I can't—'

'Martha, *dear*,' said Pam, returning a pen and pad she was holding back to her bag, 'There's no hurry whatsoever, that's not the way this works at all.'

'You know what?' replied Martha. With trembling fingers, she undid and then retied the waistband of her coat, 'I've got to go.'

'Well—' said Pam, completely astonished, and shook her head, 'But—if you'll give me—just wait a *minute*, I'll—'

'I'll walk. I want to walk—I need some air.'

Pam put down her coffee cup, and smiled awkwardly between Yousef and Amelia on the one hand and Martha on the other, increasing, as only Pam knew how, the awkwardness on both sides.

'I think I want a one bedroom thing,' mumbled Martha, her hand already on the doorknob, 'One bedroom would be more...' she said but could not finish. 'I'm sorry,' she said, and again Pam could not tell if she meant it. You can't tell anything about a one-day stand. They aren't there to be known. Pam shunted herself off the stool and put her hands out as if for something falling but Martha had already backed on to the porch. She struggled down the snowy steps, felt the same panic that rightly belongs to a fire escape. She could hear the clamour of snowman builders, speaking in tongues, laughing about something.   □

cheltenham festival of
literature

In association with **Hammicks** BOOKSHOPS

Spring Weekend **4-6 April 2003**

The Festival welcomes the dawning of Spring with a weekend's celebration of the freshest new writing. Over eighty authors descend on Cheltenham for debates, talks, performances and readings, as well as a special event featuring four of the Best of Young British Novelists.

For younger readers, Book It! offers the cream of modern children's literature, while our renowned series of courses and workshops could help you make the Granta list in 2013...

Authors appearing include:

Yann Martel • Pete McCarthy • Jane Lapotaire • David Starkey
Hari Kunzru • A L Kennedy • David Mitchell • Andrew O'Hagan
Tom Sharpe • Maureen Lipman • Graham Swift • Polly Toynbee

Bookings **T: 01242 227979**
Brochure **T: 01242 237377**
www.cheltenhamfestivals.co.uk

GRANTA

THE CYRILLIC ALPHABET
Adam Thirlwell

Adam Thirlwell was born in 1978, and grew up in north London. He is assistant editor of Areté magazine, and a Fellow of All Souls College, Oxford. His first novel, 'Politics', will be published by Jonathan Cape in August. 'The Cyrillic Alphabet' is a new story.

1

The abortion took five hours. Their appointment was for two o'clock, and they left at seven.

At half past one, they arrived at the car park of the Padre Pio clinic. With his left hand, Federico cradled the roughened skin of his wife's elbow. With his right hand, he gripped a silver-tipped mahogany walking stick. From his wrist a Maison de la Presse plastic bag sloshed and swung.

Federico de Vargas and his third wife Olga walked slowly away from the car park—leaving their car keys with the small, black car-valet. His name—*Roland*—was pinned to his tight grey smock.

Federico did not notice Roland's name.

They walked through the silent, tinted automatic doors of the Padre Pio clinic. It was a private maternity clinic, off the A10 outside Genoa, in the hills below the Alps. Despite its Catholic name, the Padre Pio maternity clinic had no theory on the nature of fatherhood. It had no strictures or beliefs.

The receptionist, perched on a high stool behind a curved strip of waist-high perspex, pointed with the cap of her black fountain pen towards the waiting room. Rotating the fountain pen cap in her fingers, she watched them walk away—gaunt Federico, taller than Olga, leaning against her, propped on his right-hand side by a stick. He dragged his left, club foot.

The receptionist was called *Renata*. Olga did not notice Renata's name.

They walked into the waiting room. There, Federico de Vargas—the recurrent darling at Cannes, Venice, Edinburgh, Thessaloniki, Gijón and Berlin; whose direction had won five Oscars, four Golden Globes and a Lifetime Achievement Award from Cinecittà; once even the recipient of the Jean Mitry Award at the Pordenone Silent Film Festival—did not read advice on the fitting of breast pumps. He did not look at the posters for antenatal classes. He did not study *Maman*, or *Bambino*—discussing massage as a viable alternative to post-natal coitus.

Nervously, he sat beside Olga, in twin Mies van der Rohe Barcelona chairs, and held her soft hand.

At the age of forty-one, Olga was pregnant. This surprised her.

She was, she thought, an obedient consumer of the contraceptive pill. And at seventy-nine, Federico was older than the average father. But, according to the theories of some theological experts, for the next four hours and thirty-three minutes, Federico and Olga were parents.

A nurse asked them to follow her to Olga's room. Safety-pinned to her left breast was an upside-down watch hung on a strap made from linked strips of stainless steel. On her right breast was pinned a laminated tag, named *Laura*.

Both Olga and Federico noticed Laura's name. She was their expert. They wanted to know her name.

They walked past the crèche—the floor a bobbled surface of miniature red and white plastic balls, like multicoloured bubble wrap. They walked past the corridor that led to the chapel of rest with its grey hoovered carpet.

Laura handed Olga a turquoise papery gown. She said that she would come back in three minutes. Olga was to take off her clothes, and then put on the gown. Smiling, Laura pushed the door open, then clicked it shut after her.

Federico loped towards the only armchair. On the miniature table beside it was a single orchid stem with three purple flowers, upright in its transparent vase. Olga went into the en suite bathroom. Federico picked up a menu printed, in italic Italian, with a range of Genovese specialities.

In the bathroom, Olga thought that her gown made her look like a boy. She was a slim and quiet beauty, with tidy breasts and subtle hips. Therefore the gown dropped, an empire line, straight from her neck. It deprived her of characteristics. But Olga was not dismayed by this. She enjoyed her boyhood. It felt safer to be unwomanly, in this bathroom, beside a toilet oddly fitted with a stainless steel basket, hooked inside the rim. Boyish was more fun.

Olga handed Federico the folded bundle of her clothes. She stood in front of him. She grinned for him. It did not occur to Federico that Olga was a boy. He only thought that she was noble and brave. She might have been five foot four, in a papery turquoise gown, but to Federico she looked Amazonian. She perched on the arm of his leather armchair, and cuddled her small breasts to his cheek.

She kissed him on the top of his head, on the tip of his nose, and on his mouth. The kiss on his mouth was the longest of these three kisses. Then she lay down. Laura knocked on the door and walked in as Federico, stretching, passed the Genovese menu to Olga.

Laura explained what she was going to do.

As they knew, because the foetus was only six weeks advanced, there was no need for an actual operation. Laura smiled. She said that this was good. She looked at Federico. She looked away. He was looking at his fingers, in his lap, nervously.

Laura would simply insert a pessary, said Laura—and she showed them, look, this was a pessary—and ask Olga to swallow two pills, and these would induce a miscarriage.

Olga nodded. She picked up the menu and asked Laura to bring her the *focaccia con le olive*, for afterwards. But this was not for Olga herself. She pretended that it was, but really it was for Federico. If he was going to stay with her all day, she wanted him to eat something.

The nurse asked Olga if she would like to insert the pessary herself. Olga replied that she trusted the nurse more than she trusted Olga. So Laura, gently, asked her to, slowly, roll onto her side. Laura pulled a translucent latex glove over her right hand, flexing her spread fingers, and rubbed the glove's wrinkles down to her wrist. She tore, from its serrated edge, the pessary's cover. She held the pessary between two fingers and pushed it, slid it, inside Olga.

Olga smoothed her turquoise gown, and lay on her back. Laura plucked each latex fingertip, then peeled off her glove. She dropped two pills into Olga's hand, and poured a glass of water from a carafe by the bed. She said that there would be bleeding. When she first thought that she could feel any bleeding, Olga should take this cardboard commode, and place it in the toilet. Then Laura would come to replace it. And Olga must make sure, said Laura, that she did not use the commode for any other need. She was only to use the commode when she felt that there was bleeding.

She touched Olga lightly, on the forearm, then walked out of the door.

From the Maison de la Presse plastic bag, Federico dragged the February issue of *Elle*. He shook its corner free from the plastic bag's handle. He passed it to Olga. Olga studied it. *Elle*'s survey, that month, was an earnest questionnaire on the difficult problem of etiquette: *When is it correct to tutoyer one's acquaintances?*

Abortion was odd, thought Federico. It happened during distractions. As an abortion took place, in the same room he sat and discussed his views on *tutoiement*. He disagreed with Olga, who believed that one should not *tutoyer* the friends of one's children. That would be, he thought, too formal. But then, while discussing etiquette, Olga would hunch her knees up to her stomach, or swish her legs, crooked, from side to side. And this was a difficult thing, thought Federico, watching Olga in occasional pain. He wanted his own pain too.

Breaking off the conversation, Olga got up, unsteadily, and went into the bathroom. In the bathroom she placed her grey cardboard commode refill in the stainless steel basket, and sat on the toilet, listening to the drip of blood. She stopped her habitual body from pissing as well. She rubbed her aching stomach, pressing it with her palms. Then Olga walked back to the bed, and pressed a small gold button to the left of the headboard, and Laura collected the commode and gave her a new grey refill.

This happened seven times.

And that was the abortion, thought Federico. It was a simple succession of facts. It was a conversation in which he discovered that his third wife had more old-fashioned views on etiquette than he did.

Both Olga and Federico wanted this abortion. It was not anguished. Olga wanted it because she did not want to interfere with the couple that was Federico and Olga. She did not know how long Federico would live, but she wanted to devote herself, forever and ever, to Fede, until he died. She was not selfish, Olga. And Federico wanted it too, because he was not selfish either. Olga was only forty-one. She was too young to be a widow with a child. He did not want to create a posthumous obstacle to Olga's remarriage.

Federico also had a more private reason for being against heredity. He did not want to ruin Olga's life, but also he did not want to ruin a child's life. He did not want to give it his club foot. Federico had read E. M. Forster's *The Longest Journey*. He had not reread this book. This was not because he disliked it, but because he did not need to reread it. For Federico, it was unforgettable. He read this novel in the Sea Spray B&B, having disembarked at Liverpool off the boat from Argentina, in 1947. Reading *The Longest Journey* was part of Federico's plan to improve his English. In the Sea Spray B&B,

beside a two-bar electric heater, he read—slowly, skipping the difficult sentences—how Rickie Elliot's daughter died, luckily, soon after she was born. Her death was lucky because, like her father, she was lame.

After the sixth grey bowl, Olga said to Laura that she thought it was over. There was something there, she said. It was lumpier, it was odder. There was something there like egg white, she said. It was only after the seventh grey bowl, however, that Laura said it was over. She handed Olga a sanitary towel, and four painkillers. She said that Olga could now get dressed.

Federico gathered up the folded bundle of her clothes.

When Olga was dressed, she came back out of the bathroom and sat on the arm of his armchair. He kissed her shoulder. He said, 'You never got your *focaccia*. You should ask for your *focaccia*.' She cuffed him, lightly, with a paw across his cheek. He kissed her shoulder again.

Then Laura came back in. Olga moved across and sat on the bed. The sheets had not been turned down. The sheets were still immaculate with their hospital corners.

Olga pressed her aching stomach with her palms.

Laura said, 'How old are you?' 'Forty-one.' 'You must come back in one month. You may feel pain for a few days, but this is normal.' Olga grinned and grunted. Federico moved his stick, like a snooker cue, up and down one arm of his leather armchair. Laura said, 'Well. Do you need me. I must ask you this, but do you need me to give you any contraception?' Olga said that she did not. 'You are not to resume relations for at least two weeks. Now you may go. Do you have, at home do you have sanitary towels?' Olga said that she did. Laura said, 'Well here are two, until then. Your car has been brought round to the front of the clinic. You will find the keys in the ignition.'

Olga and Federico walked, slowly, past the crèche and the corridor that led to the chapel of rest. They smiled at the night receptionist, called Philippe. Philippe did not notice them smile. He was pushing a block of staples into his stapler.

They walked through the silent, tinted automatic doors of the Padre Pio clinic. Federico got into the car. He leaned across to tug the plastic lock on the other door. But it was stuck. Federico groaned and pushed his door open. Then he swivelled, put his two feet down together onto the frozen gravel, into which he ground his walking stick, and pulled himself up by the handgrip. He stood for a moment, watching his breath pour out, meditatively. He slewed round, hopping slightly, and opened Olga's door with the key.

'We are getting a new car,' said Olga. 'This is ridiculous, your car. We are getting a car with centralized locking.' She was smiling. And Federico giggled. 'What is that?' he said. 'What is that in Russian?' 'In Russian. What? Central locking?' said Olga. 'I do not know. I do not know if there is a word. It is maybe. Maybe *tsentralnyi elektreecheskee dvernoi zamok.*' '*Tsentrahlnuhye elektreechkee dvernoi zamukh,*' said Federico. 'No, *zamok,*' said Olga. 'And don't change the subject.'

Federico had a reason for this impromptu vocabulary test. He was learning Russian, secretly. He had hired a girl called Pavla, recommended by his friend Yannick—the Director of the Russian Institute in Nice—to give him lessons in Russian. Because Federico wanted to talk to Olga in Russian. He wanted to argue, in Russian, about etiquette.

Federico drove back over the border into France, and along the Moyenne Corniche. Just outside the medieval, tourist village of Eze, Olga said, 'You must stop. You must stop at the next bar.' Federico stopped in a car park beside a block of flats and a shop selling souvenirs. Olga got out and walked into the bar, making for the lavatories. The barman said, 'You cannot use the toilets. Only patrons can use the toilets.' But Olga was noble. She had force. She said, 'I have a very bad period. I must use your toilet urgently.' She said this very loudly, so that the patrons of this bar could hear her. There were only two patrons. Both were men. There was a man in an Iron Maiden T-shirt, and a man with little gold-rimmed rectangular glasses and a black suit with shiny torn turn-ups. They pretended not to hear.

The barman nodded.

Olga was noble. She was Amazonian. She felt exhausted and humiliated, but she also had force.

As she left, she did not say goodbye. She got into the car.

Federico was staring at the block of flats. A man was rolling paint onto the ceiling of an empty room, lit by the shadeless light bulb, standing on a kitchen chair.

Both Olga and Federico wanted this abortion. And they also wanted the child. They wanted it, silently. They had a joint desire for a Federico and Olga child. But Olga was not selfish. And Federico was not selfish.

Because they loved each other, neither Federico nor Olga had said that they wanted this child.

Olga snuggled her cheek on the seat belt, trying to fall asleep.

2

Pavla was born in 1981, in Minsk. She now lived on the ninth floor of an apartment block in Nice's St Augustine district.

Because she was homesick, every weekend she called her mother to discuss the Russian weather, doodling in Cyrillic on a Snoopy jotting pad.

Pavla had two jobs: a full-time job that began at eight in the morning, when she started work at the Café Magnan as a dishwasher and kitchen help; and a fortnightly job that began at eight in the evening when she taught Russian to Federico de Vargas, in her capacity as an Approved Teacher of Russian Language and Culture, a certificate donated to her by a regular called Yannick. Yannick was almost a friend. He was something to do with the Russian Institute in Nice.

Pavla's homesickness had two consequences. The first was this. It had made her Slavic. Her Russian lessons were earnest, nostalgic. Discussing the nineteenth-century painter Ilya Repin, she showed Federico her stamp collection. Moving a magnifying glass, like a metal detector, above the pasteboard pages, they analysed a selection of famous Repin canvases from the Tretyakov Gallery.

The second consequence was this. Her homesickness had made her distrustful. She distrusted Federico.

After the lesson, when Federico had gone, she flopped backwards onto her sofa, and remembered Federico's Russophile Russian.

'Do not leave a name. If you have to call. Or, yes you can leave the name. But do not say it is for lesson. You must say it is for, you must say it is for, for *sous-titres*. She gets to be so. She is so suspicious, you know?'

Pavla did not like Federico. She distrusted his international charm. She did not know why he had to invent this, the most clichéd fantasy—in which Pavla was to make his wife jealous. She knew about rich old men like Federico, and their careerist wives.

Their boring sex lives bored her, she thought, as she fell asleep on the sofa, in her mother's grey cardigan with pink knitted roses on each shoulder, watching classic American hits from the Seventies on her portable TV.

But Pavla was wrong about Federico. She did not understand his need for secrecy. ☐